make up
up
break
up

make up
break up

lily menon

ST. MARTIN'S GRIFFIN
NEW YORK

First published in the United States by St. Martin's Griffin, an imprint of St. Martin's Publishing Group

MAKE UP BREAK UP. Copyright © 2021 by Lily Menon. All rights reserved. Printed in the United States of America. For information, address St. Martin's Publishing Group, 120 Broadway, New York, NY 10271.

www.stmartins.com

Designed by Devan Norman

Library of Congress Cataloging-in-Publication Data

Names: Menon, Lily, author.
Title: Make up break up : a novel / Lily Menon.
Description: First edition. | New York : St. Martin's Griffin, 2021.
Identifiers: LCCN 2020037476 | ISBN 9781250761996 (trade
  paperback) | ISBN 9781250799951 (hardcover) |
  ISBN 9781250214478 (ebook)
Subjects: GSAFD: Love stories.
Classification: LCC PS3613.E4923 M35 2021 | DDC 813/.6—dc23
LC record available at https://lccn.loc.gov/2020037476

Our books may be purchased in bulk for promotional, educational, or business use. Please contact your local bookseller or the Macmillan Corporate and Premium Sales Department at 1-800-221-7945, extension 5442, or by email at MacmillanSpecialMarkets@macmillan.com.

First Edition: 2021

10 9 8 7 6 5 4 3 2 1

For the Swoon Squad,
the most effervescent readers an author could hope for

make up
up
break
up

chapter one

♡

"Detest" was a very strong word. So were "abhor" and "despise" and "loathe." Annika, being a pacifist, preferred a different term—something her yoga teacher had said that struck a much more civil chord.

"I am elementally unaligned with you, Hudson Craft," she muttered, staring at his picture on the *Tech Buzz* magazine website. Her right hand was curled so tightly around her wireless mouse that the opalescent white plastic creaked in protest. "*Completely* and *utterly* elementally unaligned."

They were calling him "the hottest tech entrepreneur who doesn't believe in true love." It was like a train wreck you couldn't help but stare at. A gratuitously handsome, Harvard-educated, blond train wreck who had (probably) stolen her idea.

Also, that magazine feature was supposed to be hers.

When the journalist had called to interview Annika, she'd assumed *she* was going to be the feature. Instead, this was her big mention: *"'Relationships are the new frontier as far as the tech sector goes,' a local businesswoman agrees."*

That was it. That was all of it. Not only was there no mention of her business, Make Up, at all but Annika had been reduced to an anonymous "local businesswoman," just propping up Hudson Craft in all his amazing amazingness.

"Arrrrghhhh." Annika reached into her desk drawer to browse her stable of stress tools, all neatly organized using drawer separators. Mini Zen garden? Multicolored breathing sphere? Singing bowl? No, today called for something much more basic.

She grabbed the unicorn-zombie-shaped stress ball she'd lovingly named ZeeZee (he'd been a white elephant gift from one of her friends at yoga; when you squeezed him, his green brains squirted out between your fingers) and shut her drawer slightly harder than she meant to.

Spoil the ending to his book, Annika said to herself, aggressively kneading ZeeZee's brain. *Designer virus to his email address. Glitter bomb that'll take days to rinse out of his stupid golden hair.* She hadn't seen him since Las Vegas last year, but she could renew their acquaintance in a way he wouldn't easily forget.

Glancing away from the laptop screen, she let her gaze fall on the newest letter from the bank, lying facedown on her desk under an old teacup. Just like that, Annika's anger was momentarily swallowed by a wave of anxiety.

The idea of running her own business had always held a glow for Annika. Make Up was *supposed* to have been her fairy tale. She'd never dreamed of a big, fancy wedding. She'd never wanted the handsome prince or the cherub-cheeked children or the home with a yard in some ritzy Los Angeles suburb. She remembered being six years old and dressing up as Indra Nooyi, then Pepsi CEO, longtime business badass, for Halloween. No one had gotten her costume, but she didn't care. All she'd ever wanted was to be her own boss. As a four-year-old, that meant ordering Daddy around the house while wearing his suit jacket that hung to her ankles. As she got older, the dream morphed from bossing her dad around to running a company that made a difference in people's lives.

Annika stood, smoothed down her black tulip skirt, and paced her tiny twenty-sixth-floor office, still throttling ZeeZee. Her gaze lingered on the tufted velvet settee in a trendy but sophisticated plum color; the original art from LA artist Cleo Sanders, which made a statement without being gauche; the giant metal sign she'd commissioned to wrap around the walls.

MAKE UP
HAPPILY EVER AFTER, REDUX

She looked out the floor-to-ceiling windows at the bustling city below. She'd thought being in downtown LA would put her right in the middle of the action, that it would make her easily accessible to beta testers for the app—most of whom would come from the university—and to other businesses that Make Up might want to collaborate with. It was expensive, but the payout would be totally worth it.

So Annika had borrowed money from the bank and signed away her life on her zillion-dollar-a-month lease.

It worked for a time. Make Up had seemed to be touched by magic—the grant she'd won last year had been the first one she'd applied for. She had innovation, a kick-ass developer, and a relentless hunger to change the world. The deep-learning prototype was supposed to have been ready for release within six months at the latest. But that's not how things had worked out.

When Annika came up with the idea for Make Up about a year ago, she and her developer (and best friend extraordinaire), June Stewart, had designed the perfect app to help people translate their words in a way their partners would understand. The app would bridge the gap created by poorly spoken words and misunderstandings. No one had ever done that before, and that's what the Young Entrepreneur's Foundation had seen— the future, a vision, a brilliant prospect. That's why they'd given her the grant.

The bank didn't see any of those things. It saw someone who was delinquent, someone who was cash-poor, and that was all that mattered. Annika squeezed poor, beleaguered ZeeZee until his zombified unicorn brains bulged through the gaps between her fingers.

"Good morning! Did you see all those boxes in the empty office next door? I think we're getting new neighbors really soon."

Annika turned to face her best friend/partner in crime, who'd just walked in the front doors. The way she described June really just depended on the day. Annika took a deep breath and attempted a breezy tone that would conceal her roiling inner turmoil. "Hey! Yeah, I think they're moving in—" She eyed the armload of shopping bags June was carrying. "Really? It's barely past ten."

June widened her blue eyes in what she probably thought was an innocent way. "Bloomingdale's was having a sale. Besides, shopping helps me calm down. I needed it for our big meeting this morning." She was dressed in her usual flamboyant work attire: six-inch-high, leopard-print Jimmy Choos and a hot pink, one-shoulder silk dress. Her blond hair was styled in an intricate crown braid, the kind Annika could never do without the help of thirteen hair stylists.

Annika glanced down at her own understated-yet-classy burgundy peplum top, tulip skirt, and patent vegan leather slingbacks, her heart sinking. They were so different; they presented completely incohesive images of the company. The bank manager was going to think they were two flaky young women who couldn't get their shit together.

"You know," June said, studying Annika's expression. "We're totally going to win over this McManor guy. I can be the wild, creative one and you'll be the more controlled, sensible one. A little bit of yin and yang working together." She stuffed her bags in the tiny supply closet and went to sit in her (leopard-print) office chair, which was two feet away from Annika's. After sweeping a bunch of *Star Wars*–themed Funkos out of the way, she put her feet up and began tapping at her phone.

It didn't surprise Annika that June had read her mind so well. A friendship that had survived college-roommate status took on certain magical powers. "Mm hmm."

"What?" June looked up from her phone. "You don't think so?"

Annika sank into her own ergonomic chair, tossed ZeeZee onto the desk, and put her head in her hands. "No, I really don't, June. This is going to be a disaster. I can feel it. You know how strong my sixth sense is."

"It's *not* going to be a disaster!" Annika peeked at June from between her fingers as June continued speaking. "McManor's going to see that we make a dynamic, forward-thinking team and that we have what it takes to get our little cash flow problem under control. And he'll give you an extension on your loans. A big one. Everyone's finances are a train wreck these days, not just yours."

Annika sat up straight and smiled bleakly. "It's funny you say that. I was just thinking what a massive train wreck Hudson Craft is before you got here." For obvious reasons, she left out the part about thinking of him as a *handsome* train wreck. There was no need to cloud the issue. Besides, June had eyes. She knew what Hudson Craft looked like.

"Uh oh." June fired up her Millennium Falcon–skinned laptop. "Is he in another article?"

"Just emailed you the link."

She heard June click a few times, and then gasp in satisfying outrage. "*Tech Buzz*? *You* were supposed to get the *Tech Buzz* article. That journalist *said* it'd be about you!"

Annika drummed her fingers on the desk. "Read the headline; it gets better."

"No!" June cried again. "*You're* 'Mr. Relationshape: The debonair twenty-five-year-old with the *GQ* smile who's changing the shape and nature of relationships!'"

Annika raised an eyebrow.

"Well, uh—except I guess you'd be *Miss* Relationshape, and you're twenty-four. And I'd say you're more charming than debonair." June paused thoughtfully. "Also, your smile is more *Yoga Journal* than *GQ*. I knew I should've called my cousin. I'm pretty sure he has a friend at *Tech Buzz*."

Annika sighed. "It wouldn't have helped. Breaking people up is way sexier than helping them make up."

"But his business model is built on tears and heartbreak. If someone *I* was dating paid a 'terminator' to break up with me for him?" June mimed her head exploding. "Oh *hell* no."

Annika couldn't help the disdain from creeping into her

voice as she read out loud from the article. "'It's better than being ghosted.'" She looked up from her screen at June. "So—the options are being broken up with by a random 'terminator' or being ghosted? What about being kind enough to let someone down easily?"

June shook her head. "He's a complete and total ass-face, Annika. That's the only explanation."

Annika picked up ZeeZee again and pulled on the zombie stress ball's wart-studded nose. "I don't like to say I hate people, but I think I actually viscerally hate Hudson Craft. Like, I hate every single thing he stands for."

June gave her a look. *Damn.* That was the problem with having a best friend who'd been your college roommate and was now practically your business partner: They knew way, way too much. "You don't like to say you hate people? What about Fishdick Felix?"

"Who?" Annika screwed up her nose. Then her expression cleared. "Oh, you mean that guy in the freshman dorms who used to microwave fish sticks in the kitchen? *Everyone* hated him."

"Do you need a refresher?" June held up her fingers one by one. "Rehan Shah, your lab partner who chewed his gum wrong?"

"It was ridiculously noisy."

"Mm hmm. Adrian Westinger, who always said, 'GRAAAIII-INS' like a zombie to make fun of your vegetarianism? He was a jerk, but I'm pretty sure you used the word 'hate' with him, too—"

"Okay, I get it, I get it." Annika threw ZeeZee at June, who caught it midair and threw it back in one fluid motion. "So maybe I've hated a *few* more people than I thought . . ."

June laughed. "You're ruled by emotion. Messy, conflicting emotion. Just admit it."

Annika looked past her friend into the hallway outside the office. "Well, I'm feeling a lot of messy, conflicting emotion right now." She wiped her palms on her skirt and tossed Zee-Zee back into her stress drawer. "Because I think Mr. McManor from the Bank of California is walking up."

◞

Annika had never met Mr. McManor in person before. He turned out to be one of those extremely tidy, precise people who likely arranged their silverware drawers for fun on weekends and had a pair of monogrammed socks for every day of the week. He kept pushing up his little round glasses as he spoke, probably because his nose was so tiny. Annika was afraid they'd go tumbling right off his face if he made too sudden a movement. Thankfully, he was placid to the point of seeming half-dead, so sudden movements didn't seem to be a concern.

"Well." He sat very still on a floral-patterned accent chair, clutching his briefcase tightly on his lap. "I'm afraid the news isn't good, Ms. Dev. You are what we call 'grotesquely delinquent' on your accounts. Thoroughly overleveraged."

Grotesquely delinquent? Annika caught June's eye. She had the feeling he'd made that up on the spot just to be spiteful. "Be that as it may, Mr. McManor, I believe if you'd just listen to this short presentation we've prepared . . ." She nodded at June, who hopped up to her laptop and began queueing up the Power-Point slides. "You see, Mr. McManor, Make Up is not just a burgeoning young business. It's a statement about the greater good in life, about our basic humanity. The need to belong somewhere, the need to connect with another human being, the need to—"

"Press on." Mr. McManor waved a hand. "We need to press on. I'm sorry, but the time for last-ditch efforts has passed."

Annika stared into his dead-fish eyes. Coldly unsympathetic. And the bank he'd sworn his ruthless allegiance to owned both her business loan and the building where she worked. *Awesome.* "But . . . I sent you a payment. Last month."

"Ah, yes." Mr. McManor consulted his notes quickly. "Your payment of four hundred eighty dollars and . . . seventy-four cents does not come close to overcoming your rather monstrous debt, I'm afraid."

"I can keep making payments." Annika spoke firmly, willing him to see the capability in her eyes, the passion, the fire, the willingness to do whatever it took to keep Make Up running. "I can make up the back rent; I just need more time. It's a temporary cash flow problem."

"Isn't it better that you have a tenant here who's willing to work with you, Mr. McManor?" June perched on the edge of the desk. "Better the devil you know than the devil you don't, that's what my mama always says."

"Firstly, your back rent is only part of the problem. Catching up with rent has nothing to do with your business loan, on which you also owe quite a substantial sum of money. And secondly, we've had plenty of interest in the space, as it turns out. From people who would be able to afford the rent rather easily."

June narrowed her blue eyes. "Like who?"

"Gwyneth Paltrow's first cousin."

Annika blinked. "What?"

"We've been approached by a representative for Gwyneth Paltrow. Her first cousin wants to rent out this space for an interior design business she's launching. She's willing to prepay the first six months." Mr. McManor stood, brushed his suit off, and walked to the Make Up sign on the wall. The one Annika had been so proud to order. The one that had her feeling like she'd *made it*, that she'd achieved the dream, that she was unstoppable.

He turned to her, his eyes flat and distant behind those little round glasses. On anyone else, Annika might have admired them for their chic Harry Potter vibe. A beam of sunlight from the window lay in a stripe on his balding head, but he didn't seem to notice. "Unless you completely resolve your delinquency, including late fees and penalty interest, Ms. Dev, the news isn't going to be good."

"Before you go," June said. "Who's moving in next door? Are you managing their loan, too? Because maybe we'll tell them how you treated us."

Mr. McManor looked at her like she was an idiot. "Why, that is privileged client information, Ms. Stewart, and as such, is undivulgeable to you."

"That is *so* not a word," June muttered.

Annika drummed her fingers on her desk. "Interesting. But you *did* divulge that Gwyneth's cousin wants this space. Doesn't that violate some kind of confidentiality?"

Mr. McManor turned bright pink. "That was rather gauche," he said after a long pause. "I was simply . . . excited. I've been an admirer of Ms. Paltrow since her masterful performance in *Emma*."

"Excited?" Annika stared at him. "You're *excited* right now?"

Mr. McManor cleared his throat and stood up straighter, a flash of annoyance dancing across his features. It was the most animated she'd seen him in the twenty minutes he'd been there. "Ms. Dev, I suggest you do some serious thinking about your next steps. Good day." He walked away primly, his shiny black shoes whispering on the industrial carpet as he headed to the elevators.

"Why does he try to talk all British when he's not British?" June said in disgust.

"He wants us out of here." Annika sat back heavily as the full impact of his words crashed into her. She smiled bleakly at June. "Do you know how much we have in the business account right now? Less than five thousand dollars. Do you know how much we owe?" She shook her head and thought, *I am the boss. I will not cry. I will also not say how much I hate Mr. McManor.* "It's over, June."

"Sweet pea—" June squatted so they were eye to eye. "Let me give you the money. I know you're probably going to argue, but *please* just think about it. I'd really feel good about being able to help you out. Maybe I could be, like, an investor."

A fact not well-known (because June did her best to hide it) was that Violetta "June" Stewart was the only daughter of extremely wealthy movie producers. Needless to say, she didn't really need this job. June had a trust fund and lots of high-powered connections. The only reason she'd come on board was because she wanted to help Annika. Annika couldn't afford to pay her what she was really worth, but June never complained, either out of loyalty or pity. Annika was in no position to turn down, either.

Annika shook her head and squeezed her longtime friend's hand. "That's really, really sweet of you, Junebug. But . . . no. Thank you, but no. I can't take your money."

June sighed. They'd had this conversation many times before, and she knew not to expect a different outcome. Still, she was June. And that, Annika supposed, meant she had to try.

Giving up, June flopped down to sit cross-legged on the floor. Even while wearing a tight dress and skyscraper heels, she somehow managed to look more graceful than Annika, who was sitting in a chair. "What about your dad, then?"

Annika's dad was one of the leading anesthesiologists in the country. He was regularly paid to travel to various conferences and give talks because apparently, he knew more about putting people to sleep than anyone else did. Annika didn't get the specifics—she just knew she never wanted to do what he did.

That fact had almost broken his heart.

Annika still remembered her dad's face when she'd gone to him eight months earlier to tell him that, in addition to the grant money she'd won, the bank loan had also come through, and that Make Up was going to be an actual business. He'd stared at her for a long moment, scotch in hand, and then said in his deep bass voice, "But what about medical school?"

She'd graduated from UCLA two years earlier, but her dad had never let go of the dream that his only child would come to her senses and decide to follow in the family footsteps after all. Annika was all he had in this world—both his physician parents were dead, and Annika's mom, who'd been a pediatrician, had passed away shortly after Annika was born. Her dad was desperate for her to continue the family trade. Never mind that the thought of slicing into a cadaver made Annika want to suck down his unconscious-making chemicals just to escape.

Come to think of it, after he'd asked her about medical school, Annika had gotten kind of cocky. She'd raised an eyebrow and said in a very *you wanna throw down?* tone, "Just wait. In three months when my face is plastered across magazines in every newsstand between here and the hospital, you'll be singing a different tune." In her defense, things had been on the come-up then. She'd had no idea that fate would kick her in the ass just a few months later.

God, how embarrassing.

Annika nibbled on her lower lip. Far below them, a car honked in the perpetual LA traffic.

"What are you thinking?" June prompted, playing with the Baby Yoda figurine on her desk Annika had given her last Christmas.

"Well—don't get me wrong." Annika got up and began pacing, wearing a path from her desk to the window. "I believe in us. We *can* bring in a profit if we work our asses off. Our cash flow issues would be a thing of the past. But there's a part of me that's so worried I'm kidding myself—this tiny, heckling voice that just won't shut up. I expected the app to be ready for release *way* before now—no offense, I know you're working as hard as you can—and that hasn't happened. What if I've lost my fire?"

June's clear blue eyes stared right back at her. "You haven't. This is just nerves talking. You can't let McStick-Up-His-Ass win, Annika."

Annika walked over to her desk and pulled ZeeZee out again. Her heart was beginning to pound. "It's not just him. It's Hudson Craft, too. Do you know how demoralizing it is that some dude with excessively gelled hair and a toothpaste-ad smile can just come in and have everybody buzzing with his cruel, thoughtless app? Meanwhile, Make Up is going to change the way we look at technology and its use in interpersonal spaces, and we don't even get a *one-line mention* in that article? Do you know how absolutely, exquisitely infuriating that is?" Annika smacked ZeeZee face-first into the desk. He made a satisfyingly squelchy sound on impact, the force rattling the framed pictures of June, her dad, and the Make Up office that were all lined up neatly next to her laptop.

June thrust a finger at her. "There it is! Stay with that feeling. And don't forget, Hudson's a thief."

Annika couldn't believe he'd turned out to be such a jerk. When they'd met at a conference in Vegas last summer, they'd laughed at how desperate everyone was to be done with the conference so they could get to the real reason they were there: the blackjack tables. They'd bonded right away because they were both virtually the same age, from LA, and interested in starting a business soon. And later, they'd . . . well. That wasn't important.

What was important was that after she returned from Vegas, she'd found herself thinking about him often. She'd even considered reaching out to him. Until, that is, he began popping up in tech magazines and articles more and more frequently, talking about his new app, Break Up. That was when she realized he'd stolen her idea—or at least a kernel of it. "He didn't steal my whole idea. All the lawyers I called were very specific about that. He was probably influenced by it, which isn't a crime."

"Okay, so he was influenced by it. It's still totally shitty that a nasty app like his is getting all this attention."

Annika studied her best friend's flushed cheeks, her bright eyes. She felt her own temper rise another notch. "You know what? You're right. Local businesswoman agrees—he *is* a total ass, just like Mr. McMannerless. They're both douchebags who think they can just push us around. Well, they can't. We're not going to run off crying. We're here to fight."

"Yeah!" June said, pumping a Baby Yoda–wielding fist above her head.

"We can totally do this." Back in her chair, Annika spun around in a purposeful circle.

"Yeah, we can. How can I help? No task is too small."

"Really?" Annika hesitated. "Would you mind getting a whiteboard from Staples, then? It's been on my to-do list forever. I feel like I need to write stuff down where we can see it every day and be inspired. Like, for instance, we need to get ready for EPIC next month. Let's get some ideas flowing about that." EPIC—the Entrepreneurs Pitching Investors Conference—was their one big chance to turn things around.

"*Yes!* I have a really good feeling about EPIC." June clapped her hands and made for the handbag hanging on the back of her chair. "I'll go get the whiteboard, and meanwhile, you just keep thinking."

"I will." Annika hopped up again and paced faster than before. June was right; the anger helped her think. God, she should have embraced her dark—uh, hotheaded—side a long time ago.

"None of that yogi crap!" June called over her shoulder as she headed into the elevator. "Stay mad!"

chapter two

♡

"Stay mad. Right." Annika took a breath. "Stupid Hudson Craft with his patronizing smile and his—"

BONNNNGGGG!

Annika stopped mid-stride, invectives trailing off. "What the hell?"

She waited a minute, then took another step.

BONNNNGGGGGG!

Either there was a gong sounding in this trendy high-rise office building, or those nightly self-hypnosis videos had finally scrambled her brain. Either was possible; after all, this *was* LA.

She walked out of the office and followed the direction of the sound.

Weird. Muffled cheering and whooping came from down the hall, where the empty office space was. Maybe the new company had moved in? But that didn't make sense. The only reasonable explanation for the noises she was hearing was a party for demon children hopped up on sugar.

Annika picked up her pace until she found herself in front of the glass doors that led to the office next door. For a long minute, she just stood there, watching the mayhem—until an orange Nerf dart hit the glass door, pinged off in a frenzied pirouette, and shook her loose of her shock.

Her brain still refused to fully accept it, but she was definitely witnessing a Nerf gun battle between adults. Well, they were mostly hidden in their cardboard box forts, but they *looked* like adults.

Two people bolted from the opposing forts—one a pale, red-headed man and the other a woman of maybe East Asian descent. Both barefoot and in jeans and blue T-shirts, they raced around, squealing and yelling at each other like they were in an arcade. Annika watched in alarm as a Nerf dart hit a vase and it crashed to the floor. Neither of them seemed to notice. The redhead jumped on the couch, bellowing like a rhinoceros in pain. He *looked* happy, though.

BONNNNGGGG!

The sound of the gong forced Annika's eyes to the front of the room. Suddenly, her senses snapped to attention. The hairs on her arms stood up. Her vision tunneled.

And at the end of that long, dark tunnel . . . was Hudson. Fucking. Craft.

Unbelievable.

She'd spent so much time fuming about him these past few months that every single detail of his appearance was intimately familiar to her. That ridiculously thick blond hair, falling on his forehead in a wave. That square jaw, those muscular shoulders pressing arrogantly into his blue T-shirt, like he wanted to announce to the world, "*Yo! Look at me! I work out!*"

Yeah, we get it, Hudson. We get that your chiseled pecs and

your perfect six-pack usually have people under the influence of
especially strong margaritas drooling all over themselves.

What the hell was he doing here? He was perched on a little
stool, one big hand around a mallet. He punctuated every word
he spoke—strike that, *bellowed*—by swinging the mallet into a
giant brass gong. "Break—" *BONNGGG!* "—Up!" *BONNGGG!*
"Three—" *BONNGGG!* "—HUNDRED THOUSAND—"
BONNGGG! "—breakups!"

Three . . . hundred thousand . . . breakups? *What the fuck?*

Her vision suddenly expanded. Details she hadn't yet regis-
tered began to filter into Annika's consciousness.

For one, the bright blue T-shirts they all wore said Break
Up! on the front.

For another, there was the giant BREAK UP sign on the wall.

And then there was the slogan underneath, which read:
YOUR LIFE, RESTARTED. That, right there, was Reason #2,064
why Annika could never believe that this—Hudson Craft's app,
a twisted bastardization of her idea—could be a coincidence.

Anger bubbled in her veins, a furious volcano on the verge
of eruption. Not only had he probably—no, *definitely*—stolen
her idea and taken all the success that was supposed to have
been hers, he was now *in her office building?* He was in the
hallowed space she'd carved out for herself, the space that was
now in jeopardy, ringing a *gong* in the middle of a Nerf battle?
What the hell? What the actual, ridiculous hell?

Annika slammed the glass door open with the heel of her
hand, ignoring the throbbing ache. "Hey! Hudson Craft!"

They couldn't hear her over the obnoxious gong, their
own infernal screeching, and the awful "music" blaring over
the loudspeaker. As Annika marched up to Hudson Craft,
she tripped on a bright orange Nerf gun, her ankle twisting

painfully in her slingbacks. Biting back a shriek, she scooped the Nerf gun off the floor and, aiming right at Hudson, pulled the trigger.

The foam dart surged from the chamber with a satisfying *thwack!* Annika grinned, her hands gripping the Nerf gun tight, watching as the dart whistled through the air toward her target.

As Hudson whooped and banged his gong, the foam dart hit him square in the face.

"BULL'S EYE!" Annika crowed, raising the Nerf gun up high.

Hudson's eyes went wide at the sudden assault. His mouth dropped open. She brought the Nerf gun down and, almost of its own accord, her finger pulled the trigger again, the righteous urge to put another foam dart in his open mouth too strong to resist. Unfortunately, instead of smiting her enemy a second time, the Nerf gun only produced an empty clicking sound.

Dammit.

Hudson's gaze held hers for a long second. His face was a landscape of emotions: Annika saw surprise, confusion, maybe even a sliver of hurt or anger, though she had no idea what those were about. But before she could puzzle it out, he dropped the mallet, pressed both hands to his right eye, and began yelling, "Oh my god, my eye!"

Annika's stomach flipped. Immediate, flaming guilt lit up her body. This was what happened when she lost her temper. This was why she did yoga. She was a pacifist . . . until she wasn't. Underneath her calm exterior lurked a hideous, deranged, Nerf-dart murderer. "Oh, shit," she whispered, dropping the Nerf gun with a plastic clatter.

Hudson's two employees froze. "Jesus, my eye," he groaned again, leaning like he was about to keel over dead.

And then pandemonium broke out once more.

The redhead scrabbled to turn off the music and the woman said, "Oh no—oh, Hudson!" before turning to Annika. Her brown eyes flashed as she pulled a cell phone out of her pocket. "I'm calling the police. This is assault."

Annika's pulse beat a sickening rhythm. Assault. The police. She was done for. Who would ever want to hire a relationship expert who had a criminal record? She'd *known* Hudson Craft would be the death of her one day.

Suddenly, there was a muffled snort of laughter, and then Hudson spoke cheerfully to the now-silent room. "There's no need for that, Blaire. I'm fine."

"Are you sure? Because—"

"I'm sure."

Still glaring at Annika, Blaire put her phone away and crossed her arms, positioning herself in front of Hudson Craft like she was his personal bodyguard or something. The redhead was staring at Annika, unabashed. Annika could feel the waves of hostility in the room crashing over her, but she was too busy feeling relieved that she wouldn't be going to jail to care.

Hudson, his eye amazingly enough now totally recovered, folded his big, lumpy arms (some might say "muscular," but whatever) over his chest. "Well, well, well," he said slowly. "Annika Dev." He said it like he was pronouncing the name of an exotic bird species he hadn't expected to find in LA. Weirdo.

She narrowed her eyes. "Hudson Craft." She said *his* like it was the name of an oozing, highly infectious disease. "I see your eye is perfectly fine, so you were just lying. Why does that not surprise me at all?"

"Lying? I was doing you a favor. See what happens when you lose your temper? You could've gone to *prison*. Let that be a lesson to you, Ms. Dev."

He'd read her mind. Annika stood up straighter, irritation replacing all her other emotions. "*You* teaching *me* how to be a moral, upstanding citizen? Hilarious."

Hudson laughed. "I don't know—moral, upstanding citizens don't generally shoot innocent people in the face. Have to say, I'm a little surprised you went for my *face*, though. From what I remember, you were fonder of these bad boys." He made his pecs do a little dance. His employees snickered.

Annika felt her cheeks heat and balled her fists against her thighs. "You wish." She winced as soon as the words left her mouth. *You wish?* Middle school repartee was apparently the best she could do.

Hudson chuckled, as if amused by her pathetic comeback. "Anyway, we ring that gong every time we get ten thousand breakups, and we got to three hundred thousand today. We'll let you ring it at some point, too. If we haven't worn it out by then, that is." He grinned toothily, and his employees laughed.

Annika looked around at them, her blood pressure rising again. This was all just a fucking joke to them, wasn't it? It didn't matter what their boss had done to her or what a shitty person he was. Very deliberately, Annika smoothed down her hair and skirt and picked her way around the Nerf bullets to where Hudson sat, still perched on his stupid stool.

She grabbed the mallet that lay at his feet, brought it down over her thigh, and broke it cleanly in two pieces. Hudson's two Break Up sidekicks gasped.

Annika let the pieces fall to the ground. "Don't *ever* mess with me like that again."

Hudson Craft stared up at her, his eyebrows practically in his hairline. One corner of his mouth twitched with amusement. His two employees, though, were definitely not smiling. They might have looked comical if she wasn't so angry; the redhead had his hand over his mouth, like he'd just witnessed a brutal murder, and the woman named Blaire was shaking her head back and forth, as if she couldn't believe what was happening.

"You . . . what's *wrong* with you?" Blaire finally said. "You just destroyed our property!"

"What's wrong with *me*?" Annika huffed a disbelieving laugh. "Maybe you're asking the wrong person that question."

"What the hell is that supposed to mean?" Blaire's eyes glittered dangerously. The woman needed yoga.

"It's fine, Blaire." Hudson stood up slowly, looming over her now, his brawny frame blocking out the light from the windows. She had to tip her head back just to see his face. How obnoxious. "So, Ms. Dev—Annika." He rubbed his jaw and looked down at his feet, as if collecting his thoughts. Then he looked back up at her. "It's . . . been a while. How can I help you?"

She swallowed and wiped her palms surreptitiously on her skirt. "You moved *here*. Right down the hall from me."

His expression didn't waver. "I see." Annika could feel Blaire's gaze burning a hole into the side of her face. The redhead was standing back, hands clasped, watching placidly. The seconds ticked on, but Hudson didn't add anything further.

I see? What the hell did *I see* mean? "You—you stole my idea and now you're here!" Annika said in a burst, unable to take his cryptic weirdness anymore.

Hudson frowned slightly and raised one thick blond eyebrow. "I stole your idea? If I remember correctly, your idea was to play matchmaker. Mine's the exact opposite."

"*Is* to play matchmaker." Annika balled her hands into fists, realizing she'd danced right into his little verbal trap. "But I'm not *playing* at anything. Make Up's about second chances," she continued hotly. "Don't tell me this is all just a big coincidence." Annika waved a hand at the room.

The redhead coughed out something that sounded suspiciously like "Cuckoo." Blaire snickered. Annika glared at them.

"I'm sorry." Hudson's eyes were still fixed on her. It was unnerving, how he seemed to peer right into her soul. Definitely a cult leader in the making. "I'm not following. How did I steal your idea again?"

"Let me count the ways." Annika held up one finger. "First, our names. I chose Make Up and you chose Break Up? Come on—could you be more unoriginal? Second, take our slogans. Mine's *Happily Ever After, Redux* and you choose *Your Life, Restarted.* How much more obvious could you get?"

Hudson frowned. "Annika, when did you launch your business?"

"October of last year."

"Blaire, when did we launch the Break Up app?"

"September sixteenth of last year," she replied immediately, smiling triumphantly at Annika.

"So maybe *you're* copying us, Ms. Dev," Hudson said. All three of them burst out laughing.

"Ha-ha, very funny!" Annika snapped. "Look, you can't deny it. We met at that conference last summer. I . . . um, told you about my plans for Make Up—" Annika couldn't help flooding with heat at the memory of where they'd been when she'd told him. "—and then, *bam*. You launch a company that, I'm sorry, feels like a complete rip-off of mine. Beyond that, your company is anathema to mine. No, actually, it's anathema to my entire philosophy on *life*. I strive to reunite lovers and give them their happily-ever-afters, and you do your damnedest to make people miserable and alone for their entire lives."

"That's quite a story you've concocted there." The red-headed dude sniffed. "Is your real name J. K. Rowling?"

It was the weakest comeback in the history of comebacks. At any other time, Annika would've laughed in his face, but she wasn't feeling very amused at the moment. She gave him a withering look. He stepped back, looking caught out.

Hudson Craft held up a hand and spoke to the redhead. "It's okay, Ziggy. People deal with jealousy in all different ways. Annika, apparently, has opted to believe that we owe our success to her." He chuckled. "Hey, whatever floats your boat. Wish *I* was that confident. I think I'd be a lot happier about some of my more dismal failures." His lackeys laughed.

"My company is *not* a dismal failure! And I am not jealous! You just—you—" Annika pushed her fists against her head and let out a frustrated groan. "You're just such an asshole!"

She turned to stalk out, purposely stomping on as many stupid Nerf darts as she could along the way. "You just moved in and the first things you unpack are Nerf guns and a gong? You're all *adults*. Maybe act like it!" she yelled over her shoulder.

"Nice seeing you, neighbor!" Hudson called as she yanked the door open. She could hear the smile in his voice and wanted to turn around and unload another round of Nerf darts in his face. "Come by anytime! Tomorrow we'll have cookies and milk."

Cookies and milk. *Cookies and milk?* Annika couldn't resist asking, "What's next? A brown bag session with PB&J and ants on a log? Naptime?" She shut the door behind her before he had a chance to respond. Something about Hudson's easy, boastful confidence—that he had *no right* to have, by the way— really got under her skin.

It was hard to believe that *this* was the guy who'd left her business in the dust. When she'd met him at the conference, he'd seemed . . . nice. Kind. Maybe even a little lost, a little like he was searching for something. Needless to say, she'd been completely tricked. It was probably just a ploy to get her into bed. Her cheeks warmed again at the thought that she'd hooked up with him. With *him*. What the hell was wrong with her? How could she not have seen that Hudson Craft was nothing but a giant man-baby with talented pecs?

✐

Back in her office, Annika's blood pressure—or as her yoga instructor Seetha called it, her "stress elemental"—took about forty-five minutes to get back under control. She got up to open the office door and help June, who staggered in under the weight of a gigantic whiteboard, the hot pink silk of her dress all rumpled.

Annika propped the board against the wall, right under the Make Up sign. "Wow. You, um, decided to go big, huh?" The monstrosity could double as a pool table.

"I didn't want to do anything by half measures, you know?" June's face was red and sweaty. She smoothed her hair off her forehead and fanned herself. "Is the AC on?"

Cheering sounded from down the hall. June looked at Annika. "What the . . . ?"

"Our new neighbors moved in. And you'll never guess who."

"Who? Oh my gosh. Don't tell me it's Lady Gaga!"

June had a completely unhealthy obsession with Lady Gaga. Annika stared at her. "Lady Ga—what? No. This is a different performer, but one you've definitely heard of. Hudson Craft and the Break Up Cult."

"*What?*"

Annika nodded and waited for June to process through all the stages of shock. First came knee-jerk denial, which was soon followed by intense disbelief, and finally, bringing up the rear, was heated indignation. Warm smugness seeped through Annika. She had someone on her side, too. Hudson Craft and his cronies could laugh and snicker, but Annika wasn't alone in this. Not by a long shot.

June was still struggling to accept reality. "You're kidding. Tell me you're kidding, Annika."

"You have no idea how much I want to tell you that." Sighing, Annika walked over to her desk, rearranged her soothing bamboo picture frames, and sat in her chair, swiveling from side to side as she talked. "I already went over there and gave him a piece of my mind."

June took her seat, too. "No way. What did you say?"

"Just that they're all giant lying, stealing, plagiarizing pieces of shit. I also may have shot him in the face with a Nerf gun."

"Oh my god!" June clapped her hand over her mouth. "I'm sure he deserved it. Did he admit it, then? That he stole your idea?"

Annika blew out a breath. "Yeah, right. He just doubled down and tried to say *I* was jealous of his success or some such bullshit."

"Arrogant piece of—"

"It's okay." Annika looked out the window at the skyscraper-dotted view. "I mean, what else is he going to say, you know? He probably can't even sleep at night. *I* couldn't, if I was responsible for breaking three hundred thousand hearts and profiting off of all that pain. That's right—apparently they've had *three hundred thousand* successful breakups, if you can even call them that. Their app is getting insanely popular, June. It's not good."

June made loyal gagging sounds, even though Annika had rehashed her "Hudson Craft is the devil" speech about twenty-seven times a day over the past eight months.

Annika turned to her laptop and scrolled halfheartedly through her spam folder. "What the hell."

"What?"

"There's an email here from a beta tester. It went to my spam folder."

"Shit, really?"

"I am so firing our web developer."

"Are you still using him?"

"No, but . . . whatever. He's not getting any repeat business when we get our cash flow problems resolved. So many spam emails come to my inbox and the emails I actually want to see are going into the spam folder!" Annika looked up at June. "You know what the problem is? Men. All our problems can be traced back to men."

"Men," June agreed, rolling her eyes. "That reminds me, I went on that date last night?"

"Oh, the—um—the hedge fund manager?" Annika said, only half listening as she skimmed the missed email.

"Yep, Hedgefund Harry. Ugh." June began to tidy up her work surface, like she always did before getting down to coding. Baby Yoda got a prized spot right next to her second screen.

"So he got there twenty-five minutes late, just as I was leaving. He looked me up and down and was like 'Whoa. If I knew you were *this* hot, I would've shown up on time. You need to update your Tinder photo, babe.'"

Annika shuddered. "Ew."

"Where do I find these total tools?"

"Um, Tinder?"

"Right! Why do I keep using Tinder?"

Annika sighed. "Because you don't want to end up a no-life, loveless loser like me?"

"You're not a no-life, loveless loser."

Annika leaned back in her chair. "Really? Then how come every guy I've ever loved has dumped me without a second thought?"

"You know what you need to do."

"Yeah, I know, I know, but I can't just date around like you. Hookups are not my thing. *Love* is my thing." June opened her mouth to argue, but Annika was already distracted by the new beta tester's email. "Hey, should we put this guy on the calendar? Have him come in and work with OLLI?"

June came over and read the email over her shoulder.

Hi Annika,

I'm a junior at UCLA (comp sci major) and my roommate Sean said he really liked helping you train OLLI two weeks ago. Can I volunteer to do that too?

Colin McGuire

"Perfect," June said when she was done reading. "I like that his roommate's already done this, so he has an idea of how it works. And comp sci majors are normally interested in the tech, so they don't ask stupid questions like 'Who am I talking to, exactly? Why do *you* get to define sentience?'"

Annika laughed. "You really didn't like that philosophy major, did you?"

June grunted her displeasure as she went back to her desk. "OLLI's a neural network. 'Who defines sentience?' Who gives a shit? Just help me train the damn thing."

Annika grinned.

OLLI—the Original Love Language Interface—was completely innovative tech. Once it was ready, it would function as a relationship therapist people could have in the comfort of their own phones, a Google Translate for couples. You'd pull up the Make Up app, leave it on the table while you had a serious conversation with your partner, and OLLI would listen in and facilitate a healthier, calmer dialogue. If things started going badly, OLLI would flash a suggestion to fix your mistake—for example, by rephrasing something in a more compassionate, partner-focused manner. OLLI would also be able to detect anger or highly negative emotionality in your voice and push calming messages to help correct the issue.

Annika had read a book by a marriage counselor who claimed poor communication was responsible for ninety percent of divorces. Make Up could fix that. That's where the beta testers came in.

Annika and June would sit with volunteer beta testers for hours while they answered questions and role-played a communication a user might have in a relationship, to train OLLI on their voice and patterns of speech. Eventually, OLLI would get so smart and self-sufficient that it could be used by anyone anywhere.

It was, if Annika did say so herself, a completely genius idea.

It was just taking slightly longer than either of them had antici-
pated or hoped to finish the OLLI prototype, which meant the
grants they'd won were drying up and there was no new source
of income. A fact that Mr. McManor from the Bank of California had clearly noticed.

But Annika was still optimistic. Little electric sparkles of
excitement danced along her skin as she responded to Colin
and asked him to come in. This was how she'd felt when she
first came up with the idea for Make Up and OLLI, the kind
of feeling she got every time she thought about helping someone fall back in love with their loved one. The kind of feeling
she lived for. You know, not the dark, sinking desperation that
came from being cash-poor.

Once she was done fiddling with a bit of code she'd been
working on, June hung the whiteboard on the only empty wall
in their office. Annika put the heinous Hudson Craft firmly out
of her mind, and she and June spent the rest of the day brainstorming the one major hurdle Make Up still faced: its financial
shortcomings, resulting from the app still being in the prototype
phase.

Empty Chinese food containers littered both their desks,
and the scent of greasy lo mein hung like a curtain in the air.
After an hour or two had passed, the boisterous laughter and
yelling from next door had subsided, which made it easier to
concentrate.

Annika stretched, feeling her spine crackle and pop. She'd
kicked off her shoes, so her toes chafed on the tough industrial
carpet as she paced. "All right. So. Scalability—getting OLLI
ready to use by anyone anywhere—is still *the* thorn in our side.
It's the ticket to growth, which is the ticket to money, and we're
just not there yet."

June regarded the notes on the whiteboard, tapping the end of a red dry-erase marker against her chin. "Yeah. And it's proving to be a tough one to crack."

Annika nodded, coming to a stop at the window. People scurried like ants on the sidewalk below in the late-afternoon sunlight. "Right. I know it's because we're being ambitious with the tech. This has never been done before, which is precisely why *we* need to be the ones to do it. We're going to change the world."

"We'll change the world if we ever get to release." June groaned, scribbling a grumpy face in one corner of the whiteboard. "Prototyping feels like it'll never end."

Annika turned from the window to face her. "I know it does. But you know what? We'll get there."

June looked up at her and they said together, "Fail forward." June laughed. "Remember the very first OLLI?"

Annika snorted. "You mean the one we called Troll-y?"

"The iteration that hated everyone! Remember when it told that beta tester that he needed to give up and go home *while* he was speaking to you? And it told another volunteer that her partner would leave her because she sounded like an ugly narwhal pie? I mean, I know small sample sizes make neural networks weird, but WTF."

Annika perched on the edge of her desk, careful not to get anywhere near the empty food container. Grease stains were a nightmare to get out. "Don't remind me."

"But I *will* get Make Up—and OLLI—ready for release soon. I promise."

"I know you will. And if we can get it somewhere close to ready by the time the EPIC pitch contest rolls around in June, we'll blow them away."

June whistled. "Angel investors."

"Yep. It's going to be our big break. Lionel Wakefield is on the panel, and he's famous for investing in businesses that make a difference—that make the world better in some way, however big or small. So I think that's where we should begin. Let's diagram the investors and their personalities and interests—and what's most likely to capture their attention in a pitch."

"Perfect." June drew a stick figure holding a trophy in one corner. "I have a really good feeling about it."

Annika smiled, catching sight of her reflection in the window. She had bags under her eyes, but her jaw was set in a way she really liked. "Me too," she replied. "It's about time Lady Luck took our side again."

chapter three

Some people drank, some smoked pot. Others raced ferrets or composed rude letters in their heads. Annika got her high pretzeling her limbs into odd poses.

She'd been coming to the Breathing Tree Yoga Studio for a whole year now, and she couldn't dream of giving it up. Even when money was tight, even when the financial wolves were snapping at her heels, she set aside the monthly membership for Breathing Tree just like her grocery expenses. It was cheaper than therapy, and it took care of her body *and* her mind.

Yoga had started out as something Annika's dad had talked her into, but cultivating a daily yoga practice was one of the best things she'd ever done.

As a seventh grader, Annika had entered into one of the darkest and most tumultuous phases of her life. That year, it had really sunk in that, unlike all her friends, she would never have a mother to go to with questions about her period or boys.

She'd never have that nonjudgmental, unconditionally loving maternal perspective.

It hadn't seemed like a monumental loss until that year, when hormones and other unknowable adolescent stirrings had kicked into high gear. Not knowing how to cope with something as big and awful as being a motherless teen, Annika began skipping school and smoking pot until the school threatened to expel her. Her poor dad, at his wit's end, had suggested therapist after therapist, to which Annika had responded with typical teenage scorn. But then one Saturday, he'd dragged her to a yoga class at the YMCA and that was it. She was hooked.

Yoga didn't bring her mother back, obviously, but it made life a lot less shitty without one. Annika fell in love with the feeling of quietness and tranquility within her soul, which she hadn't been able to find anywhere else. She loved building her strength— loved knowing her body was resilient and healthy and able to do hard things. She'd kept with it through high school and college and couldn't ever imagine giving it up.

Now, her brain feeling mushy after all the brainstorming she and June had done, Annika strolled into studio A, the one with floor-to-ceiling windows that faced a tiny patch of grass in the back. The knot in her stomach loosened immediately, and her shoulders relaxed.

"Hey, Seetha," she called. Her Indian yoga instructor turned from fiddling with the stereo system and beamed at her.

"Annika! I was just thinking about you." Seetha, the most graceful human being Annika had ever encountered, shimmied over to her. Her gray-speckled black braid hung over one shoulder and she wore a simple diamond nose ring that winked in the light. "Ooh, is that a new outfit?"

Annika checked herself out in the mirror. She'd swapped

her office-trendy burgundy peplum top and black skirt for a purple sports bra and turquoise leggings that had silver peacock feathers printed all over. *Not bad,* she thought. Her high ponytail was bouncy, her arms and abs were toned from diligent practice, and her skin was clear in spite of all the chocolate she'd been stress-eating lately.

"Yeah, it is." Annika smiled. "I treated myself last week. Just a pick-me-up, you know. To jostle myself out of the rut." *The rut of growing an ulcer over financial issues,* she thought but didn't say.

"Well, I have just the thing to jostle you out of the yoga rut," Seetha said. "Get this, I have a new regimen for the end of class today: partner poses."

"Partner poses," Annika repeated. "Is that what it sounds like? You use a partner to do a yoga pose?"

"Precisely!" Seetha rubbed her hands together like some cartoon villainess. Annika smiled. Seetha was as evangelistic about yoga as some people were about their religion. "Elevate your practice to the next level. Get that stress elemental under control. What do you think?"

"I love it." Annika rolled out her yoga mat, eager to begin.

The class began to fill, and, after waving to a few of the regulars, Annika sat in the middle of her mat and crossed her legs, placing each foot on the opposite thigh. She closed her eyes, placed her hands faceup on her knees, and began to practice her deep breathing.

The imagery she used was always the same—pure, blue water, rippling in a burbling brook. *Breathe in, breathe out. Listen to the brook.* Annika found she could drown out practically every sound in the world with this meditation.

"Hey, Annika."

Okay, she couldn't drown out *that* sound. Annika's eyes flew open and she found herself staring at those singularly startling green irises. *"Hudson Craft?"*

He was standing there with a yoga mat dangling from his shoulder, his usual confidence marred slightly by a hint of hesitation that played across his face. He studied her with an intensity that froze her in place, an almost defensive edge to the way he held his jaw. But that made no sense. What did he have to be defensive about? This was her studio. He was the intruder.

In the next instant, the intensity, defensiveness, and hesitation were all gone, as if she'd imagined them in the first place.

"You know," he said in his casual LA drawl, "you don't have to say my full name every time." He rolled out a yoga mat next to hers and began stretching his arms, his shirt lifting up to expose a patch of tan, flat stomach and a happy trail that disappeared into his shorts. Annika looked away hurriedly, before he could catch her staring and laugh at her. *Ugh.* Why was the dude always so self-satisfied? More important, how had she ever thought he was attractive?

Sure, Hudson was conventionally—some might say Chris Hemsworth–level—handsome. He could play Thor in any remakes Hollywood might be considering. But Annika now automatically distrusted men that handsome. People with faces and bodies like that usually came with major issues. And Hudson came with a plethora, that was for damn sure.

Annika blamed her previous weakness at the conference on the margaritas. Or on Vegas. It was one of life's secret truths that almost all evil could be blamed on Vegas, margaritas, and gorgeous men.

"How's your eye, you big liar?" The words shot out before she could stop herself. "And where's your bodyguard?"

Hudson grinned, arching his back and reaching for his

toes, the ridge of his rhomboid muscle visible through his shirt. *Show-off.* "I didn't think you liked Blaire that much."

"What are you *doing* here, anyway?" She was irritated beyond reason that she couldn't seem to ruffle his feathers like he ruffled hers, and she couldn't tone down her annoyance. Hudson was interfering with all her signals, scrambling them until she couldn't think straight. "It's not enough that you move into my office building—you have to take over my yoga studio, too?"

"*Your* yoga studio?" Hudson smirked. "Nice to meet you, Ms. Tree. Or can I call you Breathing?"

Annika glowered at him, vaguely aware the class had filled with people.

He held his hands up. "Look, it was a coincidence. Both the moving-into-your-office-building part and the yoga thing. I lost a bet with Ziggy and his terms were that I take a few yoga classes. This was the closest studio to work."

Annika scoffed. "What was the bet?"

"I promised to work under eighty hours last week and didn't quite make it." Hudson quirked one side of his mouth. "I don't think I've managed to work any less since I came up with the idea for Break Up. It's important to me." His eyes held hers, and an expression flitted across his face, gone before Annika could analyze it.

He was a workaholic. Of course he was. "Working eighty hours a week pulverizing hearts is important to you. Nice. Do you have to down a bottle of NyQuil every night to get to sleep?"

"I have absolutely no problems getting to sleep. I'm doing the world a service, though you may not see it that way." Annika barked a laugh at this atrocious claim, but he continued anyway, ignoring her. "I didn't move into the building knowing you were there. Maybe . . . we just have similar taste."

Annika felt the frisson of memory between them. There were certain details from Vegas that were still sharp in her mind, like the fact that Hudson was a very, *very* good kisser. With exceptionally skillful hands. Annika swallowed and scooted a millimeter away from him. "I don't think so," she said. "We have absolutely nothing in common. *Nothing.*"

Hudson opened his mouth to respond, but Seetha spoke from the front of the room, interrupting him. With a vaguely frustrated expression, he turned to face her. *Good.* Annika hoped he'd stay quiet for the rest of the hour.

༄

It was a great workout. Annika was able to push Hudson's presence out of her head about 75 percent of the time, even though he was right next to her, his long arms and legs twisting and flexing in her peripheral vision. He was actually pretty good for someone who was doing this on a whim. And for someone with those giant tree-trunk thighs. *Of course he's good at yoga,* Annika thought, cutting him a withering glare when he wasn't looking. Hudson Craft was one of those annoying people who were naturally good at everything.

She blew out a breath and tried to refocus. Hudson was immaterial. Right now, only yoga mattered.

"And now, as you move out of vajrasana, I'd like to introduce you all to something new." Seetha's voice washed over them as she walked between rows of people. "Please take this moment to partner up with the person next to you."

Seetha walked up to Annika and Hudson. "You two can work together for this, right?"

"Uh—him?" Annika whispered, trying and failing to think of an excuse to wriggle out of it.

Seetha's dark eyes twinkled, as if she knew exactly what she was doing. "He's new, Annika, and you're such a seasoned yogi. You'll be generous with your skills, won't you?"

Annika choked on her spit, which prompted a coughing fit. Taking advantage of her inability to form words, Hudson spoke up. "Oh, Annika's very generous."

Seetha smiled, winked, and kept moving.

Once she could breathe again, Annika glared at him. Around them, people were turning to their partners with smiles and murmurs of encouragement. Must be nice. "Why do you want to partner with me, anyway?"

Hudson studied her for a long moment, his green eyes flickering with something she didn't understand. "I don't know." Then, seeming to catch himself, he added, with a raised thick blond eyebrow, "That vein on your forehead's about to assault me. Are you sure you're a practiced yogi?"

Annika groaned.

"All right, now I'd like to teach you all a new partner pose," Seetha said from the front of the class. "It behooves us all to remember that life is a partnership between us and all the other sacred creatures sharing our planet.

"Today I want us to practice ardha matsyendrasana, aka the 'half lord of the fishes' pose, with our partners. Before we begin, I'd like the yogi on the right—as you're facing the front of the room—to walk over to the mat of the yogi on your left. You'll both be sitting cross-legged on the same mat for this exercise. Right-hand yogis, please sit behind your partner."

Annika got up stiffly, and without making eye contact, went

and sat behind Hudson. He obliged by moving forward a few inches. Did he have to be so arrogantly tall? He towered over her so much, she couldn't see Seetha. Instead, she studied his back, inhaling deeply to find her center again. Even though he had a fine sheen of sweat on him, he smelled really good, like a combination of light soap, deodorant, and his own scent. Without warning, a memory of a time they'd been this close almost knocked Annika over.

They'd started drinking at the bar, and then, out of nowhere, Annika had invited him to her hotel room, surprising even herself. Later, she would think about it and realize it had been an incremental sort of thing, her lust thermometer creeping up with each quiet observation—the alpha way he strode up the stairs to take the stage and give a presentation that held their peers in thrall. Once they'd begun to form a friendship over the week of the conference, she'd been captivated by the way he bowed his head, his big hand cupped around a pencil and his eyes sparking as he outlined the ideas rattling around in his mind. But all of that would be a post-analysis. In the moment, Annika had known only that she wanted—*needed*—to be with this man.

They'd sat on the couch in her room, laughing and talking. Slowly, they'd gotten closer and closer, Hudson's arm resting lightly over her shoulders, Annika's hand on his knee. When she thought about the first time his tongue had brushed over her lips and coaxed her mouth open, tasting of sweet wine, she still got goose bumps. *Goose bumps.* As if she'd never been kissed before.

Annika forced her mind away from the memory. She shifted on the yoga mat, her heart thundering, her bones liquid. *Oh, god.* Was she actually turned on right now? She closed her eyes and gave herself a pep talk. *This is not the time to revive your sexual attraction for this man, who, might I remind you, Annika Dev, is your enemy. He thrives on helping people break up. He is poison.*

"You okay back there?"

Annika opened her eyes to see Hudson peering curiously at her over his shoulder. "Fine," she said primly, though her cheeks felt warm. Good thing it was nearly impossible to see her blushing, thanks to her extra helping of melanin.

"All right," Seetha said, in her calm voice. "Now that everyone is situated, I'd like all the right-hand yogis to turn around, so your back is against your partner's."

Annika did so eagerly, grateful she wouldn't have to stare at Hudson's perfect physique or smell him anymore. They pressed their backs together. Annika had to remind herself to breathe, which was ridiculous. Hudson Craft was just a human. Just a mound of muscle and bone, like her. So, okay, he was more attractive a mound than most people she knew, but that shouldn't matter. Yoga was about transcending the physical.

As they sat there touching, Annika found herself pressing a cool hand to the back of her neck. His body heat was intense; it enveloped her until she, too, had a light sheen of sweat all over her. A memory flashed into her mind, unbidden: Hudson unbuttoning and then slipping off her shirt, his mouth at her neck.

Goddammit. When would this exercise be over?

"Now I want you to inhale and stretch both your arms over your head," Seetha cooed, blissfully oblivious to the maelstrom in Annika's body. "As you exhale, twist to your right. Bring your right hand to the inside of your partner's left knee. Your left hand will rest on *your* right knee."

Annika's breath caught in her throat. She thought she sensed hesitation from Hudson, too, but then they were doing as Seetha had asked. Hudson's big, hot hand rested gently on the inside of her knee, his fingers putting just the right amount of pressure on her skin. The pose made them face away from each other, but Annika's mouth had gone dry. His hand brought back more memories, how it had traveled up her skirt along her inner thigh—

"Are you okay?" Hudson whispered, his head still turned away.

"Yes. Will you stop asking me that?" Annika hissed back.

"You're trembling."

He was right. She *was* trembling a little, like she was a tuning fork he'd hit. Her hand on his inner knee was shaking, too. A moment later, Annika felt his free hand over hers, stilling it.

Hudson turned his head so they were staring at each other over their shoulders. Annika couldn't help it; her gaze traveled to his lips.

"Okay, now lift your arms again, and turn to the opposite side this time."

Annika jumped as if Seetha had fired a Nerf gun at her. She wrenched her hand out from under Hudson's. She could feel his back shaking as he laughed quietly to himself. Annika narrowed her eyes and brought her other hand down hard on his opposite knee.

"Ow."

"You deserved that."

"What for? It's not my fault you still fantasize about me every time you fall asleep."

Annika's mouth fell open in outrage, even though she knew Hudson couldn't see her. "I do *not*."

"No?" His hand on her inner knee, feather-light, moved just a fraction. "I seem to remember you had a thing for my hands—and all the many ways I used them."

Annika's breaths came faster as she felt the pressure of his thumb on the back of her leg, his other fingers whispering along skin that felt like it was awaking from a deep sleep, fire dancing in her veins. Her own hand tightened, and she felt his muscled back stiffen against hers, like he was holding back some intense emotion. "Hudson—"

He turned his head, his mouth at her ear, his breath moving her hair when he spoke. "Why?"

Annika could barely breathe, let alone make sense of what he was saying. "Wh-what?"

"And that brings us to the end of class," Seetha said. "You are welcome to go into *shavasana* if you'd like to rest for five minutes. If you must leave, please leave quietly."

Annika scrambled to her feet like they, the entire studio, and the world at large were on fire. She grabbed her yoga mat without looking at Hudson and practically ran out of the room, waving quickly to Seetha.

Why had she let him get to her like that? *Incorrigible, awful tease.* It didn't help that she hadn't slept with anyone since their night in Vegas. She pushed open the glass doors, rounded the corner, and leaned against the brick wall in the alley, panting lightly as she tried to collect her thoughts.

What had she done to deserve this rush of bad luck? She'd always tried to be such a good person. Now her archnemesis had not only moved into her office building, he was taking the same freaking yoga class as her. It couldn't be a coincidence. Hudson knew the effect he had on women—he *had* to know—and he was just using that to disarm her. He had a guilty conscience because of the awful work he was doing with his app, and maybe he thought sleeping with her could somehow assuage that.

Ha. Hudson was kidding himself. Annika wanted nothing to do with him. Nothing. Zero. Zilch.

୧

Everything looked better with a cinnamon dolce latte. As Annika walked through the cool parking garage the next morning, toting her coffee and yoga gear, she was sure her reaction to Hudson had just been a reaction to work stress. In the light of day, it was even a little amusing. How had she let someone like *him* get to her? It was so obvious Hudson was trying to sleep with her as some kind of coup or a way to make himself feel better about his terrible life choices.

Annika lined up for the elevator and took a thoughtful sip of her coffee. She was wearing her red sheath dress today, the one that made her feel confident and poised—and it was working. She'd come to the realization that Hudson should be considered a speed bump in her life and nothing more. He wasn't worth the brain space she'd been dedicating to him. The elevator came and she stepped on, feeling more buoyant than she'd felt in a long time.

On her floor, there were noises coming from the Break Up office, but she kept her eyes pointed forward. They didn't exist. They were irrelevant. What mattered was Make Up, the movement she was trying to grow, what she wanted to see more of in this world. Annika took a deep, centering breath, and pushed open the glass door.

June stood by the whiteboard, dressed in a purple puffed-sleeve shirt and gold skirt, her back to Annika. She was busy writing *EPIC Pitch Contest* at the top-right of the whiteboard, obviously gearing up for another brainstorming session. Hearing Annika arrive, she turned, beaming, a dry-erase marker held jubilantly aloft. Her chandelier earrings danced. "Guess what?"

"Um . . ." Annika went to put her yoga gear into the closet. "Mr. McManor decided to take pity on us? We're debt-free? Hudson Craft fell out of his window? Gwyneth Paltrow's cousin got chicken pox?"

June mock-pouted, her hands on her hips. "Now mine is going to feel like a letdown."

Annika laughed. "I give up. What?"

"Colin McGuire, our newest beta tester, set up an appointment for tomorrow." June grinned. There were few things in life that made Annika happier than new beta testers, which meant new data points for OLLI to chomp on and grow.

"Nice. What time?"

"First thing," June replied. "I know that's when you work best."

Annika took a gulp of sweet coffee. "The more people we can get in here, the faster we can do this. It's gonna be fantastic."

"One might even say . . . epic." June raised an eyebrow. Annika laughed.

"Okay, point taken. Let's get to brainstorming our pitch. So, the contest is coming up in six weeks. That's hardly any time at all. We need to come up with something pithy, something entertaining and full of heart. I've read the investors are really into the heart-wrenching, gut-punching stories, especially Lionel Wakefield."

"Yep." June wrote down *wrench their hearts, punch their*

guts. "He was in last month's *Wired*, did you see? 'The Bleeding-Heart Billionaire,' that's what they're calling him. EPIC got a shout-out, too, something about how it's the contest to keep an eye on to see what the next big thing in tech is going to be. It's going to be huge."

"Yeah, I saw that. That's why we need to absolutely kill it."

June nodded. "Definitely. If we get our secret feature up and running in time, it'll be especially effective."

Annika frowned. "Secret fe—oh, you mean the future projection?"

"Shh." June held the marker up to her lips and gestured to the door. "There are spies everywhere." In another corner of the board, June wrote, *Super-secret feature ++Make Up.* "Okay. Do we know who the competition is yet?"

Annika walked to her desk and set her coffee down. "I heard through the grapevine that Patterns, Glow Up, and Heart Tech are all pitching, too."

June made a new "competition" section on the whiteboard and wrote down the company names. "So that's . . . an interior design app, a fashion app, and an app that wants to replace the pacemaker."

Annika put a blue X next to the first two. "I'm thinking our only real competition out of those three is Heart Tech. Patterns is too disorganized, from what I've seen of them at other conferences, and Glow Up isn't doing anything innovative."

"And their developer is better at Googling than he is at Python," June scoffed. "I met him at that workshop I did last month."

"Good for us. I don't know who else is going to be there, but I don't think that really matters. Our edge is how innovative our tech is. All we need to focus on is our energy, and make sure we convey to the panel just how big this could be." She began pacing, her brain spitting and sparking ideas as she stepped into a strip of bright sunlight on the carpet. "We're not just about the shiny new thing, right? We're not about sexy hookups or one-night stands, stuff that doesn't last. We're about long-enduring partnerships. We're about infusing love back into something that's tried and true. What's important to us is meaningful connection, making people just a little bit less lonely in this world. And we're going to use technology to help us do that. It's the perfect blend of cutting-edge tech and old-school heart." She stopped at the window and looked out at the forest of skyscrapers, at all the windows, out of which hundreds of others were probably looking out, too. None of them could see each other. "There are so many people so close together in this city. In every city. And yet we're all just like fallen leaves, scattered by the wind, swirling meaninglessly on aimless journeys. Make Up wants to give meaning to that journey."

June shook her head. "Sounds . . . lonely."

"It *is* lonely. At the end of the day, we're all completely alone. We're born alone and we die alone—didn't someone famous say that?"

"Super-secret feature? What's that—a binky for the especially needy clients?"

Annika turned at the brash, confident voice. Hudson Craft stood at the door, dressed in dark-wash jeans and a mint-colored polo shirt, flame-haired Ziggy by his side. She hadn't even heard him come in, she'd been so focused on her conversation with June.

She stared at him without saying anything. Her mind flashed confusingly with images of him whispering in her ear at yoga, his hand on her inner knee, asking her "why" (she still hadn't figured that one out—why what? Why was her app so much better than his?), the way he'd leaned in close to kiss her at the hotel in Vegas, the feeling of his gong mallet snapping in half against her thigh—and "gong mallet" wasn't a euphemism . . . though snapping *that* gong mallet in half was an option she'd consider if things got dire enough. It was easier to think of him as an inconsequential speed bump in her life if he wasn't actually in her office. Which brought her to her next thought: *What was he doing here?*

Seeing her paralysis, June stepped forward with a toothy grin, holding a manicured hand out. "Hi there," she said, her southern accent stronger than ever. Anytime June disliked someone, her accent came out even more pronounced, as though it was a shield. "How nice to meet you. I'm June Stewart. Chief Technology Officer, Make Up."

"Hudson," he said, his own brilliant smile never fading. Self-satisfied, complacent, little . . . "CEO, Break Up." His eyes danced with laughter. "And this is the partial owner of Break Up—"

"—Percy," the redhead, who hadn't stopped staring at June since they arrived, jumped in. He held his hand out, too, and June took it. "But they call me Ziggy."

"Oh." Letting go of his hand, June cocked her head and smiled pityingly at him. "You can't get them to stop?"

Ziggy let out a strange laugh, like a goose having an asthma attack. "I—I guess not." He continued to stare at June, as if he couldn't bear to look away.

Annika rolled her eyes and turned to Hudson. "Why are you here?" She hoped it sounded just as rude out loud as it did in her head.

His face was tinged with annoyance and something buried

deeper that she couldn't get to, but then he was looking past her at the whiteboard on the wall, his expression back to confident and smirky. "The EPIC pitch contest, huh? You're pitching them in June?"

Annika crossed her arms. "Yeah, so?"

"No, nothing." Hudson brushed back his hair and shrugged insouciantly, as if he were talking about the weather. "We'll be there, too."

It took Annika a beat to catch on. "You . . . you mean Break Up's going to be *pitching* the investors?"

Ziggy adjusted the collar of his crisp button-down. "Yeah, the rumor is Lionel Wakefield's really looking for a dating app to invest in right now."

"But you don't need any more money!" Annika found herself bursting out. "And you're not a dating app—you're a heartbreaking app!"

A corner of Hudson's mouth lifted in a self-satisfied half smile. "I know we look successful—and we are—but every start-up needs a steady infusion of capital to keep it going. Break Up's no different."

Ugh. Typical. Mercenary, greedy, smug *ass*. She exchanged a glance with June, who looked just as miffed as she did. This was *their* chance to turn things around, dammit. Break Up wasn't supposed to be part of the picture. She didn't want to have to worry about Hudson fucking Craft at EPIC, too.

He looked at her with a slightly pitying look on his face. "I'm not going to take it easy on you. Just FYI." Raising his chin to June's notes on the whiteboard about wrenching the investors' hearts and punching their guts, he added, "You might want a more cerebral approach than just torturing the investors until they give you money."

Annika stepped into his path, just a few inches apart from him, to block his view. Which was ridiculous, because the dude had, like, ten inches on her. Her head wasn't even in his periphery. Determinedly staring at the little white buttons on his polo shirt (she didn't want to give him the satisfaction of seeing her struggle to meet his eye), she said, "I don't *need* you to take it easy on me, Hudson. I'll be sure to send you the link to Indeed. com's job listings, though. You'll need to start thinking about a career change after we smoke you at EPIC. I hear Subway's always hiring."

There was a soft snort. Annika thought Hudson might be laughing at her but it was impossible to know for sure from this angle. Damn him and his gigantic genes. She tossed her hair behind her casually, and said, to his pecs, "It won't be so funny when I kick your ass."

"You want to say that to my face?" Laughter pushed at the edges of his words.

Ziggy snickered in response, but June was stonily silent in solidarity. She could hear them but she couldn't see them, since she was still resolutely studying Hudson's buttons. Damn. She should've come up with an exit strategy.

Hudson bent toward Annika, his eyes locked on hers. She had no choice but to gaze back. "You've got an edge, Ms. Dev. Anyone ever tell you that?"

There was a beat between them that Annika couldn't quite read. Her palms got damp. "A competitive edge, yes. All the time. I'm glad you're finally acknowledging it." Hudson didn't smile at her quip. What did he see when he looked at her? Finally breaking eye contact, she stepped back unsteadily and cleared her throat. "So, did you just come down here to tell us you're pitching at EPIC?"

"Actually, no." Stepping back too, Hudson rested his shoulder lightly against the doorjamb. It creaked, but he didn't seem to notice. Of course not. He'd be happy if Annika's office collapsed into a pile of rubble. "We're on our way to talk to someone about having a few dozen cases of champagne delivered."

Annika scoffed, abandoning her scrutiny of the doorjamb, and crossed her arms. "A few dozen cases of champagne? I know you're all about the self-congratulation, but that seems excessive, even for you."

Ziggy spoke up, his eyes bright. "We're having a 'moving into the building' party on Thursday." After a pause, his eyes darting to June, he added, "You guys should come. You know, if you're not busy."

Hudson shot Ziggy an annoyed look, but Ziggy was so busy staring at June, he completely missed it.

"Why would we *ever* come to that?" Annika asked, looking up at him.

Hudson shrugged, those big, destructive shoulders moving in his silky polo shirt. "So don't. Most of the rest of the building's already RSVPed yes. Should be a great networking event." He glanced around the empty office, raising an eyebrow. "Looks like you're having trouble attracting beta testers."

"I'm not having trouble attracting anyone," Annika scoffed. Hudson gave her a lascivious smile. "*Volunteers*," she specified, to which Hudson arched an eyebrow. Realizing how it probably sounded to someone with Hudson's twisted mind, Annika rushed on. "Anyway, we don't need your tasteless party to network."

June darted her a *what-are-you-doing* look. They'd talked about it before, how they should network with the other people in the building. It'd be good for business. But in their experience, everyone who worked there had been completely antisocial, unwilling to sit through even a brown bag lunch. Free food! What kind of people refused free food?

Annika narrowed her eyes. "But we might make an exception in this case out of pure curiosity, just to see what kind of a janky-ass party you'll be putting on." She paused, tucked a strand of hair behind her ear, pretended to check her nails. "How'd you get everyone to RSVP yes, anyway?"

Hudson flashed her his cockiest smile, as if he took her question as a compliment. With his ego the size it was, Hudson probably took comments about the weather as compliments. "All the free booze they can drink on the rooftop, served by LA's hottest models. Not many people can say no to that." He winked and turned to go.

Ziggy looked at June with a hopeful smile. "It's Thursday at five. So, will you be there, June? Because, uh—I'll—I'll definitely be there."

June gave him a polite smile. "Yeah, sure. See you then."

He left, floating down the hall as if she'd agreed to marry him.

Annika threw her hands up the moment the door closed behind him. "Free booze and hot models. Of course. Why does that not surprise me at all?"

June sighed and sank into her leopard-print chair, a dry-erase marker hanging from her limp hand. "Well, say what you want about Hudson Craft. He really knows how to give people what they want."

Annika opened her mouth, then snapped it shut. What she'd been *about* to say to June was, "Yeah, he really does." Because she'd been thinking about Vegas yet again. About Hudson's mouth, and his tongue, the way he'd pulled her hair and kissed the arc of her throat. Too bad he'd turned out to be an idea-stealing asshole heading up the world's most despicable app.

Annika glanced at June, feeling guilty. She'd never told her *all* of what had happened in Vegas, and they never kept things like that from each other. For now, though, Annika *had* to keep it to herself. Hudson was a distraction, and neither of them could afford to be distracted.

Anyway, Vegas was immaterial. Her past with Hudson Craft was immaterial.

"Let's get back to the pitch. We need to be twice as good as Break Up, which means we need to get it nailed down and ready to go ASAP."

June looked up at her, her eyes hopeful. "You think we still have a shot?"

Annika smiled grimly. "Yeah. A kill shot."

chapter four

♡

Annika sat on the tiny, definitely-not-code-compliant balcony attached to her apartment and pulled her cardigan tighter to ward off the slight chill in the air. She set her wineglass and phone on the small metal table beside her and took a deep breath. Whatever the weather, she made it a point to spend a few nights a week out here. It was the whole reason she'd gotten the place. She didn't have a great view—there was a parking lot below—but in the distance, she could see the downtown lights sparkling in the night, and somehow, that felt like home. Seeing evidence of other people, of progress, of this giant, sprawling city breathing and growing and aggressively living, helped her feel less alone. It helped her feel like she was part of something.

Describing people as scattered leaves to June earlier came from a small, scared place deep inside her. Reconnecting people to their loved ones distracted her from her secret conviction that she was never going to find what they had. Ever since she was a teen, Annika had had an abiding sense that if people were made in pairs, like socks, she was the sock the universe had lost in the washing machine. She was displaced, destined to be forever alone.

Which was fine. Everyone had their part to play, and Annika's part was the matchmaker. Always the bridesmaid, never the bride. But she was grateful she got to be part of the periphery.

She took a sip of her wine, feeling it pool in her stomach, flushing her skin with warmth. Colin the beta tester would be coming in the next day, and whatever else might be on her mind, she'd work hard to make sure his time was well spent at the office. She thought of Mr. McManor again, criticizing, weighing, *judging* her in her space, and closed her eyes, only to see Hudson Craft's face, his obnoxious smirk as he said he was doing the EPIC contest, too.

Annika took another bolstering sip of wine. He didn't scare her. Break Up might be having their day in the sun right now, but Make Up was scrappy. Make Up had a tech magic that would appeal to the investors, especially Lionel Wakefield. Make Up was about bettering the world. Surely a philanthropic billionaire would see that.

Taking a deep breath, Annika picked up her phone and dialed her father. She called him once a week, a practice that had started when she'd moved away for college and felt guilty for leaving him all alone.

"Ani," he said, using her childhood nickname, a smile in his voice. It was pronounced *Ah-nee*, and it made her feel younger instantly, safe and warm.

"Hi, Daddy." She could picture him at home in his cavernous study, a glass of expensive scotch at his elbow while he read some dusty old medical journal or other. *He* had a view of the Hollywood Hills, with nary a parking lot in sight.

"Are you coming home this Saturday for dinner?" he asked.

"Like always."

"Excellent. I'm making kalua! I had an underground oven installed in the backyard."

Annika grinned. "An underground oven? Really?" Cooking was her dad's passion; he loved foodie things more than most people loved their families. His version of a midlife crisis involved not overpriced sports cars but wine cellars and wok ranges.

"Yes, of course. It's all the rage with the homesteaders, you know. People DIY those in an afternoon."

"Did you DIY yours?"

"Well, not exactly. But Mike did."

Annika snorted. Mike was their handyman, who'd indulged many of her dad's phases. "Right. Well, I can't wait to see it."

He made a soft groaning noise, and Annika could picture him leaning back in his leather armchair, ready to have a good chat. Her heart squeezed with affection.

"How was your day, Daddy?"

"Good, good. Medicine still holds its allure for me. It's a fascinating field of study."

The unspoken addendum sat between them: *"It's not too late for you. Medical school will change your life for the better."*

He continued, "You know that surgery I was telling you about? The six-year-old with brain cancer?"

"Yeah?"

"Went without a hitch." She could hear the smile in his voice. "Everyone just about cheered when he pulled through it."

As an anesthesiologist, her dad didn't have to know much about his patients, but he made it a point to really get to know them anyway. He said the day he dehumanized the people on his table was the day he turned in his medical license.

"That's awesome! But I'm really not surprised."

He grunted, pleased. "So, tell me. How's the business? Oh, congratulations, by the way. I saw your email about the piece in that online magazine—what's it called? *Wonder Woman?*"

"*Women of Wonder*," Annika corrected, shivering lightly in the breeze that had just picked up. "I know it's no *Forbes*, but it's cool because they feature a lot of women entrepreneurs. Plus, I really liked the nickname they coined for me." She grinned.

"'Dr. Make Up, the relationship doc,'" her dad quoted. "I have to say, Annika, that's not what I meant when I said I wanted you to become a physician."

Annika rolled her eyes. "Ha-ha. To answer your earlier question, Make Up's doing really well. We have a new beta tester coming in bright and early tomorrow, a networking event on Thursday . . . busy, busy, busy." There was no good time to tell your father, who still harbored dreams of you following in his doctorly footsteps, that the bank was sending henchmen out to threaten you for being "grotesquely delinquent."

"A networking event? That could be good. You've been trying to set one up for a long time. It's nice to hear you've had success this time around."

"It wasn't exactly me who had success with it." Annika squeezed the stem of her wineglass, imagining it was Hudson's neck instead.

"Oh. Well, who did?"

Annika sighed and took a sip of wine, pulling her legs up on the chair, her feet warm in her plushy, heart-motif socks. "A new business moved in down the hallway. It's called Break Up."

"Oh, yes, they're up-and-coming, aren't they? I remember reading about the CEO in the papers last week. What was his name? Harvey Craft?"

Of *course* her dad had read about him. She cleared her throat, her hand still tight on the stem of her wineglass. "Hudson Craft."

"And you . . . don't get along with this Hudson?"

Annika closed her eyes, reminding herself of all the awful things Hudson had done. "Yeah, you could say that. Although, I'm not sure *any*one could get along with him. Do you know he's already facilitated three hundred thousand breakups with his awful app? And they hit a million downloads."

"Three hundred thousand! A million!" her dad said, totally missing the point. "Those seem like tremendous numbers. The article said he hadn't even been in business a full year yet."

Annika sighed, letting her head loll on the back of her chair so she could stare up at the ceiling, where she'd strung twinkling lights. "Those numbers aren't *that* astronomical. Anyway, Dad, you're missing the point."

She heard the smile in his voice. "And what's that?"

"That Hudson's a brash, boastful, condescending supervillain."

Her dad made a sound somewhere between a chuckle and a snort. "Supervillain, huh? Things must be bad."

Annika forced herself to mentally chronicle all the good stuff in her life. Health, friendships, father, a nice place to live, a business she loved. "No," she said, meaning it. "Things aren't so bad. I love this phase of Make Up, when we're collecting new data and everything feels rife with possibility."

"Excellent," he said, but Annika could tell he had to make an effort to sound enthusiastic.

She'd wished so many times that her father would show the same level of eagerness for Make Up as he would if she were telling him about a surgery she'd performed, or a cadaver she'd dissected. It was the one sticking point in their relationship—he simply refused to see that Make Up was her passion, her baby, something she'd created from absolutely nothing, a dream she'd concocted from thin air.

She stifled the disappointment and said lightly, "You don't really think it's excellent, but that's okay."

"No, I do. It's just that—"

Annika frowned. "Just that what?"

"I think you could be so successful as a doctor, Ani. A *real* doctor."

She set her wineglass down and hugged her knees to her chest. "Dad, you don't know that. I could *kill* people. I could be one of those doctors they profile on the news with a catchy nickname like Dr. Death. I bet you wouldn't think Dr. Make Up was so bad then."

"But how do you know that when you haven't even given it a chance?"

She glowered at her phone. "Well, I guess we'll never find out." There was a beat of silence before she added, "Good night, Dad. I'm going to bed."

"Okay. Good night, Ani. Pluto."

And just like that, her shoulders relaxed, the hurt and disappointment seeping out of her. "Pluto."

"Pluto" was what they said to each other instead of "I love you." It had become a thing because Annika's mom apparently used to say she didn't just love Annika's dad "to the moon and back," but "to Pluto and back," because that was much, much farther. Eventually they'd honed the phrase down to just "Pluto." And then when Annika came along, her dad said they would say it to her, too, though she had no memory of her mom. Now "Pluto" was a link connecting her and her dad, a way for them to signal, "*Hey, you're all I have in the world. And there's nothing I wouldn't do for you.*"

Annika set her phone down and sighed. Her dad's "Pluto" had put everything in perspective. He might not be perfect, but when she spoke to him, she felt like she belonged somewhere. She didn't need to look out at the city lights to remind herself she was here, that she mattered to someone in some way.

Annika padded back into her apartment in her socked feet, turning out the lights she always left blazing, a facsimile of warmth. After she got ready for bed, she snuggled under her covers and closed her eyes. Tomorrow was a new day. Tomorrow, she'd—

Her eyes flew open. A Hudson memory popped into her head without her permission—his warm hands encircling her waist, his fingers pressing into her bare back.

She turned the other way, pushing him out of her head. She must be way more tired than she'd realized if she was thinking of Hudson Craft in bed.

Think about . . . a nice, peaceful stream. Trees waving in a gentle breeze.

The way he'd whispered her name in her ear, sending goose bumps rushing down her arms. How he'd nipped at her earlobe, her neck, her shoulder . . . how he'd pushed her against the wall and pinned her arms above her head . . .

Her forehead was damp with sweat now, and her mouth had gone dry. She squirmed in her bed, her clothes suddenly too constricting, too abrasive. She wanted to feel the warm air on her bare skin, to feel his hands on her again—

Stop it.

Annika lay there, panting in the dark. Her hand slipped to the waistband of her shorts.

Fuck. This was a problem.

❧

The next day, Annika arrived at work at seven in the morning to prepare for Colin's arrival. The building was still quiet and almost completely empty; the security guard barely glanced up from his cup of coffee as Annika zipped her card through the turnstile reader. Once she let herself into the office, she kicked off her pumps and paced the carpeted floor in bare feet, watching the tops of the buildings turn pink as the sun seeped into the sky.

Tracing her fingers along the MAKE UP: HAPPILY EVER AFTER, REDUX sign, the metal cool against her skin, she smiled and walked to her desk to review the questions she needed to ask Colin.

June came in at eight, right after Annika finished her morning meditation. "I see we're going for yin and yang again today," Annika said, gesturing to June's metallic, zebra-print dress and hot pink pumps.

"I like the all-black look," June replied, putting her purse in the closet and running her eyes over Annika's silky shirt and pants. "Especially with that turquoise statement necklace."

Annika smoothed her hands over her thighs. "Thanks, Junebug."

"So, I was thinking that after the appointment I could review the last learning layer we added to OLLI. The aggression detection algorithm is still a little off."

Annika perched on the edge of her desk, phone in hand. "You know, I was doing some reading and I think the problem might actually be in a higher-order layer. I have some ideas about that. I'll post them on the bug tracker today."

"All right. I'll take a look—maybe it'll shake something loose." June adjusted her Princess Leia Funko and turned on her laptop. Then, a little too casually, she added, "Ziggy texted me last night."

Annika lowered her phone. "Really? What did he say?" She paused. "Wait. How did he even get your number?"

June's cheeks turned bright pink. "I saw him in the parking garage on my way out. I might've given it to him."

Annika raised an eyebrow that June didn't see, since she was steadfastly clicking around on her laptop. "Right. So what did he say?"

June shrugged, her eyes still glued to the screen. "Just that he was looking forward to seeing me Thursday at the networking event. And then we talked some tech stuff. He's Hudson's developer, you know, so we have a lot in common as far as that goes."

"June."

"What?"

"*June.*" Annika waited until June finally met her eye. "He's the enemy. Remember?"

"No, Break Up and Hudson are the enemies," June said, leaning back in her chair. "And I do remember that. It'll be good! I can keep an eye on Kingdom Break Up from the inside."

Annika sighed. "I'm worried it might get a little awkward once you've broken it off, though. We work down the hall from the guy."

"I won't let it get awkward!" June shot back, affronted. "I'm a pro, Annika. When we're done, Ziggy will think it was all his idea."

Annika smiled and hopped off her desk. "Okay, then. In that case, I hope Ziggy turns out to be a fun distraction."

June rolled her eyes. "Lord knows we could both use one of those."

They laughed and got to work preparing for Colin McGuire.

❧

"Wow. That was amazing." June sat on the edge of Annika's desk once Colin, a tall, reedy guy with a gap between his two front teeth, left. "It's such a thrill to see decision trees forming in real time." She patted her laptop. "Good old OLLI. He's really comin' along."

Annika grinned. "Yeah, it's pretty cool, right? I can't wait till we're done with this prototype phase. Maybe we can reach back out to UCLA for more beta te—"

Deep voices in the hallway made Annika look out her glass doors, only to see Hudson Craft outside, smirking at her as he spoke to someone. She gasped. "What's he doing talking to Colin?"

June followed her gaze. "Uh oh. I don't know, but you better get out there."

They speed-walked into the hall, just in time to hear Hudson say as he held out a business card, "I'm just saying. Do you know what the likelihood is of them actually getting that thing off the ground? About one in two million. Meanwhile, Break Up's already been downloaded a million times. Three hundred thousand people have used our services. You're in college, right?"

Poor Colin just nodded, bewildered.

"Thought so. Here's my card. You're gonna need it." He looked at Annika as he said it, and she got the distinct impression it wasn't so much that he needed to poach Colin for his million-dollar business but that he just wanted to get under her skin.

Well, mission accomplished.

Wedging herself between Hudson and Colin, Annika snatched the business card out of Hudson's hand, ignoring the flutter in the pit of her stomach when his fingers grazed hers. "What do you think you're doing?" She tried not to let too much vitriol seep into her tone in front of Colin, who looked confused. Turning to him, she pasted on her calm, professional smile. "Why don't I walk you to the elevator?" she said, one hand on his shoulder. "And rest assured, I'm going to talk to security about panhandlers accosting people in the halls." She darted Hudson a dirty look. He shrugged lazily, looking not the tiniest bit bothered.

Once Colin was securely on the elevator, Annika rounded on Hudson, who was now leaning against the wall, his green eyes intent on her. June had her arms crossed and was glaring at him.

"So it's not enough that you stole my idea, you have to poach my volunteers, too? You have absolutely no shame!"

Hudson pushed off the wall and walked close to her, close enough to block out the light, close enough that he was looking straight down at her. She could smell his cologne, something light and fresh and masculine. His expression was now serious, and Annika felt her pulse thrum at her throat.

"No, you're right, Ms. Dev," he murmured, those eyes suddenly searing into hers, his previous casualness gone. "It really sucks when people screw you over."

She didn't break eye contact, even though her breath was catching at his proximity, at the tension in the air between them. "I wouldn't know. I don't make a habit of screwing people."

The charged air shifted, changed. A corner of Hudson's mouth lifted, though his eyes remained intense. "Don't you? Because I remember differently." His voice was deep, growling, husky.

Her stomach fluttered, and her mind went blank. For a long moment, she was captive, unable to look away. Her fantasy from last night flitted into her mind, caressing her with its butterfly wings. In her darkened bedroom, *this* is what she'd thought about.

Then June cleared her throat.

Annika felt her face flame as she realized June was standing there, staring at the two of them, her eyebrows as high as they could go. Shit.

"I have no idea what you're talking about." Annika jerked backward and stalked back into her office.

"See you Thursday!" Hudson called through the glass door.

June came in, still staring as Annika sank onto the settee. "You . . . you and *Hudson?*" Her voice approached dog whistle–level pitches. "Why didn't you *tell* me? I can't believe you'd keep something like that from me!"

Annika massaged her temples. "I know, I know. I'm sorry. It was an impulsive mistake in Vegas, and . . . it should've never happened. You were on that Maui vacation when I got back and then a couple of months later the industry started buzzing about his app and I was too embarrassed to admit I'd slept with someone like him. Someone who had sex with me and then stole my idea, hoping I'd be too infatuated to notice." Just saying it out loud felt horrible, the worst blow to her pride. "I was hoping it would never come up, but then he moved in next door and he obviously has no plans to let me forget it."

June sat and put an arm around her. "I'm sorry. That's . . . awful. I had no idea you'd hooked up at the conference."

Annika didn't correct her. It had felt like so much more than a hookup to her back then, but it was obvious that that was exactly what it had been for Hudson. "Yeah. Not my smartest move."

June squeezed her shoulder. "We've all been there, babe." After a pause, she asked, "Was he . . . good?"

Annika glared at her best friend. "*June.*"

"What? It's a valid question. I mean, his personality's crap, but his physique is *mm-mmm.*" She closed her eyes to demonstrate her appreciation. "But what's his skill level?"

"Can we not talk about this?"

June raised a shapely eyebrow. "That good, huh?"

Annika groaned and walked to her computer. "I'm going to get to work now. Don't you have that aggression algorithm to fix?"

"You know what you need?" June said from the settee, as if Annika hadn't spoken. "A date. A really nice, handsome, funny guy to take you out and make you feel special. How long has it been since you've had sex, anyway? Has there been anyone since Hudson?"

Glaring at her friend, Annika put in her earbuds and turned her music as loud as she could stand it.

chapter five

Thursday came too quickly. Annika was keenly aware that she'd spent much of the previous night tossing and turning. She'd tried all her usual insomnia remedies—*write down what you're anxious about, count sheep, listen to soothing music.* At one point, she'd gotten out of bed to do some stretching, but she couldn't even complete one *asana* before she was stewing over Hudson's big event and how he was sure to show off about his hundreds of thousands of breakups and his hot models and his free booze and how much of a loser she'd feel like when everyone in the building except her and June was completely won over by his charm.

And . . . maybe talking with June had shaken things loose, but she couldn't help but ruminate again about the Hudson she'd known in Vegas, and the Hudson she was seeing now. There was something about him she couldn't put her finger on. He seemed to want to tease her and be in her space at the same time as she felt a distance from him, a hardness that she didn't remember being there before.

In Vegas he'd been . . . sweet. Down-to-earth. Funny. Had his success changed him that much? And then Annika was tumbling headlong down the Vegas rabbit hole, each memory like a slideshow that wouldn't quit.

She remembered Hudson telling her about his parents. They didn't have high school educations, but seeing the fire inside him, they'd given him every opportunity to succeed. They were determined their youngest son would make it. He'd shared with Annika his idea for an app that could help fine artists visualize their projects on the screen before they began. She'd been his sounding board. She'd even given him ideas about how to make it stronger.

And it had all been a giant lie.

He'd been waiting for her to drop morsels of her own as-yet-unformed idea for a dating app that could bring exes together with a touch of a button, and then he'd stolen and bastardized it. All the mind-blowing sex and vulnerable sharing had been intended to turn her head, to make her trust him even more—which it had accomplished, of course.

But she had to go to his event, because if she didn't, she'd feel even worse. She'd wonder if she'd done all she could for Make Up, especially with Mr. McManor's threats looming over her.

Annika got out of the nest of her bed, with its extra-large comforter and six fluffy pillows, shut off the alarm that hadn't rung yet, and walked to her bathroom to shower and brush her teeth. Afterward, she picked out a killer outfit that always made her feel confident and calm: a teal mermaid-style skirt, a pale coral-colored eyelet shirt, and ballet flats. Annika nodded to herself in the mirror. Bags under her eyes or not, she could do this. She *would* do this.

❧

Clutching her daily cinnamon dolce latte, Annika walked through the cavernous parking garage. She was only vaguely aware of a woman in a business suit pulling a briefcase from a silver convertible, until a man she'd never seen before approached the woman in a Break Up T-shirt and jeans. Annika slowed down to make sure the woman would be okay. She saw her look up at the guy and frown slightly.

The guy said, "Heather Formley?"

The woman nodded.

"I'm a terminator with Break Up. I've been sent by Yuri Trent to tell you he's done with your relationship and is no longer interested in couples therapy. There is no hope of reconciliation. Please don't try to call him or show up at his house. He'll have your Hello Kitty pajamas and your electric toothbrush delivered via FedEx within the week." The guy handed the woman a business card, turned on his heel, and walked off, entering something into his phone as he went.

The woman—Heather—hadn't said a word. It wasn't until the guy was out of the parking garage that she said, "Wait!" But of course, it was too late by then. The "terminator" couldn't even hear her anymore.

Annika walked up to her. "Hey. Can I do anything for you? I saw what happened. It was . . ." She shook her head.

Heather turned to her, her face a mask of bewildered shock. Her leather briefcase hung limply from one hand, the business card from the other. "What—what *was* that? What just happened?"

"Your . . . boyfriend? Yuri?"

Heather nodded. "Yeah, we've been going out a year."

Annika tried not to wince. She kept her voice gentle as she said, "Yuri hired this company called Break Up to break up with you. They're like Uber Eats or DoorDash, but with breakups instead of food. That person was one of their drivers. Look at the business card he gave you."

"He called himself a 'terminator,'" Heather said, as if she still couldn't believe this was real life. She held up the business card. It had the same Break Up branding as the guy's T-shirt. Underneath, there was a line that read, *Scan QR code for details about your breakup*, with a QR code underneath.

"Yeah. I know." Annika noticed the hard edge to her voice. "I'm really sorry."

"What . . . what'll this code do?" Heather looked completely baffled.

Annika took a deep breath and wondered how to phrase what she had to say kindly. There *was* no way to phrase it kindly. Hudson Craft had put her in this position. *Jerk.* "I think it goes to a video that Yuri's recorded for you, telling you more about why he's breaking up with you."

Heather laughed. "No way. It's got to be a joke or a scam, right? I mean, there's no way Yuri would do something—" She stopped, her eyes far away. "Except he said Yuri didn't want to do couples counseling. I only brought that up last week, and no one else knew we'd talked about it. And my Hello Kitty pajamas and electric toothbrush." She laughed again, but this time, it was a hollow, thin sound. "Right. They tell you the details so you know it was really your partner who hired them."

She scanned the QR code with her phone and a video of a thin guy with a scruffy goatee popped up. "Yuri." The defeat in Heather's voice made Annika's heart ache. "It's really him."

Seriously. How could Hudson Craft be okay with this? "I'm sorry," she said again, wishing she could say something else more helpful. "Here." She thrust her un-drunk latte at Heather. "You need this more than me."

Heather took the cup. "Thanks."

"Do you want me to walk with you? I assume you're going to work?"

Heather looked down at herself, as if she were checking. "Yeah . . . yeah, I was. But you know what?" She threw her briefcase into the back of her convertible. "I think I'm gonna take a beach day today."

Annika smiled. "Great idea."

Heather nodded, got in her car, and with a brief wave at Annika, squealed out of the parking garage.

⁓

Annika marched past her office and into Hudson Craft's, her blood boiling. She wasn't even sure *why* exactly she was going to speak to Hudson; it wasn't like he was going to suddenly change his mind and decide to join a monastery to atone for his evil ways. Maybe it was stupid, but there was a part of her that was having a *really* hard time believing that the guy she knew in Vegas was okay with what she'd just seen. A part of her felt there had to be a different explanation. She had to see what it was for herself.

Blaire was sitting in a papasan chair texting, dressed in a Break Up T-shirt and shorts, but the moment she saw Annika, she set the phone down and walked over. "Can I help you?" she said, her eyes glinting.

Blaire was the kind of person who seemed to be tethered to social norms—like not tearing out the eyeballs of someone you disliked—by only the most gossamer of threads. Annika took a hasty step back. "Where's Hudson?"

"In his office." Blaire gestured behind her. "But he can't be disturbed. He's in the middle of a really big project right now."

"This won't take more than a minute," Annika said, edging around her.

Blaire was at least three inches shorter than her, but she drew herself up. "Make an appointment."

"Blaire!" It was Hudson's voice. "If it's our nosy neighbor, you can let her in."

Blaire shook her head and stepped aside. Annika turned the corner and stepped into Hudson's office, only to find herself momentarily breathless. His office alone was about as big as Annika and June's entire space. The windows were enormous, and unlike the street view she had, his faced a gorgeous green space. Oh, the magic she could've made in a space like this one!

Instead of magic, he had a Pac-Man rug under his plain white desk, which looked like it had come from Ikea—about ten years ago. There was a malformed wooden bowl on his desk, full of an assortment of fruit. His walls were covered with retro video game posters, and one large, bare wall had a glow-in-the-dark basketball hoop screwed into it. Directly behind Hudson were framed accolades and magazine articles featuring his arrogant, smiling face. The only aesthetically pleasing thing in here was a large ombre clay pot on a shelf by itself, its turquoise hues fading to a deep blue, fading to a deep indigo, and then a pale lavender.

Hudson leaned back in his chair, which, after a second look, she realized was a giant exercise ball painted to look like a globe. As if he were *really* leaning into his evil world domination plan. "So," he said. "Is it just me or are you just . . . there every time I turn around?"

Annika rolled her eyes. "Yeah, I couldn't wait to come to this daycare of an office and be near you."

Hudson's jaw hardened, but he didn't say anything.

Crossing her arms, Annika continued, "I saw one of your terminators in action today."

Blinking, Hudson leaned forward, grabbed an apple out of the bowl, and began to eat it. "Really. What'd you think?"

She couldn't help the wrinkle in her nose, as if she'd smelled something disgusting. "It was vile. Absolutely brutal and awful. This woman had been going out with her asshole boyfriend for a year. They were going to start couples counseling."

"Oh. So they weren't happy. It couldn't have come as a surprise, then."

Annika stared at him. There was no way he really thought that. "Are you part robot? Do you not have a single feeling?"

Hudson stopped munching to think. "Oh, wait, here comes one now. It's . . . sadness? No, wait . . . it's . . . I'm . . . hungry." He took another bite of his apple, his green eyes holding hers. "Yep, definitely hungry. Does that count?"

Annika pinched the bridge of her nose, a mix of irritation and disappointment bubbling inside her. "Okay. You know what? You just go ahead and revel in your odiousness. When karma bites you in the ass, you'll be really sorry."

"Pretty sure karma's on vacation, but I'll be sure to give her your hello when she stops by."

Annika narrowed her eyes at him. She'd thought that

herself on multiple occasions before, but why the hell would Hudson think karma wasn't working beautifully for him? The man had everything. "Whatever." Annika turned to go.

"See ya at the party tonight." He paused, considering her. "I assume you're not too affronted to want to partake of the booze and ogle some good-looking men? Or women. There'll be plenty of models to choose from."

Annika shook her head. "Goodbye, Hudson."

"See you later, Annika."

෴

Visions of Heather, the terminator, and Hudson Craft danced in her head all morning until finally, at noon, Annika grabbed her purse from the closet. "I'm gonna get some lunch," she said to June, who was busy coding. "Want anything?"

June shook her head, but didn't look up from her computer, which was par for the course—when she really got into what she was doing, she'd mentally disappear for hours at a time, and the office would seem as if no one was there. Annika usually didn't mind the solitude, but today it was giving her way too much time and space to think. She wasn't even able to get into doing a pitch outline for EPIC. In any case, she still had weeks to go, so she could afford to step away for a little bit.

Annika took the elevator down and headed north on Worthington Avenue, toward the little restaurant that had the most delicious quinoa bowls she'd ever eaten. But her annoyance and disappointment weren't dissipating as she'd hoped they would.

She just couldn't believe Hudson Craft. How callous did you have to be to not care at all about people being dumped in such a cold, unfeeling way? What kind of person came up with a company like Break Up in the first place? Where was the guy who'd told her he thought the arts were seriously undersupported and that tech could be the way to change that? Where was the guy who'd caressed her cheek with such heartbreaking tenderness that Annika had pressed his hand to her face and closed her eyes, just to revel in the moment? Where was the guy who'd pulled out her chair, who'd walked on the outside of the sidewalk because he was just that chivalrous? It was like she was now getting to know his evil twin.

Telling her she needed help attracting beta testers? Ha. Make Up might not have the level of success Break Up had acquired, but they were doing okay—they'd get there one day. And to imply that she would still go to the rooftop party, eager to guzzle his free drinks and enjoy his shallow entertainment? As if she was so desperate that she needed Hudson to set up this amazing networking opportunity for her. She *had* to cream him at EPIC. It was the only way she'd ever be at peace.

There was a sudden clot of people on the street in front of her, blocking her passage. Annika frowned, trying to dodge them before she realized it was a mariachi band, warming up to play.

She stood back and watched them for a few minutes as an idea began to take root in her mind. Grinning, Annika pushed through the crowd. Hudson wouldn't know what hit him.

༄

After lunch, she strode into the office to find June still hard at work.

"Hey," Annika said breathlessly. June didn't look up. She

had the dogged look of someone with her sights on an enemy target, the keyboard her weapon, the unsatisfactory aggression algorithm the enemy. "Hellooo." Annika waved her hand in front of her best friend's face. When June finally looked up, she was dazed, as if she was surprised to find herself in an LA office instead of inside the actual code.

"Oh. Hey. What time is it?" She checked the clock and gasped. "Four o'clock? Where have you been all afternoon?"

Annika smiled at her, hoping it looked enthusiastic and not deranged. "I had the best idea. Don't worry, I'll fill you in on everything. But first, do we still have that banner from our booth at the SBA event back in January?"

"I think so." June got up and was halfway to the storage closet when Annika noticed what she was wearing.

"You changed," she said, trying not to sound accusatory. Never before in the history of June's many varied hookups had she made an effort to look *nice* for her date. She was gorgeous enough that they wouldn't have cared if she showed up wearing a giant paper bag, and she knew it.

June turned pink. Her hands smoothed down her one-shoulder black dress, which had a very conveniently placed cutout on her chest. "Kind of."

"And you're wearing your La Perla push-up!" Annika said, coming closer. "I'd recognize that level of cleavage anywhere."

"So what if I am? I'll wow our new business contacts with my brains *and* my boobs. There's nothing wrong with that."

"No, there's nothing wrong with that," Annika agreed, tapping her foot on the carpeted floor. "Except I have a feeling you have more contact than just *business contact* in mind. Especially with a particular redhead?"

June looked at her blankly for a full five seconds before she caved. "Okay, fine, so I want to get into Ziggy's pants tonight. I thought you were okay with me and him."

"You've wanted to get into a lot of guys' pants before, and it never involved an LBD and La Perla." Annika narrowed her eyes as June walked back to her chair and sat down. "You're not going to go and develop feelings for my sworn enemy's minion, are you?"

June rolled her eyes, pulled a fuchsia lipstick out, and did her lips, using her phone as a mirror. "Okay, firstly, he's not Hudson's *minion*. He's his developer, his right-hand man."

"Not the point!" Alarm bells were going off in Annika's head.

"And secondly," June continued, speaking over her as she put her lipstick away, "this is just a hookup. Seriously. June Stewart isn't ready to settle down anytime soon. You know that."

After a beat, Annika relaxed and huffed a laugh. "Yeah, I do know that. Don't know what I was thinking."

June got up and pulled the rolled-up banner from the closet. "What do we need this for?"

Annika grinned. "Walk with me and I'll show you."

❧

By the time they got up to the rooftop, the debauchery was already in full swing. Annika stood by the entrance, looking around in disbelief.

The music thumped beneath her ballet flats. A traveling bar had been set up to the immediate left, where a bartender who almost definitely played Black Panther's body double was expertly mixing cocktails with top-shelf liquor.

Although she couldn't see Hudson yet, a long line had already formed in front of the bar, consisting of people Annika vaguely remembered from their blank stares in the elevator. Now, though, those very same nine-to-five zombies had transformed into party animals—ties loosened, sleeves rolled up, bags discarded. Women were putting their hair up into no-nonsense buns to deal with the heat, losing their blazers and cardigans. Models who made Greek gods and goddesses look like trolls were already circulating around with perfect canapes, bright smiles on their beautiful faces. Next to the bartender, someone was setting up a large chocolate fountain. A man juggling what looked like glass orbs walked past them, dressed only in skintight, cheetah-print pants.

"Shit," Annika whispered, darting a glance at June, who looked impressed. Seeing Annika's face, she quickly rearranged her features into a neutral mask.

"Meh. I've seen better." She gestured to the banner and bags. "What do you want to do with our stuff?"

Annika pushed her shoulders back and shook out her hair. "Let's get in and get set up."

Chins held high, they walked across the rooftop, ignoring the curious looks they got from the partygoers, refusing every single canape offered by the catering staff. They had every right to do what they were doing. Annika refused to let herself be intimidated by superficial flashiness. The whole party might as well be a metaphor for Break Up. All flash, no substance. Those canapes were probably 90 percent air.

The east side of the L-shaped rooftop was dominated by a pergola, under which stood a small trestle table and folding chairs. Red and silver heart-shaped balloons Annika had tied up an hour ago fluttered from the pergola beams, the foil catching the late-afternoon sun. June set her bags down on the table and fished out take-out containers full of food, as well as a set of plates and glasses for each of them. After kicking off her shoes, Annika stood on the chairs and hung their banner from the pergola, then stood back and admired her handiwork.

"This is gonna be good." June waggled her fingers at Ziggy, who'd been watching them with a small frown on his face. He gave her what he probably thought was a breezy wave back and ended up soaking his sleeve with his drink. June didn't seem to notice. "I don't see Hudson, though."

Annika scanned the rooftop. "I'm sure he's around here somewhere. Let's just do our thing. He'll find us."

June nodded, and then looked toward the entrance and grabbed Annika's arm. "Oh, here they come." Her voice was high-pitched with glee.

Annika watched as the mariachi band she'd hired—expensive, but definitely worth it—filed past the partygoers, all of whom stopped to watch, their faces a hilarious mix of confusion and surprise.

"Ms. Annika?" the bandleader said to her. "Shall we set up here?"

"Yes." Annika gestured to the space beside the trestle table she and June were sitting at. "Please begin playing whenever you're ready."

The bandleader hesitated, looking at the other people on Hudson's side of the rooftop. "There is already music playing."

Annika smiled her sweetest smile. "But I rented this part of the rooftop, so we have as much right to play our music as they do." She'd made sure of this when she'd spoken to the landlord earlier. "Please begin whenever you're ready. And if you could, play the loudest, most disruptive song you can think of."

The bandleader shrugged and nodded to his fellow band-mates, and they struck up a beautifully deafening melody. Hiding a smile, Annika watched as Hudson's party music was completely swallowed by the mariachi music. His guests stood, mouths open and drinks in hand, staring at the mariachi band and Annika's side of the rooftop. A few of them were gesturing and talking among themselves. Even the juggler had stopped to watch.

Good. She had a feeling Hudson wouldn't be underestimating her again anytime soon. Score one for Make Up.

She turned to June and gestured to the take-out containers. "Shall we enjoy our dinner?"

June helped herself to a veggie taco. "Mmm. The view, the music, the ambience . . . what's not to love?"

"Exactly." Annika poured them each a glass of tamarind agua fresca, studiously keeping her eyes away from the other side of the rooftop, as much as she wanted to peek. The trick was to appear casual, totally in control, even though she knew Hudson, wherever he was, would get wind of what she'd done fairly quickly. And then he'd begin to uncoil.

She sipped her agua fresca, unable to keep the smile off her face. "I can't even hear their obnoxious music anymore, can you?"

"Nope, not a note." June swallowed, and said quietly, "In-coming."

Trying to hide her delight, Annika looked over her shoulder to see Hudson striding toward them, his eyes laser-focused on her. He'd changed out of his blue T-shirt and was wearing a Ralph Lauren button-down, his sleeves rolled up to his elbows. He moved surely through the space, as if he was perfectly con-fident he was exactly where he was meant to be.

Annika's smile faltered. Shit, he looked really pissed. She

straightened her shoulders and brushed down her mermaid skirt, attempting to appear calmly confident, even though her palms were dampening slightly.

"What the hell?" Hudson said when he was close enough to speak to her. His eyes were spitting sparks; his face was dark, a sky before a thunderstorm. Strands of blond hair blew against his forehead, but he made no motion to smooth them away. A gentle, warm breeze blew across the rooftop, carrying his scent to her. He smelled incredible. He must've slapped on a little cologne—something that made her think of ocean and sand and wind and sea salt.

"Hello to you, too," she said, raising her glass at him.

His voice was low, but throbbing with annoyance. "Annika, this is *my* event." His eyes roved over the band, her gigantic sign, and the table. June gave him a placid smile. "What the fuck do you think you're doing?"

"The building manager said you only rented that half of the rooftop," Annika said, repeating the same lines she'd rehearsed in anticipation of this very confrontation. She batted her eyelashes. "Is that not true?"

"Yeah, but that's because no one else was on the books."

Annika shrugged. "I guess you should've been a little less cheap and sprung for the whole rooftop anyway."

He stepped forward, closing the gap between them, towering over her even more because she was sitting. Annika's breath caught in her throat, but she was determined not to let him see. "I thought you were all mad about me supposedly stealing your idea. So who's stealing whose idea now?"

She stood, wishing she could look directly into his eyes. Oh, well. Looking up would have to do. "First, it's not polite to loom. And second, well, now you know what it feels like."

His gaze burned into hers. "I. Didn't. Steal. Your. Idea," he said, enunciating every word. "And this"—he thrust a hand at the band—"is beyond the pale. I'm trying to run a business here."

"Yeah. I know." Annika gestured grandly at her table. "So am I."

Shaking his head, Hudson rubbed his jaw and took a breath, muttering something that sounded very much like "stubborn" under his breath. Annika tried not to grin. Let *him* get all frustrated for a change. He studied her face again and smiled thinly, his eyes narrowing just a tad. "Okay. This is how you want to play it?"

Annika raised an eyebrow and cocked her head, but didn't say anything.

Hudson turned and stalked away to his side of the rooftop, every step brimming with irritation. As Annika watched, he went to the sound system and cut the music he'd been playing—and then, after clapping his hands to get people's attention, he announced in a voice like a foghorn, "All right, everybody! Listen up! It's a margarita mariachi party! The bartender's going to make you margaritas in flavors you've never even dreamed of before. Oh, and please, enjoy our guest band and dance the night away!" He gestured toward the mariachi band as if it were all his brilliant idea.

People cheered and roared with happiness. Catching Annika's eye across the crowd, Hudson picked a fresh drink off the bar and raised the glass to her. One corner of his mouth lifted in a smirk.

Fuming, Annika turned to June, who was looking at her with wide eyes. She took a slug of agua fresca. "Dammit."

June took a bite of her taco and watched as the partygoers

on the other side of the roof lined up to get margaritas from the bartender, who was making them in every color of the rainbow. "So . . . do you want to just sit here and eat?"

Annika looked at the people who'd already kicked off their shoes and were now dancing to the mariachi music. "Yes," she said defiantly, turning back around and heaping her plate with tacos. "Let's eat."

chapter six

After almost an hour of trying to eat her dinner in a dignified fashion, Annika sagged back against the folding chair and kicked her shoes off under the table. The other side of the roof-top was buzzing, naturally. The juggler was back on his shit, the tequila was top-shelf, and the chocolate fountain was flowing like freaking Mount Vesuvius. The mariachi band was now walking around, infusing the entire party with a sense of tropical fun. It was like she'd paid for Hudson's entertainment—a thought that had clearly not escaped him, given how many times she'd caught him looking triumphantly over at her, eyes dancing with glee.

Swells of laughter rose and fell. People milled around, chatting it up. Even Blaire, normally so terrifying, had let her hair down and was surrounded by a clot of people she was regaling with a story about working at a circus one summer. Ziggy was handing out business cards. He'd had hundreds of them at the beginning—Annika had seen the giant tower behind a table. The tower was now diminished to a stub, and Ziggy was lying in a hammock with June, who'd abandoned ship to go over to the other side.

She'd stuck by Annika for the first hour, both of them using every ounce of their energy to make it seem like they were having a great time with their sad takeout but eventually Annika told her to go have fun. There was no need for both of them to continue suffering.

Feeling a slight chill in spite of the balmy night air, Annika wrapped her arms around her torso and was just beginning to wonder if she should just go home when a frosted margarita appeared at her elbow.

She looked up to see Hudson. "Hey. You look like you could use a drink."

Annika picked up the glass and peered at its pink-and-green contents. "What is this?"

"A peace offering for the night: a strawberry-jalapeño margarita. I seem to remember you like them."

She'd almost forgotten. In Vegas, they'd had their first drink together at a dim, slightly Gothic hotel bar. She'd confessed that she'd never had a jalapeño margarita before, and, pretending to be outraged, he'd immediately ordered her one. She'd watched him over the rim of the glass as she drank and he'd watched her back, unflinchingly, the spicy drink and hot desire warming her bones and turning them to liquid gold.

Now Annika almost refused—*that* Hudson was definitely not *this* Hudson—but the thought of something spicy and tangy did sound amazing. She took a sip and closed her eyes as the tequila warmed her throat and settled into her chest like a warm ember. "Thanks." Slipping her shoes back on, Annika scraped her chair back and stood, making sure to keep an arm's length of distance between them. "Looks like your party's a roaring success."

"Wait till they light the tiki torches. No one's gonna wanna leave."

They studied each other for a long moment. Annika snorted at the same time that Hudson chuckled, the sound a deep rumble that somehow echoed in her chest.

"Well played, by the way," he said, nodding toward the roaming band. There was a shadow of real admiration in his voice. "They were a really nice touch."

"Yeah, well—you're pretty good at thinking on your feet." She gestured to the boisterous crowd. "Everyone here thinks you're a party-planning genius."

"It was touch-and-go for a minute," he said, giving her a wry look. "But I think I managed to salvage it, yes." Glancing back over the crowds of people clutching the Break Up–branded gift bags a model was handing out, he added, "I don't think they're going to forget us anytime soon." He said it casually, but Annika detected an intensity under the surface.

"So, what's the plan now?" he asked, turning back to her. A soft breeze wafted his cologne over to her. His eyes seemed to shimmer and glow in the dusky sunset. "Are you staying or leaving?"

She blinked, refusing to let him get to her. "Staying." When he began to return her small smile, though, she added, "But not with you." Taking another sip of her margarita, she began walking across the rooftop toward the crowd, unable to resist checking his reaction over her shoulder as she went.

Hudson was watching her go, his golden hair tinged red by the setting sun.

With creeping dismay, she realized she was enjoying his attention more than she strictly should. Her plan had been to treat him as an irrelevant speed bump. You didn't mingle at parties with speed bumps, and you definitely didn't accept margaritas from them.

Annika groaned inwardly as she joined the crowd, ready to network. One thing was certain: She needed to figure out why Hudson was having such an effect on her, and she needed to do it quickly.

~

For the next two hours, Annika—and June, though she seemed slightly distracted by Ziggy's attempts to impress her with his dancing abilities—went from group to group, from potential client to potential client. Annika was surprised by just how many people in the building were interested in Make Up. She had a thick stack of their business cards in her bag to prove it. When Make Up was ready to officially launch, they'd have a long list of early users.

Finally, just when her voice was getting hoarse from all the talking she'd done all night—and when the three margaritas she'd had were starting to tire her out—the party began to wind down. People started trickling out in twos and threes, most of them having called Lyfts, thanks to the potent drinks. She'd lost track of June at some point, though she assumed she was still at the party somewhere.

Hudson found her once the businessman she'd been talking to bid his goodbyes. "Rosemary Lotts just said goodbye to me. Apparently, she was really impressed by your pitch."

"Who?" Annika placed her empty margarita glass on a table. "Oh, the realtor with the blond hair? Yeah, I guess so." She added begrudgingly, "Thank you for setting all this up. I have to say, it was a success."

Hudson raised an eyebrow.

"What?"

"You just complimented *and* thanked me in the same breath. How much did you have to drink, again?"

Annika scoffed. "All right, all right, don't make me regret it."

The corner of Hudson's mouth twitched. Quietly, he said, "You have a killer energy about you when you talk about Make Up. People dig that."

"Really?" Annika asked, surprised at his sincerity.

"There are a few things about you that stick out very clearly in my mind from Vegas." Hudson's eyes were serious as he leaned against the rooftop railing. "And one of them was your passion for your idea. It was like an energy field around you. It was electric."

They gazed at each other for what felt like a full minute, Annika's knees going weak with the memories that were creeping back into her mind. What was he thinking about?

She took a deep breath to get her bearings, but caught a whiff of Hudson's cologne again, faint and masculine, and put a hand against the railing to steady herself. Turning away, she said, "I—"

And stopped when she felt an arm around her waist.

Her heart did a couple of high-energy flips in her chest. Adrenaline flooded her veins. What was he doing? Did she *want* him to be doing it?

Annika turned, her mind spinning with thoughts of what she might say.

June stood next to her, grinning. "Oh." Annika blinked. "Hey."

"Hey." June kissed her on the cheek. "I'm taking off."

"You're going home? Alone?"

Ziggy appeared at June's side, smiling. "No," she replied. "Ziggy's taking me out to eat."

"Out to eat?" Annika frowned. This was another unheard-of move in June's playbook. She went to bars with her hookups, not out to dinner. "Um, okay. Have fun. Will you text me later at some point, just to let me know you're okay?"

"Of course." Her blond hair blowing in the breeze, June hugged her and simultaneously whispered in her ear, "What's going on with you and Hot Hudson?"

"Shh!" Annika led June a few steps away. Thankfully, Hudson was talking to Ziggy and hadn't heard her. "Don't let him hear you calling him that; his head's big enough as it is."

"Well, *you* would know."

Annika groaned. "June. Seriously." After a pause during which June grinned and looked anything but abashed, she asked, "Anyway, what do you mean, what's going on with us?"

"The way you two were talking, heads together, his eyes all intense and focused on you . . . What was he saying?"

Annika rubbed the back of her neck and looked away. "I don't even remember."

June smiled at her, a wicked glint in her eye. "Liar."

"Don't you have dinner to get to?"

"All right, all right." June sighed dramatically, and walked back to the guys with her arms flung wide. "Ziggy, take me away!"

Ziggy held out his arm to her, and together they waltzed off the rooftop.

Annika watched them go, feeling slightly off-kilter for reasons she couldn't put her finger on. "Is he a good guy?" she finally asked Hudson. "Ziggy?"

"The best," he said simply. "He's one of those people you can always count on to be there for you. June couldn't have picked someone better."

Annika glanced up at him. "Oh, I don't think that's going to turn into anything serious," she said quickly.

Hudson shrugged and looked behind them at the waitstaff, who were now stacking empty trays and glasses. "Hey, they're packing up out here." A pause. "I could walk you out. I'm gonna take a Lyft home . . . I assume you are, too."

Annika looked down at the sidewalk far below, at the lights of the buildings and cars. Hudson was offering to walk with her. He was just being chivalrous, but still, she felt a thrumming under her skin, something vibrant and alive that had been long-dormant. *Stop it. This is Hudson Craft, remember? Impertinent idea stealer? CEO of Heartbreak, Inc.? Supervillain extraordinaire?*

"Um . . ." Annika glanced back at her table, still laden with her banner and paperwork.

"I'll tip Mel extra and he can take your stuff down to my office, if you want. You can pick it up tomorrow."

"Who's Mel?"

"My new assistant." Hudson thrust his chin in the direction of a scrawny white guy who was bossing some of the caterers around.

What was he, a rock star? First this giant glitzy party, and now a personal assistant?

Still, the thought of breaking down when she was tired, tipsy, and ready to go home in shoes that were really starting to hurt didn't sound especially thrilling. "He wouldn't mind?"

"Not at all."

∽

As they got in the elevator—Annika thinking about how this was the setting for the romantic scene in every rom-com

she'd ever watched, and then immediately telling her brain to
STFU—someone yelled Hudson's name.

They turned to see two women and a man racing to the
elevator, their eyes bright and cheeks flushed.

"Hey, guys." Hudson's voice was hearty as he held the elevator for them. Annika realized it was his PR voice, the one
he'd put on when he was talking to everyone on the rooftop.
Weird—he hadn't put on that voice once with her the entire
evening. "Enjoy the party?"

"How could we not?" one woman said, grabbing Hudson's
arm. "It was so much fun. You really know how to show people
a good time." She pressed her body against his, her eyes heavy-
lidded. There was no mistaking what she was trying to say.

Annika felt a twinge of irritation that she pushed aside.
What did she care if Ms. Emma Stone–look-alike was hanging all over Hudson Craft? May the force be with her! And
hopefully she wouldn't wake up to find he'd stolen her purse or
identity or something.

Hudson gently extricated himself from the woman and
smiled, looking somewhat detached. "Great. I'm glad it was
fun." He met Annika's eye and she looked away, her heart racing for no discernible reason.

This was none of her business. None at all.

⌇

Once they were outside, the trio dissipated to the right, where
their Lyft was waiting. Hudson fell into step beside Annika as
they turned left toward the end of the street, where they would
wait for their Lyfts once they called them. Annika felt her pulse
beat in rhythm with each step they took. Hudson was so close,

she could practically feel a tiny, humming current of static electricity between their arms, like a spark waiting to ignite. She blinked the thought away.

They passed a homeless man bundled up in old, ratty blankets, sitting on the stoop of a shuttered liquor store. Hudson reached into his pocket, pulled out a packet of gummy bears, and handed it to him.

"What ya got for me tonight?" The man turned the packet over in his hands eagerly. "Ooh, these are my favorite. God bless you, Hudson."

"And you, Tommy. See you tomorrow."

The man waved and tore happily into the packet.

Annika looked up at Hudson and shook her head, her curls lightly billowing in the breeze.

"What?" he asked, his green eyes luminous in the near dark.

"You give food to homeless guys, but you're okay with people breaking other people's hearts. I don't get you."

"Maybe you're not trying hard enough." He stuck his hands in his pockets.

So cryptic. "And what does that mean?"

He was looking straight ahead, but Annika saw a shadow of emotion—anger? Hurt? Defensiveness?—flit across his face. "What looks like breaking people's hearts to you might not look that way to everyone."

What was *that* supposed to mean? Annika frowned as they passed a narrow alley, where a cat was rummaging through a dumpster. "I saw that woman in the parking garage. She was in complete shock. She had no idea what was even going on."

Hudson shrugged. "Better than some other alternatives."

Annika looked at him in disbelief. "Like what? Death?"

"Like being in a dead-end relationship that both parties

know isn't going anywhere. Or being completely abandoned." He stopped to turn to her. "Or like being ghosted, having no closure, no definitive moment that felt like the end."

Annika paused, trying to read the flicker of . . . something . . . she saw in his eyes. "Hudson—I—" She stepped closer to him, and his body heat wrapped around her. "I didn't—I mean—what, um . . ." She wasn't really sure what she was trying to ask. The vibrant color of his eyes was messing with her mind again; they could be used in war zones against the enemy.

Hudson looked over her shoulder. "Come with me." And then he walked past her, his arm brushing against hers, his skin hot against her flesh.

Ignoring the jolt she felt, Annika hurried after him, through a pair of wrought iron gates in front of what looked like a hotel. "Where are we going? I still haven't called my Lyft. You're not taking me back here to mug me or something, are you? I only carry small bills."

He rolled his eyes at her over his shoulder as they walked. "Are you always so suspicious? Call your Lyft after—there's something I want to show you."

He led her around the side, away from the front of the hotel, to a stone-paved courtyard in the back. In the middle stood a fountain about twice Annika's height, the base lit with multicolored lights. Ivy crept along the ground and the iron fence around them.

"Oh." Annika took a moment to listen to the rushing water, which sounded like the meditation she used to calm herself. "This is . . . beautiful."

Hudson looked up at the zenith of the fountain, the purple, blue, and pink lights playing across his chiseled face. "Yeah. I like to come here sometimes, just to sit and think at night. It's usually empty, like it is now."

"And the hotel staff doesn't mind?"

Hudson tossed her an impish grin and sat on the lip of the fountain to dip his fingers in the water. "The manager enjoys certain . . . perks . . . from letting me come here."

Annika brushed her skirt under her and sat beside him. "Ah. Gummy bears?"

"He's more interested in Benjamin Franklin, unfortunately." Hudson chuckled and flicked the water from his fingers. A drop landed in the hollow of Annika's throat and rolled slowly down her chest and between her breasts, raising goose bumps and making her catch her breath. She adjusted herself on the lip of the fountain, feeling the hard stone pressing into her bottom and thighs, a wantonness taking over her that she hadn't felt in forever.

"Th-that's expensive," she said, when she realized she hadn't responded.

Hudson gave her a hooded look, as if he could tell where her mind had been. Annika forced herself to break eye contact and face forward, her breathing just a touch ragged.

They sat and listened to the water together, the wind rustling the leaves in the trees. Annika breathed in and out to still the thumping of her heart. It worked, somewhat. She glanced at Hudson, wondering about what he'd said just a few minutes before, about how being broken up with was better than being ghosted. What did he mean? She opened her mouth to try and bring the conversation back to it, but he spoke first.

"I didn't steal your idea, you know," he said quietly. The lights from the fountain were reflected in his eyes. "I wouldn't do that."

Annika studied his face for any signs of dishonesty or guilt,

but saw nothing but openness. "So . . . it was all just a coincidence? I told you about my idea to bring exes together, which
was kind of the kernel of what became Make Up. *You* talked
about creating an app for visual artists."

He rubbed his jaw and broke eye contact. "The visual artists
app is something I'm still playing with. I haven't given up on it.
And you telling me about Make Up . . . that's not what inspired
Break Up."

She spread her fingers flat on the cold stone of the fountain, pondering his words. "Okay. I believe you. I think." She
did, she found. Maybe this all really *was* just a coincidence,
and he hadn't thought about her at all when he founded his
company.

But it didn't completely absolve him of *every*thing. He was
still the founder of a company, an idea, that she found odious.
"So, what *did* inspire Break Up?"

But he was shaking his head slowly, his eyes searching her
face. "Do you remember Vegas at all? How we met?"

Annika dropped her gaze, her cheeks warming. "I remember."

*Annika was busy texting June as she walked into the hotel
restaurant for breakfast, which was the only reason she slid into
the chair nearest the door—only to realize, with extreme horror,
that it wasn't actually empty and that she was, in fact, sitting
in someone's lap.*

*That someone turned out to be a ridiculously gorgeous man
with green eyes that evaporated all of Annika's words. Every
single one.*

Now, at the secret fountain, she found herself studiously
avoiding Hudson's eyes. The memory—and the fact that he

remembered it, too—made her think again about what a different person he'd seemed to be then. A person she'd willingly spent an entire week with, cocooned in a Las Vegas hotel. What *had* happened?

Not really sure what else to say, Annika kicked off her shoes and turned to put her feet in the fountain. Her breath immediately *whooshed* out. "Oh my god, that's cold."

After a moment, Hudson joined her. "Fuck!"

Annika laughed. "You didn't even roll up your jeans. You're going to freeze to death. What a tragic loss for Break Up."

The corner of Hudson's mouth lifted. "And the world at large."

She rolled her eyes. "At least you're not low on self-confidence. I don't know how anyone puts up with you." She gave him a sidelong glance and wiggled her toes in the water. "Your girlfriend must be a saint."

He shook his head, looking into the water. The reflection of small ripples played across his skin. "Nope. No girlfriend. Probably a good thing, given how much I work."

A beat passed, during which Annika squashed a brief flash of happiness before adding, "It's such an enormous coincidence, you moving into the building."

He met her eye, his face serious. "Are you asking me if I followed you there?"

Annika wiggled her toes again. "Did you?"

Hudson shook his head and studied her. "No. I've had my eye on that space for a while, so when two offices opened up side by side, I knew we had to snag them. We just knocked the wall down between them to make it one giant office."

Annika looked at their feet in the water, his enormous pale ones next to her smaller, darker ones. They were different in just about every way. She didn't really know what she was doing here, sitting at a fountain and talking with him. "You're different now than you were then."

Annika lifted her cold feet out of the water and set them on the broad lip of the fountain, knees up to her chest.

"You mean in Vegas," he said, his green eyes like a lion's, intent, focused. He pulled his feet out, too, and sat in a position that mirrored hers, so they were toe to toe.

"I do." Annika saw a shadow pass over Hudson's face, but she didn't have the wherewithal to interpret what it might mean.

"Well, a lot of things have changed since Vegas." Hudson pushed a hand through his hair, leaving it mussed. "Are *you* dating anyone?"

Annika couldn't help the surprised laugh that burst out of her. "I haven't had a second date in, like, a year." *Shit.* She hadn't meant to say that. Damn margaritas.

Hudson looked taken aback. "Seriously?"

Annika shrugged and looked into the water, rippling from a slight breeze. "Seriously. It's been nothing more than a string of first dates or random encounters."

Hudson set his elbows on his knees and grunted.

"What?" Annika asked, feeling defensive. "What's that grunt supposed to mean?"

Hudson looked deep into her eyes. "I guess I just find that kind of hard to believe." He said it reluctantly. Was he afraid of offending her?

Annika didn't look away. "Why?"

The silence between them stretched, and then melted and morphed into something interesting. Annika was suddenly aware that the tips of their toes were touching. That they were completely alone in this very romantic courtyard. That the margaritas she'd drunk over the course of the night were still swimming along happily in her bloodstream, transforming the world into a glowing, sparkling phantasmagoria of romantic opportunity, inhibiting every good-decision-making neurotransmitter in her brain.

"The same reason I haven't been able to stop thinking about Vegas," Hudson said quietly, dipping his head to look into her eyes.

Annika glanced down. "Oh, stop it." She was going for nonchalance, but her voice was a little shaky.

Hudson pressed the tips of his fingers into the back of her hand for just a moment. Her heart hammered against her chest like a pitiful, confused bird. "Tell me you haven't thought about it." His voice wasn't the least bit shaky. Annika would've felt annoyed if she weren't so breathlessly, ridiculously nervous.

She met his eyes then, and the blood roared in her ears at the memories that wanted to surface. "Maybe a little," she said, her voice just a breath in the balmy night air. *If he kisses me, I'll kiss him back*, she thought. She wasn't sure whether to blame the starlit night, or the glimmers of deep kindness she'd gotten from him when he gave the gummy bears to the homeless man, or the fact that he'd said her energy when she talked about Make Up was "electric," or the way he was staring at her right then. *I want to kiss him. Right here, right now.*

He continued to stare into her eyes, the moment building and building until her blood was lava and she couldn't take it anymore. Annika reached a hand forward, her fingertips grazing the corner of his mouth. His eyes closed as he let out a long, slow breath.

Taking that as encouragement, Annika leaned forward, her pulse pounding so loudly she was sure he could hear it. And then, softly, surely, she pressed her mouth to his.

For a moment—just a breath of a moment—she felt Hudson's warm lips mold to hers, his stubble rough against her skin. She pushed herself forward, trying to deepen the kiss. In the next moment, though, he had his gigantic hands around her upper arms and was applying a steady pressure so she couldn't kiss him anymore.

Annika looked at him, her head swirling with his pheromones and her petulance. All she could manage was a high-pitched whining sound at being thwarted. "Hnnng?"

Hudson gazed into her eyes, his own burning with an intensity she found incredibly sexy. "Why are you kissing me?"

His question did not compute. "Why am I kissing you? Because I want to?" She blinked.

His eyes were two emeralds in the darkness. "You want to. Are you sure?"

Annika felt her lips lift in a smile. "Do I want to? Let me show you." She leaned forward again, but his hands were like steel clamps around her arms.

"No, Annika. You've had a lot to drink tonight." He paused, so many expressions flashing across his face, she had trouble keeping track of them all. "Believe me, I'm . . . glad you want to kiss me. But not like this."

"I'm not that drunk," she said, her eyes returning to his lips.

Hudson half smiled at her tone, but his gaze was serious when he spoke. "When I kiss you again, I want you to be clear-headed. I don't want this to be another mistake."

Annika sat back, her cheeks hot. Sure, he was saying he didn't want to kiss her because she was drunk. But maybe he was just letting her down easy. Maybe all the toying with her in yoga class and asking about Vegas had been just that—toying.

"Ready to go?" he asked, swinging his legs around and stuffing his feet back into his shoes. He didn't meet her eye.

Annika felt her heart drop, a small disappointed stone falling in her chest. "Yeah. Sure."

On the walk back to their Lyft stops, they talked about inconsequential things, and Annika rallied. She was *glad* Hudson hadn't kissed her. She was glad he'd stopped her. Because, actually, he was right. She'd clearly lost her head to want to kiss *him* of all people, Mr. Heartbreaker of the Masses, Mr. Boorish Break Up Bully. Mr. Stupid Smug Smile. Mr. Green-Eyed Devil. Mr. Powerful, Pleasing Pecs—oh. Her Lyft was here.

chapter seven

It was Saturday evening, which meant it was time for Anni-ka's weekly journey to her father's house in the Hollywood Hills. Although she'd never tell Hudson, her weekly dinner dates with her dad were the real reason why it was hard to get to know anyone. Saturday night was prime date-night real estate, and Annika knew no one would understand why she felt the need to spend every single one with her father. No one would get the guilt she still felt at leaving him behind to knock around in that giant lonely house, now that she wasn't there to fill it with a modicum of noise anymore.

She pulled up the long, winding driveway, got out of her hybrid Honda Accord, and paused. The hills loomed in the distance, dusk already wrapping them in pink and purple. She took a deep breath—even after all these years away, this felt like home.

She climbed up the wide front steps and let herself in. The massive crystal chandelier that had hung in the foyer since before she was born shimmered and twinkled, welcoming her home. "Daddy? I'm here!"

He came in from the kitchen, a striped half apron tied around his trim waist. "Ani!" He scooped her up in a hug and then held her by the shoulders, studying her with a physician's critical eye. "Have you been eating?"

Annika resisted the urge to roll her eyes. Every week, this was her dad's standing question. It was like he was afraid that without him making his delicious recipes, she'd just wither away and silently starve to death. Never mind that she'd been living on her own—and cooking for herself, or getting takeout, which was basically hunting and gathering—for six years now. "Yes, I've been eating." She gave him a peck on his clean-shaved cheek.

"Come on in. Have a glass of homemade lemonade." Annika followed him and the strains of Vivaldi coming from the direction of the kitchen, which transported her back to high school.

She would sit on a barstool doing homework while her dad bustled around cooking, Vivaldi keeping them company, drawing them together. Annika had grown up listening to classical music and nothing else. Even now, she could name composer and composition for almost any piece of classical music she came across. June found it annoying when she'd interrupt an especially poignant engagement ring or pregnancy test commercial by naming the piece of music playing in the background, but Annika couldn't help it. Her dad had ingrained that knowledge and appreciation in her.

She poured herself a glass of strawberry lemonade from the crystal pitcher and took her usual seat on a barstool. "Smells delicious!"

"Thank you." Her dad looked proud, like he always did

when she complimented his cooking. Gesturing to the bubbling pot on the stove, he said, "This is the tropical fruit chutney to go with our kalua pork."

She watched him work for a few minutes, moving efficiently in the kitchen, pulling a tray of warm Hawaiian rolls out of the oven. A feeling of contentment and ease glowed within her.

Occasionally, Hudson popped into her mind, but she pushed him right out using her meditation skills. She pictured a babbling brook instead of the way she'd leaned in to kiss him and how he'd physically restrained her to stop her. *He'd* stopped *her*. He wasn't even supposed to be more than a speed bump in her life.

She pictured the babbling brook running right over his face.

"What are you thinking about?"

Annika almost choked on her lemonade. "S-sorry?"

Her dad waved an oven-mitted hand in the air. "You looked completely lost in thought, like you were trying to map the genome in your head."

"Oh. Um, no. Definitely not trying to do that." She attempted a light laugh. She knew what was coming.

"It's not too late for medical school." There it was. His back was turned to her, but she knew the look on his face: equal parts grave, concerned, and patronizing.

"Which would be helpful if I wanted to become a doctor. But I don't."

He turned and considered her, the recessed lighting shining in his impeccably groomed silver hair. "And why not?"

Annika threw up her hands. "Dad. Can you not? We've had this conversation so many times. I have a job, remember? I have my own business. How do you think it makes me feel when you keep bringing up medical school?"

Her dad frowned. "Makes you feel?" he said, as if those words didn't make sense.

Oh my god. Why was it that every time they had an argument, Annika felt like she'd been sucked into a vortex and was fifteen years old again? "Yes, makes me *feel*! People have feelings, Dad, and you're not making me feel good ones right now."

He still looked confused. "But this isn't about feelings. This is about making a financially secure career decision, which has nothing to do with emotion."

Annika glared at him. "There's more to life than money." She knew she wasn't being completely fair. Her dad was not the shallow type, and he'd always been very generous with her. But he was getting on her nerves.

"I know there is. And when you have money, you can enjoy those other things a lot more. Let me tell you, Annika, not once since about five years after medical school have I had to worry about how I was going to pay the bills." He leveled a glance at her. "Can you say the same?"

Annika felt her blood pressure rising, along with her embarrassment. "No, I can't. Not yet. But that doesn't mean it'll always be this way."

"Do you have an idea of when that'll change?"

Annika gripped her glass, her fingers sliding in the condensation. "We have a few things we're playing with. The money will come."

"*How* will it come? Do you have a plan in place so that financial stress doesn't become a pattern? How are you going to take care of yourself? How will you support your family one day? These are the things you need to be thinking of and planning for now."

"Dad, please. I'm nowhere near having a family. And I'll figure it out, okay? Lots of new businesses deal with this."

"I'm just worried about you, Ani."

"Well, there's nothing for you to worry about! I'm a grown woman. I can take care of myself. I don't need you to worry."

He smiled a little. "I'm your father."

Annika shook her head and got to her feet, abandoning her lemonade. "I'm going out on the balcony for a little while."

She strode out before he could respond, down the hall to the great room and through the French doors onto the enormous deck, which faced the mountains in the distance. It was almost completely dark now. Annika lit the outdoor gas fireplace, watching the flames dance for a moment.

Her dad loved her, this she knew. She had never doubted that. But every time he pretended that Make Up wasn't a "real" business and that running it wasn't a "real" job, she felt like he was questioning who she was. She stood on the balcony for a long time, until she heard him walk up behind her.

He took his place right beside her. "Pluto."

Her shoulders relaxed. "Pluto."

"Your mother loved this view, you know. The city lights in the distance, the silhouette of the mountains in the dusk until the night takes them away . . . I think the view was what sold her on this house. She used to say she'd raise you on this deck." He chuckled.

"Is that why you don't want to leave?" Annika asked, glancing at him. "Because it reminds you of her?"

He swallowed. "Yes. It's too big for me, but . . . leaving would feel like leaving her behind."

That's how I feel about Make Up, Annika thought, but couldn't quite muster up the nerve to say. She didn't know if her dad would understand or dismiss her out of hand. Make Up was an homage to her parents' love. Ever since she was four years old, the one thing Annika had wished for was to give her mom and dad a do-over, to somehow change the past. She'd realized how impossible that was as she got older, but she'd thrown herself into doing for others what she couldn't do for her parents.

"Do you regret it, Dad?" she asked softly. "Do you ever regret falling in love with Mom so hard, and then . . ."

"Losing her just as we got started?"

Annika nodded.

Her dad smiled. "Never. First, she gave me you." He rubbed her back, and Annika smiled, too. "Second, how do you regret the single most beautiful thing that ever happened to you? Do I wish she hadn't got cancer, so she could still be here with us? With every single breath I take. But regretting falling in love with her would be like regretting witnessing a meteor shower because it didn't last forever. You don't, though, do you? You just enjoy it while it's happening. You're mesmerized and enthralled and completely happy for as long as you get to witness it. And then you always look back fondly on the time you got to see it."

"That's a really inspiring way to look at it." She laid her head on his arm. "Do you ever get lonely?"

Her dad patted her head. "With you coming to visit me every week? Not a chance."

But just underneath the surface, she could hear the emptiness.

∽

They ate not too long after that. Even as someone who was vegetarian with the exception of when she was at her dad's (he worried enough about her protein intake as it was), Annika had to admit the pork was every bit as delicious as she'd expected. "Mmmm." She closed her eyes and savored her last mouthful. They were sitting at the table out in the backyard, the landscape lit with glowing string lights and lanterns. In the distance, a rock waterfall gushed down a gentle slope. "Seriously, Dad, you could quit your job and go on a cooking show and become a famous chef somewhere."

He chuckled and dabbed at his mouth with a napkin. "Oh, cooking's just a hobby. But I'm glad you enjoy it. Your mother always thought I was a tad too adventurous."

It's like she's still here, Annika thought. *She's in nearly every conversation we have, and she's been dead almost twenty-five years.* "Well, I love it. Is there more I can take with me?"

Her dad grinned, genuinely pleased. "Of course."

"Awesome." Annika sat back, her belly pleasantly full and her body warm from the glass of red wine she'd had.

"How's June?" June was one of her dad's favorites. The only thing he enjoyed more than feeding Annika was feeding June, on the rare occasion she made the trek out here, too.

"Great. She's got her eye on someone new."

"Oh, really? That hedge fund man she was excited about?"

Annika screwed up her face. "No, not him. That didn't work out; he turned out to be something of a jerk. But the guy she's into now seems nice. He works just down the hall. He's a partial owner of this business, Break Up."

"Oh, yes. Next to the man you told me about. What's his name again?"

"Hudson." Annika's pulse beat a little bit faster. Memories of the night at the fountain resurfaced once more, like a nest of bugs you thought you'd gotten rid of but were hiding in a little hole in your house somewhere. She took a deep swallow of ice water. "Hudson Craft."

"Right, right, Hudson." There was a pause, as they both wandered around with their memories. The twinkling lights reflected like stars in the lenses of her dad's glasses. "So, do *you*?"

"Do I what?" Annika wondered if she'd missed something because she'd been thinking about Hudson again.

"Have your eye on anyone new? Like June?"

No, and the last guy I tried to kiss practically ran away from me. Not very flattering. Annika waved a hand. "I'm too busy for all that."

Her dad leaned back in his chair, the wicker creaking with the movement. "Really? Too busy? Do you think that's ever going to change? You have to make the time."

"Not everyone can be lucky enough to meet their soulmate at twenty-three, Dad. Besides, I'm happy how I am."

Her dad patted her hand. "Of course you are," he said, but she saw the concern in his eyes again.

Just for once, Annika wished she didn't feel like she was letting her dad down on all fronts.

❧

The next afternoon, Annika sat on the floor of her apartment in an old UCLA T-shirt and sweatpants, using tweezers to paint by stickers.

As organized as she liked to keep the office, her apartment was the exact opposite. It was the one place she didn't have to worry about looking put-together or in control. Here, she could let her inner slob shine, and no one cared.

Dust mites floated in the sunlight that streamed from the

glass doors to her right. The throw pillows were tossed on the floor, where Annika frequently sat. On the coffee table was a pile of books—business memoirs, tech start-up manuals, and, of course, romances. June's cup of coffee rested next to a potted plant on her end table, which was really just a collection of twigs, the plant having died from overwatering many weeks ago. *Sleepless in Seattle* was playing on the TV, though neither she nor June were really watching; they had all the lines memorized anyway.

"That looks tedious," June remarked from where she was sprawled on Annika's navy-and-white-striped couch. She was wearing old shorts and a crop top, but somehow still looked as glamorous as an Old Hollywood starlet.

"Mm. It's relaxing." Annika carefully laid a slice of purple sticker on the lion's nose.

"Well, I found out something that's not going to make you feel so relaxed," June said, her nose wrinkled. "Ziggy said that *Time* is doing this big profile on Hudson and Break Up. 'His meteoric rise in the tech sector,' that kind of thing. They're going to make it look like he's the next Zuckerberg."

Annika squeezed her tweezers. "Of course they are. And of course the investors at EPIC are going to see it and be all impressed. Shit." After a pause, she added, "But you know what? Let's talk about something else." She'd spent enough time stewing about Hudson Craft and the almost-kiss and what it meant that she'd wanted to kiss him, her mind going around and around in useless circles, like a merry-go-round that wouldn't stop. Her brain was such a muddled puddle that she hadn't even mustered the energy to tell June what had happened. Annika glanced at her best friend. She would—soon.

Just not right at this second. She didn't need to stress about the *Time* interview this minute, either. There would be time for damage control later. Right now, she was mentally exhausted and needed a reprieve.

Glancing up at June for just a second, she said, "You and Ziggy went out again last night, right? How was it?"

June's gaze dropped to her hands, which were obsessively playing with a couple of errant threads on the couch. Annika resisted the urge to stop her before the entire couch collapsed in a heap of thread and batting beneath her. "It was . . ." June sighed. "I don't know."

Annika looked up from her picture, the amber-colored sticker that was meant to go on the lion's eyeball hanging precariously from the tweezer. "Uh oh. That doesn't sound good."

"Well, it started off fine. We went zip lining—oh my god, *what* a thrill. I'm serious, Annika, the next date you go on, make sure it's something that gets your adrenaline going. Our cheeks were flushed, our hearts were racing . . . *talk* about an aphrodisiac."

Annika half smiled. "Thanks for the tip. Not that I'll need it anytime soon." June frowned and opened her mouth to say something, but Annika waved her off. "Continue."

"Okay, and then we went to dinner at La Rouge, and then . . . I suggested skinny-dipping."

Annika laughed and chose another sticker. "That sounds about right."

June shook her head and sat up, crossing her legs. "He didn't *want* to go skinny-dipping."

Annika's eyes went so wide, her eyeballs felt like they were in danger of popping out. "Wait, what? He didn't want to go skinny-dipping with *you?*"

June bit her lip, tracing a finger down a stripe on the couch. "He looked at me in the moonlight and said, 'You're beautiful. And you don't know how hard this is for me to say, but . . . I don't think we should. I want to take this slow.'" She put her face in her hands. "I'd already started stripping, and then I had to pull my top back on. It was *awful.*"

Annika set her tweezers down and reached forward to squeeze her friend's knee. She suddenly realized this was June's first time ever being rejected by a guy. "I'm sorry. But—"

June peeked at Annika from between her painted fingernails. "But what?"

Annika shrugged and said hesitantly, "It sounds like the reason he said that is because he *likes* you. Like, he *really* likes you."

"No!" June said immediately, as Annika had guessed she would. She picked up her coffee cup. "He doesn't *like* me. Come on—we barely even know each other. He's probably just weird about sex or something."

Annika considered her friend for a moment. "What would you do, though?" she pressed. "If he does really like you? Would you continue to see him?"

June looked at her over the top of her coffee cup, her pale face swathed in steam. "I—I don't know," she said, looking completely thrown.

"Whoa." Annika stared at her. "This is the first time you've ever responded with anything other than, 'Move on because men are like trains. There's always another one coming.'"

"Doesn't mean anything," June said, but she wouldn't hold

Annika's gaze. *Fascinating. Very, very fascinating.* "Can we talk about something else now?"

"Sure." Annika picked up her tweezers again and turned to study the palette of colored stickers. "Of course."

If there *was* something going on here—if Ziggy really was somehow worming his way into June's heart—she would be really happy for her. Happy like from-the-head-to-the-toes-of-her-soul happy. But there was a small part of her that felt . . . "jealous" was too strong a word. Call it . . . "unsettled." Yes, unsettled had a better ring to it.

June was the one who went out on strings of first dates because she *wanted* to, not because they never called back—unlike Annika. She was famous for saying that her twenties were all about sowing wild oats and her thirties would be about wedding dresses and babies. She had a timeline all planned out, a timeline that made Annika feel infinitely better about not having a serious boyfriend yet. And now, here they were, all of twenty-four years old, and June seemed to be changing her mind. Wasn't it a bit early for that?

And if *June* had found The One when she wasn't even looking, what did that mean for Annika, who'd always been open to something serious? Was she completely hopeless and destined for solitude?

"Hey." June snapped her fingers. Annika blinked and looked up at her. "What're you thinking about? You look like Eeyore after his dog got run over."

Annika forced a smile. "Nothing! I'm just . . . musing about dating and stuff. That's all."

June narrowed her eyes, not one to be fooled so easily. "Mm hmm . . ."

Annika set her tweezers down and pursed her lips, unable to keep the secret any longer. "Something happened on Thursday night."

June took a sip of her coffee, biding her time. She knew Annika well enough to know when to push and when to wait.

"With Hudson. After the rooftop party." Annika took a deep breath, placed her hands flat on the coffee table, and said in a rush, "He told me he couldn't stop thinking about Vegas and I told him I've been thinking about it, too, and then I got caught up in the moment and tried to kiss him and he physically held me off and rejected me. Oh, and I don't think he stole the app idea after all."

June set her mug down slowly. "Whoa. That is a *lot* of information."

"Yeah, I know. I'm sort of a Dumpster fire."

"So he thinks about you."

"Yeah."

"And you think about him."

Annika winced. ". . . Yeah."

"And you tried to kiss him, but he said no?" June frowned. "Why?"

Annika leaned against the couch and groaned. "He said it was because I'd had a lot to drink and he wanted me to be clear-headed when he kissed me, but I don't know. That was probably just an excuse. Right?"

June shrugged. "I don't know. I mean, I saw the way he was stealin' looks at you that night. I don't think there was any part of him that *didn't* want to kiss you." She paused and leaned forward. "Is there any chance he's just . . . a gentleman?"

Annika scoffed. "The creator of Break Up, a *gentleman*? I don't think so."

June sat back. "But you don't think he stole the idea for Make Up and turned it into Break Up."

"No. He seemed pretty genuine about that. I'm not sure why he came up with Break Up, but . . ." She trailed off and shrugged, picking up her tweezers again.

There was silence, apart from Meg Ryan's character talking to that fiancé everyone knew was no good for her.

"But you don't want to date him," June said casually, as if the answer didn't matter to her one way or another.

"No!" Annika looked up at her. "June, me and Hudson? Can you really see it? It wouldn't work on any level. Our philosophies on life and doing the right thing are so diametrically opposed that the universe would combust if we dated."

"Okay," June said, shrugging. "I get it. But, um, if you're not going to date *him* . . . Ziggy told me about this guy he knows, this Greek dude named Alesandro. He's really successful, he has his own bakery, and—"

Annika held up a hand. "I'm gonna stop you right there and say no."

June pulled a pillow onto her lap and squeezed it just as her phone pinged with a text. She glanced at the screen, set the phone aside, and made a face. "Ew. Hedge Fund Harry. He's been trying to set up another date." She turned back to Annika. "But seriously, Alesandro could be so great! I'll see Ziggy for a bit, you'll date Alesandro, we'll go on double dates together . . ."

Annika put a sticker on the lion's snout and raised an eyebrow at her best friend's very convenient selective memory. "Are you serious? I've been on two blind dates in my entire life, and they were both ginormous disasters."

"Come on. What are the chances Alesandro's hair will catch on fire? Or that he'll get hit by a bike messenger while you take a romantic walk in the city?" Picking up her mug, she waved it around, not noticing the tiny splash of coffee that sloshed onto the carpet.

Annika sighed and grabbed another sticker from the sticker book, slightly ripping a corner in her agitation. "I don't know, but with my luck, probably a hundred percent."

June grabbed her phone off the side table. "Okay, but just look at his picture. Doesn't he look like the sweetest man? Plus, you wouldn't have to worry about the universe combusting if you dated him. Y'all have a lot in common." June held her phone out to Annika.

Alesandro was an olive-skinned man in his late twenties, with brown eyes that crinkled at the corners when he smiled. He was dressed decently, too, in a button-down shirt with an open collar and dark jeans. His hair was thinning, but that wasn't a big deal. He *did* look like a nice guy. It had been a long time since Annika had gone out with a nice guy.

She sighed, and June's smile got bigger, as if she could sense weakness. But she sat quietly.

"All right, fine," Annika said, turning back to the sticker book. "I'll do it. You can tell Ziggy to tell Alesandro I'm in." A couple of thoughts flashed through her mind: *Would Ziggy tell Hudson? Would Hudson get jealous?* She shook her head, annoyed at herself. Why would Ziggy bother telling Hudson? Besides, she couldn't afford to think like that. She and Hudson were never going to work. Did she find Alesandro as attractive as Hudson? Not really. But that was neither here nor there. Everyone knew physical attraction should be a very small part of the equation. And the emotional attraction would probably come very soon. Like June said, she and Alesandro had way more in common than she and Hudson did.

June squealed and began typing furiously on her phone. "Okay, it's done. I'll let you know which days work for him and we can go from there."

"Great." Annika placed a white sticker on the lion's mane, feeling nothing but a deep sense of foreboding. Here she was, putting herself out there again. Her string of first dates in the last year alone already told her it wouldn't amount to anything, but at least June was happy.

June's phone bleeped with a text and she giggled before responding. Annika sighed.

chapter eight

♡

On Monday morning, June was already at her desk typing away industriously when Annika walked in at eight. "Oh, hey," she said, setting her latte down on her desk and stashing her yoga gear in the closet. Thankfully, after that one time they'd run into each other at Breathing Tree, Hudson had stopped going to her classes. Something that required as much internal strength and awareness as yoga was probably a bad match for him. "You're in early."

June met her with a beaming smile. "Yes, I am. And I've had a breakthrough with the aggression algorithm. I'm just finalizing the last bit of code."

"Awesome!" Annika booted her laptop up and took a sip of her coffee as she waited, glancing around at the office in satisfaction. Her enclave. The place she felt *right*. The windows threw sunlit squares on the wall, highlighting the painting above the settee. "When you're done, I'd love to take a look at it."

"Sure." June turned back to her computer for a second

before looking back up again. "Oh, by the way. How are you feeling about that tech volunteering thing this afternoon?"

Annika shrugged. "Pretty good. Early to Tech, Early to Rise is one of Lionel Wakefield's favorite charities. It should be fairly low-key, and I'm hoping it'll be an easy way to get into his good graces before EPIC. Plus, they do really good work, so it was a no-brainer to volunteer Make Up's services."

June leaned back in her chair. "It's basically just Make Up and a couple of other start-ups doing presentations for a bunch of high school–aged entrepreneurs, right?"

"Right. Apparently, the CEO of Early to Tech is best friends with Lionel. So if we can really impress her, it'll feed to Wakefield—and then we just might have EPIC in the bag." She grinned, loving the adrenaline rush right before an event she knew she was going to slay.

June nodded. "I'm glad you're feeling good about it." She kept staring at Annika, now fiddling with her Darth Vader figurine.

"What?" Little niggles of worry began to replace Annika's excitement.

"Nothing, just that . . . Ziggy said Break Up was invited, too. Hudson will be speaking."

Annika stared at her. "What? Since when?"

"Apparently since forever ago. Didn't Early to Tech, Early to Rise tell you?"

"No. They definitely didn't tell me."

June quirked her mouth. "But . . . it's fine, right? Since you feel good about it and everything?"

Annika quickly turned back to her laptop. "Oh, no, yeah. Totally fine. Why should I care whether or not he'll be there?" She and Hudson hadn't spoken at all since the weird almost-kiss at the fountain on Thursday. Which was fine. As far as she was concerned, there *was* nothing to talk about. Period dot.

"Why, indeed? It's just Hudson Craft, and y'all sabotage each other with every opportunity you get. No big."

Annika glared at her. "Are you teasing me?"

June opened her blue eyes wide. "Of course not." There was laughter in her voice. "I'm just saying, you know he's going to be up to something if you guys are part of the same thing."

"Oh, I know. He's *always* up to something. You can't ever have your back to him." Annika reached into her drawer for ZeeZee and began kneading him. "But you know what's great about Hudson? He always underestimates his opponent. And I'm not nearly as sweet as I look." She smiled the most vicious smile she could conjure up. "So you tell Ziggy to tell Hudson that."

June groaned. "It's like high school again." When she saw Annika's narrowed gaze, she quickly added, "Okay, okay, I will. But first I'm putting the finishing touches on this code right here and then I'll upload it to the repo."

"Sounds good." Pushing thoughts of Hudson and the tech forum from her mind, Annika tossed ZeeZee back into the drawer and pulled up the Word document in which she'd begun to outline the EPIC pitch.

She read through all the bullet points and then read them again. Her pulse began to quicken; her palms tingled. She could see it—she could see the direction she needed to go.

She pulled her laptop closer and began typing up her vision furiously, barely hearing June when she said, "Someone's going down the rabbit hole."

When Annika emerged from the rabbit hole three hours later, Hudson was knocking on their door and letting himself in.

She sat up straighter and pushed her chair back, even though there was barely any room to maneuver in her office with him taking up so much space. She blinked, feeling dazed from all the ideas that had been tumbling through her mind only moments before. "Oh."

June's desk was empty. She hadn't even heard her leave. Annika blinked and rolled her neck, coming slowly back to the present. Right. Hudson was here. Her discomfort surged at the memory of how they'd ended their last encounter. "What, um—what are you doing here?"

He smiled lazily, as if he could read her mind. "It's time for the tech forum. Thought we could all go together. Ziggy, Blaire, and June are by the elevators."

"What, already? What time is it?" She went to get her bag in the storage closet.

"Around noon."

Right on cue, Annika's stomach grumbled. She realized she hadn't had her midmorning snack.

"You should feed whatever's in there," Hudson joked.

Annika tossed him a dirty look as she started toward the door. Was he just going to pretend everything was fine between them? That his whole rejection thing had never happened? Or that they were friends now, or something? "Some of us actually work hard for a living, and that means forgoing the occasional meal." Even if it was an accident.

He didn't seem fazed by her rudeness. "Oh, I ran into Seetha in the parking garage on the way into work today. She said you missed yoga Friday, so I said I'd stop by and say hi." He paused and leaned against the doorjamb, his arms crossed. He was wearing a green button-down today, which perfectly matched his eyes. "Hi."

Annika glanced at him as she walked into the hallway, her chin up. "Hi."

After a pause, he trailed after her. "You nervous? About having to talk to people at the same time I'm talking to them?"

Annika rolled her eyes. She could hear June and Ziggy down the hallway, just around the bend. She was so close to freedom, to not having one-on-one Hudson attention. "Yeah, I'm so nervous about how great I'm going to look after they spend two seconds listening to your arrogant ass."

No response. Annika turned around to see Hudson cocking his head as he watched her. "You're mad because I didn't kiss you," he said finally, giving her a smug, lopsided grin. "I can remedy that right now, you know. You haven't had anything to drink today, have you?"

Annika spluttered for a good ten seconds before finding her voice. "Incorrigible," she muttered loud enough for him to hear, as she turned back around and began marching to the elevators again.

He laughed. "Admit it. It bothers you."

Clutching her bag tighter, Annika picked up the pace and refused to respond, not wanting Hudson to know how right he was. "Hey!" she said to June, as soon as she rounded the corner to the elevators. "We're riding together, right? You and me?"

June smiled at her. "Actually, Ziggy already said he'd take me and Blaire." She leaned forward and whispered in Annika's ear, "But I was sure you wouldn't mind riding with Hudson."

What? *What?* What had she ever said to make June think she wouldn't mind riding with Hudson Craft?

"Yeah," Ziggy said, before Annika could set her best friend right. "My car can only fit four, so would you and Hudson mind riding together?"

"Of course not!" Hudson replied heartily, from behind Annika. How had he caught up with her so fast?

She turned to him, trying not to glare. "I can drive myself, thanks."

"Annika." Hudson sounded shocked, though his eyes were twinkling. "Think of the environment."

She glanced at June, who shrugged, as if to say, *He does have a point.* "I have a hybrid," she said, eyeing him haughtily. "The environment will be fine."

❧

The tech forum was being held at the Manhattan Beach Library, a giant glass structure with views of the ocean from its top floor. The wide-open space had been converted for the event, with a small stage set up in the front of the room, complete with a podium and projector. The rest of the space was filled with about two dozen chairs, presumably for the high school entrepreneurs, who were yet to arrive.

Annika, June, Hudson, and his team fanned out across the space, the Break Up team talking among themselves about some award they were getting from *Tech Now* and how they should find a way to slip that into conversation with Rita Davenport, the CEO of Early to Tech, because it would definitely impress Lionel Wakefield. Occasionally, Hudson would catch her eye over Ziggy's or Blaire's heads, but she forced herself to look away immediately every time. She would *not* get sucked into the Hudson vortex.

She walked with June to the windows, where they stood looking out at the ocean for a while. Annika took a deep, calming breath. "This is pretty cool, getting to meet the young techie minds of the future. How many girls do you think will be in the group?" When she got down about not making progress as quickly as she'd like with Make Up, Annika liked to focus on the fact that she was showing other young women entrepreneurs out there that they could do it, too. The glass ceiling might still be there, but it was smashed and splintered almost beyond recognition.

"I'm hoping for half this time," said June, ever the optimist, turning to Annika with a brilliant, fuchsia-lipsticked smile.

"Annika Dev? Hudson Craft?"

Annika and Hudson both turned toward the voice to see a Black woman in her midthirties striding toward them. She was dressed in white sheath dress and espadrilles, and held out her hand to each of them, a winning smile on her face. "I'm Rita Davenport. We've been speaking via email. Thank you so much for agreeing to present to our teens. You don't know how much it means to them, and to our organization."

Hudson took her hand and gave it a firm shake. Annika made sure her handshake was even firmer. "It's our pleasure, Rita," Hudson said, smiling in his annoyingly charming way. *Ugh.* Annika could *see* Rita being dazzled in real time. "Break Up is all about giving back."

"Ha."

Rita, Hudson, and June all turned to look at her, Hudson's eyes flashing in annoyance. *Oops.* She hadn't meant to say that out loud. Looking pointedly at Rita, Annika said, "Sorry, tickle in my throat. Anyway, it's the same for Make Up. We're all about giving back—only we give back to both the community *and* the people who use our service. We want to make the world a better place all around." She tossed a glance at Hudson, whose eyes were narrowed, as if he was calculating his next move.

"Wonderful," Rita said, looking a little taken aback. Rallying, she added, "Well, I *have* heard that you're both going to be participating in EPIC in June. I can see there's already some friendly rivalry here." She laughed throatily and Annika forced herself to chuckle right along with her, though she made sure her eyes narrated a very different story to Hudson. *You're going down, Craft. May the best me win.* He didn't seem too intimidated, but that meant nothing. Wait till she outshone him in every way in front of Rita.

"Anyway," Rita continued, oblivious, "the other entrepreneurs should be arriving any moment, and we'll have the students file in when everyone's here. Would you like some tea or coffee?"

"I'd love some tea, thank you, Rita." Annika smiled warmly. "But first, would you mind telling me where it'd be best to plug in my laptop?"

By the time Annika finished plugging her laptop into the only available outlet beside the stage, the other tech entrepreneurs had arrived. One was a tall Korean American man and the other a short bespectacled white man. Rita made the introductions as they stood by the refreshments table and then walked off to welcome the first of the arriving high schoolers.

Hudson shook the other two men's hands, and then said, "If you'll excuse me. I have the first presentation, so I want to make sure the AV setup's all good."

Annika watched him go and then turned to the Korean American man, whose name was Tom. "I'm next, and I think you're third?" Tom nodded. "Well," Annika continued, "I hope your presentation goes well. I think the three of us"—here she included the white guy, Gavin—"are going to really blow this away."

Gavin took a bite of a chocolate-glazed doughnut. "Oh, I don't know. Break Up is pretty good. I think they might steal the show."

Annika laughed. "They're all smoke and no fire, Gavin. I wouldn't worry too much."

"It's not a competition, though, is it?" Tom pulled at his collar, looking nervous. "I thought this was just a presentation to benefit the kids. No one told me we were supposed to compete."

Annika looked at Hudson, who was fiddling with the mic onstage, and narrowed her eyes. "Oh, it's *always* a competition."

⁓

She had to hand it to Hudson: He had great timing. His presentation was short, funny, and timed down to the second. He was done at seven minutes exactly, with three minutes left for the Q&A. It was just too bad she hadn't had time to plan some sabotage.

Annika stood by the refreshments table and watched as the high school kids, all of whom had been quiet aside from laughing at the appropriate times, shot their hands in the air when he asked if they had questions.

"I saw online that Break Up was in the top twenty most downloaded dating apps this month. So, what does success mean to someone like you?" a short Black boy with a full, curly head of hair asked in a rush.

Hudson spoke confidently into the wireless mic he took off

the podium, his big hand clasped firmly around the handle. "Success, to me, is the only way forward." He shrugged, but his green eyes flashed, intense. "Success is the way you prove to yourself that you've earned every single sacrifice someone else had to make to get you to where you are. Success means nothing if you don't push yourself every moment to top the previous day's efforts. It's the way you say thank you for everything you've been given."

Annika frowned as she chewed the last of her raspberry Danish. For someone who was already close to the top, he sounded . . . obsessed.

"The whole concept behind Break Up is dope. How'd you come up with the idea?" This one came from a pale, lanky boy, his face bright red.

Hudson's eyes flickered over to Annika for a second. "Thank you," he said to the boy, walking a few steps forward. "It was a complicated process. When I thought about the way we date—or don't date—in most of Western society, I realized there was so much lacking. We don't communicate. If given the chance, we'd rather run away from our messy feelings. And running away from feelings . . . well, that just creates more mess. I created Break Up for people who don't know how to say two simple words—'it's over.'" Here, he looked at her again, raising his eyebrows a bit.

Annika raised her eyebrows back and shrugged. Okay, so on the surface, his explanation seemed . . . reasonable. Maybe even noble, in some sense. But the bottom line was Hudson was hurting people with his app. It was being used by people like Heather's boyfriend, the woman she'd seen in the parking garage being broken up with. It was brutal.

Her thought process was interrupted by the thunderous

applause for Hudson. He set his mic back on the stand and twisted the knob to tighten it before raising a hand and hopping off the stage, right toward her.

Annika straightened her shoulders and surreptitiously brushed Danish crumbs from the corner of her mouth. "I could tell you did your best," she said, when Hudson was within earshot. "But let me show you how to do it better." Flashing him June's trademark southern *bless-your-heart-but-not-really-because-I-detest-you* smile, she started for the stage.

"I hope you can do it with a laptop that's woefully low on power," Hudson said casually, smiling and popping a cream puff into his mouth.

"Wait, what?" Annika spun to look at her laptop at the front of the room. Her charger wasn't plugged into the wall anymore—it had been replaced with a cell phone cord that was now charging a phone that wasn't hers. "What the hell? Did you *unplug* me? How petty can you be?"

He swallowed his cream puff thoughtfully. "Well, I was listening to some really great mariachi music on the way over and it did a number on my battery." Annika flushed. "So I needed to charge my cell. I *hate* when it goes below ninety percent."

"You—you complete—" Annika's anger was fire. "How am I supposed to . . . *arrrhhh!*"

Hudson chuckled, looking unfazed. "It looked like you only had about five percent left, so I guess you better talk fast."

Balling her fists at her side so she wouldn't do something that would land a felony on her record, Annika stormed to the front of the room and looked at her laptop. It was already at 4 percent—definitely not enough to get through a ten-minute presentation. *Shit.* Hudson was right; she'd have to talk fast and maybe even improvise the ending.

She tossed him another dirty look and flounced up to the podium with her dying computer. While the crowd sat stock-still and silent, watching her, Annika quickly looked around for a place to charge it on the makeshift stage. Of course, there wasn't one.

Pasting a smile on her face, she placed her laptop on a small wooden stool, hooked it up to the AV wires, and lowered the mic from Hudson's height to hers.

Well, she tried to, anyway. He'd tightened it extra hard—probably just to watch her struggle, red-faced, as she was doing right now—until finally, she snatched it off its stand entirely.

"Hi." She sounded a little savage, and the high schoolers winced at the initial squeal of feedback, but she kept going. "So nice to see all of you! I'm Annika Dev, CEO of Make Up." Hazarding a glance at her laptop, Annika saw it was now at 3 percent. "Okay, so without further ado, I'm going to get into the presentation. What I have here"—she gestured to the screen as she spoke, rapid-fire—"is a prototype called OLLI: the Original Love Language Interface. OLLI is a deep-learning network that we feel is really pretty innovative." She caught June's eye in the very back of the room. She kept miming for Annika to slow down, but of course, she couldn't. "Umanyway," Annika continued, seeing the 2% flashing on her screen, "thisisbasicallyawayforpeopleinrelation—"

A boy with red hair that almost exactly matched Ziggy's raised his hand. "Excuse me?"

Annika tried not to groan in frustration. "Yes?"

"I can't understand you."

A laugh floated up from Hudson's side of the room. She glared in his general direction and turned back to the boy, forcing a smile. "Okay. I'll slow down a bit." Taking a deep breath, she said a little slower, "As I was saying, OLLI is basically a way for people in relationships to communicate better with each other. So, for instance, if you look at the screen . . ." She forwarded through the slides as quickly as she could without looking like a complete lunatic or getting called out by another teenager.

Hudson was swilling coffee from a plastic cup, which he raised to her, a mischievous grin on his face, as if he were at a particularly entertaining party.

". . . and we hope to have the entire app up and running within a few months. We're confident we can make it." Annika beamed at the audience.

A boy who was slumped in his chair as if ready for a nap called out, in a laconic drawl, "Yo, your laptop died."

Annika turned to see a blank screen. *Dammit.* She turned back to the audience, a bright smile on her face, her hand clamped in a death grip around the mic. "Uh . . . yes. Yeah. I know. I'm . . . finished. Let's head into Q&A!"

The teens in the audience looked less than impressed. She heard a snicker from Hudson's end of the room.

Another boy, this one wearing a backward baseball cap and a football jersey, raised his hand. "Yeah, uh, do you have a boyfriend?" he asked, a lazy smile on his face. The group of boys sitting around him immediately burst out into laughter.

Annika's eyes unwittingly darted to Hudson, who was watching the exchange with a slight frown on his face. "No, I don't," Annika said into the mic, even though she could see

Rita Davenport giving her the *you don't have to answer that* signal. "But," she continued, "I have a first date I'm really excited about soon. So." She smiled a victorious, *see-I'm-not-even-thinking-about-our-almost-kiss* smile in Hudson's direction, only to see him straighten, a muscle in his jaw jumping as he set his coffee cup down.

Feeling slightly off-kilter, Annika turned to the audience again. A Latina girl in the front row raised her hand. "Your tech sounds really cool," she said, in a high, sweet voice. "And, um, you said your developer is also a . . . girl?"

Annika grinned. "Yeah. I have a kick-ass developer, June Stewart. She's right back there, actually." She pointed toward the back of the room. June smiled and waved.

The girl looked back up at Annika, her brown eyes wide. "I want to do that one day."

"You totally can," Annika said seriously. "Don't let *anyone* tell you you can't, okay?"

The girl nodded.

Another hand shot up, this one belonging to a brown-haired girl with braces in the third row. "You said you won the Young Entrepreneur's Grant last year, right? That's really hard to do. I was reading that only one percent of the applicants get picked. So, like—why do you think you were chosen?"

Annika paced a little as she spoke. "Well, you know, I think it all started with the fact that I was—I *am*—really, really passionate about what I want to do in this world. I want to bring people together, and every day I go to work excited that our app will help us do that. Honestly, even if we hadn't gotten that grant, I'd still consider us a success. You know why?" The girl shook her head, her gaze riveted on Annika. "Because success means doing good in the world. It means waking up every day knowing you made the world better in some way, big or small."

The girl's face broke out in a big smile. "Cool. I want to make an app that pairs service dogs with disabled people according to personality and lifestyle needs."

Annika clutched the mic with both hands. "That is an *awesome* idea. What's your name?"

"Taylor."

"Taylor, if you ever have any questions about the tech world, feel free to email June or me, okay?" Taylor nodded enthusiastically, and Annika looked over at the Latina girl. "And what's your name?"

"Angelica."

"Angelica, you too. In fact, any of the girls in this audience— take a business card and take us up on it. Because we're out there doing the work and we want you to do that, too."

The space exploded in applause—the girls were the loudest, but so was June. And—ha! So was Rita Davenport. *Yes.* And . . . Annika did a double take. Hudson was clapping, too.

She walked off the stage and right over to him. "So you thought you'd sabotage me, did you?" she said, as Tom made his way onto the stage.

He looked down at her, a slow smile spreading on his face. "Not bad, Ms. Dev. You almost convinced them you're successful."

She tipped her head back and looked down her nose at him, an impossible feat, considering the height differential. It was the intent that mattered. "And *you* almost convinced them you're human. Let's hope you learned your lesson, Mr. Craft. I'm invincible. I'm unstoppable. And I *will* kick your ass at EPIC."

Annoyance flashed across his face as he turned to the refreshments table and poured himself a new cup of coffee. "I wouldn't go that far."

Annika tossed her hair over her shoulder and went to join June. She could tell, even without looking, that he was watching her go. An onlooker might accuse her of swaying her hips *slightly* more than necessary, but they'd be wrong. Totally and utterly wrong.

chapter nine

After Tom and Gavin finished their presentations, Annika and June spent a few minutes speaking to small groups of the high schoolers, including the two girls who'd asked questions. Finally, Rita Davenport went onstage to thank all the entrepreneurs, marking the event over. The high schoolers said their goodbyes and began to pack up.

Rita walked up to the entrepreneurs, beaming. "Thank you all for doing such a splendid job!"

The four entrepreneurs expressed their own niceties, and shortly after, Tom and Gavin made their excuses and left. Rita stepped closer to Hudson and Annika. Her warm brown eyes sparkled. "I have to say, you two were definitely the biggest hit with the students. To see two incredibly successful—" *Ha!* Annika flashed Hudson a smug smile, but he remained impassive. "—young entrepreneurs doing what they love and speaking to them so candidly about it . . . you really have a knack for this. You should consider volunteering with us more often."

"I would love to," Annika said, and meant it. "This is really a great organization."

"Agreed." Hudson looked around at the kids, some of whom were still getting their bags together and walking out. "You're planting seeds that'll grow into mighty oaks soon enough."

Rita looked impressed with his metaphor. Ugh, he was such an ass-kisser. "Well, I'll be sure to let Lionel know just how fantastic a job you both did. And good luck at EPIC."

"Thank you," they said, and then, under his breath so Rita wouldn't hear, Hudson added, "She's going to need it."

～

After they'd said their goodbyes, Annika and June walked to Zero Gravity, a trendy chrome-and-leather bar down the road from the library that was running a happy hour special on all their margaritas. Ziggy had wanted to take June out, naturally, but she'd told him she and Annika needed to debrief, for which Annika was thankful.

They grabbed a corner table in the dimly lit, mostly empty interior. Annika sighed. "That went well, don't you think?"

"Definitely." June smiled just as a waitress with a nose piercing came over to get their drinks order. Once they'd ordered their drinks—a cosmo for June and a mango margarita for Annika—June continued, "The kids were obviously into Make Up and what you do there. And I got a bunch of questions about being a developer at the end, so that was cool, too."

"It's just so nice to talk to students, especially the girls. I remember this one time in high school, they had a small business owner come speak to us for Career Day. She ran a printing shop, but still—I remember how amazing it was to hear a *woman* talking about being her own boss, about having the power to make *all* the decisions. That's when I first began to think that maybe I could do that, too. Although—did you happen to catch any of Hudson's answers?"

June shook her head. Annika groaned. "You're lucky. He's insufferable. I don't know what kinds of mental contortions you have to do to frame your heartbreaking business as a *good* thing, but he's doing all of them. He thinks the world's a stage and he's the main attraction that we've all been waiting twenty-five years to see."

June nodded. "Ziggy thinks they're doing good work, too. He says Hudson's a visionary."

Annika nearly choked on her own spit. "A *visionary*? Of what? Broken dreams and oceans of tears? Ugh. Poor Ziggy. He's obviously been indoctrinated." She shook her head. "Whatever. I'm just looking forward to relaxing and putting Hudson Craft out of my mind for the rest of the day."

June made a face and looked past Annika. "Um . . . then you might not like what's coming."

Annika looked over her shoulder to see Hudson and the Break Up team heading their way. "Oh, great," she muttered, just as they walked up.

Ziggy went to stand by June, but Blaire stayed behind Hudson, her face a steel mask. She'd never forgiven Annika for the Nerf gun move that very first day.

"Hello again, Hudson," Annika said, making a monumental effort to be polite.

"Annika," he said, inclining his head a bit.

"Oh my god," June said suddenly, her voice low. She leaned forward, ducking her head.

Annika turned to her. "What?"

June's hands were fists. "Hedge Fund Harry," she whispered, jerking her head toward the door.

Annika turned to see a tall, slim man in an expensive-looking gray suit. His dark hair was combed straight back, and he wore a planet-sized watch on one wrist.

"Who's Hedge Fund Harry?" Ziggy asked in a normal voice, following their gazes.

"Shh!" June said, but it was too late.

Hedge Fund Harry turned in their direction. Annika saw the spark of recognition as he took in June, and then he was sauntering over, an easy smile on his very square face. He had a dimple in his chin—June's Achilles' heel. "June!" he said, too heartily. "I've been texting you."

Ziggy's hand was resting on the table, and June took it. Annika raised her eyebrows, but didn't say anything. "I've been busy," June said.

Hedge Fund Harry looked from their hands to June to Ziggy, as if assessing this new development. "All right," he said slowly, holding his hands up. "You're taken. I don't trespass on another man's territory."

June stiffened, and Ziggy said, "She's not my terri—"

"You're pretty, but I don't date Asian chicks anymore." Hedge Fund Harry was looking at Blaire. "Ever since my last girlfriend's tiger mom destroyed our relationship. She was Korean." He brayed a laugh.

"Somehow, I'm certain Asian women everywhere will survive this setback," Blaire deadpanned, her face still an immovable mask.

Hedge Fund Harry's eyes lit on Annika. "Well, hey there," he said, flashing what he thought was a winsome smile, no doubt. "What's your name?"

"I'm Indian American, which qualifies as Asian," Annika said, taking a sip of water. Beside her, Hudson snorted.

"Indian is hardly Asian," Hedge Fund Harry countered. "And anyway, I think we can make an exception this one time. . . ." His smarmy smile got bigger.

Hudson took half a step closer to him, putting himself between Annika and Hedge Fund Harry. "I think it's very clear she's not interested." His lips were set in a firm line.

Hedge Fund Harry looked at him in annoyance, but realization dawned on his face a second later. "Hey." He held out a hand. "You're Hudson Craft. The Break Up guy."

Hudson stared at his hand, pointedly not taking it. Then, turning to Ziggy, he said, "I guess I'll—"

But Hedge Fund Harry wasn't going to be thwarted so easily. "Bro, you have saved my ass so many times, I can't even tell you. Ever since I downloaded your app, I feel like my life is mine again. I don't have to deal with all those messy tears and all the shrieking when I'm breaking up with a chick anymore. You know how it is. Time is money."

Hudson looked at him, his eyes cold. "That's not the intent of Break Up. It's supposed to be a way for a clean, easy break for both parties." Hedge Fund Harry opened his mouth to say something, but Hudson cut him off smoothly. "Anyway, I'm taking a break from work at the moment. If you'll excuse me."

Hedge Fund Harry looked uncertain, as if he wasn't used to people telling him to leave. "All right, bro. Take care." Executing a one-handed, low-effort wave, he made his way to the bar, checking out every woman under fifty along the way.

They watched him leave in silence. June let out a noisy sigh. "Oh my god. Can you believe that guy?"

Hudson turned to Blaire. "Hey, are you okay? What he said about Asian women—"

Blaire waved him off. "Heard it all before. Dude wasn't even original." She met Annika's eye. "Nice deflection, by the way."

Annika tried not to show how surprised she was at the compliment. "Yeah. Thanks." She glanced up at Hudson. "And, um, thanks for standing up for me."

He was looking down at her, his expression inscrutable. "Anytime." The weight behind his words made it seem like he really meant it.

Annika felt her cheeks heat. She kept her gaze on her glass, only glancing up once to find he was still staring at her. She looked around at the others, sure they must've noticed, too. But they were all talking to each other about something different, completely oblivious. She looked back at Hudson—he was *still* looking at her.

"Do I unsettle you, Ms. Dev?" he asked, a smile in his voice.

She forced herself to look up at him again, even though it felt impossibly difficult. "N-no." Annika held her chin up. "Not at all."

He stepped closer, close enough that the silky fabric of his pants brushed her bare leg. Close enough that her heart juddered, her breath catching in her throat. "Are you sure?"

Her mouth was dry. She couldn't look away from him, couldn't set her water down, couldn't speak a word.

"I don't think your *date* will have quite the same effect on you, do you?" he pressed, looking at her like she was the only one in the bar, the only one who mattered.

She began to shake her head to agree with him when the waitress came by with her and June's drinks, breaking the spell. Annika let out a ragged breath in relief.

"We should go order, too," Hudson said, after one long look at Annika. The Break Up team wandered off to get their own table—but only after Ziggy had planted a soft kiss on June's lips. She watched him go, a hint of a smile on her face that Annika was sure she didn't realize was there.

Annika sipped her margarita to quell all the disconcerting feelings—about the effect Hudson had on her, about how June was interacting with Ziggy—in the pit of her stomach. "Mm. This is good."

"So is this," June said, sipping her cosmo. "Oh, Alesandro said he could do this Friday at seven, at Neon. You'll go, right? You'll really make an effort?"

Annika's gaze fluttered to Hudson's table a few yards from hers, where he sat with his elbows on the sleek wood. "Uh, yes, I'll go." She forced her eyes back to June and sat up straighter. "And I'll make an effort." She'd be damned if she was going to let Hudson ruin her date.

June patted her hand, looking maternal. "Good. I think you'll have fun."

Annika allowed herself a noncommittal grunt. "Anyway, how's the prototype shaping up?"

"Excellently." June sipped her cocktail and smiled. "I'm feeding the algorithm lots of data so it's coming along at a good clip."

"Nice." Annika traced a drop of condensation down the side

of her glass. "And the new feature we've been talking about—the future projection? I know you're working really hard, but have you had a chance to look at the notes I sent over?"

"I have! I think it's going to be so good. That was a flash of brilliance on your part, honestly."

Annika waved her off. "I mean, it's all about execution and that's all you. But yeah, if we can project a realistic future for the couples who use Make Up based on data, I think the app will be so much more powerful. Not to mention it'll make them so much more likely to try and fight for their relationship if they think it has a sustainable future."

"It'll make things real," June agreed, playing with her napkin. "It's ambitious, but I think we can pull it off. Your notes and ideas were detailed enough that I have a good stepping-off point."

"Good." Annika took a sip of her margarita and watched a guy at the bar try to get the bartender's attention in vain.

"Oh shit, I almost forgot to tell you." June set her drink down with a clatter. "Guess what?"

Annika raised her eyebrows. "Um . . . Alesandro's on the FBI's Most Wanted list? Lady Gaga wants to feature you in her next music video? Princess Leia invited you to high tea on Alderaan?"

June sighed. "Stop it. And high tea would be impossible, considering Alderaan was destroyed by the Death Star in the original 1977 film." She took a breath. "Anyway, you know how *Time* is doing that big spread on Hudson?"

Annika took a morose sip of her margarita. "Yeah. I remember. We still need to figure out damage control for that mess, how to offset it and impress the EPIC investors in our own way."

A sneaky smile spread across June's face. She leaned forward, her hair falling in her face. "Weeeellll . . . we might not have to. I just happen to know Megan Trout, who's a senior editor for *Time*, who also happens to be BFFs with Emily Dunbar-Khan, who's doing the piece. Megan put me in touch with Emily, and I said, 'You know what, Emily? There's a great businesswoman who runs an app that does the exact opposite of Break Up. While Hudson Craft pries people apart, Annika Dev *lives* to bring them together. Wouldn't it be fun to pit them against each other? Let readers decide who they want to side with—the heartbreaker or Dr. Make Up.'"

Annika set her margarita down slowly, her heart thumping. A large, noisy group of people walked past her, bumping her chair, but she barely noticed. "What did she say, June?"

June grinned. "She said yes, Annika. You're going to be in *Time*! *Make Up* is going to be in *Time*!" She paused. "I haven't told Ziggy. And I figured I'd leave it to you to break the news to Hudson."

Annika snorted. "First I have to come up with a few strategies to offset whatever he's going to lob my way at the interview. You know he's going to put up a fight, especially now that we're elbowing our way in there, too."

June patted her arm. "You can handle him. You always do. So what if it's *Time*?"

Annika stared at her, shaking her head. "*Time* fucking magazine," she whispered, her mouth going dry as the realization fully hit. "Oh my god."

"The interview's in about two weeks," June said. "So we just need to get you in tip-top shape before then. Emily said she'd send a few of the questions over this week, so I figure we can practice until you're super-polished. This is going to be so good for EPIC in June. It's going to put us on the map, right beside Break Up!"

Annika raised her glass. "To you, Junebug."

June clinked her glass against Annika's. "To kicking Break Up's ass."

Annika laughed. "To taking over the fucking world."

chapter ten

It was Friday after work, which meant one thing: date night. June glanced at the clock. "Five-thirty!" she announced, beaming as she turned off her monitor and grabbed the purse hanging on the back of her chair. "You going to get ready for *Alesandro* soon?" She said his name with a flourish, rolling her *r*.

Annika laughed and looked at her best friend over her laptop screen. "Yeah, soon. I'm going to work on this pitch for a little while longer, though."

"Mmkay." June walked over and kissed her on the cheek. She had a date with Ziggy that night, but unlike Annika—who had to dress to impress on this first date—*she* was dressed in jeans and a peasant top. "Have fun and text me to tell me how it's going, if you get a chance."

"Okay, you have fun, too. Tell Ziggy I said hi."

June waggled her fingers and walked down to the elevators. A moment later, Annika heard Ziggy say she looked beautiful. She turned back to her computer.

The sky outside got darker and darker as she worked, the evening settling in for good. Finally, once she'd gotten to a good stopping point, Annika turned off her laptop and rolled her wrists. She walked to the storage closet to grab her date-night clothes and makeup and headed to the bathroom. She was going to keep her expectations low this time, she decided, and hope to be pleasantly surprised.

Annika kept her head high as she walked past the Break Up office. She could see a light on in Hudson's office through the glass door, but his door was closed. Good. Maybe she could get dressed and out of here before he saw her.

But when it came to Hudson, things never worked out quite how she thought they would.

She ran into him in the hallway on the way back from the bathroom, where she'd changed into a black bodycon dress with sparkly spaghetti straps and a low back, which she'd paired with red stilettos. He was wearing faded jeans and a Break Up T-shirt. She felt massively overdressed and, somehow, completely vulnerable.

Hudson looked her up and down, his eyes going dark. Her stomach flipped. "You have your date tonight."

It wasn't a question, so Annika didn't say anything.

"I would say have fun, but I wouldn't mean it." He stepped closer and she smelled the warm fragrance of his skin wrap around her like a cloak.

The hallway was empty, like the rest of the building. Most people cut out early on Fridays, but not her. Not Hudson.

"Why not?" she demanded. The slight tremble in her voice was, she hoped, easily masked by false confidence.

He ran a feather-light finger down her chandelier earring, making it bounce. Annika's heart pounded, as if it were trying to escape her chest. "I think you know the answer to that question, Ms. Dev."

Annika mustered a response, a mixture of defiance and desire warring inside her. "I really don't. Now, if you'll excuse me." But she didn't move to brush past him, even though she knew she should.

He leaned in close, dipping his head so his mouth was at her ear. His breath tickled her ear, raising goose bumps on her arms and legs. "If it were up to me, I'd pick you up and take you into my office right now. That dress wouldn't last ten seconds."

Annika swallowed, the sound thunderous in her ears. Her own pulse racing, she put one hand over Hudson's heart. Her hand looked ridiculous, small and inconsequential on the broad span of his chest. She could feel his heart pounding, heavy and strong. His pupils dilated at her touch. "I have a date with someone else," she said, her voice a touch shaky. "This is completely inappropriate."

He ran a finger along her collarbone, leaving a trail of fire in its wake. She closed her eyes. "I would buy that if you weren't trembling under my hand." His voice was husky, barely controlled. "You seem . . . confused about me." His finger traced over her shoulder, down her arm. "Am I wrong?"

She wasn't breathing in a normal, controlled manner anymore. "Alesandro," she gasped, somewhat incoherently. "Neon. I have to go." And she forced herself to turn and walk away, feeling the heat of his gaze on her back.

❧

As Annika's Lyft driver—she figured she'd be drinking tonight and didn't want to drive—pulled up to Neon, a flurry of butterflies swooped in her stomach at the memory of running into Hudson in the hallway. But she commanded them to get their shit together, got out of her Lyft, and looked at the bright, trendy exterior of the restaurant. It wasn't surprising that the crowd waiting to get in spilled out onto the sidewalk, especially on a Friday night.

She pushed the door open with a renewed purpose, smoothed down her LBD, and scanned the crowded interior for anyone matching the one picture she'd seen. There were neon lights around the bar, outlining the floor that led down to the main seating area. Large metal sculptures hung from the ceiling, also highlighted with bright pink neon lights. The crowd was loud and hip—mostly young professionals who were gearing up for the weekend, and a few well-dressed couples in their twenties and thirties. Annika's stomach rumbled as a waiter passed by her with a platter of grilled vegetables and bowls of soup, the savory smells flooding her senses.

"Hi." A young waitress, her arms covered in tattoos of the Mad Hatter, approached Annika. "Looking for someone?"

"Yeah, I think the reservation's under Alesandro Makos?"

"Your party's already waiting. Follow me."

Annika followed, feeling a spasm of nerves at having to sit through yet another first date that would probably be just as tiring as all the other ones before it. Why had she agreed to this after a long day at work? The brain-scrambling interlude with Hudson certainly hadn't helped. She was suddenly afraid she'd forgotten to refresh her deodorant, but a quick sniff told her she was okay. Smiling, the waitress stepped out of the way and Annika saw the man from June's cell phone photo.

He was dressed in a crisp pink button-down and dinner

jacket, his long fingers drumming on the table. He looked around, checked his phone, and set it back down.

He was built long and lean, with a narrow face. He was tall, but his shoulders weren't quite broad, and his arms were slender. He was completely unlike Hudson—at least, physically.

Annika frowned. Comparing Alesandro to Hudson was unproductive.

Releasing a breath, she walked forward and held out her hand. "Alesandro? I'm Annika."

His hand was powder-smooth, his handshake firm. "Hi," he said, smiling broadly to reveal a set of very straight white teeth. "So nice to meet you."

"You too." She took a seat, and the waitress handed her a menu.

"Can I start you off with some drinks?" the waitress asked, looking between them.

"A chardonnay for me, please," Annika said.

"I'll have the same," Alesandro added.

"Of course. I'll be right back with those."

"So." Annika smiled resolutely. She was going to give this a fair shake, dammit. "Did you . . . have a good day at work? June tells me you own a bakery?"

"I do." Alesandro nodded several times, as if Annika had said something fascinating. "We specialize in traditional Greek desserts. Our baklavas were featured in the city paper recently. We got five omelets." Seeing Annika's confusion, he added, "That's their rating system—omelets instead of stars."

They laughed, and Annika couldn't help but realize Alesandro had a very warm smile. "Well, that's fantastic," she said. "Congratulations."

The waitress returned with their wine in miniature wooden wine barrels that had the Neon logo stamped on the side. Alesandro swirled his around and smelled it before taking a small sip.

"Are you ready to order?" the waitress asked, pulling a notebook from the pocket of her sleek black leather apron.

Annika's stomach rumbled again at the mention of food. "Yes. I'll have the large tofu bowl with tahini dressing."

The waitress turned to Alesandro, who was closing his menu. "I'll have the pasta carbonara with a basket of breadsticks and a side of fresh fruit. And could you please bring me the brownie sundae for dessert as well?"

"Coming right up." Smiling, the waitress took their menus and walked off.

Alesandro turned to Annika. "I'm carb-loading for the marathon I'm running tomorrow."

"Oh, you're a marathon runner!" Annika exclaimed. "That explains your—" A warmth crept to her cheeks. What she'd been about to say made her sound like a total perv. "Your, um, physique."

Alesandro beamed, as if he was pleased and not at all weirded out that she'd noticed and commented on his body. "Yes," he said, smiling gaily. "I'm definitely built like a runner. What about you? Do you run?"

Annika laughed. "Oh, no. I tried it once and couldn't take the feeling of my lungs about to explode. I do yoga, actually."

"Ah. Yoga." Alesandro closed his eyes for a moment, as if taking a moment to appreciate yoga in all its nuances. When he opened them again, he added, "I love yoga. I do it every morning on my balcony."

"Oh." Annika smiled. In her experience, most men had a pretty condescending view of yoga, or only did it under duress. Like Hudson. "I do too, actually."

They smiled at each other for a moment, and then Alesandro asked, "So, tell me. I hear you're a business owner yourself. How's that going?"

Annika took a sip of her wine; it was cool and crisp, exactly what she needed. "I don't know who I'd be without my business. You know? It's like a calling. Maybe that's silly to say if you aren't, like, a doctor or nun or something, but—"

"No, I totally get it," Alesandro said earnestly, one hand around his wine barrel. The back of his hand was covered in black hair. "I've known I wanted to own a Greek bakery ever since my parents got me a play kitchen when I was three."

Annika laughed. "That's amazing. What sorts of things did you bake in your play kitchen?"

"Oh, I made the *best* imaginary baklava and basbousa, hands down. I even got stellar reviews from all the big critics—you know, my mama, my baba, my pappous."

Annika grinned. "But of course. I'd expect nothing less." Feeling a little pinch of hurt, she said, "They must be so proud of you."

Alesandro's expression got somber. "I lost my pappous a decade ago, and my parents died three years apart when I was in college. It's just me now. That's why I do so many marathons. Most of them are charity runs for the things my family struggled with: strokes, heart disease, Alzheimer's."

Annika leaned forward. "I'm so sorry. That's terrible. I know a little of what it's like to lose your family—I lost my mom to cancer when I was a baby. My dad raised me by himself."

Alesandro gazed into her eyes. "So you know," he said softly. "You get it."

Their hands were close together on the table, and Alesandro

made a move to touch his fingertips to hers. This was as real, as romantic, as *connected* as first dates got.

But Annika found herself moving her hand to smooth back an invisible strand of hair. Disappointment flashed across Alesandro's face, and Annika coughed to distract from the ruined moment.

Alesandro cleared his throat. "Excuse me a moment—restroom," he said, giving her a small smile as he scraped back his chair and stood.

Annika watched him go, feeling a thump of disappointment—not at the ruined moment, but at herself. She was always pining after that rosy relationship glow, always stressing about how her first dates never went anywhere. Well, here it was—a great first date, handed to her as if on a platter, and she'd basically just knocked the platter to the floor. What was *wrong* with her? Alesandro was handsome and passionate and kind and it seemed like they had a lot in common. And yet . . . she felt nothing. Not the tiniest spark, not even a lukewarm ember.

Oh, come on, Annika. Not every relationship is going to start off with a sizzle. It's not always going to be fireworks and breathlessness, goose bumps and pounding hearts. Give it a chance. Make an effort.

She heard Alesandro's chair being pulled back and looked up with a beaming smile, determined to give it a sincere try. "Oh, hi. I was just—" She stopped, her smile sliding off her face. It wasn't Alesandro seated at her table. It was Hudson Craft.

Annika stared at his clean-shaven face. The recessed lighting emphasized the square planes of his jaw. In contrast to how she felt, he looked completely at ease. He'd changed since she saw him in the hallway, and was now dressed in an expensively cut gray blazer—probably bespoke—and a peacock-blue shirt that brought out the green tones in his eyes. A shiny, voluminous lock of his blond hair sat on his forehead, as though he was in a shampoo commercial. "Date ditch you already?" he asked, crossing his arms and cocking his head.

"Are you stalking me? And no, he hasn't," Annika bit out, glaring at him. "He's in the bathroom."

"I have a dinner reservation with a potential investor in about twenty minutes. I like to be early." Then he asked with a conspiratorial smile, "Are you sure your date didn't run out the back exit?"

"I'm sure," Annika said, narrowing her eyes. "Why is it so hard to believe that he'd want to stay on this date with me?"

Hudson studied her for a long moment. She began to squirm under his intense gaze. "Actually, I find it hard to believe that any guy would leave you alone for any length of time."

They stared at each other, the butterflies once again in full force in Annika's stomach.

"Excuse me. That's my seat." Alesandro was back from the bathroom, a winning smile on his face once more. He'd apparently rallied after Annika's brush-off.

"Yes, it is," Annika said in relief, turning back to Hudson and forcing a slightly poisonous smile. "So goodbye, Hudson." She could see Hudson sizing Alesandro up, taking in the crisp lines of his ironed shirt and his olive-toned, kissed-with-health skin.

"You know each other?" Alesandro asked, obviously oblivious.

"We work in the same building," Hudson said, beginning to stand. "But I won't intrude. I have an event to get to any—"

"No, sit, sit," Alesandro insisted, grabbing an empty chair from a nearby table. *What?* Annika stared at him in disbelief. He turned his thousand-watt smile on her. "I'd love to get to know one of your friends."

Oh, god. He'd gotten the wrong idea. "He's not my—"

"Great idea," Hudson said, speaking over her. "Thank you." He flashed a smile at Annika that rivaled Alesandro's in its brightness.

The waitress came by with a huge platter of food and began to set things down in front of Annika and Alesandro.

Hudson studied the spread. "Wow."

"I'm carb-loading," Alesandro explained. "For a marathon tomorrow."

Annika tossed Hudson a victorious look. "Yes, a *charity* marathon. Alesandro's very philanthropically minded. He's working to make the world a better place."

"Carb-loading helps me keep my energy up." Alesandro dug into his carbonara. "I want to shave another minute off my time." With his fork in one hand, he mimed running, pumping his arms by his side and puffing out breaths of air. "I think tomorrow's the day."

Hudson glanced at Annika, his eyebrows raised, as if he were saying, *"Really? This guy?"*

Like *he* was such a prize. Annika sat up straighter and said, "Alesandro also owns a Greek bakery. He's *very* successful."

"Oh, I don't know about that," Alesandro protested, going back to his food.

"He's just being modest," Annika said, looking at Hudson pointedly. "Modesty's so hard to come by nowadays, don't you think?"

Hudson turned to Alesandro. "Are you into Nerf or paintball at all? Because those pastimes become a real liability around Annika."

Alesandro looked perplexed. "Oh, okay—"

Annika leaned forward, clutching her miniature wine barrel. "Well, don't let Hudson near your bakery. He can't attract customers on his own, so he likes to poach other people's—ones they came by honestly, with hard work and diligence and ethics, things he knows nothing about."

Hudson raised an eyebrow and looked at Alesandro. "Annika likes to accuse people of stealing her ideas with absolutely zero evidence. Has she accused you of stealing a family recipe yet? Because she will; it's just a matter of time." He leaned forward and spoke sotto voce. "You should get out while you still can."

Annika felt anger engulf her. "I do not just randomly accuse people—"

"Is there something going on here?" Alesandro asked, setting his fork down and looking from Hudson to Annika. "Between you two?"

"Nothing besides animosity," Annika said, barking a laugh. "Seriously, Alesandro, I—"

"She's always been obsessed with my pecs," Hudson said, crossing his arms.

"What?" she spluttered. "Alesandro, don't believe—"

"Yeah." Alesandro patted his lips with his napkin. "I thought so." He looked at Annika. "You weren't connecting with me tonight. I felt it, you felt it. And I think I know why now." He scraped his chair back.

"Ale—"

"No, it's okay." Alesandro smiled a little. "I understand. I've been hung up on other people before, too. Just call me if this doesn't work out, okay?" He gestured at Hudson and nodded at the two of them. "I'll settle the bill before I leave." Without another glance backward, he strode toward the hostess stand.

They watched him go for a moment, and then Hudson turned back to her, his eyes sparkling with mirth. "Seriously, if he scares *that* easy . . ."

Annika glared at him. "For your information, he was a *very* nice guy. And this was the best first date I've had in a long time. But you had to go ruin it. You messed with me before in the hallway, and then you just show up here. What's your *problem?*" To her alarm, her eyes began to fill with tears.

But she had no one else to blame except herself for this date going to hell. "Go ahead," she said, refusing to look at Hudson and brushing her tears away with a rough fist. "You can laugh. I know you want to."

"I would never laugh when you're crying." She looked up at his tone. Lines of concern had appeared between his brows, and there was no trace of his trademark teasing smile on his face. He reached for her, seemed to think better of it, and set his hand on the table. "I'm sorry. I didn't know . . . the date was important to you." His Adam's apple bobbed as he swallowed.

Annika shook her head and took a deep drink of water. "It's not about this particular date. I mean, I wanted to give it my best shot, but I don't think it was going anywhere, to be completely honest. That seems to be a theme with me." She took a centering breath. *That's enough vulnerability for now.* "But that's okay." Pasting on a bright smile, she added very deliberately, "It gives me more time to prepare for my *Time* interview. Or should I say, co-interview, with you?"

He paused, his face confused at the change of topic. And then his brow cleared. "Wait. What? How do you know about my *Time* interview?"

Ha. She sat back and crossed her arms. "Our *Time* interview." She paused, savoring his silence. "Whoa. Hudson Craft, with nothing to say for the first time in his life. Maybe I should take a picture." She put on an innocent expression. "Emily Dunbar-Khan hasn't told you yet? Mm, well, she will. It's not just a profile on Break Up anymore. It's a 'Make Up and Break Up go head-to-head' kind of thing." Smiling, she took a slow sip of her wine. "Much more interesting for readers that way."

Hudson shook his head slowly and began to chuckle. The neon lights frosted the tips of his blond hair pink. "You still don't get it, do you?"

Annika narrowed her eyes, not liking his reaction one bit. "Get what?"

He looked at her, cocking his head. "You think you're getting one over on me. But all you're showing me—by rushing into my office and accusing me of taking your idea, by renting out a corner of the rooftop during my event, by co-opting the interview I was going to do by myself—is that you can't bear to be apart from me."

Annika stared at him, her cheeks flaming. "C-completely, utterly ridiculous." It wasn't a full thought, but it was all she could manage.

"Is it? I'm not so sure." Still smiling, Hudson pushed his chair back and stood. "I'll see you later, Annika. I'm sure you'll find a way to make that happen." He stuffed a hand in his pocket and walked away, melting effortlessly into the crowd.

Annika sat looking after him, her heart beating furiously in annoyance. After a minute, she sighed, put her napkin on the table, and stood. This was all too much. Alesandro had the right idea; she was going home, too.

～

Back home, Annika kicked off her shoes, pulled off her bra, and threw it on the floor on her way to the living room, her eyes catching on the evidence of a life lived alone: one cup on the kitchen counter. One forgotten plate on the coffee table. The remote stuck between the cushions, where she'd last left it.

She began switching on lights as she went. The darkness only made her apartment seem emptier, emphasizing how alone she was. No one else would go into a room and turn on a light.

Her stomach growled as she walked into the kitchenette and peeked into the freezer with a single-minded purpose: ice cream. It was definitely an ice-cream-for-dinner kind of night. She grabbed a spoon, a glass of water, and a pint-sized tub of Ben & Jerry's Cherry Garcia, then padded back to the couch. Flopping down, she turned on Netflix and began to browse.

She found what she wanted to watch in an instant—*Hacker Love Story*, a rom-com about two hackers who tried to out-hack each other but ended up falling in love. It was exactly the kind of funny, low-stakes, everything's-gonna-be-all-right world she wanted to lose herself in.

Annika was only fifteen minutes into the movie—right at the part where the male hacker hacked into the female hacker's computer and left her a video message—when she realized she was barely following along at all. Her thoughts were too tangled, too messy, too loud.

She pulled a fluffy throw over her and pushed her spoon into the cardboard container of ice cream, watching it get swallowed up. She hadn't even been the tiniest bit disappointed that Alesandro had left, that their date was basically over before it began.

A slow, undeniable realization sank in: The most fun she'd had was at the beginning of the night, when she'd run into Hudson in the hallway. When he'd crashed her date, her heart had lifted before she'd squelched the feeling. Annika groaned and stuffed a spoonful of cherry ice cream into her mouth. What was wrong with her that she'd rather spend time with someone so arrogant, so smug, so *detestable*, than a perfectly nice bakery owner who ran charity marathons?

She was completely hopeless when it came to matters of the heart.

Her phone beeped. It was a text from June.

How's the date going??

Annika squeezed her eyes shut and sighed. She'd respond to that later. Currently, all she had the energy for was ice cream.

ᔐ

Early Monday morning, June pulled into the mostly empty parking garage, turned off her Porsche, and faced Annika. "So what if things didn't work out with Alesandro? There'll be other guys. Lots of other guys."

"You know, I'm fine with it," Annika lied, grabbing her yoga gear and handbag. She'd had all weekend to think up her response, and she didn't want June feeling bad for her. She was tired of being the one people had to feel bad for. "I just need to focus on the EPIC pitch and keeping Make Up going. That's just the season of life I'm in."

June studied her for a moment before opening her door and getting out. "That's a great attitude." Pausing, she looked around at the empty garage. "Hey, maybe we need to work on

off-hours. Would you look at this place? Traffic on our com-
mutes would be so much easier, too."

Annika laughed. "Easy parking and no traffic *are* tempting,
but not tempting enough to get me to give up my early morn-
ings, late nights, and weekends."

"Yeah, plus your dad wouldn't like you skipping your Saturday dinners."

"That's very true. Hey, I feel like a little fresh air—want to
go the long way around?"

June nodded and they walked out of the garage and onto the
street in the direction of their huge steel-and-glass office building.
The early-morning air was cool and slightly breezy, and Annika
took a deep breath, imagining she could smell the ocean in the
distance. In this moment, she felt light. She felt . . . optimistic.

"Maybe we could expand one day," June said, spreading her
arms wide, apparently feeling it, too. "I could head up the office in Paris."

Annika laughed. "You *might* be getting a little ahead of
yourself there."

"No way," June insisted as they walked into their building
and headed to the elevator, their heels clip-clopping against the
gleaming floor. "We're totally going to slay at EPIC. You know
there are rumors that we're the ones to watch? Well, us and
Break Up, but you know we're going to win it."

As the elevator pinged and opened onto their floor, Annika
smiled at her, her eyes shining. "Yeah, I have heard that. I think
Rita Davenport at Early to Tech has a lot to do with it, actually.
Rumors about the *Time* article are creating buzz, too, I can tell.
I have to admit, I know we're overleveraged, but . . . I'm feeling
good. Like something's about to change. You know? All our
money troubles are going to be behind us soon."

They got out and headed toward their office. "Absolutely," June agreed. "But now I need to run to the potty. Too much coffee on the ride over."

After Annika unlocked the door and stashed away her bag and yoga gear, she grabbed the mail and rifled through the envelopes. *Bill, bill, a membership offer for Idealists Anonymous of Los Angeles* . . . Annika glared in the general direction of the Break Up office. Wonder who signed her up for that. Turning back to her mail, she saw there was an offer to upgrade her Wi-Fi service, and—Annika frowned as she landed on an envelope from the Bank of California. From Mr. McManor, to be precise.

Annika walked back to her desk and tore into the Bank of California envelope. Her heart was jumping in her chest, and her palms were slightly sweaty. *It's fine,* she told herself as she smoothed out the paper. *It's probably just a reiteration of what he told us at our meeting. Nothing new, nothing to worry about.*

19909 La Casita Ave
Los Angeles, CA 90079
May 20, 2021

Annika Dev
Make Up
2160 8th Street, Suite #2688A
Los Angeles, CA 90055

Dear Ms. Dev,
Pursuant to our meeting on May 10, this is a follow-up to remind you that as of the writing of this letter, your account

continues to be in a delinquent state. After a thorough review of your account, the Bank of California has decided that, should your debts not be sufficiently settled by July 1, 2021, you will be evicted from your office space at 2160 8th Street, Suite #2688A in Los Angeles, CA. At that time, we will also begin legal proceedings to recoup losses via Make Up's capital assets.

Please contact our offices immediately to make arrangements for payment to avoid this outcome. If you have questions, please reach out to me via the address above or via telephone at 213-555-7343.

Sincerely,

Irvin A. McManor

Financial Manager, Bank of California, Los Angeles

The letter fluttered from Annika's fingers to the desk, where it landed atop ZeeZee. July 1. She had until July 1 and then they were . . . they would . . . Annika felt her throat tighten painfully. Tears sprang to her eyes, but she blinked them away. She looked around at her haven, her beloved office space—at the big metal sign on the wall, the settee, the painting right above it, June's enormous whiteboard. Her fairy-tale cottage. Her space for people to believe in true love again. To believe in *themselves* again.

And the bank would take it, just like that. Cast her out with nothing to show for all the love and effort and thought she'd put into making Make Up what it was today. And could she really blame them? They were a business, too. A crushing wave of guilt and shame and fear threatened to swallow her. She was failing. Just like her dad expected her to do.

And what about her future app users? What about all the people out there who lay tossing and turning, lonely and cold, wishing they knew how to convey to their estranged lovers all the things that went unsaid in their hearts? If the bank kicked them out, Annika would never have the chance to help them. She'd never be able to give them their happily-ever-after.

"Did we get anything good in the mail?" June walked in, smoothing her hair back. She'd put on some mascara, too. When she saw Annika's face, though, she stopped short. "You okay? What's going on?"

Annika picked up the letter wordlessly, her hand shaking, and handed it to June, who scanned it, her frown deepening as she went.

"Well, this is just bullshit!" she said. "We're gonna have to talk to a lawyer. They can't just force us out."

Annika shook her head slowly. "We're really overleveraged," she said, her voice suddenly hoarse. "He warned us when he came."

"They're just doing this because they want Gwyneth's cousin to move in here! That's gotta be illegal."

"That might be why they're doing it, but it doesn't change the facts. I just . . ." She looked at June, stricken. "Six weeks, June. And if we can't pay the back rent by then, we'll be forced to declare bankruptcy on top of being evicted. That'll effectively be the end of Make Up." A wave of panic overcame her; she was afraid she was going to start crying. Did she have to see this letter *today*, when she'd been on such a high, when she'd felt like things were finally changing for Make Up?

"That's not going to happen, though," June said defiantly. "We work our *tails* off, and that means a lot."

Blinking hard, Annika walked to the window to look down over the still-quiet city streets, at the glint of sunlight on the steel skyscrapers around her. "You're right," she said quietly. "It means a lot to us. But it means nothing to the bank."

"That's because they're a bunch of bloodsucking leeches." June walked over and put her arm around Annika's shoulders.

"They're just doing their jobs," Annika said, feeling a tremble at the edge of her words.

They stood watching the burgeoning traffic together for a few minutes.

June spoke into the silence, her voice resolute. "You know what? Our big chance to get some capital was to ace the EPIC pitch anyway, right? So that hasn't changed. The pitch is on June thirteenth. That's a full two weeks before the bank deadline. If we win that, we can show the bank we'll be coming into funds and they'll let us stay."

Annika pinched her thumb and forefinger to the bridge of her nose. "We need to *really* wow the investors to win EPIC. And the way to do that is to show them a completed—or nearly completed—prototype, which we don't have."

"But we have all the work we've done so far on it. We can show them that. And you said yourself that energy and passion are what matters! Do you want to work on the pitch together right now?"

Annika turned to her with a wan smile. How could she explain to June how she felt? The bank letter had just confirmed her worst fear: that she wasn't fit to be a business owner, and everyone else seemed to know it except her. Maybe tomorrow she'd have the energy to rally and see a solution. But right now there was nothing but the bitter tang of defeat and the crushing fear of failure. Her business, her love life—nothing was going right. "I think I want to get some work done by myself," she said finally. "Sorry, I just need some time."

June studied her expression, biting her lip. "Okay, hon." She nodded as Annika walked back to her desk on wooden legs. "I'm here if you need me."

∽

Annika wasn't surprised to only get approximately thirty minutes of sleep that night, which were not only spent upright in her chair on her rickety little balcony but also happened without her permission. It was like her body was trying to shut itself down so her brain wouldn't keep going around and around in panicked little circles.

Eviction.

Bankruptcy.

Eviction.

The words were a tinny heartbeat in her ears. She heard them when she got home, she heard them as she climbed the steps to her apartment, she heard them as she undressed. She had a feeling she'd never stop hearing them. Sitting on her balcony in the near dark, looking out at the cold city lights, shivering lightly in her T-shirt and boxer shorts, Annika felt like an enormous failure. No one in the world had ever failed this epically. This was it. This could be the end.

She picked her phone off the tiny table next to her and dialed, tears streaming down her face.

"Hello?"

"Daddy?" she said, her voice catching. "I know I missed our dinner Saturday night, but . . . can I come visit? Tomorrow night?"

A pause while her dad scrambled to understand what was happening; it was clear from his voice that he'd been asleep. "Of course you can," he said at last. "You can always come home, Ani."

She closed her eyes and let the tears flow.

~

Annika felt a wave of nausea as she walked up her dad's wide, sloping driveway after another restless day of work, her shoes clip-clopping on the concrete. It was quiet here, especially after the hectic bustle of the city, and she took a moment to stop and listen to the birds chirping in the oak trees, filling her lungs with silken air that carried the faint scent of eucalyptus. She and June had barely spoken to each other all day, June sensing that she still needed space. And thankfully, the Break Up team had been off attending some workshop together, so the floor was quiet for what felt like the first time since Hudson had burst back into her life.

The lack of sleep definitely wasn't helping her nausea, nor was the realization that it *wasn't* all a horrible dream from which she'd soon awaken. The idea of telling her dad about the eviction was . . . well. Not the bright spot of her week.

She wasn't worried he'd be unsupportive. Sure, he hadn't exactly been the most enthusiastic about her plan to go into lots of debt and open Make Up. He hadn't understood why she'd choose such a risky proposition over the steady income generator that was being a physician. His past actions weren't exactly a ringing endorsement of his faith in her ability to carry this off. But the bottom line was that he loved her. Her dad was her dad, as June said. He had to be there for her. It was in the contract he'd signed when she was born or something.

She couldn't exactly wail to June about how unnerved she was feeling. June wasn't just her best friend, she was her employee—she needed to see Annika take charge and be in control. She needed to see Annika say, "Okay, we're headed into a storm, and this is how we need to steer this ship."

Today, she was hoping her dad would be the sounding board she needed, so that she could figure out what her next steps would be. Maybe she wouldn't be able to save the office space, but there could be an alternative to shuttering the doors that she hadn't thought of yet. Her dad had successfully run his own private practice for almost twenty years. He *had* to have some advice.

"Ani," he said when he answered the door, looking freshly showered in a pale purple polo shirt and linen pants, his salt-and-pepper hair still damp. His eyes anxiously searched hers behind his wire-frame glasses, taking in the sight of her, her rumpled cotton dress, the bags under her eyes, her hair pulled back in a frizzy ponytail. "Are you all right?"

"I'm fine, Daddy." She stepped forward and put her arms around his waist, inhaling the comforting scent of the Armani Autumn Smoke cologne he'd worn for as long as she could remember. They didn't even make it anymore, but her dad ordered it from some warehouse in Milan that specialized in out-of-stock luxury items. That was how unwilling he was to try anything new.

Pulling back, she smiled up at him. "Can I get some of your mango juice, though?"

"Yes, of course," he said, stepping out of the doorway so she could walk in. "Let's sit down in the great room."

❧

Annika took a deep gulp of the fresh-squeezed mango juice her dad always had in the fridge. "Mm." She closed her eyes. "So good. Thanks, Dad."

"Of course." He patted her knee and sat back in his leather armchair, watching her from behind his glasses. Annika could tell it was taking every fiber of his willpower to not demand she tell him everything.

Setting the juice on the coffee table, Annika folded her legs on the couch and settled back against its comfortable taupe cushions. She pulled a cashmere throw over her legs. Playing with its fringe, she said quietly, "I got some bad news about the business. From the bank."

She didn't dare look up at her father; she wanted to give him the chance to rearrange his face into an expression other than fear or concern or worry. There was silence for a moment or two.

"What kind of bad news?" her dad asked stiffly.

"They're going to begin eviction proceedings," Annika said, her voice barely above a whisper. "In July. We were supposed to have our prototype ready for this big pitch contest coming up, but it's not ready, which means we probably won't win. And if we don't win, we won't have money to pay the bank." When she finally did look up at her dad, she found him gazing steadily at her.

He nodded once. "Okay. I'll make some calls."

Annika's heart leapt. Of course! Her dad had connections everywhere. She'd thought they were all medicine related, but he had a lot of money—it stood to reason that some of his connections would be in the financial sector. "Really? You'd do that for me?" It just went to show, your dad would always be on your side. It didn't matter if you butted heads.

"Yes. The dean of medicine over at UCLA is an old friend. I'm sure he could slip the dates a bit for you. If you hurry, you can take the MCATs and fill out an application. He can get you in in the fall semester."

Annika stared at him. Her heart plunged into the pit of ice water that was her stomach. "You . . . you're talking about medical school."

"Well, yes." He knitted his eyebrows together, as if this should've been obvious. "What else is left to do?"

Much as she was trying to restrain herself, Annika could feel her emotions beginning to bubble over, like they usually did around her dad. It was like this house was a time-traveling capsule; she got whooshed back to her teen years the moment she stepped through the door.

Annika threw her hands up in the air. "I could try to save my business? I could maybe not give up so easily?"

Her father watched her like she was an alien descending from a giant glowing spaceship. "Why are you getting so upset?"

Annika spluttered. "Are you serious? Dad, we've been having this same exact conversation for almost a year. You just refuse to listen. I. Don't. Want. To. Go. To. Medical. School. I'm a business owner. My business is called Make Up."

Her dad cleared his throat, as if he were buying time, trying to think about how to say what he wanted to say. "But . . . will you *have* a business by the end of the summer? It doesn't sound like it."

Annika grabbed her head with both hands. "Dad! Don't you see how unsupportive that is? Don't you understand that your complete lack of enthusiasm for my career, for my *passion*, is a constant cloud hanging over my head?" She took a breath and looked her father in his bewildered face. "Do you know you're half the reason I even came up with the idea in the first place?

"I wanted to do something that would be an homage to your love for Mom. I couldn't give you guys a second chance, but maybe I could give other people that chance. I wanted Make Up to be a place where lost, lonely people could come to believe in the power of love again. Sure, I'm stumbling right now. But I refuse to believe it's over." As she spoke, Annika realized it was true. She couldn't give up. Not now, not ever. This was Make Up, her *baby*. She wasn't going down without a fight.

Annika flung the throw to the side and stood. Her voice shook as she said, "I'm just sorry you don't see that. I'm sorry you don't believe in me or my dreams. Because I really could've used your support." Brushing away her tears with a fist, she walked to the door.

"Ani," her dad began. "Wait."

"No, Dad. I'm done talking about this." She yanked open the heavy front door and strode into the fading light of dusk, got into her car, and drove down the street before pulling over and texting June.

We're not gonna give up without a fight.

June's response came back immediately. No we are NOT

Annika sat back and smiled. They would do this. She was going to save Make Up with every last scrap of ferocity she had in her.

Her phone dinged again. Does this mean you're in the mood to go to that housewarming party with me tomorrow night? Didn't want to remind you before . . .

Oh, right. She'd completely forgotten. Yeah sure. Sounds like it'll be a good networking event. Let's do it.

THAT'S MY BAD BITCH RIGHT THERE

Annika laughed, feeling a spike of energy and confidence, and began to drive again.

~

On Wednesday night, Annika and June made their way up to the penthouse suite of a high-rise in a special, gold-dusted elevator.

"This elevator has a touch screen," Annika said, staring. "I've never seen that before."

"It's really flashy, right?" June looked impressed, even though she herself had grown up in a twenty-bedroom, four-kitchen mansion. "This guy must be doing well for himself."

Annika frowned. "You really don't know whose housewarming party we're going to? Are you sure this is going to be okay?"

June waved an ombre-nail-polished hand. "Lucy said it'd be fine. She got to invite whoever she wanted, and she wanted to invite me." She flashed Annika a big smile. "And *I* wanted to invite *you*. Look at it this way, sugar. After your disastrous date with Alesandro and subsequent ambush by Hudson, you deserve this night. Maybe you'll meet your prince in this palace!" She swept her arm around her in a grand, very June gesture.

Annika shifted her present from one hand to another. "Okay, but if I get thrown out by a scary bouncer, I'm blaming you. Also, by the way, who throws a housewarming party on a Wednesday night? That's so random."

The doors pinged open onto a marble-floored foyer. A wave of sound swelled and crashed over them; there had to be two dozen people here that Annika could see, clustered around the canape table and standing near potted palm trees.

June raised an eyebrow. "I guess all *these* people don't mind."

Annika adjusted her purse strap with one hand, shifted the present she was carrying for their unnamed host in the other, and followed June out, suddenly wobbly in her stilettos. She checked herself out in an enormous mirror opposite them. She looked pretty good, she thought, in a green wrap dress and a simple emerald pendant her dad had given her when she graduated college. She had a bit of cleavage on display, but not enough to be gauche. June, of course, looked stunning in a bright yellow dress and shiny hot pink Prada pumps.

"This must be the present table." June set her prettily wrapped box next to hordes of others on a gleaming wooden table off to their left. Annika followed suit, looking around at the other guests at the same time.

Oh my god. "June." Annika grabbed her elbow.

"What?" June looked completely unbothered, her blue eyes roving the crowd. She grabbed a champagne glass off a silver tray a waiter brought by.

"I think I just saw Briana Grant," Annika hissed. "Right there." She tried to gesture discreetly with her chin.

June waved a casual hand, causing her Tiffany bracelets to clink together. "Oh, don't worry about all her Grammys. Briana's really easygoing. You want me to introduce you?"

"You *know* her?" Annika knew June had connections thanks

to her parents, but she'd always told her she hated the celebrity scene and tried to keep a low profile.

"Well, not *know* her, exactly—we're more like acquaintan—"

She was interrupted by high-pitched squealing. *"June Stewart?"*

They both turned in the direction of the French-accented female voice. A thin, tall red-haired woman dressed in a sparkly tulle dress was making her way toward them. Annika recognized her immediately; she'd been in practically all the *Vogues* all over the world.

June stepped forward with her own shriek of recognition. *"Lucy! Sugar!* Thanks for inviting us!"

The two air-kissed and hugged, and then June turned to Annika, her eyes bright. "This is my friend and boss, Annika Dev. She's the owner of Make Up! Remember I told you about her?"

"Oh, *oui*, of course!" Lucy grinned. "The creative genius!"

Oh my god, Annika thought. *Lucy Bilodeau just called me a creative genius.* She took Lucy's hand and felt one of her giant diamond rings press into her flesh. Shaking her hand was worth the pain. "It's so good to meet you. And thank you so much for the invitation. Although—June didn't seem to know—whose house *are* we in?"

Lucy shrugged, her statement bell necklace tinkling a little. "I was invited by my friend Katie. I'm sure whoever it is will make an appearance at some point." She turned to June suddenly. "Oh my god. Speaking of Katie . . . have you heard the news about Aidan?"

"No, what happened?"

"Oh, it's the saddest thing! Remember that snake venom diet he saw in *Vogue Italia* and wanted to try out? Come with me, I'm sure Gabrielle will want to tell you more . . ." Lucy began to lead June away.

June turned. "Wait, just a minute. Annika—"

Annika waved her away. "No, go. I'll be fine. I'll just mill around and hopefully find the host so I can say hi."

"Are you sure?"

"Yep!" Annika forced an easy smile, as if milling around a bunch of beautiful, famous people was her usual Wednesday evening activity.

Her smile faded as June was swallowed into a group of people and more shrieking arose, likely at June's appearance. Annika was three steps into the fabulous condo, and she was already lost and alone. She glanced at herself in the mirror again. "Stop it. You are Annika Dev. You don't need June or anyone else to hold your hand. This is for Make Up." She took a glass of champagne from a nearby waiter, tossed her hair back, straightened her shoulders, and stepped into the elegant melee.

chapter eleven

Oh, god. Celebrities were exhausting.

Just when you thought one of them looked friendly and approachable enough to not obliterate your ego, they would be approached by other celebrities who were much, much cooler than you. Annika stood awkwardly on the balcony among small clusters of people. Only she was cluster-less, like a free-floating dandelion fluff. All the other fluffs clung to their seedpods or whatever, happily belonging. Annika was sure there was a neon sign above her head in her blind spot that said, LOSER. DO NOT ENGAGE.

She took another sip of champagne and wandered around until she came to a small group of people standing under one of the hanging lanterns. There was a middle-aged man in a red Hawaiian shirt, a woman in a flowy purple tunic, and a younger man in trendy glasses.

"I heard this year's EPIC is going to be completely dominated by Break Up," the younger man said to the other two. "I'm not even sure who else is competing."

"Well, they shouldn't." The woman laughed, tapping away at her phone. "Break Up's obviously going to take the prize. Come on, I'm dying for a drink." They wandered away.

What? Annika walked over and smiled at the man in the Hawaiian shirt, who hadn't said anything and was left behind. "Hi." She reached into her purse with her free hand for her card. "I heard you guys talking about EPIC. I don't know if you've heard, but there's this new app, Make Up, that's a serious contender. I'm Annika Dev, and I'm the CEO and founder." She held out her card, but the man looked at it blankly, as if he didn't know what it was. Perhaps he was from another culture, where cards weren't passed out regularly. "This is my business card," Annika explained. "I own a business, Make Up—"

The younger man with the trendy glasses noticed their interaction and rushed back to the middle-aged man's side. "Sorry, Phil's on a vow of silence right now. He can't talk." The younger man gazed deeply into Phil's eyes before turning back to Annika. "But Phil would like you to know that you have very nice chakras."

Phil nodded seriously and bowed.

Annika blinked. "Oh. Um, yeah . . . okay then." She pulled her business card back. "Good luck with the . . . the vow. Of silence." Not completely sure she wasn't being trolled, she walked off and stepped back into the house.

"Oh my god," someone said, but Annika kept walking; surely they weren't talking to her. But then she felt a tap on her shoulder and turned to see a young woman with a sandy-colored, geometric bob staring at her like she'd invented pumpkin spice lattes. "Oh my *god*," the young woman said again, her palms pressed up against her cheeks. "I am *such* a huge fan."

Annika frowned. "Of . . . ?"

"You! You were hilarious in *Bollywood Mix-Up*! I read your books, all of them, and they changed my li—"

"Um." Annika looked around, as if someone would materialize to help extract her from this hideous situation. "I'm not . . ." She leaned in close. "I'm not Rosie Singh." The woman just stared at her. "The Indian actress? I'm not her."

The woman laughed uproariously, the ends of her bob bouncing. "Oh my god, that's so *funny*. Are you, like, incognito right now? I promise I won't tell anyone else. But if you could sign my napkin, that would be *so* amazing." She brandished a cocktail napkin.

Annika stared at it, and then at the woman. Another swell of laughter rose behind her; clearly people were merrily unaware of the train wreck of a conversation taking place right in front of them. "No . . . seriously. I'm not Rosie. Like, at all."

The woman mimed zipping her lips. "I promise I won't breathe a word to anyone. Please? It would mean so much to me—you have no idea." She pulled a pen out of her purse and pressed it into Annika's hand.

Annika had the distinct impression she wasn't going to get out of this one. Pausing to look at the woman one more time, she took the napkin from her. "I'm . . . going to sign this, then."

The woman nodded, her palms pressed against her cheeks. She looked like she might cry.

Awesome. Annika looked around for a spot to put the napkin and the woman said, "Here, let me." She turned around, offering her back. "Can you make it out to Stacy?" she asked over her shoulder. "Just a 'y,' no 'e.'"

Annika pressed the napkin against Stacy's back, careful not to let the pen puncture through the napkin and into Stacy's back—it would be *such* a shame if that happened—and scrawled a signature that could've really said anything—Annika, Rosie . . . it could've been a sketch of a groundhog carcass. "Okay. All done!"

Stacy turned and took the napkin, beaming like she'd swallowed a light bulb. "Oh my god, thank you, thank you! You're so amazing. Keep being you." She scurried off, and Annika heard her say, "Oh my god, Ava, you're never going to believe what just happened!"

Sighing, Annika walked through the living room, which was full of a cacophonous mixture of pulsing music and chattering, squealing, and laughing. She pushed past clusters of people who looked either über-techie, sadly underfed, alarmingly over-tanned, or completely wasted—sometimes all at the same time. No one gave her a second look. She'd lost sight of June a long time ago, and whoever the host was, they were not easy to find. Deciding she'd take a quick break in a quieter part of the house—if she could find one—Annika picked her way down a long hallway.

⁓

There were fewer people in this hallway, but still enough chatting together in tight clusters that Annika had to shove some of them out of the way before they'd step aside. She continued her path through the haze of perfume and cologne. Closed doors greeted her on either side, and the hallway dead-ended in a large pedestal, on which was poised a gorgeous, sinuous sculpture made of iridescent white stone.

At first Annika thought it was a teardrop, but then she noticed arms folded against a shapely torso, a neck bent with a head on the end like a dandelion at the end of its stalk, and realized she was looking at a sculpture of a woman. Gently, she ran her fingers over the cool stone, marveling at the craftsmanship.

Raucous laughter echoed behind her. She didn't want to shove her way back through the crowds to go back to the living room, so on an impulse, she reached for the doorknob of the door closest to her and turned it. The heavy door swung silently inward. With a quick glance over her shoulder to make sure no one was about to stop her or accuse her of being a thief, Annika stepped into the dark, cool, quiet room and shut the door behind her.

Ah. Blissful quiet.

She turned the light on, dimmed it, and looked around. It was an enormous bedroom, with a minimalist bed on a raised platform. The bed was fitted with taupe and black sheets and several overstuffed pillows. Three of the bedroom's walls were glass; they looked out over the city and its breathtaking assortment of roads and skyscrapers and the red glow of brake lights, like a string of rubies on a necklace. Annika noticed more sculptures on the nightstand and dresser as well, which were smaller and more brightly colored than the one in the hallway, but similarly languid in style. They were mounted on wooden stands.

Annika walked forward, her heels sinking into the plush carpet, her eyes running along the painting at the head of the bed. It looked like the Himalayas, but she wasn't sure. This bedroom was an oasis, she realized, for an artistic, sensitive soul.

She threw her purse on the floor and flopped backward on the bed, throwing her arms out to the sides. In the quiet, she took a deep breath and turned her head to stare out at the twinkling lights of the city. It smelled good in here, like faint ocean-scented cologne and something else—something fresh and cottony, like soap and clean pajamas.

She knew she couldn't stay here for the rest of the night, in some random stranger's private bedroom, but this felt good. Like a little enclave, suspended in a castle. A private bubble, where no one could find her and where she didn't have to pretend to be a grown-up with enough self-confidence to walk among snooty celebrities who didn't want her around.

The door clicked open.

Annika scrambled up to a sitting position. The man in the doorway was dressed in straight jeans and a simple white button-down that accentuated his tanned skin and green eyes, ridges and planes hinting at the stellar anatomy underneath the fabric.

Hudson Craft.

He narrowed his eyes at her, the silence ticking on. "Oh. Um, hi," she said finally, because it was clear *he* wasn't going to speak at all. Weirdo. "What . . . are you doing here?" But of course, he was probably BFFs with the gazillionaire host of this party. He was Hudson fucking Craft.

"Well," he said, closing the heavy door behind him and turning back around, a faint smile playing at his lips. "Anything I want, I guess. Seeing as how this is my bedroom."

Annika's eyebrows shot up to her hairline. She scrambled to get off the bed, her cheeks flaming. "This . . . this is *your* place? What are you, a multimillionaire?"

Hudson leaned against the door, hands in his pockets, and chuckled. "Just bought it a month ago. And no, just a millionaire.

Though I *am* working on the 'multi' part." He gave her a boyish grin.

"Oh." Annika stood there awkwardly. The reminder of his millionaire status drove home the feeling of failure the eviction letter had brought with it. She pushed the thought from her mind. "I swear I'm not barging in. June invited me, and she was invited by her friend Lucy, who was invited by *her* friend Katie—"

Hudson waved her explanation off, his eyes holding hers steadily. "I'm glad you're here."

Did he mean *here* in his house or *here* alone with him in his bedroom? In his plain-but-very-stylish clothes, he belonged in this room completely, with its clean lines and expensive but understated décor. Annika suddenly had a vision of him, shirtless and dressed only in plaid pajama bottoms, reclining in his bed, his hair damp and his chest and abs covered in droplets of water. And another vision of herself, startlingly similar to a memory she had of Vegas, kneeling beside him and licking each of those droplets off.

Her skin began to pulse with desire. Really, she should leave. Hudson Craft was still Hudson Craft; nothing had changed. They weren't compatible. Couldn't be compatible. She should just stride past him, open the door, and be gone.

But she didn't want to. She wanted to stay here, to get a glimpse behind the curtain, to see who Hudson really was. And that was a problem.

Abruptly choosing to ignore the tiny voice of reason that was getting smaller with every breath she took, Annika turned to look out the glass wall again, then sat on the black leather bench at the foot of his bed, her mind carefully skirting all the reasons she shouldn't. "Your view is killer."

Hudson pulled a standing swing chair over and sat, too, facing the glass wall across from them. "I like it. In fact, I think it was this view that sold me on the house."

Annika gave him a look.

"What?"

"Nothing." She shook her head and ran her fingernail along the stitching on the leather. "My dad said the same thing about his house and my mom. She wanted to buy it just based on the view from the deck."

"Smart lady," Hudson said. "I haven't regretted waking up to this so far. How does your mom like her view?"

Annika paused. There was never a good time to lay this on people; they always got really awkward and strange when she did. "My mom died a long time ago, when I was a newborn. Cancer."

Hudson turned to look at her. "I'm sorry," he said simply. "That must've been really hard, growing up without a mom—never knowing her, always wondering what could've been."

Huh. No one had ever said that to Annika, apart from the therapist she saw briefly as a teenager, for what her dad called her "unprocessed abandonment issues"—by which he meant he was mad that Annika had started having sex and didn't know what else to do about it. Everyone else always assumed that just because her mom had died when she was a newborn, she must not have too many feelings about it. "Thanks. It was. But my dad definitely made up for it. I never felt alone." *Shut up, Annika. He doesn't care.* Why was she sharing all of this with him?

But if he noticed her blathering, he didn't say anything about it. In fact, Annika thought, he was . . . different tonight. That hard edge she'd noticed before wasn't present now, though she had no idea what had changed.

Hudson pushed back with his legs so he swung slowly in the chair. "Nice. I have two parents and a brother and I can't say the same."

Annika turned sharply to look at him. There was that disorienting feeling again, the same one she got when she swam in the ocean, the feeling that there was an entire universe beneath her that she had no idea about. It was both terrifying and thrilling. "*You* were lonely growing up?"

His expression didn't even flicker. He shrugged. "My point is, you're lucky to have the dad you do."

Annika hesitated. "I am."

He studied her, his eyes probing. "But?"

She shook her head and traced the stitching a little faster. "Nothing. I really am lucky. I just . . . I wish my dad and I saw eye to eye on my career, that's all."

"He doesn't agree with the choices you've made?"

"More like he isn't very enthusiastic about them. He's still holding his breath, hoping I'll go to medical school."

Hudson scoffed. "Medical school? You?"

Annika glared at him, her fingernail digging into the leather. "What? You don't think I'm smart enough to be a doctor?"

He looked at her steadily. "You're definitely smart enough, you know that. I just can't see you doing something so mechanical, so . . . routine. You're too creative for a job like that."

Annika looked down at her shoes, her stomach feeling weird and swoopy. "Doctors can be creative," she mumbled. Why was she getting all tongue-tied? Why was she letting him get under her skin again? This was the problem: Being attracted to Hudson was like being attracted to two completely different people, Dr. Jekyll and Mr. Snide. He flirted with her just to see her blush, teased her mercilessly, and also owned a horrible, soul-sucking business like Break Up, which was flourishing while her own lovingly nurtured business was wilting. But he *also* did nice things that made her heart melt.

She, Annika Dev, could *never* go out with someone like Hudson Craft—evil millionaire who was in the professional heartbreaking business. It didn't matter if she was going to die alone. She could never live with herself if she dated someone like him, who put out so much negative energy, so many dark, sad vibes into the universe. Plus, how would she feel if, against all odds, she really did have to close down Make Up in a few weeks? How could she continue to go out with him without it making her sick to her stomach? What she was *going* to do, like the mature, responsible person she was, was get up and let herself out of this room. And possibly out of this party, which happened to be *his* party, because of course it was.

Instead, Annika found herself getting up and walking to the sculpture on his sleek, otherwise empty nightstand. *Come on, Annika. Just leave.* But she couldn't. It was like Hudson had his own gravitational field, and he'd pulled her, a tiny, helpless star, into it. Escape was impossible. "I like all of these sculptures. What's the story behind this guy?"

Hudson walked to where she stood, all tall and delicious-smelling. She made a point of not letting her breath waver. "I made that in college."

Annika turned to him. "*You* made that?" He'd mentioned visual arts in Vegas, but never specifically sculpting.

He huffed a breath and put a dramatic fist on his hip. "What? You don't think I'm creative enough to be a sculptor?"

Annika crossed her arms. "To be honest? No."

He laughed easily. "Ouch. Quick and painful."

"Sorry," she said, feeling a *little* bad. She turned back to the teal-and-gold sculpture, tracing her finger along the liquid curves and voluptuously rounded edges. Everything about it was soft and vulnerable, so different from the Hudson Craft she knew. So Mr. Merciless-*Forbes*-Millionaire-Businessman had an artistic side. There was that disorientation again. She couldn't keep up with his two halves.

"It's fine. I don't really talk about it much. I actually used to want to be a sculptor, but then I realized I wouldn't make any money that way. And that wouldn't be of any help to my parents."

"Oh. They owned that convenience store in rural Ohio, right? And you wanted to help them retire?"

Hudson looked taken aback. "How do you know that? I don't remember that being in any articles."

"It wasn't. I remembered you telling me in Vegas."

They studied each other for a beat, his eyes softening. "Vegas. Right."

Annika went back to studying the sculpture, a little unsettled. What was he thinking? Why could she never tell with him?

After a beat, he added, "Well, they're retired now and their house is paid off. But I still send money home to them every month to keep them comfortable."

"They must be really proud of you."

Hudson only shrugged.

Annika remembered how intense he'd been at the tech forum, talking about how success was a way to give back to the people who'd helped him become who he was. Was that what he meant? She didn't know how to ask. It was a deeply personal question.

Clearing her throat, she said, "So what do you like about sculpting?" She just couldn't picture him in a sculptor's studio, his hands all messy with clay. She half wondered if he was just bullshitting her.

But Hudson didn't smirk or laugh. He ran his index finger gently over the sculpture she'd been admiring, his touch tender and soft and . . . respectful, somehow. "I like that I'm completely at the mercy of the clay, of the form trying to emerge. There's no rushing the process. Sculpting's a labor of love—painfully slow, surprisingly emotional. You have to be okay with failure." He traced his finger over a tiny divot at the top of the statue that Annika hadn't noticed before. "You have to learn to live with the imperfections and the flaws in each piece, maybe even come to love them."

As Annika listened to him, she realized that everything he loved about sculpting was exactly the opposite of Break Up. Break Up was about *faster, higher, more*. It was quick and brutal and savage and cold, with no room for softness or emotion. She found herself shaking her head slowly.

He caught her eye, and his misty, soft expression cleared. "What?"

She stood there, her upper thigh pressed against the nightstand, acutely aware that Hudson was just a step away. Faint laughter drifted in from the hallway. She breathed, "Why do you act the way you do?" instead of the million and one more appropriate things she could've said.

Looking confused, he pushed a hand through his hair. His blond hair flopped onto his forehead. "What do you mean?"

Shit. The moment stretched on, Annika's mouth opening and closing futilely. Well, it was too late to backtrack now. *Just rip off the Band-Aid, Annika.* "You . . . you're all over the place. You commandeer my first date with a perfectly nice guy and you ruin it for me. You're completely fine with breaking people's hearts and being some kind of hero to douchetruffles like Hedge Fund Harry. You tell me you think about Vegas and yet you act like I have a communicable disease when I try to kiss you. You're constantly in my space and you're constantly in my head and I don't know what to do with all that." She stopped, aghast. She should never have brought up the kiss, or told him he was in her head. Never, never, never. "You know what? Never mind."

He considered her for a long moment and then rubbed his jaw, looking away. "Annika, I'm not trying to be confusing."

She waited for more, her heart thumping. So they were back to this again? She should tell him it didn't matter, that she shouldn't have brought it up. She should *leave*. Being in a room alone with Hudson Craft, even when she hadn't been drinking, was a heady experience—one in which she didn't trust herself. When he was silent, she said, "Right. That's just your natural state, then. Confusing as hell."

His eyes burned into hers. "Maybe I can make things a bit clearer." He stepped forward, so they were just a breath apart. Placing a big hand on her arm, he said, his voice a rumble, "I meant what I said at the fountain. I haven't stopped thinking about you since you quoted Florence Nightingale to me in a dim bar in Vegas: 'Happiness is the gradual realization of a worthy ideal or goal.'"

Annika's heart thudded in her chest. *Walk away*, she instructed herself firmly. *Nothing good will come of this*. Even though she wanted to hear what exactly he'd been thinking about her, and even though she was dying with curiosity about how he was going to make things "clearer," she was definitely going to walk away. She was going to turn right around and go find June—

Hudson closed the gap between them, the hard lines of his body molding to her soft ones. She tipped her head back and stared into his green, green eyes, her breathing coming in shorter, quicker pants. There was a smile on his face—just one corner of his lips tipped up. She placed her hands against the firm muscles of his chest, intending to push him away, to wipe that smirk right off his face, to tell him she was no Hudson Craft groupie.

But he took her touch as an invitation. The smirk disappeared as he cupped her cheek in one enormous hot hand, the other at her waist, tugging her even closer, impatient, demanding. And then his lips covered hers.

Annika's body responded before her brain could yell its outrage. She was enveloped by his clean smell and brilliant, radiating warmth, like a surfer being swallowed by a wave. Her cheeks burned where his stubble scraped against them, just the right amount of rough, sandpaper against silk. His mouth claimed hers, equal parts firm and soft. He kissed the way he did everything else—sure and self-assured. He nibbled her bottom lip, no tongue, smiling against her mouth, teasing her even now, in this moment. She nipped at his lip in response, hard, and he laughed gently before opening his mouth wider, giving her what she really wanted.

When his tongue caressed hers, Annika moaned softly, and he kissed her deeper in response, the hand on her cheek slipping to tangle in her hair, as if he couldn't get close enough. She ran her hands down his pecs to his stomach, feeling the taut muscles, her bones going soft, melting so she was nothing but a puddle of hot desire.

Her fingertips hit the button on his jeans and she heard the sharp intake of his breath. He was hard, pressing against her, and she was so wet, so open, so ready to take this further.

And then reality slammed into her. This wasn't just some guy she was hooking up with in some random bedroom. This wasn't a date with someone she cared about and trusted and saw a future with. This was Hudson fucking Craft. And Hudson Craft—keeper of Break Up—was anathema to her soul.

She pulled back suddenly, pressing one hand against his chest again. But this time, the message was clear: *Stop.* His eyes were wide, his dark pupils dilated against the green. Annika took some pleasure at the way he was breathing, hard and ragged, his cheeks flushed.

"Hudson . . . it's—this is not a good idea."

"I beg to differ," he murmured, trying to close the gap between their mouths again. Annika wanted to let him; desire was making her toes literally curl in her shoes. Any gap between them felt criminal in this moment, utterly unthinkable. She wanted to feel his hands everywhere. She wanted to feel every part of *him* under her palms.

But she forced herself to take a step back. "I mean it," she forced herself to say, even though her voice shook and her body was screaming, No, *you don't, you moron!*

Hudson rubbed a hand across his swollen lips as he realized she was serious. He frowned. "Did I . . . do something wrong?"

"No, I . . . you didn't. I just . . . I don't see *this* going anywhere, Hudson. You're you, and I'm me."

He looked confused. "Yes, we're the people we are."

Annika sighed. Of course he wouldn't understand. He'd made a million dollars with his app. He was considered a visionary, a genius. He didn't have an eviction letter in his drawer at work, in spite of how hard he'd tried to do something good in the world. "Don't you get it? We're like if a tree and a forest fire wanted to go out. It just doesn't make sense." She walked to the leather bench to get her purse as Hudson watched in silence, one hand rubbing his jaw. "It would make more sense if we shared the same values, if we were even *friends* first. You and I . . . we have so little in common."

Hudson stood there, one hand braced on his nightstand. Frustration flashed across his face; his jaw was clenched. "We *were* friends. We spent an entire week together in Vegas. I'm not even sure why that week ended, because I sure as hell had a good time. More than a good time."

"Me too." Annika bent to scoop up her purse and looked at him. "But I think we both know why it ended. Vegas was a bubble. It was unsustainable. That's not how things work in the real world." She gestured between them. "Look at us now. *This* is the real world, Hudson. And in the real world, the CEO of Make Up and the CEO of Break Up don't belong together. I should go," she added, slinging the purse over her shoulder. "I've got to wake up early for work anyway."

"Annika." Hudson stepped forward, though he still kept a few feet between them. The soft lights of the room cast shadows under his eyes. "I'm more than just the CEO of Break Up."

She shrugged. "Maybe. But Break Up's obscuring what I suspect are the best parts of you. I can't see anything else." And then she strode to the door and let herself out.

chapter twelve

The next day was such a blur Annika could barely make time to blink, let alone tell June about kissing Hudson or stew about why exactly she'd kissed him.

After three consecutive phone calls with beta testers—the first two punctuated by gong sounds she had to scramble to explain—Annika stood and stretched. She glanced over at June, who was rolling her wrists around, taking a break from squashing bugs in the app.

"Hey," Annika said. "Want to take a quick stretch-your-legs break?"

June grinned and pushed her chair back. "Thought you'd never ask."

They walked out into the hallway, and Annika glanced toward the Break Up office. The gong sounds from earlier this morning had thankfully stopped, but the lights were still on. She could hear faint laughter floating their way. June headed down the hallway, but Annika grabbed her elbow.

"Hey, uh—do you want to go the long way around to the bathroom?"

"What?"

"You know, around the elevators," Annika said, feeling sweat prickle under her arms. She was a terrible liar on her best days, and this wasn't her best day. Images of kissing Hudson Craft kept playing in her head, but right now in the hallway was not the time to tell June what had happened. And she *really* didn't feel like continuing her conversation from the previous night with Hudson. She forced a happy smile. "It'll be good exercise, okay?"

"O . . . kay." June frowned, but she followed Annika nonetheless. Bless her. "Are you okay?"

"I am," Annika began, dying to tell June what was going on, now that they had a moment. "I—"

"Annika?"

Shit. Shit, shit, shit. There was no mistaking that deep voice.

It was Hudson, and he must be heading down the hallway toward her. There was no way she wanted to have this conversation with him here, now, and talk about their kiss and what she'd said and how he made her feel and—no way. Not now, not with June standing there, totally innocent and clueless.

Annika began speed-walking down the hallway, hoping to get to the bend and lose Hudson before he could catch up to her. "Come on!" She tossed June a maniacal smile over her shoulder. "It's good exercise! Let's go!"

"Annika," June said, speeding up. "I'm pretty sure Hudson's looking for you."

"No, he's not!" she insisted, grabbing June's arm as she raced along. The bend was just ahead, thank goodness. "You must be hearing things."

"Actually, she's not." Hudson stepped around the corner,

his cheeks pink, his hair less than immaculate. Dammit. He must've sprinted here to cut her off. He folded his arms and leaned against the wall, his eyes boring into hers. "Hey."

She stumbled to a halt. "Oh. Um, hey. I didn't hear you there." She laughed weirdly, her voice too high.

June, who'd begun lagging again, caught up to Annika, huffing and puffing. "That was *not* easy in six-inch heels, missy." Then she caught the look Hudson was serving up and looked slowly from him to Annika, falling quiet.

"Training for a 10K, Ms. Dev? I only ask because you were running the last time I saw you, too." There was a small smile at Hudson's lips. *Rude.* Plus, his tanned skin was practically glowing, even under industrial recessed lighting and against cement-gray walls. *Extremely rude.*

Annika crossed her arms, too. "I'm trying to escape the relentless gong sounds emanating from your office. Some of us have serious businesses to run, you know."

Hudson laughed. "Hey, that's the sound of success."

There they were, their diametrically opposed life philosophies on glaring show. "No," Annika said, cocking her head. "That's the sound of *heartbreak*, Hudson."

Hudson blinked and looked away for a moment, and then turned to gaze back at her. "Can we talk?" he asked more seriously. His eyes flickered to June and then back to her. "Somewhere private?"

"Sure, why don't I—" June began, but Annika cut her off.

"There's nothing more to say," she said, cupping her elbows with her hands. "I'm sorry, but there's just not." Unless he'd sold Break Up and was here to share the good news.

He huffed a breath and ran a hand through his hair. "Annika, come on."

"What's changed since last night, Hudson?"

He didn't say anything, but frustration was painted all over his face.

"Didn't think so," she said quietly, brushing past him and turning toward the bathrooms. She looked over her shoulder. "June, you coming?"

She heard June murmur something, and then she called, "Yep!"

As they walked into the bathroom together, Annika couldn't help but glance at Hudson. He was standing in the same spot, looking after her, his jaw hard, his expression a blend of frustration and dissatisfaction. That made two of them.

 ~

In the bathroom, June rounded on her as soon as the door shut behind them. "What is the *deal* between you two? Something happen last night?"

Annika went to the nearest sink and ran cool water over her wrists. She closed her eyes and took a deep breath. "Okay, so we haven't had a chance to really talk since early in the party," she said, when she was capable of speaking.

"Uh huh." June hopped up on the counter beside her. "I left with Lucy and her friends at the end of the night, but you were long gone at that point."

"Right. And we texted a little about how it was Hudson's party and all that, but I didn't tell you . . ."

June looked at her agog, as if she knew something juicy was coming.

Annika shut off the faucet and leaned against the sink, hanging her head. "I ended up in his bedroom and . . . we kissed."

"Like, a *kiss* kiss?"

"Oh, it was a real kiss."

June grinned, a wicked little thing. "How was it?"

Annika threw up her hands. "It was great! It was exactly what you'd want a kiss to be! He was decisive and teasing and he smelled good and he *really* knew what he was doing—"

"So what's the problem?" June asked, ever the short-sighted optimist.

Annika gave her a look. "What's the *problem*? June, we've talked about this. This is Hudson Craft. You know, the one in the business of bringing misery and loneliness to the world?"

"All I know is that you're always talking about him, whether it's to complain about him or plot against him," June said, shrugging. She looked in the mirror and used her nail to get a smudge of lip gloss off the top bow of her lip. Turning back to Annika, she added, "Maybe you just need to see what's there. Maybe y'all need to rekindle what happened in Vegas." The wicked smile was back again.

Annika shook her head. "A hookup is never just a hookup to me. Make Up is who I *am*. And Break Up's the exact opposite of that. And now . . . with the eviction hanging over our heads while they just keep ringing that stupid gong and accumulating more breakups? It all just feels *wrong*." She took a deep breath as memories from the night before washed over her. "Plus, you know what he told me? His *real* love is sculpting."

June blinked uncomprehendingly for a few moments. "Oh, right. A sculptor. Ugh . . . sculptors. Yuck?" She gave a theatric shudder.

"No!" Annika paced from one end of the empty bathroom to the other. "Not only is he running a completely vile busi-ness, he's not even being true to himself. He's a sculptor, an *artist*. And he's going to stomp that part of him down, to, what? Break even more hearts? Make even more obscene amounts of money?" She paused. "Besides, you heard him, lording his 'success' over me! How do we know he's not just trying to get in my head, get me to forfeit the EPIC pitch? I think he knows we have an actual shot at this thing. I can't afford to let him do that, not with eviction and bankruptcy being actual possibilities."

June wrinkled her nose. "Do you really think he's *that* sneaky? The way Ziggy talks about him, Hudson's really not that bad of a guy. Ziggy says he's got more integrity than anyone else he's ever worked with."

Annika rolled her eyes. "Yeah, right. Of *course* Ziggy has to say that. It's called cognitive dissonance." Seeing June's blank look, Annika shook her head. "Doesn't matter. Let's just get back to work. I don't want to think about all of this anymore, okay? We need to focus on kicking ass."

After a pause, June hopped off the counter, brushed off her dress, and checked her hair in the mirror. "You're right."

Annika grinned. "Let's show 'em how it's done." And she forced all her other feelings into a little box in the corner of her mind.

chapter thirteen

♡

Annika took a sip of Peet's herbal tea, trying to keep her freshly manicured hands from shaking. "It's *Time* magazine," she whispered, vaguely aware that she'd already said this about six times in the last ten minutes. "*Time. Magazine.*"

June, dressed in loose linen shorts and a tank top, squatted in front of the stool Annika was sitting on and patted her knee. "Yes. And you're going to kick ass."

They'd arrived twenty minutes early for makeup before being shuttled into a large, many-windowed, industrial-looking room in a warehouse. One corner of it had been converted into a dressing area, where Annika sat at a vanity table. The makeup artist was finally finished blow-drying her hair and dabbing foundation and lipstick and eyeshadow and blush onto her face. All that was left now was . . . the interview.

The interview area was about twenty yards away, in the center of the enormous space. They'd put up a backdrop of the city skyline, and created a makeshift "techie" office in front of it, complete with sleek, neon-lit chairs and a clear acrylic table, staged with lots of slim electronic gadgets.

Annika's gaze fluttered over to Hudson. He'd been finished with his makeup in about half the time she was finished with hers, and was now on a couch in the corner with Ziggy and Blaire, all of them scrolling on their phones and speaking in low, urgent tones. Annika's stomach clenched with nerves.

"I'm going to be sick," she said, and took another sip of her tea. Good thing her lipstick was smudge-proof.

"No, you're not," June insisted, getting up and dragging a stool over to sit with Annika. "You're fine. You've done interviews before, too."

"Yeah, but nothing like *him*." Annika thrust her chin over at Hudson's cozy Break Up huddle. "He's done *Forbes* and *Glitz* and *BizTech* and—"

"Doesn't matter," June said firmly. "What matters is you're comfortable and confident in what you say. You know why you created Make Up; you know the good we do in the world. That's all you have to talk about. Just speak from your heart."

Annika took a deep breath. "Right. Just speak from my heart. Easy-peasy." She paused. "What do you think Hudson's up to? You know he's going to try and get one over on me somehow."

Hudson looked up at her at that very moment, even though it was impossible that he could've heard her. His hand slowly adjusted the deep green silk tie at his throat, but his eyes never left hers. Annika's pulse thrummed at her throat. She forced her eyes away. Nothing had changed since their kiss at his condo, so why was her heart pounding like that? The thing was, her heart was quite possibly very stupid.

"Whatever he's going to do, you can do better. You're quick

on your feet. Just remember, we're going to *cream* them at EPIC. Take that energy with you."

"Take that energy. Right." Annika blew out a long breath and took another sip of tea. "I can do that."

"Yes, you can." After a pause, June added, "And you look *really* good." She adjusted a lock of Annika's hair over her shoulder. "Wouldn't it be great if we could just have a makeup artist follow us around all the time?"

Annika pulled on the slim black belt she wore at the waist of her slightly-too-tight red pencil skirt. "Right now, I'd kill to be in something comfortable like you've got on," she muttered. "I feel like I can't breathe." She glanced down at her black suede Prada pumps. "But thanks for lending me these shoes. They're fantastic."

June smiled, satisfied. "They are, aren't they? I got them at—"

A tiny woman in a black pantsuit bustled up to them, interrupting June. She was barely five-foot-one in heels, her dirty-blond hair like a lion's mane around her shoulders. "Annika!" she exclaimed, holding out a minuscule hand. Annika took it gently, and almost gasped in pain at the woman's bear-trap grip. "I'm Emily Dunbar-Khan. I'll be interviewing you today. Are you ready?"

"Hi, Emily," Annika said, setting her tea down on the table and sliding off the stool. Her mouth felt parched, but there was nothing to do about that now. At least the interview wasn't being taped. You couldn't see nerves through a photograph. Or so she hoped. "I'm so ready. Thanks for bringing me on!"

"Of course!" Emily smiled at June. "By the way, thank you. When Megan told me you'd called her with the idea, I lost my shit. It's such a dynamic point of view! A woman-owned app all about giving people their happily-ever-afters goes head-to-head with a wildly popular app that's all about breaking people up." Emily clutched her tiny hands to her heart. "Perfection."

Annika smiled, though she didn't like the thought of Make Up being contrasted with Break Up's "wild popularity" as some tiny, loser app.

"You're welcome," June said, glancing at Annika. "Although I wouldn't be surprised if by the time your article comes out, Make Up's much more than 'wildly popular.' It's going to take the tech world by storm."

Annika gave her a grateful look, but Emily just laughed. "Sure, sure, we'll see what develops." She turned to Annika, her eyes gleaming. "Let's go."

chapter fourteen

♡

Annika took a seat in one of the chairs lit up with LED lights. The chair next to her was empty, and she managed to avoid craning her neck to look for Hudson. There was no reason to make him think she was eager, because she wasn't. She was cool. She was collected. She was going to pretend this was an interview for a college lit mag instead of *Time*.

"So Callum's going to get a couple of pictures of the two of you." Emily gestured to a blond young man with a goatee who was wielding a giant camera. "And then we'll do the interview. Sound good?"

"Sounds great."

The reply came before Annika could say anything, and she turned to see Hudson striding confidently toward her, adjusting his cuff links. "Hey, Emily," he said, as he got closer. "Good to see you again."

"Hudson. Always a pleasure." They shook hands, but Hudson didn't flinch at Emily's superior grip.

He turned to Annika before he sat, a small smirk at his mouth. "Ms. Dev. You look positively ravishing today."

Annika narrowed her eyes. Even though his words would be construed as a compliment by everybody on this planet, his tone implied he was making a joke of some kind. Maybe this was how it'd be during the interview, too—him saying things that would be great in print, but would be obviously condescending and aggravating in person. Well, fine. Let him play his games. Annika was too smart to fall for them. "Compliments to throw me off? Isn't that a little obvious for you?"

He squinted his eyes in confusion, but the photographer spoke before he could.

"For the first picture," Callum said, "let's get the two of you with legs crossed, elbows resting loosely on the chair arms, giving me your best competitor face. Really cold, really calculating. This is a cutthroat world, and you're at the top of your game."

Annika felt like a total idiot giving face as Callum took a series of pictures, but June stood behind him, shooting her lots of thumbs-ups and big grins. Annika kind of wished she wouldn't; Hudson's team was still coolly hanging out on the couches, as if this was all old news to them.

"Great, great," Callum said, adjusting something on his camera. "Now how about the two of you stand? Let's get the chairs and skyline behind you. Good, now turn so your backs are against each other and cross your arms, but look this way."

Annika did as he asked, her mind racing. Feeling Hudson's firm back against hers reminded her of their yoga session. The way they'd been partnered up, the way Hudson had whispered in her ear, his fingers on her inner knee—

"Now that's very seductive, Annika," Callum laughed. "But can we get a little more cold, calculating businesswoman?"

Annika's cheeks heated as she caught June's wide eyes. Hudson chuckled knowingly behind her, as if he knew exactly what she'd been daydreaming about. Anger crept up Annika's face, like a living mask.

"Excellent!" Callum called out. "Now we're seeing it, Annika—you're merciless, you're murderous, you're savage!"

"It's easy when you actually feel that way about your opponent," Annika said. Both Callum and Emily laughed, but Hudson, she noticed, was very quiet. His back had stiffened.

"Save it for the interview, Annika!" Emily called, and Annika grinned at June.

Once all the pictures were taken, they took their seats again, and Emily pulled up an extra chair to sit in front of them. June walked off to speak with Ziggy in the corner, and Annika sat up straighter. It was showtime.

"Let's start with an easy one," Emily said, smiling. Her canines were very, very pointy, Annika noticed. "Both of your businesses deal with relationships in very different ways, and yet both of you rely on pretty innovative app technology to provide customers what they want. Can you speak to why you wanted to marry—pun intended—technology and a time-honored tradition like courtship?"

Annika began speaking before she'd fully articulated an answer in her head. She was going to say her piece, and she wasn't going to apologize for it. "Technology is the perfect vehicle for love," she found herself saying. *Yes! Pull quote potential!* "Intertwining the old with the new, the fairy tale with science, is exactly what Make Up is all about." She'd practiced that with June, and it flowed out of her seamlessly now. "Why not give customers every advantage we can while still preserving the magic of love and second chances?"

Emily looked impressed. "I see. Hudson, do you agree?"

Hudson chuckled and rubbed his square jaw in that insouciant, confident way he had. "Not at all, Emily. It should come as no surprise that I don't believe in fairy tales or happy endings for most people. The cold, hard truth is, people are busy. Technology makes our lives easier in almost every arena. So why should relationships be any different? We have apps that make it easier for people to find others to hook up with, date, marry, whatever. There was a gap when it came to breakups, and that's what we're here to fill."

Ugh. Robot. Total robot. Did he think people's lives were widgets to be fixed?

"Interesting," Emily said, studying Annika's expression. "Annika, what do you think of Hudson's summarization?"

"Frankly, Emily, it baffles me," Annika said, shaking her head. "How can someone sit there and be so dispassionate about bringing heartache to hundreds of thousands of people around the country? I go to work every day feeling optimistic and happy about what I'm putting out into the universe. I know Hudson can't say the same."

Emily looked like all her Christmases were coming early. "Really!" She turned to him. "And what are your thoughts, Hudson?"

Hudson's green eyes were narrowed; he was staring at Annika as if Emily hadn't spoken at all. "Our app has been downloaded over a million times," he said. "What about yours?"

"It's not all about downloads and money and popularity!" Annika said, throwing her hands up. "Right there is exactly why this would never work!"

Hudson froze. Emily, on the other hand, looked thoroughly confused. "What would never work?" she asked, checking her notes as if the answer might be there. "A . . . collaboration between your businesses?"

Annika felt her cheeks get warm. *Shit.* This was a *Time* interview, not a reason to rehash the reasons she couldn't be with Hudson. Not daring to look at either June or Hudson, she cleared her throat. "Yes, exactly. Our business philosophies are just completely opposite one another." She attempted a smile and continued, "Yes, a business is about making money. But is that the *only* reason to own a business? Shouldn't it also be about what you're doing for the world? Shouldn't it be about *people*, taking care of them and making sure they have their shot at happiness? Otherwise, what's the point of anything? What is all of your money, all of your success *for*?"

"My success is so I can give back to the people responsible for where I am today," Hudson said slowly. In spite of his measured cadence, one big hand was curled tightly around the arm of his chair, and Annika was a little afraid he'd crack the plastic. Why was he getting so bent out of shape, anyway? "It's how I can tell whether my days on this earth have been worthwhile or not."

Ziggy and Blaire broke out into spontaneous applause. Annika was less than impressed. So was he saying he was successful for other people? What sense did that make?

Annika leaned forward, her eyes flashing. "So how much are you going to keep giving back to them? Is it ever going to be enough? And, anyway, who says *money* is the definitive way to give back to the people who supported you along the way? Isn't the way you treat other people, what you put out into the world, a bigger payment?"

Here, June cheered, much louder than Ziggy and Blaire put together. Annika smiled at her. Hudson glowered, his jaw set.

"Annika, how would *you* define success?" Emily grinned and crossed her legs on her chair, obviously enjoying the direction this was now taking. "At the end of your life, looking back, what would prompt you to say you'd been successful?"

Annika took a moment to think about it. "I would like to look back and think that I helped every single person who reached out to me," she said, hastening a glance at Hudson. It was exactly the kind of romantic notion he'd generally ream her for. But right now, his grip on the chair had loosened and his face was free of derision. His expression was soft, thoughtful, considered. She looked away, back at Emily. "I would love to have a big stack of holiday cards or wedding invitations from happy couples who are together because Make Up gave them their second chance." She blinked, her throat suddenly tight as she thought of the letter from the bank that was sitting in her desk drawer. She couldn't let Make Up go. She *wouldn't* let it go.

"Really," Emily said, with a bit of an evil smile. "That's a pretty *idealistic* view of success, wouldn't you say, Hudson?" She was clearly trying to start something. "Do you think it's realistic to run a business that way?"

Annika looked full-on at Hudson, ready for him to unleash his arrogant sarcasm on her. But his eyes were soft as he regarded her. "Is it idealistic?" he asked, almost wonderingly. "Sure, I guess." He shrugged and continued, "Is Make Up clearly the more moral company? I'd say yes. Does Annika do more good in the world than I do? Again, the answer is yes. Hands down."

Annika's mouth popped open. Of all the thousand and twenty verbal insults she'd been mentally preparing for Hudson to lob at her, she hadn't expected him to actually say something so . . . so nice. "Um—" She tucked a lock of hair behind her ear, unable to think of a single thing to say. She'd been disarmed. Completely, thoroughly disarmed.

Wait a minute. Was this just one of his verbal kung fu tricks? Giving her a compliment to keep her on her toes? Saying seemingly nice things with a patronizing, arrogant edge? Maybe she'd just missed the edge because she'd been mentally preparing a response. "I don't need your pity," she snapped. "Make Up's doing just fine being the more moral company. Moral doesn't equal unsuccessful or pathetic, Hudson."

She expected him to laugh, to have a pithy rejoinder at the ready. Instead, his eyes widened just a touch, and he looked almost . . . hurt. It was a minute change, and probably wouldn't be noticed by anyone else except her, but he looked like he'd really meant what he'd said, like he'd put a bit of himself out there, and she'd just shit all over it. What the hell was going on? Annika blinked, feeling disoriented—which wasn't uncommon for her around Hudson Craft.

Emily grinned. "Well, on that note: Are you both ready to go head-to-head at the EPIC pitch event in Napa? From what I hear through the tech grapevine, Make Up and Break Up are two of the top contenders. I've heard the board of judges has a soft spot for businesses that have a philanthropic or humanistic bent, Annika, but on the other hand . . . Break Up's been steadily getting more and more popular. It has a working business model. Who wouldn't want to be part of all its success?"

"Break Up's ready," Hudson said, his confident smile back like it had never slipped at all. "We're going to go in there and really dazzle those judges, Emily. It's not our first time pitching at such a large-scale event."

"That's right," Emily said, making a note on her pad. "Annika, any nerves about going in front of a lineup of superstar judges, one of whom is world-renowned billionaire businessman Lionel Wakefield?"

Annika laughed, an easy laugh she'd practiced with June over an entire afternoon. It came out pitch-perfect, and for a moment she was disappointed there *wouldn't* be video. "Lionel Wakefield is known as the *bleeding-heart* billionaire. Who do you think he's going to identify with more, Emily—a business that specializes in tearing people apart, or one that Hudson Craft himself calls the more moral company?"

Emily laughed, but Hudson was quiet. "Great point, Annika! Could you tell me a little bit about the tech Make Up is using? I hear it got a lot of attention when you first announced what you intended to do. You even won a prestigious grant."

Annika took her eyes off Hudson to answer the question, though something about his posture bothered her. He was still—*too* still. Gone was the brash confidence, the boastfulness, the aggravatingly self-assured way he talked about Break Up and his role in its success. He'd folded into himself, which was . . . disconcerting.

Tucking her hair behind her ear, Annika put on another smile for Emily and brought her thoughts back to what she was here to do. "Yes. My developer's building a deep neural network. We've named it OLLI—the Original Love Language Interface—and the idea is that it'll function as a Google Translate for couples who need help with their communication patterns. OLLI will be the relationship therapist you don't have to pay two hundred dollars an hour to see." She took a breath, mentally rehearsing the next thing she wanted to disclose. She and June had decided the *Time* article would be the perfect vehicle to introduce it to the public. "I'm also really excited to talk exclusively with you about something we've been working on in conjunction with the main framework of OLLI: We're also working to create a future projection feature, in which people can upload their social media profiles and pictures to view a custom video predicting a future for them. Our hope is that it'll inspire people to keep working on their relationship, to not lose sight of what could be."

Emily looked genuinely impressed as she scribbled away on her notepad. "That sounds incredibly ambitious, but if you can pull it off . . ." She shook her head, her dirty-blond hair flouncing. "That could be a game changer."

"Exactly." Annika propped her elbows on the arms of her chair, pleased. "You can count on it, Emily. We're going to change lives." She darted a look at Hudson to see if he had any reaction, but his head was bent, his fingers tracing the texture of his slacks.

Emily beamed at them, seemingly failing to notice that he'd withdrawn. "Well, I know that I, for one, am going to be at the edge of my seat, waiting to see the outcome of that event."

Annika sat back against the uncomfortable chair, knowing she should feel triumphant about the way she was handling herself. *And I am*, she thought, as she glanced sidelong at Hudson's profile. She felt good about how she'd represented herself and Make Up. But there was also a part of her that was . . . thrown by the things Hudson had said and the way he was acting. A part of her that felt bad because, oddly enough, she may have unintentionally hurt the CEO of Break Up.

Who *was* he really, under all that bravado and masculine rakishness?

⁓

"Megan, my friend at *Time*? She says Emily thinks this is going to be their most popular article next month when they publish it." June grinned at Annika across her desk, which now featured a taped-up photograph of her and Ziggy dressed like Princess Leia and Han Solo from a recent nerdy convention—Cosmic Con—they'd been to. June had blushed furiously while taping it up, insisting they'd given her the photograph for free. That didn't explain why she was taping it to her desk, but Annika hadn't pushed.

"Good!" Annika clapped her hands. It had been a couple of days since the interview, and though she felt confident about how it had gone, she'd been nervous. "That makes me feel so much better."

It was a slow day, so Annika, dressed in a T-shirt and capris because they weren't expecting any visitors, had decided to take the day to really prepare for the EPIC pitch next month. She'd been pacing the office barefoot with her flash cards, trying out about four thousand different permutations of the pitch for June.

The pitch was to be no more than ten minutes long. In just ten minutes, Annika had to convince a panel of four extremely high-powered strangers—Lionel Wakefield being the most famous of them—that Make Up was worth investing in. That *she* was worth investing in. She couldn't fall, not even a little. She couldn't stumble, she couldn't pause, and she definitely couldn't show any hint of uncertainty.

From all the online reading she'd done, all the podcasts she'd listened to, and all the YouTube videos she'd watched until her eyes felt like they'd burn right out of her head, she knew that angel investors wanted to see passionate, bubbly, excited people whose energy blew them away. They wanted to see people who looked like the next Steve Jobs, Whitney Wolfe, or Mark Zuckerberg. They didn't want to know about your insecurities or your doubts. They wanted a dream they could invest in, and that's exactly what Annika would give them.

"Okay, how about this?" Annika said, scribbling a note on her flash card. "I believe in happily ever after, even if it doesn't take the first time. I believe in happily ever after, redux."

June grinned and pumped her fist. "That's it!" Then, looking solemnly at Annika, she added, "We're going to get it."

Annika blew out a breath. "I really want it. I really, really want it." She got ZeeZee out of her desk and squeezed him.

"I'm looking for Make Up." An authoritative male voice drifted to them from the hallway.

June frowned. "We're not expecting a beta tester, are we?"

"No," Annika said, frozen. "I think I know that voice." She slipped her sandals on and walked down the hallway.

Her dad stood by the elevator, talking to a man dressed in a suit and carrying a briefcase.

"Daddy?"

He looked over at her, his face breaking into a smile. "Ani!"

"What . . . what are you *doing* here?"

The suited man watched them, bemused, until the elevator doors dinged and he got on.

"I wanted to pay you a visit!" her father said, as if his presence here was the most natural thing in the world, as if he frequently stopped by to check in on her, when in reality he hadn't visited her since the very first day she'd opened up shop. Even then, his visit had lasted all of fifteen minutes before he'd jetted off to his practice. "I had the hardest time finding your office, though."

"It's . . . this way," Annika said. They began walking back together. "So . . . you're just here to visit me. That's it?"

As they entered her office, her dad said, "Well, that's not

all." He cleared his throat and smiled at June. "Hello, June. How are you?"

June's gaze flickered toward Annika before landing back on her dad. "Um, great, Dr. Dev! Just, you know, workin', workin', workin'!"

Annika led her dad to the couch, where he promptly plopped down, feeling the velvet with his big hands. "Yes, yes, very nice." He looked around the room. "Nice art. And nice sign. You've done a good job, Annika."

If she weren't so furious with him, she would have laughed. He and the purple settee looked ridiculously incongruous, especially with his custom charcoal suit and bland, expensive haircut, both of which screamed, *"My gold wedding ring is the flashiest thing I own!"*

He smiled and gestured at her T-shirt and messy bun. "So . . . is this workplace casual?" When he saw her expression, he rushed to add, "I like it!"

"Dad," Annika said, folding her arms across her chest. "What are you really doing here?"

He glanced at June, who'd been watching them with avid interest. "Oh!" she said, her cheeks getting pink. "I'll just . . . um . . . see if there's some, ah, tea." She ran out of the office, closing the door behind her.

Annika turned back to her dad.

"Will you sit down?" he said, gesturing to the seat beside him. She'd never seen her dad nervous, and he didn't look it now, either, but there was something about him that seemed off. He was discomfited, Annika realized, and that threw her. Her dad was *never* discomfited.

She sat next to him on the settee, but left enough space between them so that she could turn slightly to look at him.

He took a moment to polish his glasses with authority, his brown eyes thoughtful. When he finally looked at her, he said, "I'm sorry."

"For?"

He took a deep breath that made his shoulders heave. "When your mom and I found out she was pregnant with you, you know one of the first things she told me?"

Annika shook her head.

"She said, 'Raj, one day this little being is going to go off and live her own wild life, making decisions that *we'll* deem mistakes and *she'll* deem adventures. We're going to want to toss a cold bucket of water on her, to wake her up, to slow her down. Let's make a promise right now that we'll stop each other from doing that. I'll be your checks and balances and you'll be mine." He smiled, and Annika saw his eyes were misty. Her own throat felt tight. She blinked hard. "After you walked out Tuesday night, I kept thinking about your mom. What would she say if she could see you now? What would she say if she could see me?" He shook his head, lines of pain etching his forehead.

"I think about that a lot myself," Annika admitted, her voice high-pitched with the effort of trying not to cry. "I hope Mom would be proud of me. But I don't know."

Her dad scooted closer and put a warm hand on hers. "She would be," he said, with such determination that she believed him. "I have no doubt of that." He put an arm around her and continued, "Ani, this place is beautiful. It's full of your personality and it's . . . I never could've thought all of this up, not in a million years. And I haven't taken the time to really reflect on the magic of that. You've always been one to march to the beat of your own drum, and I was trying to squelch that. I was trying to make you into a mini model of me and your mom, because . . ."

Annika laid her head on his shoulder. "Why?"

"Because . . ." Her dad cleared her throat. "It felt like losing you. It felt like losing your mom again, to not have you follow in her footsteps."

"Oh, Dad," Annika said. A tear slipped out of the corner of her eye. "I did this so we'd always have a token of your love for Mom. I want her love for us to live on through Make Up."

Her dad kissed the top of her head. "Good," he said gruffly. "Good. Then you should do that. I'm sorry I ever stood in your way. You're doing such good in the world, Ani."

"Well, it's not surgery," Ani said, looking at him wryly.

He smiled. "It doesn't have to be."

She let his words wash over her. *It doesn't have to be.* He was finally seeing her venture for what it was. He was finally accepting what she was trying to build.

"So," he said, reaching into his coat pocket. "I'd like to invest in your business. As a way of showing my faith in you. Will you let me?"

Annika stared at him, feeling a swell of relief. *Yes.* It would be so easy. Her dad could make a huge dent in her back rent and business loan, and she could work out something with the bank for the rest of it. It would take her forever to pay her dad back, but she knew he wouldn't ask her for it. And he clearly wouldn't be hurting for the money, either. Not to mention, it'd take all the pressure off the EPIC pitch. It wouldn't be such a do-or-die thing anymore. She opened her mouth to tell him the exact dollar amount she needed, knowing he'd write a check without a second thought.

And then she closed her mouth again.

"Ani?" He dad frowned.

Annika forced herself to shake her head. "N-no," she heard herself saying. "No, that's okay, Dad. I need to do this on my own."

Her dad gave her a quizzical look. "But didn't you say the bank was beginning eviction proceedings in July?"

"Yes." Annika's mouth felt suddenly dry. She licked her lips. Forcing herself to look into her dad's eyes, she added more forcefully, "But I need to figure this out for myself. And I will." After a pause, she added, "All my life, you've been there with your checkbook. But Make Up is different. This is my creation, and I want to be responsible for it." She shrugged. "That's how it is. Whether I sink or I swim, I want the onus to be on me and no one else."

Her dad nodded slowly, though she could tell from his face that he was wrestling with a million things he wanted to say and advice he wanted to give. "Okay," he said in the end, patting his coat pocket, as if resigning himself to the fact that his checkbook would have to remain there. "If you're sure."

She smiled. "I am. I'm sure. In fact, that's what June and I are doing today. We're working on this pitch for an angel investors' event in Napa on June fourteenth. And I had an interview in *Time* magazine with Hudson, the guy who owns Break Up."

"*Time*?" her dad said, his eyes wide. "Ani, how fabulous! Of course you're going to win the pitch!" It was obvious that he meant it. Annika smiled.

"So, the pitch event . . . I'd like to fly out there to support you. If—if you want me to, that is."

Annika studied her dad's hopeful eyes, knowing this was another extension of his olive branch. How could she refuse? "I'd love that."

"Good." Her dad patted her hand and then frowned. "Wait. Did you say the *Time* interview was with Hudson Craft? I thought you didn't like him."

Ani sighed. "He's probably the most irritating, aggravating man I know. But it was kind of his article. June was able to leverage her contacts to get me in on it, too."

"Well, it's good to keep your enemies close in business, Ani, especially the well-connected ones. You get to know them, and maybe you don't *like* them any better, but you understand them and they understand you. It makes things infinitely easier."

Annika made a noncommittal noise she hoped her dad would take as agreement, so that she wouldn't have to talk about Hudson anymore. The truth was, even a couple of days post-interview, Annika was still thinking about the things Hudson had said—how she did more good in the world than he did, how Make Up was the more moral company. There hadn't been an iota of sarcasm in his voice. He'd been honest. Maybe even a little earnest. It confused and unsettled her.

They turned at the sound of the door opening. "Our neighbors wanted to meet you!" June said, walking in with Ziggy close on her heels. And right behind him was Hudson. Annika stiffened, and June gave her a look.

"Right," Annika said, forcing a smile. "Dad, this is Ziggy and that's . . . Hudson Craft."

Her dad stood and shook both their hands, his grip firm and sure and confident. Hudson's was, too, she noticed. "Nice to meet you both."

"Dr. Dev, it's a pleasure," Hudson said, smiling easily.

Her dad studied his face, and Annika could tell his wheels were turning. *Uh oh.* Nothing good ever came from her dad's wheels. Before she could open her mouth, though, he was speaking. "So, Hudson—Annika tells me you're both going to be in *Time*."

"That's correct," Hudson said, his gaze coming to rest on hers. "It was a great interview. Annika was fantastic."

Annika felt her cheeks warm at his tone and the way he was looking at her.

"Very good, very good," her dad said thoughtfully. "You know, I don't know if Annika's told you, but she comes over for dinner every Saturday. Is there any chance you could use a home-cooked meal this weekend?" *Wait. What?* "I make far too much food and it goes to waste anyway. How about it?" He looked at June and Ziggy. "You're both invited, too, of course!"

Ah, right. He was implementing his "keep your enemies close" strategy. Dammit. Now Annika wished she'd told him she hated the idea. She tried to laugh. "I don't know, Dad. I'm sure they're all very busy. Plus, it's kind of a long drive—"

"It's not that long a drive," he countered.

"I'd love to come," Hudson answered, catching Annika's eye. He looked completely serious; this wasn't one of his games. Annika wasn't sure how to feel about that. "I assume that's okay with you? I'd love to see where you grew up . . . maybe even a few baby pictures." He grinned suddenly and brightly, the corners of his eyes crinkling with mirth.

Her dad had just waved the white flag. She knew very well that if she was rude and told Hudson that he couldn't come, her dad would be hurt. So what if she had to endure one evening with this new Hudson, the one who left her feeling unsettled and confused? At least it'd be on her turf. And June and Ziggy would be there, too. She could just spend the entire evening talking to them. Annika pasted on a smile. "Of course it is."

"I wish we could," June said, the absolute traitor, "but Ziggy and I have a wedding to attend in San Diego this weekend."

Shit—that was right. She'd totally forgotten June had agreed to be Ziggy's plus-one at a wedding. Another first for her.

"Well, then, it's decided," Annika's dad said. "Hudson, I'll see you and Annika next weekend."

"I can't wait." Hudson nodded at Ziggy. "We should take off. We've got a meeting we don't want to be late for."

After they were gone, Annika turned to her dad, her hands on her hips. "Don't you think a homemade dinner is taking things a little too far?"

Her dad frowned. "Annika, this is a good thing for you and for Make Up. Hudson obviously gets invited to lots of prestigious things. This is an opportunity for you both to bury the hatchet and get to know each other a bit more. Business is ten percent business, ninety percent networking."

Annika and June exchanged glances and then Annika sighed. "Okay, fine. It's just one meal, anyway. But I think we need to get back to work on this pitch—"

"Right, of course. I better get going anyway." He took her by the shoulders and kissed her cheek. "I'm proud of you, Ani. Never forget that."

As she watched him leave, she knew she never would.

chapter fifteen

♡

Annika checked her lip gloss in the rearview mirror one last time, her nerves jumping, before she got out of her car. She'd parked in one of many guest parking spaces assigned to Hudson's penthouse, ready to pick him up and take him to her dad's house for dinner. They'd decided to drive together, since Hudson didn't really know where it was.

As she gave her name to the doorman and got on the penthouse elevator, Annika couldn't help but think about all the different shades of Hudson she'd gotten to see lately, like a multifaceted onyx she held in the palm of her hand. Not just flat black, but purple and red and blue and green, too many hues for her eyes to hold on to and appreciate. What colors would she find tonight?

She pressed the button that would alert him he had a visitor. "Annika?" his voice crackled over the intercom.

She felt a fresh flurry of nerves, which she tried to quell. So *what, so what, so what.* It was just a voice. He was just a man. "Yeah." *Her* voice was slightly squeaky.

"Come on up." She heard a slight smile in his voice.

For the first time since high school, Annika found herself wondering what her dad's place would look like to a stranger—especially Hudson, who came from a working-class family. Hopefully he wouldn't think she was a spoiled princess who'd grown up with everything she could ever want. Plus, *hello.* She'd seen his penthouse, and it wasn't exactly Skid Row.

Oh, come on, she told herself sternly as the elevator zipped upward. *What do you care what Hudson Craft thinks of you or how you grew up? It's immaterial.* She shouldn't care. She didn't.

There was a ping as the elevator came to a stop at Hudson's, and the doors slid open noiselessly. Annika straightened her shoulders, her heart pounding just a little bit faster than necessary.

"Good evening," Hudson said, as soon as she emerged into his living room. He bent down to air-kiss her, smelling fresh and expensive, dressed in a crisp turquoise polo shirt and long pale yellow shorts.

"You look summery," Annika said, stepping back to size him up, though it was almost too much to actually meet his eye. She was feeling . . . shy, she realized. "Smell like it, too." Her hands tightened into fists as she heard herself. *What the actual hell?*

Hudson looked amused, though his cheeks were faintly pink, like he was feeling a little hesitant around her, too. Annika cleared her throat and stepped off to the right, toward a nook in the wall that held a pedestal and a sculpture of a bird poised to take flight. "Anyway. Wow. This is gorgeous." She stroked the iridescent feathers on the bird's extended wing, as exquisitely fragile and silky-soft as if it were the real thing. She glanced up at Hudson. "Is it new?"

He was watching her admire the sculpture with a peculiar look in his eye. He blinked it away when he saw her looking. "Ah, no—no, it's not. I made that a couple years ago. Just found it in a moving box the other day, actually."

"Mm. The longing on its face is . . . haunting."

"Longing?" Hudson walked closer to her, so they were standing side by side, their arms just a hairbreadth away from touching. She felt his warmth seep into her skin, and had to blink to focus. "You see longing there?"

"Sure." Annika studied the bird more closely. "There's longing in every one of its features, in the way it's holding its wings, its posture. It's poised, ready to take flight, but it hasn't quite achieved what it wants yet." She realized Hudson was watching her intently and felt her face get warm. Maybe she'd said too much. Art was an oddly intimate thing. "What?"

"Nothing." Hudson shook his head, a faint smile at his lips. "I made that as sort of an experiment, but I wasn't sure it would work. I tried to make the bird ambiguous in its intent—its expression, its posture, whether it's poised for flight, as you said, or whether it's landing. Everyone who's looked at it so far has said something different. No one's talked about the longing the bird feels."

Annika's face got even warmer. "Oh, great. So I'm weird, then, is what you're saying."

"Not at all." Hudson kept looking at her until she met his eye, reluctantly. There was no trace of humor or sarcasm there.

"So what do *you* see?" Annika asked. She was genuinely, truly curious about what his artist's eye saw.

Hudson looked at the bird and Annika looked at him, hoping he wouldn't notice. She shouldn't do it so openly, or even at all, she knew. Not after what she'd said to him in his condo the other day; she'd drawn a line then, and she intended to stick by it. But the way he shimmered and shone like a nearly opaque lake, with Annika only barely able to glimpse what was underneath, was . . . compelling.

"I see entrapment," he said finally, jarring her out of her reverie. He stroked the bird's wing gently with one finger. "It wants to fly, but it's not sure how. It's been anchored to the ground against its will, almost—and yet, the ground is all it knows. The world is its cage, but the sky beckons, unattainable."

Annika stared at him. Hudson rubbed the back of his neck. "Too bizarre?" he asked, laughing as if her answer didn't matter, but she could sense the vulnerability behind the question.

"No, I just . . . you sounded like a poet just then."

"Is it surprising that I might be poetic?" His expression was full-on cocky now, his eyes glittering.

Annika folded her arms and leaned back against the wall next to the nook, putting a little distance between them. She needed to remember who she was talking to here. "Um, yeah. I don't remember any poetry in the *Forbes* article that came out last month."

Hudson stepped a bit closer. Annika's traitorous heart thumped in response. "That's because *Forbes* doesn't exactly inspire poetry." His eyes held hers.

"And . . . what inspires poetry in you?" Annika managed to ask.

Hudson put one hand on the wall behind Annika's head,

his face mere inches from hers. She knew she should move, but she couldn't will her legs to listen, like a doe paralyzed by a lion. Her gaze was riveted to his, and her heart pounded out a rhythm against her rib cage.

"Lately, it's been just one subject," he murmured, his eyes drifting briefly to her mouth. Annika had a flash of memory: her in Hudson's bedroom, his teeth nipping gently at her lips, teasing her.

She struggled to blink it away, her knees going weak. "Oh, yeah?" she managed, her voice breathy. "What subject is that? Ancient history?"

Hudson ran a fingertip from her temple to her cheekbone to her chin, as if her skin was the most beautiful thing he'd ever seen, and Annika was afraid, actually afraid, that she might pass out from hyperventilating. He leaned forward so their mouths were basically sharing the same air, their lips poised to touch but still unbearably apart. "I think you know," he whispered. He was so close that all she could see, all that existed in the universe, were his green eyes.

Do not *kiss him*, her brain telegraphed, the letters neon-red and flashing a panicked beat. *This is* Hudson Craft. *Anathema to your soul, as I recall.*

But . . . a small corner of her heart whispered back. *He's not all bad.* She tilted her head forward, just a millimeter, until her lips brushed his and both brain and heart fell silent. All that remained was her body, and every nerve ending, every fiber inside her was glowing, a filament in an incandescent bulb. She wanted to kiss him; she *needed* to kiss him.

There was a *ping!* as the elevators opened, just a few yards away. Annika froze as a young white couple in T-shirts that said Elite Housecleaning Services stepped into the living room, saying something about the heat. Hudson looked over his shoulder at them, took a small side step away from Annika, and called out, "Hey, guys. We'll be out of your hair soon."

The couple jerked their heads toward him at the same time, their mouths falling open. "Oh, Mr. Craft," the woman said. "We're so sorry. We thought you'd have left by now."

Hudson held up a hand and walked toward them smoothly. "No worries. It's my fault. We *were* supposed to be out of here. I got . . . distracted." His eyes flickered to Annika, and she felt her cheeks get warm again. "I need to grab something quickly, but are you ready to go?"

"Yep." Annika smoothed down her hair and cleared her throat, unable to look at the couple. *We weren't even* doing *any-thing!* she thought, exasperated at herself. Why was her guilty conscience always so out of proportion to her actual crime? Which, in this case, wasn't even a crime—it was Hudson's house; he could do what he chose. And she was a consenting adult.

The young couple made their way to the kitchen with their cleaning supplies, and then Hudson walked into the foyer with a bottle of wine in a bag. "Let's do this."

They traveled down the elevator in relative silence, though Annika couldn't help darting glances at him during gaps in their conversation about traffic out to the Hills and her dad's culinary skills.

He caught her staring once, and gave her a lopsided smile. "I'm going to finish what I started, you know."

"What?" Annika squeaked. The elevator doors slid open.

Hudson considered her for a full second, his gaze lingering on her in a way she found maddening, before walking out into the parking garage. A valet greeted him by name and asked if he'd like his car pulled around, but Hudson shook his head. "I'm going to finish that kiss," he said to Annika when she caught up to him, his voice low and intense.

She almost tripped over her own feet, her muscles going mushy at the command, the husky desire, in his voice. "Probably not at my dad's house," she managed weakly, and he laughed.

"No," he conceded. "Probably not there."

They'd reached her Honda, by which point she was eager to change the subject. Kissing him, allowing him to *talk* about kissing her—it was probably giving him the wrong message. She needed to remind him, and maybe even herself, why they couldn't go out: Nothing had changed, not really. He was still the CEO of Break Up. Sure, she'd seen sparks of something deeper, something more to Hudson's relationship with Break Up that he wasn't divulging. But she still wasn't sure what. Watching him get in, his long legs folding so he could fit, she remembered what he'd said at the *Time* interview— the way he'd looked at her, almost hurt, when she'd taken his comments as sarcasm. What did it all *mean*? "Anyway, um, thanks for the bottle of wine. You didn't have to bring anything."

Hudson set the wine in the back seat and buckled in. "I hate going to parties empty-handed. It makes me feel like a free-loader. Speaking of gifts, thank you for the book you got me for my housewarming. I hope you got my thank-you card?"

Annika laughed as she began to back out of the space. "Yes, and it was very proper of you."

"What? That's not *proper*. I'm not stuffy. I'm just . . ."

"Stuffy." Annika gave him a sidelong glance as she pulled out of the garage and signaled right, the ticking filling the car.

"It's okay, Hudson, just own it. Really lean into that fussy, fancy side of yourself."

He laughed. "Okay, I can be kind of fussy and fancy. But only when it comes to parties and thank-you notes. It's a weird thing my parents drilled into me. I guess I just never got rid of it." He adjusted the seat so it was lower and farther back. "Who was riding in here last, a kid?"

Annika snorted as she went around a BMW that was going ten miles under the speed limit. "That would be June. And she's actually pretty tall, for your information."

Hudson leaned back in his seat. "I'm happy for them," he said thoughtfully. "Ziggy and June. They seem good together, don't they?"

"Well, I don't know if June would agree they're 'Ziggy and June.' She's kind of guarded when it comes to love. But I *am* glad she seems to have found . . . the Han to her Leia. Even if she doesn't know it yet." She could feel Hudson looking at her and glanced over at him. "What?"

"Do you ever wonder why some people get lucky in love and others don't? What's that about?"

Annika rolled her eyes. "I don't know. Maybe I did something bad in another life."

"Do you really think that? Do you believe in karma and all of that?"

"I believe in kindness coming back to you," Annika replied carefully.

Hudson tapped his fingers on the center storage compartment. "Right. And yet, from what I can see, you're nothing *but* kind. That's why I really wonder about karma sometimes. If there is such a thing, though, I'm not sure I'm helping my chances by owning a company like Break Up."

Annika glanced at him sharply before watching the road again. "You know what you said at the *Time* interview? How you think Make Up is the more moral company?"

He nodded, his eyes straight ahead.

"Do you really mean that? Do you have . . . doubts about Break Up?"

He scratched the side of his jaw, looking torn. "It's complicated," he said finally, his voice distant. "Anyway." He turned on the radio, clearly finished with the conversation for now. "Let's get some music on, what do you say? Maybe some mariachi?"

She huffed a light laugh, even as she clutched the steering wheel tighter. Here was a crack in his armor that she could peek through—a hint, a hope of change. Maybe Hudson Craft *wouldn't* always be at the helm of Break Up. And then what? What might that mean for them?

❧

Her dad opened the door wearing a Why Whine When You Can Wine apron. Hudson shot her a smug look, clearly self-satisfied with his choice in a gift for the host.

"Yes, yes, you're a genius," Annika said, stepping in to give her dad a hug.

"Dr. Dev," Hudson said formally, extending a hand. "Thank you so much for having me. I brought you some wine."

Her dad accepted the wine and checked out the label. "A 2013 Côte-Rôtie la Landonne! Nice choice, Hudson. Very nice. Thank you."

Hudson smiled as they walked through the foyer. "This is a stunning home. Is that a replica of a chandelier from the Hall of Mirrors in Versailles? It's exquisite."

Annika's dad beamed. "It is indeed. Annika's mother had that commissioned many years ago. We have an identical one in the master bedroom as well. Why don't you come in? I'll show you the thirties-style lighting I had installed in the kitchen."

They walked in, talking about lighting and floors and faucets. Annika followed, smiling a little.

❧

They sat out in the backyard under the pergola, pink honeysuckle entwined in its wooden beams, creating a sweet-smelling canopy above them. Lanterns hung from ropes tied to the beams, casting a soft golden light and flickering shadows around them. The feast her dad had laid out looked like enough to feed twelve people, but Hudson was making a valiant effort to eat it all.

"It's so good," he said, stuffing more naan into his mouth. "I mean, I thought I'd eaten good Indian food in restaurants, but this . . ."

Her dad chuckled. "You can't beat family recipes. Of course, Annika thinks my food is far too spicy."

Hudson raised his eyebrows at her. "Seriously?"

She glared at him over the top of her silver glass of lassi. "What? Just because I'm Indian I need to like spicy food?"

Hudson laughed. "No, you need to like it because it's delicious."

Her father chortled. "Hear, hear!"

Annika turned to him. "Daddy, have you been sleeping? You have bags under your eyes." His hair was grayer than she'd noticed when he visited the Make Up office, too. For the first time, it occurred to Annika that her dad was . . . aging.

"Oh." He waved his hand and took a sip of the wine Hudson

had brought, instead of answering. "This is drinking nicely, Hudson. Excellent choice."

"Thank you," Hudson said, glancing at Annika.

"Dad. You don't think you're going to fob me off that easily, do you?" Annika pressed.

Her father sighed. "I'm fine, Ani." He looked out past her to the swimming pool, which glimmered in the distance like an aquamarine jewel. The lantern lights reflected in his glasses. "This is just . . . a big house, you know? And sometimes I realize it'll never be full again and it makes me think."

Annika frowned. "Think about what?"

He shrugged. "Just . . . what I want to do now. Or in the future. Do I want to stay here in a year's time? Five years?"

"You—you mean you might want to sell the house?" Annika tried not to show how much the thought unsettled her.

Her father shrugged. "Perhaps. Do I really need all this?" He gestured around the expansive backyard, with its neatly trimmed hedges and citrus tree groves and multiple seating and grilling areas.

Hudson studied Annika, a sympathetic look on his face. She took another sip of her lassi. "What about—but you bought this house with Mom," she said softly. "I thought you didn't want to move on from it because it'd feel like leaving her behind."

"That's what I've always told myself," her dad said, finally meeting her eye. "But maybe that's foolish. Maybe it's time to leave the past where it belongs."

"Is it?" Her heart was hammering in her chest. More talk of leaving her mom's memories behind. "Or should we honor the past by taking it with us wherever we go?"

Her dad looked at her for a long time, his features soft and sad. "I don't know, Ani," he said, shaking his head. "But I wish I had the answers."

"You'll feel better soon," Annika said firmly. "Maybe go golfing tomorrow. You're probably just overworked."

Her father smiled a little, his index finger circling the rim of his wineglass. "Maybe," he said. "Maybe you're right."

chapter sixteen

Annika and Hudson stood on the deck with their glasses of port, looking out at the sparkling city lights. Her dad was in his study, calling a patient who'd come out of surgery a few hours ago and was asking to speak to him.

"It's very peaceful here," Hudson said. "I can see why you come every weekend."

"Well, I come mainly for my dad."

Hudson smiled lightly. "I think he's part of what makes it peaceful. There's a feeling of family here that's pretty incredible."

Annika swirled her port slowly. "Yeah, I guess there is."

There was a pause, and then Hudson said carefully, "Are you worried your dad might sell this place?"

"No. Yes. Kind of?" Annika shrugged. "It's all I have of my mom. I feel like she's everywhere here, you know? I feel her so much—I can see the things she picked out. I know some of her likes and dislikes because of this house. Maybe it's silly, but I almost feel like I know *her* because of this house."

"I don't think that's silly," Hudson said, leaning his elbows against the railing. "She put a lot of herself into this home. It seems to me that it's kind of a legacy she left behind for you."

"Exactly." Annika stared at him. No one had ever put it that way before. "That's exactly it."

He nodded, holding her gaze for a while before looking away at the hills in the distance. "You know what you asked me, in the car? About whether I have doubts about Break Up?"

Annika's heart thumped. "Yeah. You said it was complicated."

Hudson met her gaze again. The outdoor gas fireplace was on behind her, and the flames flickered in his eyes. "It *is* complicated. My brother . . . he's a mechanic in Swanson, the same town I grew up in. He doesn't make a lot, and he already has three kids. My parents have run the same convenience store for thirty years; my mom inherited it from her parents. I knew from the beginning that if anyone was going to support my parents, it'd have to be me. They always expected that of me, you know. I was always supposed to be the one who got away, and the one who'd get successful and take care of them in their twilight years."

Annika shook her head, reeling from the fact that Hudson was actually sharing something deep with her again. But she wanted to keep up; she didn't want him to stop. "But you said you helped them pay off their house and retire, right?"

Hudson nodded and leaned back against the railing. A light breeze tousled his hair. "Right. But it feels like there's always something else. Their car breaks down, they need a new one.

Or my brother needs help, too—his kids need school clothes, or medicine because they're sick, or he doesn't have the money to get them stuff for Christmas." He smiled, clearly remembering something. "My nephews are really cool kids. I *want* them to have fun birthdays and Christmases. So I'm happy to help out." He shrugged and took a sip of his port.

Annika wondered how to phrase the next question. She knew she had to step delicately. "But when . . . when do you stop? When will it be enough, what you're doing?"

Hudson looked down into his glass. It sparkled under the muted lights of the deck. Somewhere in the distance, a dog barked in the night. "I don't know. I ask myself that sometimes. And the answer I always come up with is never. My parents never gave up on me, and I can't ever stop the pace at which I'm making money, either."

Annika stood in silence, listening to the wind whisper in the trees. "But?" she asked finally, when Hudson didn't fill the space.

He let out a deep, heavy sigh and tipped his head back to look at the dark sky. "But you're right. I do have doubts. The way I think about it—about *never* being able to stop—might be untenable. And the way I'm supporting them by running Break Up . . . the entire thing chills me to the core. The people who employ our services, like that guy we saw in the bar after the Early to Tech event. The men who clap my back and thank me for making it easy to juggle multiple women and then toss them aside when they're done. The businesspeople I'm always meeting with, with their slick, slimy smiles and their ingratiating compliments. I know they'd be gone the instant my financial situation faltered. The journalists who want to know if I think the future of relationships is a game of survival—who gets to use up whom first, who gets to do the discarding. The thing is, I'm sick of it all. This is not who I—this is not how I pictured my life. This can't last. I can't be the face of Break Up forever. I don't have the passion for it that you do for Make Up." He pushed a hand through his hair and shook his head. "Sorry. That was a lot of information. It's not something I really like to talk about, so I'm not sure what happened."

Annika's pulse thumped in her throat and her wrists while her heart did a tap dance in her chest. He was saying what she thought he was saying, wasn't he? He didn't want to be at the helm of Break Up anymore. He hated it as much as *she* hated it. It was just a matter of time before he walked away.

"Don't be sorry. Thank you for sharing that with me," she said, her voice steady in spite of the tumultuous emotion she was feeling. He was going to give up Break Up—she was almost sure that's what he was saying, without actually saying it. He'd said it felt untenable. He'd said the whole thing chilled him to the core. He was still going to compete against her at EPIC, but . . . this was a shift, wasn't it? An important one, even.

Hudson laughed and set his drink down on a nearby table with a glassy *clink*. "It sounds like I'm having a quarter-life crisis. Jesus."

Annika managed a weak smile. "It's not just you, believe me. A lot of us are completely confused about our lives." She drained her port in one gulp and set her glass down, too.

"Really?"

She looked at him, chewing her lower lip, her fingers tracing the curved metal edge of the table near them. "Really." She paused. "I—I got a letter from the Bank of California. They're evicting us. We're so far overleveraged that we can't keep up with rent. And we're ridiculously behind on payments on our business loan, too."

"Shit." Hudson looked genuinely devastated. As he spoke, the firelight caught the tips of his golden hair, threading it with glimmers of red. "That fucking sucks."

Annika managed a smile. "Yeah. It does. But we're not going down without a fight." She put her hands on the railing, looking out onto the night-darkened hills in the distance. A few lights dotted the vista, like jewels set against black velvet. "EPIC is my chance to bring Make Up back. And I have every intention of winning." She glanced at Hudson. "Did I just make it awkward?"

Chuckling, he joined her at the railing. "Maybe a little. But you know what? I'd expect nothing less of you." He paused, rubbing his thumb along the edge of the railing. For some reason, the movement made Annika's face warm. "And anyway, I can't imagine a world where I *don't* get to annoy you with my gong. So, you know. I feel like it'll all work out one way or another."

Annika laughed and pretended to punch his arm. His muscle didn't even move; it was like hitting a wall. "Thanks—I think."

They stood in silence for a moment, just staring at each other, their smiles slowly fading into something serious.

"Hey," Hudson said softly. "There's something I want to ask you."

Her heart began thumping in her chest again, a rabbit in a trap. A cool, citrus-scented breeze blew in, rustling through the deck, caressing her skin and making her shiver lightly in her thin cotton dress. "Okay."

Hudson regarded her, crossing his arms slowly. "Why don't we both call a truce from now until after EPIC? No sabotaging, no tricks, no pranks."

Annika thought about it while playing with her hair. Hudson's eyes fell to the nape of her neck, just for a second. "A truce? Like a cease-fire?"

"Exactly."

A curl blew across her cheek. "I don't know . . . that sounds like something an Idealists Anonymous member would do."

Hudson smiled. "Ah, so you got the membership invitation."

Annika snorted. "Yeah, thanks for that." After a pause, she looked up at him. "So . . . why exactly do you want to call a truce?"

Hudson leaned closer to her. The port had imparted a rosy glow to his cheeks. "I'm hoping it'll endear me to you a little bit. I like to finish what I start. Like I said earlier."

Annika's heart began beating out an erratic rhythm, her fingers tracing her collarbone lightly. "Right," she said, her eyes moving down to his lips of their own accord. "I do too, as it happens." If he was going to walk away from Break Up . . . was there really any reason she should keep fighting what she felt for him?

Hudson took a half step closer to her. "Good." She turned and pressed her back against the railing, looking up at him, her pulse flying. Even though she still had her doubts, a part of her wanted to let him corner her here, wrap his big hands around her waist and pull her against him, snug. Her knees felt strangely shaky, as if her bones were made of melting wax.

"Parents make the worst patients," her dad said loudly, bustling out onto the deck.

It was like both Hudson and Annika had grabbed an electric fence at the same time. They flew apart, Hudson rubbing his jaw and clearing his throat, and Annika blinking, dazed and confused.

"W-what?" she asked, her brain struggling to catch up to where she was: with her *dad* on his deck, not in some hotel room alone with Hudson.

Her dad, completely oblivious, waved an impatient hand. "The kids are fine, you know. Really resilient. But the parents? They want me to calm their anxieties. This is the sixth call today from the same family. I sympathize, but also, your child's fine! Let him sleep off the post-op urinary retention from the anesthesia! The nurses and the attending doctor are perfectly capable of keeping an eye on him."

Annika very pointedly kept her eyes on her dad and not on Hudson. She wasn't sure what the expression on his face would be, or how she might respond. "Right—but don't you give your cell number to all your patients?"

Her dad chuckled. "Aha! So you're trying to say I brought this on myself. Fair point, fair point."

Annika walked over to him and slung an arm around his waist. "You can't help that you care about your patients so much. It's what makes you a great doctor."

Her dad kissed the side of her head. "Hey, not that I want to break up this party, but it's getting late. Do you want to stay the night? You're welcome to as well, Hudson."

Annika swallowed. "Um . . . no. I think we'll head back, Dad. But thanks." She nodded to Hudson. "You ready to go?"

His gaze never leaving hers, he answered, "I'm ready."

A soft shiver went through Annika's body at his words; they held a promise for things to come. Things were changing with Hudson . . . but she couldn't—wouldn't—hold back at EPIC.

Napa was going to be a very interesting experience.

chapter seventeen

Annika arrived in Napa on a perfect Friday afternoon. The skies were an exquisite crystal blue, with just a few picturesque clouds scudding across the surface. Her dad and June would fly in tomorrow, and EPIC would be on Sunday morning, which gave her all of today and tomorrow to rehearse and re-rehearse her pitch. She'd done it dozens of times already, but it paid—literally—to be perfect. Better than perfect, even.

Thoughts of the bank letter darted into Annika's brain as her Lyft pulled into the large circular driveway of the hotel, but she pushed them out again. This weekend was about positivity and confidence. She was determined not to let anything mar her mental state between now and Sunday.

She glanced up at the hotel as her Lyft driver helped her unload her suitcase. The Hotel Monte Vista looked like a medieval castle, with flags waving from its roof. Somewhere inside, Hudson would be settling into his room. They were back in a hotel again, just like in Vegas.

Annika blinked the thought away. This time, she was here to kick his ass, truce or no truce.

◦⁓◦

She stood in the check-in line of the grand hotel lobby, looking around as a harpist in a floaty white gown played a gentle melody in the corner. A monstrous crystal chandelier was suspended from the vaulted ceiling—threateningly, Annika thought, though none of the other guests seemed too concerned. Like every five-star hotel, the air was softly scented with money, as if to lull guests into feeling right at home. *"You're exactly where you're supposed to be,"* the hotel seemed to murmur soothingly. *"You're among friends. You're—"*

"Daydreaming?"

Annika spun around to see that she wasn't the last person in line anymore. Hudson smiled down at her, one side of his mouth higher than the other, his trademark look. He was dressed in a button-down linen shirt that emphasized his broad chest and shorts with palm trees embroidered on them. Very preppy. Very I'm-on-a-working-vacation-in-beautiful-Napa.

Annika felt the tips of her ears heat. "Oh, hi." She was not ready for this. Yes, they'd called a truce, and she did feel like she'd gotten to know him a lot better at her dad's, but . . . he was still Hudson. How was she supposed to *be* around him if she wasn't actively sabotaging his every move? She tucked a lock of airplane-flattened hair behind her ear and smoothed down her pink floral jumpsuit, just now noticing how rumpled it had gotten on the flight. "How—um, did you just get in?"

"An hour or so ago. I was waiting in the restaurant while they got a room ready for me."

Annika nodded, trying desperately to think of something to say that wasn't snarky. "Um, so . . . where are the others? Blaire and Ziggy?"

"They'll fly in tomorrow. I wanted a day to unwind and get my bearings. Plus, this is a gorgeous hotel, might as well enjoy it a bit." He gestured at the big glass windows overlooking rolling hills in the distance.

"Right, yeah—me too. I mean, June's flying in tomorrow. With my dad."

Oh, god. This was too weird. They were making awkward conversation like two acquaintances or boring colleagues. Was this how she wanted the whole weekend to be? Annika glanced at him from underneath her eyelashes and quickly looked away when she saw he was watching her.

"I have a question for you."

Annika stepped forward as the line moved up, her hand clasped around the handle of her rolling suitcase. A businessman in a suit lined up behind Hudson, tapping away at his phone. "Okay." If he asked to see her pitch, she was going to laugh in his face. Truce or no truce, Hudson was still on the opposing team—the *losing* team.

He scooted his duffle bag forward with the side of his shoe. "Will you go to dinner with me?"

"Oh." Her hand jerked up, hitting the handle of her suitcase. It fell to the floor with a clatter, causing everyone in line to turn around and look at her. Her cheeks burning, Annika knelt to pick it up.

Hudson smiled, a touch of mischief dancing in his eyes. "Is that such a scary thought?"

Annika barked a laugh. "I'm not scared of *you*."

He continued to smile, as if he could see her nerves shimmering around her like an opalescent wall. "So? What do you say, then?"

Dinner with him? Was he . . . asking her on a *date*?

As if reading her mind, he said, "I mean, neither of our teams are here yet." It was nice of him to call June her team. "You'll have hours until then to rehearse your pitch, and if you feel like a break . . ." He shrugged.

Annika thought about it. "Well . . . I mean, we *are* both going to be in the hotel. It seems silly not to—uh—take some time to unwind."

His eyes twinkled as they moved forward another step. "Exactly. Plus, you don't want to be over-rehearsed."

Annika shook her head solemnly, even though Hudson was the last person she'd take tips from on this topic. "No, definitely not that." Her heart thumped as she looked up into his eyes. "So . . . dinner. Tonight. You and me."

He bowed his head. "Dinner tonight. You and me. Say, seven-ish? We can meet here in the lobby."

"Okay."

They stared at each other for a long moment, not saying anything else. Annika's heart thumped again. He made it sound like a casual thing—just something to do, since they were both here and would otherwise be bored.

The man behind Hudson cleared his throat, which made

Annika jump. "Excuse me," he said, looking a little irritated. "They're ready for you."

Her face warm, Annika walked up to the counter, pretending she couldn't hear Hudson chuckling at her obvious blunder.

"See you tonight," he called after her. She swallowed hard.

Yep. Tonight. The CEO of Make Up having dinner with the sexy CEO of Break Up. No big deal.

෴

Her room was beautiful. Gorgeous gold curtains framed a large window, which looked out onto a garden. Annika kicked off her sandals and turned on the glowing lamplights, the cool, air-conditioned air whispering over her skin. Then she sank into the crisply made sleigh bed and, falling backward, closed her eyes.

She hadn't said anything further to Hudson, except to wave as she walked off to the elevators. Dinner with him—she still wasn't convinced it was a good idea. She needed to focus on EPIC. And yet . . . after all he'd told her at her dad's, there was a part of her that was curious to learn more about him. She wanted more of that other Hudson, the one who'd said Break Up chilled him.

Annika sat up and walked to her suitcase. There was no time for all that right now. She had a few hours today to practice for her pitch on Sunday morning—plus whatever she'd do tomorrow—and she intended to make good use of them.

Eventually, the fading light outside her window alerted her to the fact that she'd been working longer than she'd realized. A quick peek at her phone told her she was right; it was already six-thirty. *Time to get dressed.* Annika's stomach lurched like she was on a roller coaster. *Stop it*, she told herself sternly as she walked to the bathroom, peeling off her clothes as she went. *It's only Hudson Craft.* The thought didn't help as much as she wanted it to.

After a quick shower and a change of fresh clothes (a pair of linen shorts and a floaty cami top—cute but not "I think this is a date" cute), Annika FaceTimed June.

"I'm going to dinner with Hudson," she said in a rush, as soon as June answered. "That's a bad idea, right? I mean, I need to focus on defeating Break Up on Sunday, not gallivanting with the enemy."

June shrugged. Behind her, there were rows and rows of colorful book spines, and a teen in glasses and a Yoda T-shirt brushed past her. "So why are you going?"

Annika chewed on her lip for a moment. "I think it's because of what he said on my dad's deck. You know, about his involvement with Break Up being untenable?"

June nodded; they'd already dissected that night in detail. "Right, but you know he might not bring that up again tonight."

"Oh, I know." Annika leaned back on her bed on one elbow, letting herself sink into the plush mattress. "It's probably best not to push him on that. He'll get there when he gets there." She adjusted the phone in her hand. "But I guess the fact that he even *said* that, that the writing's pretty much on the wall . . . he's basically ready to give up Break Up. It's a matter of *when*, not *if*."

A group of loud teens passed behind her. June turned, trying to find a quieter spot. "And that makes you . . . want to get to know him better?"

Feeling restless, Annika hopped off the bed and perched on the blush-pink accent chair by the window, watching the trees sway in the breeze in the garden. "Exactly." She screwed up her nose. "Is that a bad idea, though? I mean, we're competing in two days."

"You should still go. Have fun."

"Really?"

"Really." June adjusted her grip on the phone, the video tilting as she did. "Annika, Sunday's a big day, and you're already *really* well prepared. Plus, you have all of tomorrow to rehearse, too. It's more important that you're relaxed. It's just dinner, right?"

"But this is the last big push to save Make Up." Annika pulled her legs up on the chair. "It feels kind of . . . I don't know, irresponsible, to just go off and do this."

"Do you know the pitch forward and backward?"

"Yeah."

"Right. How much more can you do right now? Don't overthink this. Just go out, give yourself a night off," June said, as a very pale man in a Darth Vader hat walked by.

"That makes sense." Annika sagged back against the chair and let out a breath. "I *did* already go over everything for the last few hours."

June smiled. "There you g—" The sound of deafening cheers suddenly drowned her out.

Annika squinted and sat up straighter. "Where *are* you?"

"Oh, Ziggy and I are at a book signing for Timothy Zahn." She grinned and panned the phone so Annika could see Ziggy, who waved. He was wearing what looked like a vintage *Star Wars* T-shirt. "I'm gonna get all fourteen of his Star Wars books signed."

Annika laughed. "Okay, well, it sounds like the crowd's really riled up, so I'm gonna let you go. Love ya."

"You too! Remember: Just relax. Your dad and I will see you tomorrow." June blew her a kiss and they ended the call.

Annika looked at herself in the mirror across from the chair, feeling pinpricks of doubt now that June's reasonable voice was gone. "Just a casual dinner. You can handle this, Dev."

Her pep talk almost worked.

∾

She stepped off the elevators and into the marble-tiled lobby, which smelled of citrus water and expensive bouquets of lilac. She wiped her palms on her shorts. The gilded ceiling seemed miles above her. There was another harpist in the corner, nearly indistinguishable from the one who'd been there earlier. The music tinkling in the air should've calmed her nerves, but it didn't. As she walked toward the seating area, Annika had a feeling that nothing would.

When she came closer, she caught sight of Hudson sitting in an overstuffed paisley armchair by a potted palm tree, his head bent over his phone screen. He looked far too big for the chair, his legs and arms and shoulders jutting out past its boundaries, as if he couldn't be contained. He hadn't seen her yet, so Annika took a few seconds to take him in and observe the way he seemed to command the space without even seeming to try, the way he looked utterly at ease in his surroundings, no matter where he was.

She began to walk again after a moment, clearing her throat. Hudson looked up, and as his face creased into a smile, she found herself feeling just a bit giddy. Her nerves softened and reshaped into something a little more fun, just for a moment, before snapping back into their old, tense shape.

"Hey," he said, his voice soft and smooth as velvet as he stood to greet her. He'd changed into a dark-green button-down, paired with dark-rinse jeans that hung just right on his slim hips and long legs. "You look . . . really nice."

Annika glanced down at herself, her hands fiddling with the drawstring on her shorts. "Oh—thanks. Um—so do you." In fact, it was kind of hard to look directly at him. No one man should hoard so much beauty like that. It was immoral.

"Rose? Rose for the lady?"

They turned to see an old man in a tweed suit who'd wandered over to the sitting area, holding a basket full of pale pink roses. He smiled at them, his teeth too straight and even to be anything but dentures. "Beautiful couple. Rose for your lady, sir?"

Annika jerked her head to look at Hudson, her eyes wide, her cheeks warm. Turning back to the old man, she began to say, "We're not a—"

"I'd love to," Hudson interjected, reaching smoothly for his wallet.

Annika couldn't breathe. She wanted to laugh and tell Hudson to stop being silly, but that part of her was very small and . . . quiet. After all, they'd called a truce, he was rethinking running Break Up, and June *had* told her to relax. And maybe because of those things, a bigger part of her *wanted* him to buy her a rose.

The man took the money, stuck it into his pocket, and handed the rose to Annika. She took it with trembling fingers, the stem firm and cool under her skin.

"Wish you both a happy life!" The old man waved and

walked away with his basket, his eyes set on another couple across the lobby.

Annika turned to Hudson, swallowing. "Thank you. You didn't have to do that."

He grazed his fingers over the rose petals and Annika's body responded as if he'd touched her instead; her skin tingled like a hundred butterflies had fluttered their wings against her. *Ridiculous, hopeless idiot.* "I wanted to," he said.

Annika attempted to distract herself from her traitorous body by looking around them at the busy lobby. "So—where are we going? The hotel restaurant?"

Hudson cleared his throat and rubbed the back of his head. "Actually, uh—I took the liberty of getting us two tickets to the Napa wine train, if you'd like to go? It's the moonlight tour of the vineyards in the area; I heard it's supposed to be really good. Plus, it still counts as dinner. They serve a meal on the train."

She didn't laugh at his attempt at a joke. There was a heavy moment between them; his eyes looking for answers in hers. If she didn't want to, this was the time to say so. A moonlight tour on a train wasn't the casual dinner she'd been expecting. It would be perfectly fine to tell him she'd prefer to eat an avocado sandwich at the hotel restaurant. She took a breath, fiddling with the stem of the rose, preparing to say no.

"Um, sure. That sounds cool."

"Yeah?" He was still searching her face, wanting to be sure he wasn't forcing her into it.

Annika smiled a little, trying to invoke June's carefree spirit. "Yeah. Let's do it."

The wine train was a vintage locomotive sitting on the tracks in the last of the dusky sunlight like a big, eager caterpillar, ready to take them all on a wonderful journey.

Annika and Hudson were the first two to climb aboard. She looked around her with a fizzy sense of anticipation, distracted from EPIC and Hudson and everything else on her mind—for the moment, at least.

"This is *amazing*." They climbed the stairs into the dome car, which was 90 percent curved, clear roof and enormous windows. After taking a seat in a private booth, Annika carefully set her rose on the seat next to her. There was a small crackled-glass vase of flowers on the table, next to a flickering Moroccan-style lantern. Golden light filtered over everything, suspending them in a gilded soap bubble, a dream.

Annika's stomach flipped as Hudson took a seat across from her and folded his big hands on the table. He'd picked the moonlight tour instead of, say, a more casual restaurant—like Subway—for a reason. This wasn't the kind of dinner you had with a colleague at a conference, especially a colleague who might obliterate you in a competition two days away. Hudson clearly had a specific agenda in mind. The thought made her gulp.

"It's nice, isn't it?" He looked around. A few more couples were climbing aboard; all of them looked deeply in love.

"Really nice," Annika replied, her fingertips grazing the flowers in the vase. Her mind was elsewhere; she needed to tell him what she was thinking. It might ruin everything—it might totally kill the vibe—but she had to be honest. Looking back up at him, she said, "Hudson. I'm playing to win at EPIC."

He leaned back against the booth, his expression unbothered. More people walked in and drifted past them. "As am I."

"Only one of us can win," Annika pressed, as if he didn't already know that. "No matter how many train rides we go on, or how many roses you buy me. That changes nothing. I'm going to be ruthless."

He put his elbows on the table and smiled at her, the lantern light reflecting in his eyes. "This isn't a bribe, Dev. Besides, that's one of the things I like best about you."

She raised an eyebrow. "My ability to kick your ass?"

Hudson chuckled and ran a hand over the lantern, making shadows play across the table. "The fact that you're a worthy opponent. It wouldn't be fun otherwise."

"Right." Annika felt a little bubble of relief. He felt the same way as her about EPIC. As for what he'd said on her dad's deck about Break Up—they'd get to that, maybe after the pitch contest. Which meant . . . maybe, just maybe, she could sit back and enjoy the ride. Literally. She let herself smile as she looked around them. The last of the passengers were on, and the train doors had closed. "I have to say, this is the perfect way to relax before the big pitch Sunday."

Hudson held her eye, not returning her smile. "I don't want to talk about work anymore tonight."

Her blood began to hum. She didn't want to talk about work, either, she realized. Now that EPIC had been settled, she wanted . . . she wanted Hudson to lean into her, to murmur jokes in her ear, for them to sip each other's wines. She wanted *him.* "Okay," she said quietly.

"You're not fighting me so much anymore," he murmured, oblivious to all the chatter around them.

Annika shook her head, unable to look away. "No. I'm not. I think I might be done fighting."

Before Hudson could respond, their waiter came into the

aisle to introduce himself and tell them all about the tour and the two vineyards they'd pass. It was going to be a three-hour trip—three hours to sit with Hudson, to look into those unnerving green eyes. It was only mildly terrifying.

Annika settled back against her booth.

chapter eighteen

♡

"Here's a question I love," Annika said, waving her wineglass around.

They were about an hour into the trip and the sommelier kept coming around, pushing a "full-nosed" this and a "bouquet" of that. She'd accepted a couple of glasses of rosé and was deeply, deeply enjoying the wine. She'd been worrying for nothing—what she really needed to do was relax before her big day, just like June had said.

"If you had a magic wand and you could wave it to have the perfect life when you woke up in the morning, how would you know your life was perfect when you woke up? I heard it at this seminar I went to in college. It's supposed to help you create a concrete plan to get to your perfect life."

"Hmm." Hudson sipped thoughtfully at his merlot as the train rocked them gently. "Let's see. I guess, for one, I'd be completely happy. I wouldn't wake up and think, 'Here we go again.'"

Annika blinked. "That's what you think now?"

He nodded his head slowly. "Every day."

"Because of Break Up?"

"Because of what it means that I'm the public face of Break Up. I'm a little mired in the existentialism of it all. Plus, like I said before, I don't see myself doing this forever."

"Okay." Annika reached into her purse and pulled out her little notebook and pen. Her palms were actually damp. Holy shit. What she'd told June was a thousand percent true—Hudson was going to give up Break Up for good. Probably very soon.

Her fingers shaking slightly, she wrote "Hudson's Magic List" at the top of the page and added, "#1: No more public face of Break Up." Nodding at him seriously, she said, "Got it. What else?"

He looked at her, amused yet oblivious to the maelstrom inside her. "I guess . . . I'd have a full sculpting studio set up in my condo. So I wouldn't need to rent out space anytime I got the itch."

"Mm hmm." Annika jotted that down. "Studio for sculpting. Done. Anything else?"

When he was quiet, she looked up at him—and froze. He was studying her with an intensity that made her stomach flip. "I'd like to be in a relationship with someone I care about and respect. Someone who shows me new ways of being."

"Okay," Annika said, hyperaware that her voice was a little squeaky. With a trembling hand, she wrote "#3: Relationship, care, respect." What did he mean by that? Did he mean he wanted to be in a relationship with *her* specifically, or just in a relationship with *someone*? She wanted to ask him, but her mouth felt glued shut.

They gazed at each other across the flowers and the lambent lantern flame. Hudson's eyes shone a golden green in the fading dusk. "What about you? What would be on your list?"

A waiter came by with their second courses before Annika could respond. When he was gone, she took her time cutting a piece of her smoked eggplant and chewing it carefully. Then, looking up at Hudson, she said, "More than anything, I want Make Up to work out."

After a pause, during which they both ate their food and drank their wine in silence, listening to the hum and rumble of the train, Hudson said, "What else would be on your list? Just Make Up?"

There was a look in his eye, a shadow of the question he really wanted to ask. Annika's stomach fluttered.

"Well, I want my dad to be happy, of course," she said formally, buying time.

"Of course," Hudson said, just as formally, cutting his fish.

Annika took a gulp of her wine. Her palm was actually sweating around the glass. Yuck. "And . . . you know, I might want to start dating. A little bit. Maybe."

Hudson's face was casual as he nodded. "Hmm. Interesting."

"Isn't it?" Annika said, her heart hammering pitifully against her chest. "I mean, you want a relationship, I'm thinking about dating . . . it's definitely like we're moving along. On similar paths, one might say."

"One might," Hudson agreed, watching her.

The waiter cleared their plates. When he was gone, Hudson said, "I'm serious, you know. About being ready for a relationship." He leaned forward, his face unreadable, his hand mere centimeters away from hers on the table.

"S-so am I." She couldn't look away. "About dating."

Soon, the waiter began his trek down the aisle, depositing people's third courses as he went. Hudson held Annika's eyes. "I'm not that hungry anymore. I think I might go to the viewing deck for a bit." He paused, and Annika's pulse beat against her throat like a trapped hummingbird. "Will you join me?"

Join him. On the viewing deck. They'd be the only two there, because everyone else was enjoying their award-winning dinner. She swallowed. "Okay." Her voice was hoarse, barely more than a whisper.

Hudson dabbed his mouth with a napkin, set it on the table, and walked down the aisle, murmuring something to the waiter as he went. The waiter glanced at Annika—who felt her cheeks redden—and nodded with a knowing smile.

Relax, Annika, she told herself, patting her lips on her napkin and reapplying her lipstick quickly.

Taking a breath, she slid out of the booth and walked down the aisle to the viewing deck, doing her best to ignore the wild thrumming of her pulse.

⁓

Dusk was rapidly spooling into nighttime. The viewing deck was a small, secluded balcony-like setup on the far side of the train, just big enough for two people to squeeze in side by side. The car attached to it was empty and shrouded in almost complete darkness. Outside, a full moon had already risen, coating the vineyards with its silver light, purple shadows dancing in deep pools. Annika slotted in beside Hudson, who was watching the vistas pensively as they trundled on.

She glanced at him, her head swimming pleasantly from all the wine. "I like this train. I wonder if I could pay rent and just live on it."

He smiled, still looking straight ahead. "You could do yoga on the roof."

"Yeah, kind of like a *Polar Express* situation, but less creepy."

Hudson laughed and turned to her, the tips of his blond hair blowing in the wind. "You found *Polar Express* creepy?"

She turned so she was facing him, too. "Didn't you? The Tom Hanks character on the roof gave off major predator vibes."

Still chuckling, Hudson tucked a loose strand of her hair behind her ear, his warm hand caressing her skin. Without thinking about it, Annika leaned into it. "You have a very unique view on life," he said, his handsome face serious, no sign of his trademark smirk anywhere.

They reached for each other at the exact same time. Hudson's hands wound around her waist, hers around his neck. He pulled her against him with urgency, his desire burning in his eyes like green embers.

"Hudson," Annika murmured, sliding her hands down to his chest, feeling his incredible pecs through his shirt. Her legs felt like they were made of melting rubber, like they couldn't possibly hold up her weight much longer. She couldn't stop staring at his lips, at his strong jaw, at the hint of blond stubble. How he towered over her, how she felt completely safe in his arms. How he took up space with authority, as if standing here on the viewing deck was something that had become part of his life naturally, as most great experiences did.

"Annika," he said softly, her name like poetry on his lips.

"Do you know how long I've been waiting to hold you like this?"

"Really?" she whispered, looking up at him.

"Really," he said, his face solemn. "I can't stop thinking about you. I can't stop laughing at the things you say, even when you're not around. Ziggy and Blaire think I need help. Every morning when I wake up, I don't think about what I'm going to *do* at work—I think about who I'm going to *see*. Will you walk past? Will you stop in to talk to me? How can I organize a group lunch so you'll come? A party, so I can invite you? Every time I open my mouth, I want to tell a story about you. Believe me, this is not normal. Not for me."

"I can't stop thinking about you, either," Annika whispered, so close to his lips that the words were trapped between their breaths. "And . . . I don't want to stop thinking about you."

Then his mouth was on hers, his lips warm and firm, his teeth scraping her mouth, his tongue tasting her like she was the most decadent morsel he'd ever had. Annika sank into his kiss, her body molded so closely to his she could feel his erection, his desire, his absolute *want* for her. His hand slid up her bare thigh under her shorts, and cupped her ass. She moaned slightly as his fingers slipped forward, gently teasing her along the lace edge of her underwear.

"Hudson," Annika whispered again, as his fingers slipped farther in. "Not here—someone could walk out." But her body belied her words; she parted her legs slightly.

His mouth dipped down to her throat. "I want you so badly," he said, pushing the crotch of her panties aside, just the tip of his fingers entering her. "Right now. I've been thinking about this, about you, since last summer. Since Vegas."

Annika gasped and his other hand tightened around her

waist, steadying her. She could feel his mouth curving upward into a smile.

"If you really want me to stop, Ms. Dev, I will," he crooned, letting his fingers slide into her just a fraction more, leaving her gasping.

"No." Her eyes slipped shut. "Don't. I've been thinking about you, too." Annika didn't think she could stand anymore; her legs were now incapable of supporting her. She wanted him to lift her up, to set her against the wall, to have his way with her.

"I think it's down this way."

They flew apart as soon as they heard the voices trailing down the previously empty train car. Hudson's eyes were wild, feral, his pupils dilated with desire. His cheeks were flushed, and Annika knew she looked just as unkempt as he did. Patting down her hair, she turned to look out at the view, Hudson holding himself awkwardly, thanks to certain parts of his body that still hadn't calmed down. Their hands lay next to each other on the railing, and he gently edged his pinky onto hers. She smiled at him just as an older middle-aged couple rounded the corner.

"Oh!" A man wearing a plaid newsboy cap said. "I didn't realize there was someone else up here!" His wife smiled at them.

"It's okay," Annika said, with a questioning glance at Hudson. "I think we were done here?"

He nodded. "Yeah, we're done." Then, looking right at her, he said in a voice that was half-growl, half-command, "For now."

Annika swallowed and managed a smile as they brushed past the older couple and made their way back down the train car. Other people were finishing up their third course and moving on to their third. Their magic moment was over . . . for now.

⤸

How long could foreplay last? Annika didn't think she could Google it without Hudson seeing, but she was really curious. As the train neared the station, she got up twice and checked her makeup in the bathroom, reapplied a little perfume, and teased her hair at the roots so it had more volume. She didn't know if he noticed these things, but *she* noticed them. If she wanted to tap into her inner femme fatale, she needed to harness everything in her tool kit.

For his part, Hudson seemed to be trying to drive her crazy while maintaining an unbelievably cool composure himself. Once, his foot found hers under the table, and he drew his leg up against hers, the denim of his pants rough, so inviting against the smooth silk of her skin. Her breath caught in her throat as she looked across the table at him, but he glanced at her and then away, even as his leg continued to brush up against hers.

Another time, he reached across and fed her a grape, succulent and sweet, his fingers lingering in her mouth just a fraction too long, her tongue reaching out to dart across his skin—only to have him pull his hand back, leaving her panting, leaving her wanting.

Hudson had awakened something long-dormant inside her on that viewing deck. She wanted more from him. She wanted to see more of *this* Hudson, the one who was in courting mode, the one who wanted a relationship, the one who was pursuing her with a single-minded purpose that made her dizzy. She wanted his deft, sure fingers again; she wanted to taste him, and she wanted him to taste her. She wanted her mind blown, and she knew he was the one who could take her there.

For now, though, she had to sit rigidly in her seat as the train pulled into the station, hissing and groaning. The waiter came by to thank them all and wish them a good night, and everyone began to disembark. She and Hudson were the last to get off.

Annika felt her heart pounding in her chest, her palms dampening again as they walked together toward the shuttle, not saying anything, buoyed by the slight chill in the air and the muted chatter of the other passengers, all of whom looked more tired than she felt. Each one of her nerves was on high alert, her entire body thrumming with desire and wanton need. She glanced at Hudson, but his face was impassive, unreadable. What was he feeling? What was he thinking?

On the shuttle ride back, Hudson told her stories of vacationing in the Midwest as a kid, how he'd stayed at his family's cabin and read in the attic while his parents and brother had gone fishing, how they'd come back and he'd fallen asleep up there and they were all panicked, how he'd come downstairs just as they were mobilizing the neighbors into a search party. She laughed at all the appropriate parts, but her brain was hyperaware of each time his hand brushed hers or her knee, arguing with herself about whether it had been on purpose or accidentally-on-purpose or just an accident.

She could tell nothing from the way he spoke. She couldn't exactly ask him, either, because a gay couple across the aisle had heard him talking and chimed in with their own "summer in the Midwest" stories. Annika was forced to nod and smile and listen, while every cell within her sang in hope and anticipation. Her blood pulsed, her skin felt alive and alert—every body part consumed with desire. Her head felt foggy, *actually* foggy, like sexual attraction was the most potent opiate and she'd just slammed a concentrated vial of it.

Once the shuttle had deposited them back at the hotel foyer and the gay couple said their goodbyes and good nights, Annika and Hudson regarded each other in the glowing chandelier light, the harpist still playing her tinkling, inoffensive music in the background.

"So." Annika looked up at him. Her knees were getting weaker the longer they locked eyes. He was unsmiling, so serious, so very intent.

He nodded. "So."

She waited a beat, but nothing came. "So . . ." Feeling flustered, she scratched the back of her neck. "Um, I just, I didn't know—"

"Annika."

She looked back up at him.

"I'm going to my room."

"Right," she said finally, nodding briskly. "Good idea. We have an early start tomorrow, and I can't sleep in hotels, so . . . yeah. Good." *Ugh.* She sounded completely unconvincing and defensive. Blinking, she looked at the harpist playing her happy little song, entirely oblivious.

"Annika."

She forced herself to look at him again, rearranging her expression so it was not at all hurt, not at all vulnerable. When their eyes met, though, her mouth went dry at his intensity— the deep desire, the laser focus.

"I'm going up to my room, and I'd very much like it if you would join me." He took her hand.

Oh. *Oh.* Annika felt her hands begin to tremble. "I'd—I'd love to," she said, unable to breathe.

Smiling faintly, Hudson laced his confident fingers around hers, stilling them. They walked to the elevators together in silence, her hand practically singing at his touch.

chapter nineteen

His room was extravagant—twice as big as hers, and on the top floor, with a sweeping view of the vineyards and fields that were now bathed in ribbons of moonlight and shadow. The walls were wallpapered in textured white linen shot through with silver threads.

As her eyes swept over the gold sofa by the window, Annika suddenly remembered their time in Vegas, when they were draped over each other on the couch in her room.

Well, to be fair, *she'd* been the one to drape herself over Hudson.

> "*It's going to be about second chances,*" she told him, sitting so close their thighs were touching. She leaned over in a way she knew exposed her breasts in a very flattering way. "*Maybe bringing exes back together or something. Happily ever after, redux.*"
>
> "*Right.*" His eyes dropped to her cleavage, as she knew they would, but unlike most guys, he made a valiant and successful

effort to look back at her face. "That's a really good idea," he said, *sounding like he meant it.*

"And maybe it'll monitor their vitals to read their comfort level," Annika continued. "Maybe via their smartwatch." She *caressed his wrist lightly, her fingers moving to the underside of his arm, finding his pulse.* "It would read an elevated heart rate. Things like that."

Hudson looked at her, his eyes drifting to her lips. "Really? What's my heart rate like right now?"

She smiled and moved in closer. "Pretty high, Mr. Craft. I think you're in dire straits."

His hand found the edge of her pencil skirt and began sliding up her thigh. "Mm," he said, *placing his lips over hers.* "I think you might be right."

Hudson walked closer, bringing her back to the present, her cheeks warm from the memory. After he flicked on the gas fireplace, he turned back to her. Other than the small lamp on the desk and the flickering firelight, the room was dark.

Annika hovered by the bathroom, feeling nervous and fluttery, like she was a high school student about to have sex for the first time—which was so far from the truth, she would've laughed if she didn't feel like gulping down twelve gallons of water for her parched throat and running away.

Hudson approached her, his eyes determined. He was lithe, confident, not a trace of uncertainty about him. He ran his fingertips feather-light down her arms, then laced his fingers with hers. "Hi."

She had goose bumps all over her skin. "H-hi."

"You sound nervous." He said this in an assessing way, without judgment or amusement.

"I kind of am," Annika laughed. "Which is ridiculous, I know. We already hooked up in Vegas, but—"

"But this feels different," he said, his face softening.

Annika nodded.

Suddenly, he was smiling the most deliciously devilish smile she'd ever seen. "A bath would relax you."

"A—a bath?"

Taking her by the hand, Hudson led her into the giant bathroom. In dead center was an enormous polished granite tub. Coming up from behind her, he pushed her hair to one side and kissed the nape of her neck. Annika closed her eyes.

"I could draw you a bath," he whispered against her skin, his hot breath tickling her. "How does that sound?"

"Yes. Okay. Good." She was incapable of speaking any more syllables. Already, her shirt and shorts felt like too much clothing, too much restriction.

"Good." She could hear the smile in his voice. Straightening, he walked around her and began to fill the tub, dumping in a generous helping of the freesia-scented bubble bath that sat in a little wicker basket next to the washcloths.

Then he walked to the phone mounted to the wall, grabbed the handset, and pushed a button. "A bottle of your best champagne," he said, looking right at her. Her stomach flipped.

"Why the champagne?"

He hung up. "We're celebrating."

"Celebrating what?" Her voice got hoarser the closer he came. He was like a proud lion in the jungle, king of all he saw. Including her.

Gently, using just his fingertips, he slipped the straps of her camisole down her shoulders. "You. Us. Here, together."

Feeling a burst of confidence at his words, Annika pulled

her camisole over her head and slipped out of her shorts. She could see his breathing pick up as he looked at her in her black bra and lace underwear. Then, reaching behind her, Annika unhooked her bra and let it fall to the floor, relishing the cool air against her breasts, making her nipples erect. His reaction was immediate; his pupils dilated; his breathing got harsher. Next she slid out of her underwear, already feeling how wet and ready she was, and without meeting his eye, she climbed into the bathtub.

Hudson swallowed visibly; it helped her to see *him* discombobulated for a change. A rush of exhilaration overtook her as the hot, foamy water slipped over her bare skin, making her sigh. She looked up at him. "Now what?" she asked softly.

He turned off the faucet and sat on the wide edge of the tub. It was maddening in the best way, being completely naked while he was fully clothed. "Now I'll wash you," he said, his voice husky.

She held his gaze for a long moment and then nodded, her body melting into the water.

As Hudson retrieved a washcloth and soaked it, Annika lay back and closed her eyes. A moment later, she felt the texture of the warm fabric traveling down her arms, first one, then the other. He wiped her face gently, starting at her forehead, then traveling slowly over the bridge of her nose, caressing her mouth and chin. The washcloth traveled lower still, down the arch of her throat to her shoulders. Her pulse hammered wildly.

The washcloth slipped down to her chest, and then, slowly, almost reverently, over her right nipple. Annika couldn't help it—a soft moan left her mouth before she'd even known it was coming.

She heard Hudson suck in a breath and opened her eyes.

"You're fucking beautiful," he growled abruptly, as if holding back some great emotion.

Annika's eyes slipped shut again as the washcloth traveled lower, into the water, along her diaphragm and across her stomach. She parted her legs in the water, aching to feel the fabric between them.

Hudson swiped the inside of her right thigh, then her left, each motion of his wrist making her pant, making her writhe with absolute desire. Even now, even as she struggled to keep her composure, he was in control, his movements never hesitant, his face a mask of calm as his eyes blazed a trail of fire over her skin.

"Hudson—" she found herself saying, his name a sizzle on her lips.

"What?" he breathed huskily, dipping his head down to hers, nipping at her lips. "Tell me what you want."

Annika put a hand on his strong wrist in the water. "I want you to touch me," she whispered against his lips.

His hand moved with aching slowness, the washcloth shivering over her inner thigh and then slipping between her legs, swiping with just the right amount of pressure, both soft and rough, over her sex. Annika gasped, throwing her head back as Hudson worked the washcloth over her. He kissed the arch of her throat, moving upward until her earlobe was between his teeth.

"Give yourself to me," he whispered, his voice commanding but fraught with desire.

She did; she had no other choice. As one hand rubbed her with the washcloth, the other cupped her breast, the ball of his thumb roving her nipple. Annika's hips moved in rhythm, her body quivering on the edge, almost flying over—and then he removed his hands completely. Panting, she opened her eyes and looked at him, dazed, frustrated.

He was flushed, his eyes almost black with desire, but he was sitting up and away from her. "Not yet," he said, tracing his finger over her lower lip, his eyes on her mouth, her throat, her breasts. "I have plans for you, Ms. Dev."

"But—" Annika couldn't formulate a response. Her mind was spinning, her body crying out for his hands. "I—"

He grinned, a lopsided, mischievous thing that made her want to rip his clothes off. "Good things come to those who wait."

There was a knock on the door. "Room service!"

"I'll be right back." Hudson draped the washcloth over the edge of the tub and strode toward the hall, closing the bathroom door behind him.

Annika sat up straighter, her body buzzing, every nerve ending eager for more of his careful, tantalizing attention. What kind of lover *was* Hudson Craft? When they'd been together in Vegas, he'd been . . . talented, of course, but she hadn't seen this part of him. She hadn't yet been *seduced* by him.

A thrill went through her as she heard the front door close. A moment later, Hudson walked in with a bottle of Dom Pérignon and two champagne flutes on a silver tray. He smiled at her and set the tray on the counter, popping the cork and pouring two glasses in silence. Annika could hear the drinks fizzing, the bubbles popping against the sides of the flutes.

Hudson brought her a glass and she took it, gulping down a deep swallow. "Mm." She let her eyes drift closed for a moment. "That's good." Setting the flute on the edge of the bathtub, she leaned back, watching as Hudson sipped his champagne and walked back to sit by her.

"Now," he said, a glint in his eye. "Where were we?"

"You were washing me," Annika said, the wantonness in her voice both surprising her and not.

The glint in his eyes graduated to a veritable spark of lust. "That's right." Then, smiling that devilish smile again, he said, "But you know what? I think it's time to take a break and wash your hair now."

Annika wanted to groan in disappointment and frustration. She was ready. She was *so* ready. "What about *your* clothes?" she asked petulantly, splashing the water. "Why am I the only one naked?"

Hudson leaned forward in response. Annika felt her breath hitch as he came closer. She could smell the faint fragrance of his aftershave, combined with a very Hudson scent—masculine and strong. She felt her breathing get shaky as he got closer still, his eyes burning into hers. And then he dipped his head and laid the softest trail of kisses from the spot behind her ear to the hollow of her neck. Annika heard a moan, and realized it was coming from her throat.

"Patience," Hudson whispered again, against her skin.

"I don't know how much longer I can be patient," Annika managed to say. Hudson pulled back and chuckled.

He grabbed the shampoo and Annika slid forward so she had enough room to tip her head back. The idea of Hudson shampooing her felt . . . strangely erotic, though she wasn't sure why. It was just shampoo. It was just hair.

"Tilt your head back," he said, gently moving her chin with his fingers. She did as she was asked, her eyes fluttering closed. The warm water from the shower head flowed over her, and she felt herself relaxing amid the lavender fragrance of the shampoo.

Then his fingertips were in her hair, massaging it into her

scalp. He used just the right amount of pressure; never had a hairdresser come close to getting it so right. His fingertips moved from the crown of her head to its curve to the nape of her neck and back up again. He massaged behind her ears, and with every point of pressure on her scalp, Annika felt the stress and tension in her shoulders dissipate. A slight headache she hadn't even realized she'd had began to disappear.

"You're smiling," Hudson noted, and though her eyes were closed, Annika could hear the answering smile in his voice.

"That feels incredible," Annika said, and then she felt his finger trailing down the column of her throat. Her heart began trip-hammering.

He stopped at her chest, right over her heart. "Good," he said, his voice deep, authoritative. "Isn't it so much more fun when you're nice to me?" He used the showerhead to rinse out her hair thoroughly, his fingers handling each lock with gentle care, the hot rivulets of water like strips of silk against her sensitive skin.

When he was done, Annika opened her eyes. Without looking at her, Hudson got her a towel and brought it over, all business. She stood and wrapped it around herself. Her wet hair dripped onto her shoulders and upper back, soaking into the towel.

She climbed out of the tub and stood there, looking at him. He watched her with the same intensity she'd seen before, focused, alert, but with just the slightest hint of hesitation, like he was holding himself back from what he really wanted to do.

What does he really want to do? The thought made Annika's knees nearly buckle. She was done with this. She was done with being the only one naked, with him toying with her, with this gradual inching forward toward what they both wanted.

Annika took a breath, and then let the towel fall. She stood completely naked in front of him again. Her knees would knock together if she weren't holding herself so rigidly. "Your turn," she said, making it a command.

His eyes roved her body for a full five seconds, dark and hooded, his breathing getting harsher and faster. It was obvious he was hard; he wanted her. He wanted her just as badly as she wanted him. "Are you sure?" he asked, teasing her even now, in this moment, when they were both almost mad with lust. "Any second thoughts about sleeping with the enemy?"

"As long as the truce is still on," Annika joked, though her voice came out breathy and trembling.

Hudson unbuttoned his shirt slowly, one button at a time, until she could see his pecs and abs. They were as perfect as she remembered; it was like he was sculpted from stone. He shrugged off his shirt, let it fall to the floor, and then reached for his belt.

When he kicked his pants and boxers to the floor, Annika couldn't help staring. He was . . . flawless. Every muscle was gorgeous—streamlined and powerful. In the dim ambient lighting of the bathroom, his skin seemed to glow. "How is that, Ms. Dev? Am I to your satisfaction?" His eyes studied her reaction.

Annika walked forward, into his arms, running her hands over the planes and contours of his body, feeling the toned hardness of his muscles. A groan left his lips at her touch, first feather-light and then more intense, more desiring, greedy.

"I think you'll do, Mr. Craft."

When she reached between them to feel his hardness in her hands, he brought his mouth to hers in a devouring, all-consuming kiss.

There had never been a kiss like this. Never before had she been held this way, with passion and gentleness and roughness and caressing, with heat and fire and confidence. When his hand reached between them to slip between her legs and finish what he'd started, Annika closed her eyes, letting her head fall back.

He kissed her throat as his fingers found her most sensitive spot. She moaned, her back arching as his fingers slipped and slid, working in circles, his voice coaxing her, bringing her to the balls of her feet, to the apex. "Oh god, Hudson," she panted, her fingers digging into his strong shoulders. "I want you inside me."

He grabbed her by the hips and picked her up. "Say it again," he commanded, his voice low and husky, his eyes feverish with need.

Annika didn't hesitate. "I want you. *Now*." She wrapped her legs around his waist and pulled him close, feeling his erection pressing against her, steel-hard.

He propped her against the wall, his mouth devouring hers before pulling back to murmur, "Do you know how long I've wanted to do this? Do you know how crazy you've been driving me, pushing me away and drawing me close?" He ran a hand through her hair, pulling her head back with just the right amount of force so he could nip at her throat.

"I thought about you even when I didn't want to think about you," Annika gasped, feeling the slick wetness at her core, wanting him inside her even as he stayed right on the edge, teasing. "You're in my head all the time, messing with my sleep, my thoughts, my plans. Do you know how *infuriating* that is?"

Smiling that lopsided, wicked smile, he plunged inside her, filling her up in a way she'd never been filled. Her moans echoing in the enormous bathroom, Annika let herself get lost in a fog of pure ecstasy, her eyes closing.

They worked together in rhythm, his big hands cupping her breasts, tweaking and pulling her nipples, sending electric currents of desire and heat pulsing through her. She gasped his name, again and again and again, the frenzied need of the moment overtaking all her senses until his voice was all she could hear, his scent was all she could smell, and his lips were all she could taste. Their climaxes built together, until, at last, Hudson was calling out Annika's name and she was clutching him, holding on as if he were her last hope.

≈

Morning came in drifts and shakes, like confetti raining down from a brilliant blue sky. Annika's eyes fluttered open. She was lying on her side, naked underneath an enormous white comforter, facing the window. The AC hummed lightly. They'd only drawn the gauzy curtain last night, not the blackout, so sunlight filtered in and warmed her face. She felt an arm around her waist, a big, warm body curled around hers, a chin resting lightly on the crown of her head. *Hudson.* She was still in Hudson's room.

Annika smiled as memories from last night flickered across her mind: how he'd carried her to the bedroom, how he'd held her hands above her head once they were in bed, his face smiling above her own, her breath catching in her throat as he moved lower and lower down her body. How skilled he was with his tongue, and how generous, the way she'd arched her back, grabbing his hair, shaking as she came. The way he'd grabbed her waist when she was on top and clearly tried not to squeeze too hard as his pleasure peaked. The way they'd stared into each other's eyes, drinking each other in. The way she'd felt so close to him—so protected, so completely safe and *right*.

She turned over under his arm and kissed the tip of his nose. "Good morning."

Hudson's eyes opened, and a slow, sexy smile spread across his face. "Good morning indeed." Then he kissed her, slow and languorous and warm, his hands slipping down to caress her ass. "Mm," he murmured against her mouth.

Annika laughed. "Didn't you get enough last night? I feel like I burned off all the dinner and alcohol from the train."

He gazed at her frankly. "I don't think I'll ever get enough of you."

Annika felt her cheeks heat up and she snuggled under his chin, against his warm chest. "That's . . . a pretty incredible one-eighty from the first time I saw you in my building."

He chuckled. "I don't know. I was pretty smitten with you from the beginning, Annika. I think you were the one who hated me. Remember the Nerf dart?"

She pulled back and gave him an outraged look. "I was mad! You couldn't stop teasing me—not to mention one-upping me and sabotaging me at every turn."

He rubbed a thumb over her lower lip. "Sabotaging you was just a way to pull you closer. I wasn't sure you felt the same about me as I did about you. Until you kissed me drunkenly at the fountain." He laughed.

All out of arguments, Annika stuck her tongue out at him.

He nipped at it with his teeth and then they were kissing, slow and deep and languid.

When they pulled apart, he cradled her face in his hands, searching her face, as if weighing something in his mind.

Annika smiled. "What?"

Hudson pulled back and got out of bed, leaving her cold as he padded out into the living room. "I have something for you."

"Okay, but you should come back quickly before I turn into an icicle." She snuggled farther into the blankets. "Although I *do* like to watch you walk away . . ."

His laughter drifted to her, making her smile. He returned just a moment later, sliding under the covers, his back propped up against the leather headboard. In his hands he held a big wad of pale pink tissue paper, the kind used in gift bags.

"What's that?" She sat up, too. The covers pooled around her waist, exposing her breasts, but she didn't care. After last night, she didn't feel even slightly self-conscious around Hudson. Some invisible barrier had broken between them, once and for all.

"It's . . . something I made for you." Hudson turned the package over in his hands, his eyes thoughtful. "Well, actually, it's something that was *inspired* by you. I just finished it, and now . . . I want you to have it." He handed it to her gently, his quietness a testament to the fact that he was giving her something important, that he was being vulnerable.

Annika took the package carefully and unwrapped the layers of tissue slowly. She gasped softly when her eyes fell on a sculpture, the curves and lines coalescing into one unified image. "I love it," she whispered, tracing her finger over the figurine, which was about the size of her palm. "Is this . . . me?"

It was a woman yogi in *vrksasana*, or tree pose. Her left leg was lifted, with her left foot balanced on the inside of her right thigh. Her arms were tall above her head, and she had a small heart cupped between her palms. Hudson had glazed the entire ceramic sculpture an opalescent white, and it caught the light in iridescent twinkles as Annika turned it this way and that.

"It is," he answered, touching the heart between the figurine's palms. "I wanted to capture you as I see you: graceful, peaceful, planting love everywhere you go."

Annika blinked back tears. No one had ever said—or done—anything like this for her. "It must've taken you forever to do," she said, choked up. "Are you sure you want to give it to me?"

Hudson put a hand over hers. "I'm sure." He smiled. "I began making it that day after our first yoga class—you know, with the partner poses?"

Annika stared at him. "But that was so long ago."

He grinned and planted a soft, sweet kiss on her lips. "I told you. I've been smitten for a long, long time. I'm just glad you've come around. I've had to work my ass off."

Annika laughed and set the sculpture carefully on the nightstand beside her. Turning back to Hudson, she said, "Do you want to know what was holding me back? And what changed?"

He nodded, smiling still.

She took his big hands in hers and looked into his eyes. "Every time we talked, I got the sense that there was so much more to you than the papers said—so much more than a millionaire playboy who didn't care that he'd made his money off the pain and tears of so many people." Annika smiled. "As soon as you let slip that you were going to resign from Break Up, I knew—"

Hudson frowned. "Resign from Break Up? I never said that."

Annika chuckled uncertainly. "Um . . . yeah, you did. Several times."

Hudson's frown deepened; a muscle ticked in his jaw. "Like when?"

Annika slowly took her hands away from his and sat up

straighter, pulling the covers back up over her breasts. Why was he acting like this was all news to him? "Like on the night we had dinner at my dad's? You said you were sick of it all, that you didn't want to be the face of Break Up forever. And you said the same thing on the train last night."

"Right . . ." Hudson said slowly. "I meant that I might step aside and take up a secondary role in the company. Maybe let Ziggy take over as CEO."

Annika waited for his smirk, for him to tell her he was joking, that he was teasing again. But it didn't come. "Are you serious?" she said, unable to stop her volume from rising. "What about guys like Hedge Fund Harry? What about the fact that this isn't how you pictured your life or that you're not even happy when you wake up every day, Hudson?"

"I don't know!" he said, pushing his hands through his hair and leaving it messy. "I didn't say all those things so you could pressure me into doing what *you* think is right!"

"I'm not pressuring you!" Annika shouted. "I'm just repeating back all the things you've said to me. And now you're telling me you want to *stay on* at Break Up? That's just not going to work for me!"

Hudson stared at her. "What are you saying?"

"I'm saying I can't be with someone who's willing to run a company like that—who's willing to do that to other people, to do that to themselves!"

Hudson snapped the covers back and got out of bed. As he slid into his pants, he said, "And I can't be with someone who wants to change me and can't understand why I have to do what I do."

"You *don't* have to do it! Why can't you see that?" Annika flung the covers back and leapt out of bed, throwing on her camisole from the night before. As she thrust her arms into it, her hand hit the sculpture on the nightstand, knocking it to the floor.

She gasped, reaching to catch it before it hit the tiled floor, but her fingers were a millisecond too late.

The sculpture smashed into pieces, the heart broken in half. Annika stood staring at it, her hand over her mouth. "I'm—I'm sorry," she said, her voice just a whisper in the sudden quiet. "Hudson, I didn't mean to—"

But he was already turning away from her, his face a mask of pain and regret. He grabbed a shirt, walked out of the room, and a moment later, Annika heard the front door thunder shut behind him.

In the cold, empty room, she knelt before the pieces of the sculpture and picked them up gingerly. Then she dressed, not looking at herself in the mirror, and slipped away.

chapter twenty

Annika would always remember what she'd been doing when she got the phone call.

She was in one of the many hotel gardens, watching brightly colored birds peck at the ground, searching for seeds. Her mind was numb, her fight with Hudson an analgesic rubbed over everything. It had been four and a half hours since she'd last seen him, since she'd cried until she was al-most sick, since she'd scrubbed herself clean in the shower and vowed not to cry another tear today. The EPIC pitch was tomorrow, and she knew she should feel a rush of adrenaline, of excitement. She'd try to muster that then. Today was just for feeling nothing.

Her phone beeped with a text. It was June.

Hey! We landed about an hour ago. Your dad and I split up to go get our rentals. I got mine and I'm headed to the hotel.

K thanks, Annika typed. She should be hearing from him

soon, then. They'd probably do dinner tonight; Annika wondered if she'd have the energy for that.

How's H??? 😁

Annika closed her eyes for a moment. Talk later. She put her phone away and didn't respond to the ???? June sent her in response. She just didn't have the energy.

She wasn't sure how much longer she sat there, watching the birds peck around her with their sun-dappled feathers. She sat so still, they crept closer, keeping a watchful eye on her. Her mind was curiously blank. She wasn't thinking of much at all—wasn't feeling much of anything.

And then her phone rang with an unknown number, as if the universe was saying, "*I'm going to* make *you feel something.*"

Annika answered, worried that it might have something to do with the EPIC pitch. "Hello? This is Annika Dev."

"Ms. Dev, this is Dr. Gregory. I'm the attending physician at the ER at Queen of the Valley Medical Center in Napa." Annika's heart began to race. Her mouth suddenly tasted metallic. "I have your father Raj Dev here. He's been in a bad car accident."

Annika clutched the phone to her ear, her hands frozen. "Is he—is he alive?" her voice broke on the word "alive."

"Yes." A relieved breath *whoosh*ed out of her. "But I'm afraid he hasn't regained consciousness. He has significant swelling in his brain, multiple contusions, and a spleen bleed. It's too soon to say how things are going to turn out from here."

Annika's entire body began to shake. A sob escaped her lips, loud and abrupt, and the birds who'd gathered enough courage to peck near her feet flew away in a coordinated wave. "I—I need to see him. I'm going to be there as soon as I can. I shouldn't be more than an hour at the most."

"I'd suggest you have someone drive you, Ms. Dev," the doctor said kindly. "We'll see you soon."

She ended the call and ran toward the hotel entrance, dialing June as she went.

❧

She shook the whole time she was waiting for Dr. Gregory to come out and talk to her. June was rocking her in her arms, but Annika couldn't stop shaking. She was cold, colder than she'd ever been in her life. She was afraid her heart was turning to ice.

"It's going to be okay," June kept saying, her voice thick with tears. Her ponytail was rumpled, her eyes red and puffy. Had Annika been crying, too? She honestly couldn't remember. "Your daddy's going to be fine."

But June didn't know that. No one did.

Finally, Dr. Gregory came out to speak with Annika. He was a gray-haired man in his fifties, tall, with a big belly and kind blue eyes. A stethoscope hung around his neck, a clipboard in his hands. "Ms. Dev?"

She stood; her knees buckled, but she managed to stay upright. June stood beside her, a hand on Annika's elbow. "Yes. How's my father? Can I see him?"

Dr. Gregory looked at her sympathetically. "Yes. He's stable now, but he's unconscious, as I said on the phone. He won't be able to respond to your presence."

Annika couldn't see the doctor through her tears. "I don't care," she whispered.

"And—" The doctor looked away before looking back at her. "He looks rough. He took quite a beating in the crash. From what I understand, he was T-boned by a drunk driver in a truck much bigger than what your father was driving." He looked at June, as if to impress on her the impact of what he was saying. June nodded; Annika didn't. She had only one thought: She wanted to see her dad.

Finally, the doctor led them down the hall to her dad's room. "He'll be moved to the ICU soon," the doctor said. Then, nodding at the two of them, he slipped out of the room and shut the door.

Annika stood in the doorway, staring at her dad for a full twenty seconds, not moving, not saying a word. She heard June's soft gasp from beside her, but she didn't react. Couldn't react.

Her father lay in the clean, white hospital bed, a number of tubes protruding from him, a nest of monitors beeping and glowing like angels guarding his unconscious form. His head had been shaved and a shunt placed through his skull, the skin around it a discolored purple and black. His entire face, Annika noticed, was discolored: Great patches of purple and blue bruises covered his cheekbones, his jawline, his nose. Elsewhere, he was covered in stitches and bandages where the doctors had attempted to piece him back together again, to make him whole, to delay his leaving.

His leaving.

A sob crawled up her throat. Annika walked to his side on shaking legs, her body once again trembling, as if it couldn't hold this excess of emotion. June followed silently, a pale ghost behind her friend.

Annika took her father's hand, one of the only visible parts of him that wasn't damaged—and even then, it had an IV sticking out of it, denying her the veil of normalcy. There was nothing normal about any of this. "Daddy," she whispered, even though she knew he wouldn't wake up. She'd been warned that he couldn't even hear her. "Daddy, I'm here. Pluto." The tears were steady streams now, spilling from her eyes and running down her cheeks, drip-dropping on her lavender top, staining it dark purple.

She heard June sniffling behind her, and then her fingers were threading through Annika's free hand. They stood like that, standing vigil, until the light outside the window turned blue, then deep purple, then inky black. The color of her father's bruises.

⌘

Later, they sat in the hospital cafeteria, Annika staring into her now-cold cup of black coffee. It was close to one in the morning, several hours since they'd arrived at the hospital. The fluorescent lights seared into her retinae, making her eyes burn. Her head was buzzing. She could feel the electric current running through her skull. "He's a doctor," she said quietly. June took her hand from across the table, where she was nursing her own bad hospital coffee. "He's supposed to take care of other people. It shouldn't be happening this way."

"No, it shouldn't." June squeezed her hand firmly. "This is nine kinds of fucked-up."

Annika nodded, staring at the Formica table, seeing patterns in it that were likely not there. God, she was tired. And she would never sleep again. "What if his brain's not okay? What if he doesn't wake up? Or what if he does, but he's not himself anymore? What if he doesn't recognize me?" She raised the coffee to her lips, her hand trembling so much, the coffee sloshed over the side and onto her shirt. So she'd smell like coffee and tears for the rest of the night. It seemed fitting.

"You can't think like that, sugar," June said, leaning forward to catch her eye. "You've got to keep positive. That's what the nurse said, remember? They're taking really good care of him."

"Right. Yeah. Sure." She was just saying what she thought June wanted to hear. She had no idea if he would be okay, or if anything would be okay ever again.

Her phone beeped. When she flipped it over to check the screen, it was a calendar reminder: EPIC pitch!! Woo hoo!! starts in 8 hours on Sunday, June 13th. Annika stared at the reminder blankly. She'd set it to alert her in the middle of the night so she could see it first thing upon waking. She'd meant to wake up at five, with several hours to practice and refine her pitch.

For just a moment, her heart had surged with a desperate hope that the notification was a text from Hudson, that he was reaching out to say he was sorry and that he was coming. For just a moment, she felt a fierce burning to be held in his strong arms, to be comforted the way only he could comfort her, to be spoken to in the way his heart could speak to hers. But of course it wasn't him, because Hudson, too, was gone. He wasn't who she'd thought he was. It had all just been one big illusion, a magic trick her heart had been desperate to believe.

June cleared her throat and tapped Annika's phone screen. "Don't you worry about that. I'll withdraw us. I already told Ziggy we were probably going to do that, and he said it's an easy process. You just have to tell the—"

"I don't want to withdraw." Annika frowned at June. It was hard to get the words out; they stuck in her throat like tar. "I have to do the pitch. There's no other way to save Make Up."

June's face crumpled, pale and sallow under the harsh hospital lights. There were red half-moons under her eyes, as if she'd rubbed the skin there raw. Annika wondered what she looked like. She hadn't even looked in a mirror when she'd used the bathroom, she'd been so desperate to be with her father every minute she could. Even sitting here drinking a coffee for ten minutes felt wrong. "Sweetie, no one expects you to do it. Not now. Not with your Daddy . . . the way he is."

"June." She looked at her best friend for a long moment, her brain addled. "June . . . he's half the reason I *created* Make Up. Him and my mom." Her voice wobbled on the word "mom," but she kept going, refusing to think that she might potentially lose both her parents. "If I don't do this pitch, I'll lose it. I can't lose so much all at the same time. I just can't." Tears slipped down her cheeks. She hadn't realized she was crying. When had she started? Had she ever stopped?

June's eyes filled with tears in response, her nose getting red. "Okay. Okay, babe. Then I'll do the pitch. Okay? Let me do it. I've heard you practice it; I can probably pull it off."

Annika shook her head. "No. That won't work. I'm the one who knows it best. You haven't practiced it once, and I'm the CEO. I'm the one who's practiced it until I could recite it in my sleep, who has the passion for the business. That's what they're going to look for. They want to see that deep, personal connection. I have that, not you." She took a sip of her coffee, exhausted by all the words she'd just spoken. Taking a deep breath, she added, "I'll do it. I can do it. You can help me by staying here and looking after my dad."

There was a long pause, during which June came around the table and pressed Annika to her. "Okay," she whispered, kissing the side of Annika's head. "You can do it. And I'll support the hell out of you, however you want."

Annika nodded and they sat there, hugging, crying, and holding vigil, through the night.

Dressed in a crisp black pantsuit and pearls back in her hotel room, Annika put everything out of her mind. She'd reluctantly left the hospital two hours ago, once her dad had been transferred to the ICU. June, the doctors, and nurses repeatedly reassured her that they would let her know the instant her father's condition changed. Still, she'd placed a tender kiss on his broken cheek, promised him she'd be back as soon as possible, and made June vow not to leave his side except for biologically necessary functions.

Now it was time for the pitch. She took one look around the cool, silent hotel room, bathed in blue morning light, made sure she had everything she needed—laptop, briefcase, check—and let the door lock behind her as she strode down the hallway to the elevators, her pumps whispering along the carpet. Her mind kept returning to thoughts she didn't want: her father, Hudson. Hudson, her father. Her father, her father. She kept redirecting herself to the pitch. Everything else out. Pitch in. That was all she could handle right now.

Annika stepped into the elevator and checked herself in the mirror. The blood vessels in her eyes were a bright crimson, standing out in stark relief against the whites. In spite of her heavy hand with concealer, there were purple shadows under her eyes, but that couldn't be helped. She took a breath and faced forward, checking her phone for a message from June or the hospital. Or Hudson. Nothing.

Since it was such a small pool of contestants, they'd all been given an individual time slot and strict instructions not to arrive early. This was apparently to keep them from seeing or intimidating each other. It had seemed a silly rule when Annika had first learned of it, but she was immensely thankful for it now. She couldn't handle seeing Hudson again, not so soon after they'd broken up, not when her father lay in a hospital bed, not before the pitch.

Annika emerged from the elevators and walked across the hotel foyer down a carpeted hallway to wait in a small room that was outfitted with frond-y potted palms and small leather armchairs just outside of conference room A. She wondered whether Hudson was in there right now, just a few dozen yards away from her, and pushed the thought out of her mind again. She couldn't think of him, not while her heart felt so pulverized and raw. But sitting here, in the quiet, wasn't good for her, either. Her mind kept turning to things she wanted to keep locked away.

Luckily, she only waited two more minutes until a diminutive man in a mint-green suit and purple glasses stepped out of the conference room and called her name.

She entered through the open conference room door, her head held high and her shoulders back, looking—she hoped— more energetic and confident than she felt. There was a small headache starting behind her eyes, but there was nothing to be done about that now.

This was it. This was her chance to save Make Up. She couldn't afford to fuck it up.

෴

Conference room A was large and corporate looking, like any conference room in any big hotel in any city anywhere in the world. The windows were hung with garish gold drapes, and fake potted plants decorated the room's corners. A projector screen hung on one end of the room, next to a wooden podium. The panel of angel investors, seated behind a large burgundy-tablecloth-covered table on the opposite side, was all male—three of whom were white and one Latino. Lionel Wakefield sat in the center. He was a sixty-something-year-old white man, with a head full of woolly hair the color of snow, a mustache that was still mostly salt-and-pepper, and a known propensity for brightly colored ascots. Today, he was wearing a canary-colored striped number, at which Annika had a hard time not staring.

"Thank you, gentlemen, for taking the time to let me pitch you today. Mr. Wakefield, I've been a huge fan of your many philanthropic ventures for a long time now." Annika forced herself to smile brightly and walked to the podium to set up her PowerPoint. It was cold in conference room A, as if to keep the contestants from sweating themselves into messy puddles.

No one said anything, but Lionel Wakefield nodded solemnly from behind the table. She'd been hoping for friendlier, but that was okay. She wasn't feeling too bubbly herself right now. Maybe they'd be less apt to notice.

Tucking a lock of hair behind her ear, Annika pulled up the first slide, which simply stated the name of the business and their slogan. "My name is Annika Dev, and I'm the founder and CEO of Make Up. Our motto is *Happily Ever After, Redux* because that's what we believe in—second chances at true love." She forwarded to the next slide, which was a picture of June and her in the Make Up office, in the middle of a discussion. "We are a woman-owned business that wants to do good in the world. We're not about short, snappy solutions to problems. We want people to make meaningful, long-term connections. We want them to see that how they've been living—pining away for a relationship that doesn't work anymore, sleeping in separate beds because they're just so tired of fighting—doesn't have to be the end of the story. We want them to see that happily ever after is within their reach.

"Let me introduce you to OLLI—the Original Love Language Interface. OLLI is the cutting-edge AI we're training with the use of deep-learning techniques over an artificial neural network." She forwarded the slide to show a ten-second video of the app and OLLI in action, narrating what they were seeing while the video played while wishing she could fast-forward through it all. "Users interact with OLLI to teach it about themselves—their communication patterns, the cadence and pitch of their voices—and once OLLI learns all of this information, it can communicate to the user, via the app, when they need to rephrase what they're saying, how to steer the conversation back on track, etcetera."

Dammit. There was supposed to be a joke there that she'd completely glossed over. She couldn't even remember what it was now, to weave it in later. *Oh well. Keep moving, Annika. Just deliver the pitch and get back to the hospital.* She took a breath. "There's also a component that hooks up to the user's smartwatch and monitors their biometric data to look for spikes of anger or anxiety. But as intimidating as that might sound, as you can see, my developer and I have worked hard to ensure that the experience is both user-friendly and user-engaging. We're working to increase the app's scalability, which will allow users to train OLLI from the comfort of their own homes . . ." She advanced through the rest of the slides, keeping an eye on each of the four men.

They had to be the most stoic men in the history of stoic men. The first one, David Smith, may as well have been asleep or dead. He even sneezed without changing expression.

The second guy, Jim Hernandez, had his eyebrows raised the entire time, which Annika at first took to mean he was interested or surprised by what she was saying. It turned out his eyebrows were always like that.

The third guy, Lewis Stenton, took a lot of notes—a copious, frenetic amount. He barely looked up from his notebook, in fact. Annika wondered if he was writing a book. *What a Pitch: Hilarious Tales from a Not-So-Angelic Angel Investor.*

Lionel Wakefield seemed the most sympathetic. He made eye contact and even smiled at Annika encouragingly when she stopped mid-sentence for a second, losing her train of thought before continuing. But she shouldn't have done that. She could feel the other investors taking note and docking her points.

David Smith was the first to speak, slowly and deliberately, as if he'd finally woken from his deep slumber. His voice was very baritone for someone so short and slender. "So, Ms.—" He consulted a clipboard on the table. "—Dev." Really? He'd already forgotten her name? "You stated that you began prototyping back in September, but that you're still not done. What's taking so long?"

"That's right," Annika said confidently. "Our tech is really very innovative, and no one's done what we're trying to do, so we're blazing a completely new path. As such, we've overcome many novel challenges in the area of deep learning with neural networks that we didn't previously foresee. There's also a compelling future predictor feature we're working on and hope to have release-ready soon—"

"Thank you," David Smith said, sounding bored.

Rude little annoying—

"And how many are on your team?" Jim Hernandez asked, still looking as astonished as if he'd just learned an alien bug colony had taken up residence in his nose.

"Two right now," Annika said, weariness threatening to drag her down. She hadn't slept at all last night. Not even a catnap. It was a wonder she could string coherent sentences together. She tamped down her urge to check her smartwatch again. Her heart was at her father's hospital bedside, not here with these cold, soulless men who would decide the fate of Make Up, an app built around love and passion. She wanted to save her business desperately, but her father took precedence over everything else. "My developer, June Stewart, and me. Of course, we do have plans to expand, but knowing how many new businesses go under by expanding too quickly, we're biding our time in that arena. Having just the two of us makes us nimble and adaptable, which we feel is important in this economy. When June needs extra assistance, we hire developers on a freelance basis."

Lewis Stenton finally looked up from his notebook. "You said the idea came to you after learning your parents' love story."

"Yes, that's right." Annika attempted a smile, though she could tell it wobbled. She took a deep breath and added, "My father—" Her voice choked up on the word "father," but she rushed on, hoping she wouldn't break down completely.

"—used to tell me stories about their time together instead of reading me books at bedtime. Their love story became my lullaby. My mother died when I was very young, and them not being able to have their second-chance romance inspired me to found Make Up." She sniffed at the end, in spite of her best efforts. Actually sniffed. *Dammit.* She was completely fucking this up.

Lewis Stenton leaned forward. "So, you might say you have a very emotional connection to your business."

Annika wasn't sure what to make of his glinting eyes, which were reminiscent of Mr. McManor's. "Yes. I believe most people who launch start-ups are emotionally invested in their businesses."

"Hmm." He sat back. "But perhaps some more so than others. And perhaps emotions of that level don't have a place in business."

"I think emotion is what makes a business more than just a job!" Annika said hotly. She wanted to grab her laptop, wrench the door open, and go back to the hospital. How dare this random jerk imply she shouldn't be emotional about her father, who lay unconscious in the fucking hospital? Instead, she took a deep breath and said more composedly, "Emotion is what makes it a calling." She didn't want to piss this guy off, but she also didn't want the last message she gave to be that she was an emotional train wreck or whatever he was trying to imply. Too bad her voice trembled, cutting back on the effectiveness of her message. She wanted to tell them the truth: Her heart wasn't in this. Her father was hurt, and he was all she had in this world, and she really, really needed to be with him. But she was afraid she'd lose all credibility if she did.

"Ms. Dev," Lionel Wakefield said. She turned to him, bringing her attention back to the present. "I, for one, absolutely love the creativity and the personal connection you've brought to your business. The blend of old and new, the idea of a second-chance love story for those who need it most . . . all of that really resonates with me. In the world we live in, we could use every bit of happily ever after we can get."

Annika managed a smile. "Thank you, Mr. Wakefield," she said, trying to infuse some ebullience into her voice.

Wakefield paused before adding, in a more somber tone, "It does concern me that you have such a small team. Just two people? I'm not sure how sustainable that is. And since you haven't yet launched the app, Make Up has no track record of profitability." He sat back and regarded her frankly.

Annika tried to force her brain to come up with a pithy rebuttal to his concern, or even just a way to assuage it, but her mind was blank. Something about being . . . nimble? But she'd said that already. Before she could say anything at all, though, another investor was speaking.

"Yes, well, that brings us to time," David Smith said, stifling a yawn. "Thank you. Please leave your financials outside with Tori."

"Thank you all for your time. I really appreciate it." Trying not to rush, Annika gathered her laptop and her bag and walked to the exit quickly.

～

She sat by her father's bedside again, her blazer hanging on the back of the hospital chair. It was a tremendous relief to be back here with him, to be able to see him and touch him and talk to the medical staff anytime she wanted. "So there was no change? None at all?"

"No. I'm sorry." June stood beside Annika, rubbing her eyes. "He slept peacefully the whole time."

"Thanks for staying with him," she replied, keeping her eyes on her father. "I got back as quickly as I could."

"Of course." June squeezed her shoulder. "So . . . the pitch went okay?"

Annika let out a breath. "It could've been better." She looked up at June. "I'm sorry. I messed up a couple of times and my heart just wasn't in it. I'm pretty sure they could tell. Wakefield seemed impressed by the idea, but I'm not sure I gave him anything to really hold on to." When she looked down, a few tears dripped off her eyelashes. "I think we're going to lose." And Break Up would win. She would've felt worse about it, but she'd hit the limits of negative emotion.

June wrapped her arms around Annika and gave her a quick hug. "Let's just wait and see what the results come back like tomorrow. Anyway, you did the best you could with what you had. That's all anyone can do, sugar. That's all anyone can do."

"Thanks, June." Annika pulled back and looked at her friend's drawn face, her eyes puffy and red, her expression slightly dazed. "You should go back to the hotel, though. Get some rest."

June frowned. "What about you?"

"I'm going to take a nap in this chair. I can't go back to the hotel; I won't be able to sleep."

After a moment, June nodded. "Okay. But text me the moment something changes? I'll be back in a couple hours."

Annika managed a thin smile. "Sure."

❦

Once the nurse took her father's vitals, Annika slumped down in the chair and closed her eyes. Her body began to sink into sleep almost immediately, the craving for rest becoming too much for her conscious mind to handle. Images and thoughts began flashing through her mind, the precursor to sleep: her father, smiling at her and handing her a glass of mango juice; Hudson gathering her into his arms, smelling like the ocean; the investors' blank looks as she tripped and fumbled her way through the pitch.

And then, finally, there was darkness as she slept fitfully, pieces of her broken heart rattling in her chest.

"Ani."

Her eyes flew open before her brain fully processed what was happening. The clock on the wall said she'd been asleep for about two hours. "Daddy," she gasped, rushing to his bedside.

His eyes were open, eyelids fluttering. His gaze roved her face. "What—what's happening?"

Annika pushed the nurse's call button. "You were in a car accident," she said, her voice wobbling. Tears streamed down her face as relief coursed through every muscle, every nerve-ending, every artery in her body. He was awake. He was speaking. Her father was here with her. "You've been unconscious almost a full day."

His face was uncomprehending, though he winced, as if he were in pain. "An accident?"

Annika rubbed his arm, hating how her normally robust father looked so confused, so frail. "Yes. You're in Napa, Daddy.

You rented a car and then a truck hit you. But you're okay. I'm here."

The nurse rushed in, took one look at Annika's father, and said, "I'll get the doctor!" before rushing back out.

Her father watched the nurse go. "The doctor?" he said. "I think that's supposed to be me." He grinned at Annika. That's how she knew he was going to be okay.

chapter twenty-one

Because her father was her father and was able to articulate eloquently and at length why he would thrive getting care closer to home, the doctors agreed to transfer him to Cedars-Sinai in Los Angeles, where he'd practiced for decades and felt more comfortable. His brain swelling had completely subsided, as far as the doctors could tell. The only symptom of the injury to his temporal lobe was short-term memory loss. His spleen would recuperate perfectly as well. In other words, he'd gotten massively, massively lucky.

"So, are you going to sue the drunk driver who hit you?" Annika asked. She and June sat beside her father's bedside, watching him eat minestrone soup while propped up against the pillows. Suing was something she and June had talked about, but of course, it was ultimately her dad's decision.

He looked up at her, his poor bruised face contorting into a small smile. They'd given him glasses because he'd made a quip that he liked to see the food he was eating, even if it was hospital food. "Oh, I don't know about that, Ani. They tell me the poor man had been sober for twenty-five years and fell off the wagon because his only daughter was diagnosed with a brain tumor." He took a deep breath, shaking his head slowly. "I suppose we all have our burdens to carry in this life."

"How did you find that out?" Annika asked, frowning.

Her dad grinned and continued to eat his soup. "People tell you all kinds of things when they find out you're a doctor."

Annika shook her head, smiling. "Hey," she said to June. "You should go to the hotel and get packed. Our flight's in a couple of hours. I'll meet you there in a bit."

Her father would be using a medical transport since he was still a little weak from all the time he'd spent unconscious, but since he was doing so well otherwise, he'd told Annika to fly home with June separately.

"Okay." June hopped up from her chair, slipped her phone into her pocket, and pecked Annika's dad on the cheek. "See you on the flip side, Dr. Dev."

"Bye-bye, June."

After she was gone, Annika's dad turned to her, his expression serious. He set his spoon down. "Annika, I need to say something."

"What is it? Do you need me to call the nurse for pain meds?"

"No, it's nothing like that." He took a deep, steadying breath. He was still attached to an IV, but most of the other machines had been removed. "I've just been thinking about a lot of things these past couple of hours. Almost dying in a car accident will do that to you, I suppose. I feel like I've gained more perspective now than I did in fifty-six years of being alive." He smiled before continuing. "I am so proud of you for following your heart. I know I haven't been the most supportive, and I've been trying to change that as of late, but . . . you're an incredible woman, Ani. And I'm so happy you're pursuing your dream. Your mom would be so proud."

Annika blinked back tears. She hadn't told him about flubbing the pitch; she didn't want to upset him. Hearing this now, when she could very well lose Make Up in two weeks to bankruptcy, felt bittersweet. She sniffed and squeezed her dad's hand. "Thanks, Daddy. That means a lot to me."

"I have another thing to say." He stopped to reach for his water, wincing a little as the IV pulled at the back of his hand. Annika handed the water to him and he thanked her, took a deep swallow, and set the cup back down. "I realize I've been living my life in fear." He stared off into space, lost in thought for a moment. "I've been afraid to move on from the house even though it's too big for me, because of what it might mean for your mother's memory. I've been afraid to date for the same reason. I didn't want to do a disservice to her, or even risk forgetting what she and I had. I didn't want you to start your business and say no to medical school, because I was afraid you wouldn't be safe—and also because I was afraid, yet again, that your mother's memory would be tarnished in some way because she was a physician."

He looked at Annika, smiled, and shook his head. "But I see now that that's no way to live your life. Being afraid hampers your ability to be in the moment. And if there's one thing this accident has taught me, it's that the present moment is all that matters. You just never know if you're going to get another."

Annika sank into the chair at his bedside, her hands clasped loosely between her knees. A prickle of nerves tingled under her skin. "So . . . what are you saying?"

"I'm saying things are going to change," her father said, his brown eyes serious behind his wire-rimmed glasses. "I'm going to sell the house and downsize. I'm not going to fret so much about whether you're eating or how you're going to pay your bills because I know you're fully capable of taking care of yourself. And . . . maybe it's time I sought out some companionship. Gave myself another chance at love."

"Wow." Annika got up and walked to the window, her brain tumbling with a thousand thoughts. She looked down at the hospital courtyard, where a woman in a wheelchair sat surrounded by her family, all of them laughing and talking in the warmth of the afternoon sun. Then she turned back to her dad, remembering all the times she'd worried about him in that enormous house, all by himself. "You're right. I'm going to miss the house, but you have to do what's best for you. I think we've all seen up close how short and precious life is. As for dating . . ." She took a deep breath and smiled. "I'm really happy for you, Dad."

"Really?" He searched her face, not returning her smile. "You don't feel like I'd be forgetting your mother?"

Annika sat on the edge of his bed. "No. I'm not a little girl anymore. You deserve to be happy, Daddy. More than anything, I want to see you live your life with joy."

He squeezed her hand. "I want that, too, Ani. For both of us. I want that, too."

〜

The next twenty-four hours were a haze of flying back to LA, getting her dad checked in to Cedars-Sinai (where he was being treated like royalty, of course; as soon as Queen of the Valley Medical Center informed them about his accident, the other doctors even bought him an all-inclusive trip to Aruba for when he fully recovered, and they were all going with him), and facing the very real possibility of having to close Make Up and declare bankruptcy.

At her desk the next morning, before June came in, Annika reached into her bag and pulled out the broken sculpture Hudson had made her. She'd tried to glue it back together, but it was still very clearly damaged, the seam in the heart glaringly ugly. She set the sculpture on her desk, sat back, and looked at it in the crisp, cool quiet. Without warning, her eyes filled with tears.

Burying her face in her hands, Annika let herself cry.

She cried for the Hudson she thought she'd met, but who had never been there at all. She cried for the Annika who'd wanted so badly for this to be a fairy tale, a love story with a happily-ever-after. She cried because it had turned out to be just another failed first date, just another sign from the universe that maybe, just maybe, she was meant to be alone. She cried because she hadn't cried for all those things yet, since she'd been too busy crying for her father. And then, finally, she cried because she was just so tired of crying.

Thankfully, by the time June arrived, Annika had managed to dry her tears and muster some semblance of normalcy. She needed to appear at least slightly put together today. It was the day they'd learn the results of the EPIC pitch.

❧

Annika sat at her desk later that morning, deep-breathing in time to the anxiety app on her phone. "It's all fine. I looked it up and actually, filing for business bankruptcy is a very straight-forward process."

June studied her from behind her desk, her eyebrows knitting together as she played with her Yoda figurine. "But you don't know yet if we've won." Glancing at the clock on the wall, she added, "We still have an hour until EPIC officially notifies the winner. It could be us!"

Annika breathed in for a four-count, held it, and let it out for a four-count before responding. "If one thing's become clear to me with a little time and sleep, June, it's that I did a really, really poor job with that pitch. I was emotional and distracted and . . ." She shook her head, feeling a pinprick of guilt. "I know I did the best I could, given what was going on at the time, but . . ."

June was nibbling at her lip, her eyes watchful.

Annika sat back in her chair. It squeaked softly under her weight. "Mm. Now that's an 'I have many questions' face if ever I saw one."

June fiddled with Yoda's oversized ears. "No, it's just that with everything going on, we haven't really talked about Hudson."

Annika focused on the anxiety app's encouraging, glowing orb and took a deep breath again. "Ziggy didn't tell you?"

"No. Actually, the last I heard from him was yesterday. He said some stuff was going on that he needed to take care of, but that he'd call me later today. None of them are back in the office yet." June paused. "I wondered if that had anything to do with you and Hudson, but I didn't ask. I wanted you to be able to tell me on your own time."

Annika smiled a little. "Thanks, Junebug. You're a good friend. What am I saying? You're the sister I never had."

June's eyes got misty. "Same."

Sighing, Annika got up from her tufted office chair, sat on

the settee, and motioned for June to join her, which she did, her eyes full of questions. Annika studied their thighs, pressed against each other. They'd sat on this settee together and had countless conversations over the past almost-year. She wondered if this would be one of the last times.

"Hudson and I broke up." She heard the words fall into the room, harsh as broken glass, pricking all the soft parts of her.

An intake of breath from June. "Broke up? So . . . were y'all together?"

Annika bit her lip, blinking back tears that were threatening to fall. She played with her seaside charm bracelet as a way to distract herself. When she was able to speak again, she said, "I guess not. We weren't dating or anything, not officially, but . . . I wanted to be with him, June. It was all a big misunderstanding, though. He's not ready to give up Break Up at all. He's willing to hurt himself by not being true to his heart or what he wants. And I just can't reconcile myself to dating him when he hasn't figured any of that out." She brushed at the tears about to spill from her eyes. "And it fucking hurts and it sucks but that's just the way it has to be."

June's arm snaked around her shoulder. "I'm sorry, sweetpea," she said, her voice choking up, too. They'd both cried so much during the past two days. "I'm so sorry."

"It feels like almost everything's going to shit," Annika said, shaking her head. "But at least I have my dad back now. I have to focus on that."

"And you have me," June said firmly, kissing the side of her head. "That'll never change."

Annika gave her a rueful look. "What about if you and Ziggy decide to get married?"

June scoffed. "Me, get married? Not until I'm at least thirty."

Annika didn't believe that for one second, but she didn't say so. "Right." She smiled. "I am happy for you, though. Please don't feel like you have to hide your relationship stuff from me just because Hudson and I . . ." She swallowed, trailing off.

"I don't," June said quietly. After a while, she added, "You deserve to be happy, you know. You told me you said that to your dad, but you deserve it, too. And I know in my heart you'll find it one day."

Annika was able to muster up a wan smile, though she wasn't nearly as optimistic as June. "Thanks, babe. That means a lot to me."

⁓

Annika and June went back to work, just to keep their hands and minds busy. Annika kept glancing at the clock on her laptop until she forced herself to switch Word over into Focus mode, so she could see nothing but the screen. *Twenty-two more minutes.* She'd know in twenty-two more minutes who'd won EPIC. In her heart, she was sure Break Up had taken it away. But there was a tiny, tiny part of her—that stupidly idealistic part—that kept saying it wasn't over till it was over.

"Holy shit!" June yelped, and Annika started, her heart pounding.

"What? Is it EPIC? Did you hear something?"

"No, I'm sorry." June gave her an apologetic look. "But I think I just got the future projection feature to work."

"What? Are you serious?" Annika peeked at June's laptop. "Can you show me?"

"Sure." Grinning, June clicked on the screen. "So, I fed data points from a fictional couple into the computer."

"Who?" Annika asked.

June wrinkled her nose. "Um, Sam Baldwin and Annie Reed?"

Annika laughed. "Tom Hanks and Meg Ryan's characters from *Sleepless in Seattle*?"

"Hey, it's what popped into my head, okay? And check this out." She clicked the as-yet-rudimentary "go" button on the program. A short movie began playing.

It showed Tom Hanks and Meg Ryan together, at the top of the Empire State Building, kissing. Then it showed them on a computer-rendered wedding day, cutting cake in front of a dozen wedding guests. Afterward, it showed the couple with three children in Green Lake Park in Seattle, a golden retriever romping around them with a Frisbee in its mouth. And finally, it showed them on twin rocking chairs on a porch, watching the sunset.

"Wow," Annika breathed as the picture faded to black and returned to June's programming screen. "It . . . *works*. It really works."

"Yeah, but I haven't fed it real-couple data yet," June cautioned. "So we'll see how well it works then. But at least we know it's possible." She grinned up at Annika, her blue eyes shining. "Isn't it great? When we roll the app out, this feature's going to kick major ass."

Annika got serious again. "*If*, June. *If* we roll the app out." June had done so much work on it. It would break Annika's heart if it had all been for nothing, but she had to be realistic.

She glanced at the clock on the wall at the same time as June, and they looked at each other.

"Ten minutes," June said, blowing out a breath. "They're going to call all the participants, right? No matter whether they won or not?"

"Right. So we'll know for sure, one way or the other, in ten minutes." Annika began to pace to the window and back to the desk. "I need to burn off some energy."

June hopped off her chair and began to do toe touches. "Me too."

Annika snorted. "I'm glad no one can see us right now." And then she went back to pacing.

Her phone rang exactly ten minutes later, noon on the dot. June stared at her, her face flushed from the toe touches. "Oh my god. This is it. This is *it*."

"Yes." Annika took a deep breath. "No matter what, we played our hearts out. And we should be proud of that."

June nodded, breathless, as Annika pushed the button to take the call. She put it on speaker and said, "This is Annika Dev with Make Up."

A woman's voice came through in a clipped tone. "Ms. Dev, hello. My name is Tori Thompson, and I'm one of the board members for the EPIC pitch contest. I'm notifying all of the participants of their status in the contest."

Annika's heart sank. This was not how you'd begin the call for the winning team. There was no excitement or enthusiasm in the woman's voice at all.

"Okay," she said quietly, unable to meet June's eye. She didn't want to see the dashed hope there, not while she was nursing her own.

"Your app, Make Up, was the winner. Congratulations. We will set up a meeting to discuss details, but the EPIC investment team will be putting forward a minimum sum of five hundred thousand dollars into your company."

Annika stared at the phone. In her peripheral vision, she could see June jerk her head up. "I—I'm sorry?" Her voice croaked, but she didn't care.

"Congratulations," the woman said again, more slowly. "Your app, Make Up, was the winner."

"Oh my god," Annika said, her skin rippling with sudden goose bumps. "Oh my god—we *won*?" She looked at June, who began jumping around the office, her mouth open in a silent scream, tears of happiness rushing down her face. "We *won*?" Annika said louder.

There was a long pause. "Yes. You are the winner." The woman was clearly not a fan of emotions or inflections of any kind. "Since the investors were too busy to call everyone themselves, we asked them to write the winner an email. You should see that arrive in your inbox any minute now."

"Wait, wait," Annika said, sensing that the woman was about to end the call. "What about—what about Break Up? Were they a close second?" She looked at June, who'd stopped jumping. Annika couldn't believe Break Up hadn't won, especially when she'd been *so* not on her game.

"Break Up withdrew from the competition."

Annika's breath caught in her throat. "What? When?"

"The morning of EPIC. The CEO cited personal reasons as the cause for their inability to compete."

"Personal reasons" was purposefully vague. "But . . . but why, specifically?" She looked at June, whose hands were now clapped over her mouth.

"I'm sorry, I don't have any more information. Now, do you have any questions for me?"

"No," Annika said, blinking to refocus. They'd *won*. They'd won EPIC! "Thank you very much."

She ended the call and looked at June, a slow smile creeping onto her face. Screaming, they reached for each other, hugged, and began jumping around again.

"Okay, okay, but we have to read the email from the investors," June said. "Right?"

"Right." Annika rushed to her laptop and clicked on her email. There it sat in her inbox, with the subject line *Congratulations, EPIC winner!* "This is surreal," Annika muttered, clicking on it. She and June read the email silently.

Dear Annika and Make Up team,

Congratulations on your spectacular win at EPIC! We were completely bowled over by your pitch. The emotion that imbued every word as you spoke about your parents, about how your father had relayed his love story with your late mother to you every night, was what gave you that winning edge over the competition. We also understand that you've signed up to volunteer regularly at a very worthwhile charity in your area, and for that, we commend you.

We know you will do a world of good with your app, and we're delighted to be able to have some small part in your success.

Cheers! Here's to you, and to changing the world.

Best wishes,

Lionel Wakefield, Jim Hernandez, David Smith, and Lewis Stenton

Annika sat back as the breath *whoosh*ed out of her. "Wow. Wow. They actually *liked* how emotional I got! It worked in our favor." She laughed. "Well, I say 'they,' but that email has Lionel Wakefield written all over it."

June did a little dance all over the office, and after a moment of laughing until she couldn't breathe, Annika got up and joined her. When they were both exhausted and collapsed on the settee in two graceless heaps, June said, "Five hundred grand. *Minimum.* With that kinda money, we can afford to hire a freelance developer or two for a decent amount of time. With three of us working on the scalability issue, we're going to have the prototype up and running within a couple of months. And then we can actually put the app out there, for people to buy and download." She whistled. "All of our money troubles are effectively over! Are you gonna call Mr. McManor and tell him?"

"I'm tempted to let the five hundred grand do the talking for us, but yeah. I guess the more professional thing to do would be to give the man a heads-up before he keels over of shock." She chuckled. Then, after a moment: "June?"

"Hmm?"

"Why do you think Break Up withdrew? Do you think it was because of what happened between Hudson and me?" The thought stuck in her mind like a pebble in a shoe. She didn't want Hudson to have forfeited because of their breakup. It didn't feel right.

"I don't know, sugar." June patted her arm. "But . . . maybe you should reach out to him?" When Annika opened her mouth to say she didn't see the point, June rushed to add, "For closure. Get some answers. And then you can say goodbye."

Annika closed her mouth and swallowed the lump in her throat. *Say goodbye.* Deep inside, Annika knew that Hudson forfeiting EPIC meant something bigger. It was, at least in part, a rejection of her; it was him saying, with finality, that they were done. He didn't want to compete with her anymore; he didn't want anything to do with her at all. "Okay," she said quietly. "I think that's a good idea."

When June went to make herself some coffee, Annika got her phone and texted Hudson.

Hi. Heard about the pitch. Can we meet?

The response came back less than five minutes later. When?

chapter twenty-two

June left early to meet with Ziggy. Apparently, he'd texted her to say he had a few things to tell her, and asked to meet for an early dinner. June looked nervous, but Annika knew Ziggy wouldn't tell her anything she didn't want to hear. It was probably work stuff to do with Break Up withdrawing from the pitch.

She herself was meeting up with Hudson in a half hour at a bar down the street. She'd refreshed her deodorant, reapplied some of her makeup, and now she sat in her chair, tapping her nails on her desk. It was so quiet on their floor. Too quiet. It gave her too much time to think. She considered calling her dad again, but she'd already called him twice (once to break the news of the win; he'd yelled so loudly, the nurses had come rushing to his room) and visited once. She knew he was fine.

Gently, Annika ran a finger over the glued-together sculpture Hudson had made her, her finger snagging on some of the sharp corners that were left over from its break. After a moment, she clicked to wake up her laptop and opened the cloud service June stored her work in. She knew June's future projection program was stored there, too.

Without thinking too closely about it, Annika fed her social media accounts to the program, which were its main source of data points unless they were manually entered, as June had done for the fictional Annie and Sam. Then, she fed it Hudson's social media.

A message popped up on the screen: *Processing, please wait . . . and while you wait, enjoy this scene! May the Force be with you!*

A small video player popped up, featuring an epic battle scene from the first *Star Wars* playing on its screen. Annika snorted. This was so June. She was halfway through the scene when it abruptly disappeared. It was replaced, instead, by Annika and Hudson's projection.

Annika's breath caught as she watched herself and Hudson doing yoga together on the beach at sunset. Then, hand in hand, they strolled through an open-air market, picking out flowers and fruit, talking together, Hudson's head dipped toward hers as he whispered something in her ear that made her laugh. There was Hudson, down on one knee, proposing to her in a hotel room with a view of the Seine, while she cried unabashedly and said yes. There she was, walking hand in hand with a dark-haired toddler in overalls, Hudson taking a picture of his little family. And finally, a rendering of her and Hudson as older adults, sitting under a pergola in a beautiful garden, reading together in the dappled sunlight.

The screen faded to black.

This was the future OLLI had predicted for Hudson and Annika, based on their personalities and how they interacted with the world. This was one possible future of many, she knew that. None of them might come true; it wasn't magic. It was just one machine's idea of what might happen.

Annika pushed her chair back and stalked to the storage closet to grab her bag, suddenly annoyed that she'd fed the program her and Hudson's information. At any point, she could've realized what a stupid thing she was doing, that it was an exercise in frustration. She was annoyed that OLLI hadn't shown them arguing or fighting or getting divorced. She was annoyed, most of all, that it had made her long for something that could never be hers.

Grabbing her phone, Annika turned out the lights and stalked to the elevator. She and Hudson were never going to be together. They'd lasted less than a full *weekend* before breaking up; that's how incompatible they were. OLLI was wrong—completely, breathtakingly, stupendously wrong.

Once out of the elevator, Annika crossed the foyer and walked into the balmy evening toward the bar where she was meeting Hudson. She'd have to tell June the program wasn't working nearly as well as she thought it did.

⁓

Hudson was already waiting when she arrived. Annika pushed the door open and stood there, her hand still on the handle, staring at him. She could barely breathe.

He was sitting in a dimly lit corner of the stylish bar, under repurposed wooden shelves that held antique liquor bottles. A chandelier hung in the center of the bar, throwing pinpoints of light all over him. He wore dark jeans and a wrinkled button-down rolled up to his elbows, and he had a day's worth of stubble he was rubbing. He wasn't on his phone, wasn't reading a book, wasn't doing anything except gazing off into the distance. What was he thinking? Had he been so busy since the pitch that he hadn't had time to shave or dress as impeccably as he usually did?

Annika's heart hurt. She wanted to rush up to him, curl up into his lap, nuzzle her face into his neck, and breathe deeply. She wanted him to rub her back, smooth back her hair, take her lips between his teeth, and tease her. But the time for all of that was over.

Clearing her throat, she let go of the door and stepped all the way inside, making way for the young couple coming up behind her. *Pull yourself together, Annika.* She glanced at her reflection in the distressed wooden mirror on the wall; her hair was pulled back in a ponytail, and she was wearing mascara, lip gloss, and a simple cotton dress. Not the best she'd ever looked, but not horrible. Not that it mattered to Hudson anymore.

She made her way to his table, her heart beating furiously. He looked up, met her eye, and stood to greet her. No smile.

"Hi." His green eyes held her with the fiery intensity she already missed.

She leaned forward to kiss his cheek, her pulse jumping at the contact. His stubble scratched her skin and she made a valiant effort not to inhale. She didn't want to smell him—she *couldn't.* "Hi." When she pulled back, she noticed he had his eyes closed, but he opened them again immediately. Annika took a seat across from him. "Thanks for meeting with me."

He nodded and took a sip of his water. There were lines around his mouth and slight bags under his eyes, like he hadn't been sleeping.

"You look . . . like you've been busy."

Hudson smiled, but it was mirthless and didn't reach his eyes. "You mean I look rough."

She didn't say anything. That *was* what she'd meant, but she was curious what he'd been up to. The waitress came by and Annika ordered a Coke. She wanted to keep a clear head. Hudson ordered a whiskey sour, apparently having no such concerns. *Guess he's able to keep a clear head around me no matter what.*

After the waitress left, Hudson rubbed a hand along his jaw and looked at Annika. "Congratulations on your win. I'm really happy for you." Though he didn't smile, she could tell he meant it.

"Thanks," she said quietly. "But that's actually why I wanted to talk to you."

"I'm assuming you heard we withdrew from EPIC."

"Yes." She crumpled Hudson's straw wrapper between her fingers. "Did you do that because of . . . us? Because of our fight?"

Hudson shook his head, a lock of his hair falling across his forehead. "No. I did it because I heard what happened to your dad."

"Oh." The word escaped Annika's mouth, just a breath of air. "How is he?"

"Okay. Much better now. It was really scary for a while, but . . ." Her voice wobbled and she cleared her throat. Hudson frowned, as if in pain. "He's at Cedars-Sinai now, and they're taking good care of him." She paused and bit her lip. The bar was filling up, happy people taking up tables near them. It felt odd to be in such a festive place when her own conversation and feelings were so solemn. "Why—why would *you* withdraw because my dad was in an accident? I thought you—Break Up—needed the capital from the investors."

"We did." The waitress placed their drinks in front of them and left. Hudson took a swig of his drink before continuing. "But I didn't want to win like that, Annika. I didn't want to go up against you when you were hurting, when your whole world was collapsing around you. I thought it was fucking brave that you still wanted to pitch. When June told Ziggy, I knew what we had to do."

Annika picked her Coke up with a shaking hand and took a sip. He thought she was brave. "You—but—what will you do now for capital? Find another investor?"

"I suppose we could." Hudson sat back and watched her for a moment. "But I've decided to close the company down instead."

Annika almost snorted Coke up her nose. "You what? Completely?"

Hudson nodded grimly. "Completely. The news will break later this week. I've already contacted Emily Dunbar-Khan at *Time*. They're going to rewrite the article so it's about you and your success at EPIC. I'm sure she'll be in touch soon."

Annika shook her head. This was all happening so fast. "Wait, but . . . why? Why would you close the company down? What about your parents—sending money home, wanting to be successful for them?"

Hudson leaned forward, setting his elbows on the dark wood. A group of people behind Annika laughed uproariously at something, but his eyes didn't so much as flicker toward them. He was intently focused on her. "You were right, Annika." His voice was low, but full of emotion. "When *was* it ever going to be enough? When was I going to loosen my grip? When was I going to reconcile who I am with what I do for a living?" He pushed a hand through his hair, shaking his head.

"You asked the tough questions, and at the time I couldn't see that they were the *right* questions. I was losing myself to Break Up, and it took you pointing it out for me to see it clearly."

Annika's hands were trembling. She balled them into fists against her thighs. "What . . . what about Blaire and Ziggy? What will you do now?"

"I talked to them before I withdrew. I told them what it meant for me and that I was done. That I didn't want to run a company like that; a company I didn't believe in anymore. They were a hundred percent behind me. We've all had time to build our savings up with Break Up's success, so money isn't going to be an immediate issue.

"As for what I'm going to do next . . . I'm going back to the visual arts app I told you about in Vegas. Blaire and Ziggy want to come along with me." He smiled faintly and took a sip of his drink. "And in my free time, I plan to work on a dream I had—my sculpting. I'm converting my second guest bedroom into a studio." He reached forward, his fingers hovering above Annika's hand. Her heart raced, her skin aching for the contact. But he curled his hand into a fist and placed it back on his side of the table. "Thank you. For being so honest with me. For seeing something that I didn't see myself. You've changed my life." There was that faint smile again. "But I suppose that's par for the course for you."

Annika's throat felt painful and tight for reasons she couldn't articulate. Swallowing a sip of ice-cold soda, she opened her mouth to say he was welcome. Instead, she found herself saying, her voice barely a whisper, "You didn't call or visit. When you heard my dad was in the hospital."

He squeezed his eyes shut for just a moment. "I wanted to. I thought about you constantly. I got updates from Ziggy, who got them from June. Thirdhand updates." He shook his head. "It was torture. But I didn't think . . . the way we left things, I thought I'd be the *last* person you'd want to hear from. I didn't want to add to the nightmare."

She shook her head slowly, a tear leaking down her cheek. "I wanted to hear from you. I kept wishing you'd call. It felt like—like you didn't care."

Hudson closed his eyes again, just for a moment, his face a mask of regret. "That is . . . that's not at all how I felt." His voice was tight, controlled.

"I still don't understand," Annika said, brushing the tear off her cheek. "You were so different in Vegas. The guy I met there didn't even have Break Up in his mind. So . . . why? Why did you change your mind?"

Hudson held her gaze. The way the fading sunlight was coming in through the windows, his eyes seemed to glow green-gold. "You."

Annika shook her head, frowning. "I don't understand."

"It was you. Don't you remember how we left things?"

Annika woke up and rolled onto her side. Hudson lay sleeping beside her, one arm tucked under his head, his other flung over her waist. Already, she was learning him. Already, she knew that if she slid out of bed before seven o'clock, he wouldn't stir.

She was usually a morning person. Seeing the sunlight filtering through the curtains generally filled her with delight. But not today. She knew what today meant. She knew it meant goodbye.

She and Hudson hadn't discussed what their summer dalliance meant, or whether they were going to see each other again. She wanted to; she thought about it all the time, what it might be like back in LA with him, having coffee together in her favorite coffee shop or going to a concert over the weekend. But she knew what she felt was one-sided. He'd never brought up the future. She, on the other hand, was the hopeless romantic—the one who always fell too fast, and too hard. She was a first-date girl, not the one men wanted to date for any length of time. And she just couldn't face that rejection again. Not from Hudson Craft.

Besides, they were both young professionals, busy with apps they wanted to launch into the world within the next year. Annika knew what this meant as well as he did: This week was all they had. Seven days; no more, no less. And now it was over. She and her foolish heart would take a long time to get over this, and she might never have another week like the one she'd spent with him ever again. But Hudson would move on. He'd forget about her soon enough.

Reaching over carefully, she planted a kiss on the corner of his mouth. He didn't stir. She thought for a moment, and then wrote him a note on the pad on the nightstand.

"This was fun. I wish you well. Annika x"

Not too clingy, not too sad. A goodbye that let her leave without feeling the sting of rejection she knew was coming once he woke up.

She stood at his door for just a moment longer than necessary, watching his sleeping form. Goodbye, Hudson Craft. Then she turned and walked away.

Annika frowned at Hudson, the background full of clinking glasses and merry laughter. "I . . . I left you a note."

His eyes were somber. "You ghosted me. No number, no email address. You didn't want me to find you. After everything we shared that week, I thought we had this—this real connection. And to wake up to that empty bed and that impersonal note . . ." He shook his head. "It fucking hurt."

Annika's brain was having trouble comprehending this. "What? Why?"

Hudson laughed incredulously and took a gulp of his drink. "Isn't it obvious, Annika? I fell for you. Hard. I thought maybe you felt the same way, or at least on the same spectrum as me. But then you treated me like a one-night stand—excuse me, a seven-night stand—that you picked up at a frat house." He took a shaky breath. "You were the best and worst thing about that summer."

"But—but *I'm* the one who always falls for people too fast. I left you that note because I thought there was *no* way you felt the same about me. I didn't want to put you in an awkward position, or—" She shook her head, trying to drown out all the sounds around her. "But you never brought up the future. You never said you wanted to continue to go out in LA."

He leaned forward, his hands flat on the table. "I was going to, that last day. I didn't want to scare you by bringing it up too early, but that was my plan. I wanted to have your number, take you out on a proper date once we got to LA."

Annika licked her dry lips. "I—I had no idea. I thought you were going to walk away and I couldn't face that."

Hudson held her eyes, not saying anything.

She pushed a hand through her hair, still having trouble believing what she'd heard. "You were hurt by *me*. And that's why you came up with Break Up." She began to laugh. "Hudson—"

Hurt flashed across his face, the skin around his eyes tightening. "I don't see what's funny."

Annika shook her head, trying to catch her breath. She

reached out and took his clenched fist in her hand. "I'm sorry. I'm laughing because . . . do you know why I came up with Make Up?"

"Your parents," Hudson said carefully. "You couldn't give them the second chance they deserved, so you wanted to give it to other people."

"That's *half* the reason I came up with Make Up." She held his eyes to make sure he was listening. "The other half was you."

Hudson's face changed, a mixture of hope and confusion splashing across his features. "What do you mean?"

"After I . . . ghosted . . . you, I suppose, though it didn't feel that way to me, I was heartsick. I convinced myself that I cared about you way more than you cared about me. I was always the hopeless romantic, falling in love too easily, getting my heart broken. The one who was perpetually alone." She squeezed his big hand, feeling the dense bone under his skin, a sculpture all its own. "And you . . . you were so gorgeous and talented. I was sure you wouldn't think of me again. But then I thought, *What if I could bring people together?* Not exes, as I'd originally imagined, but people who were on the cusp of losing each other and *knew* what they stood to lose, unlike me. Unlike us. What if I could help people realize what they were going to be giving up if they walked away? I wanted to prevent what happened to me from happening to other people."

"Annika," Hudson said, his voice barely controlled, its echo a rumble in her chest. "What are you trying to say?"

"I'm trying to say I fell for you, too, Hudson Craft. I fell for you then and I fell for you now and I'm still falling." She shook her head, her lip trembling, the tears starting to fall. "I'm in love with you."

Suddenly he was on her side of the table, lifting her out

of her chair, his hands cupping her cheeks. His mouth found hers, hungry, wanting. Annika sank into his arms, letting him dip her back, letting him in again, apologizing with her tongue, with her mouth, with her lips.

Finally, she pulled back, breathing hard. "I'm sorry," she said, looking into his eyes. "I'm sorry for the way I've behaved, for the ways I've hurt you."

He shook his head, the evening sunlight from the windows playing with his hair, turning it to burnished gold. "I'm sorry, too. For being a fool. For not realizing sooner that it's *you*. You're the one I love, Annika Dev. And I don't want to be apart from you for a single minute more."

The smile that burst out of her was like sunshine. She wouldn't have to leave the lights on in her apartment anymore. Never again.

"I love you, too." Laughing, she collapsed against Hudson's chest. He held her there, his arms strong and firm around her, as if he'd never let go.

It was summer and their future was ahead of them, brilliant and shining, a sculpture as yet unformed. Annika couldn't wait to see what they'd build together.

acknowledgments

Words cannot express the delight I'm feeling while writing the acknowledgments section of my very first adult romance novel. I've dreamed of this moment since I was about nine years old, and it's finally here!

I'd like to thank my editor, Eileen Rothschild, who made this happen by reaching out to my agent and asking if I'd be interested in writing an adult romance for her imprint. I don't think I gave them the chance to finish the question before I was hopping around my office yelling, "YES PLEASE!" Thank you to my literary agent, Thao Le, who has seen me through many years and many phases of my career. Thank you to the whole fabulous team at St. Martin's Griffin for making this book-shaped dream come true. Thanks also to my readers—the Facebook Swoon Squad in particular, who are so unrelentingly encouraging and enthusiastic about my work, and who treat One-Line Wednesday like it's Christmas. You are a vital part of my writing life and I appreciate each and every one of you. Cupcakes for all!

A special thank-you to Anisha, who provided me with the idea that Annika could fantasize about spoiling the ending to Hudson's book! Brilliant and petty and I love it!

And last but never least, thank you to my steadfast, loving husband who read so many, many drafts of this book and encouraged me to keep going even when I was ready to toss the whole thing into the fire. You are my sun, my moon, and all my stars.

about the author

LILY MENON has always been enamored of romantic comedies and happily-ever-afters in all shapes and sizes. Her very first love story, written at age nine, was about a handsome boy who wooed the heroine with books, chocolates, and a very fat puppy. Now Lily lives with her own handsome boy (who indeed wooed her with books, chocolates, and fat puppies) in the mountains of Colorado, where she spends her days dreaming up kissing scenes and meet-cutes. Visit her on the Web at www.lilymenon.com.